FEARLESS

Crescent Cove Romantic Suspense, Viper Force, Book One

MARLIE MAY

Hummingbird Press

ASIN: B07PPW1LR1
ISBN: 9781099347511

Hummingbird Press

✿ Created with Vellum

There's a bit of each of my friends in these pages.
Jessica for reading this book a billion times.
Lee, my bestie, despite the fact
that she lives on the other side of the world.
Stephanie, my very first CP.
Jes for listening to my endless venting.
And Renée, Alex, Katrina, Laura, Amber, Kim, & Lana.
I'm grateful to have all of you in my life.

For Mom. Miss you.
For Laura, Jessie, & Elizabeth
who were also taken too soon.

For my children who give me endless support.
And, last, but not least, for my own personal hero,
my retired Seabee Chief husband.
I couldn't do this without you.

Cover art by Black Bird Book Covers
*Find them on Facebook **here***

**Their second chance at love
turns lethal when a man
from her past is
determined to see her dead.**

Navy Chief Cooper Talon is on leave to clean out his dad's house and shut the door on the abuse he suffered there. He takes a break to go camping with a buddy, never expecting to run into his friend's younger sister, Ginny—the girl he secretly adored twelve years ago. With an upcoming deployment, he can't make a play for her heart. But when someone stalks her, his protective instincts kick in.

After an abduction overseas, travel photographer Ginny Bradley returns home to Maine. A camping trip with her brother will put her nightmares to rest, and meeting up with Cooper makes the weekend complete. Thousands of miles will soon separate them, but something powerful draws them together. Then someone threatens her life.

With time ticking down to Cooper's deployment, they must discover who wants to hurt Ginny. Long-distance romances rarely survive, but they end permanently when threats turn lethal.

This book was a 2018 RWA® Golden Heart Finalist.

Ginny

Instinct told me to run.

As I hurried down the path between the campground and the lake, the forest loomed around me. Air heavy with the scent of decomposed leaves and earth filled my lungs. It hadn't rained for weeks, and brittle grass crunched beneath my sandals like tiny bones.

And while it had to be at least eighty out, my skin prickled with goosebumps.

Switching my tote bag from my weaker to my stronger arm, I deliberately slowed my pace. Told my heart to stop racing. If anyone saw me scurrying like a spooked rabbit, they wouldn't believe that for the past ten years, I'd traveled the world all by myself. I'd walked through the countryside near Cairo. Spent days backpacking on the Isle of Crete. I'd even hiked for a month in the Kalahari region of South Africa. More often than not, I hadn't known where I'd wind up the next day, let alone where I'd lay my head that night.

And now, I was so chickenshit, I could barely find the courage to walk through a wooded campground alone.

"Here's the white-hot truth," I whispered to myself. "No one's going to snatch you up and carry you away." This was Maine, the laid-back place I'd grown up in. Not Istanbul, where my confidence had been shattered.

It wasn't easy facing the fear I'd lived with for three months, but I'd come camping this weekend with my older brother to find a way to start moving past it.

I emerged out onto a beach that sloped down to the lake. Ahead, the water gleamed, blue glass broken by only a few boaters and swimmers. On the shore, two little girls splashed under their mom's hovering gaze. A bald man sat on the dock with his feet dangling in the water. And farther out, teenagers hooted as they cannonballed off a float.

"See?" I mumbled. "You're fine."

A solo walk was the first challenge I'd set for myself. Next up? Swimming alone. After staking out a chair with my towel, I pulled off my sundress and waded into the lake. A sweaty mess after helping my brother set up our campsite, the cool water gliding over my skin felt fantastic. I turned onto my back and floated, my hair tickling my shoulders like blonde seaweed. The sun beat down, dulling my senses, and I relaxed.

Pushing my resolve, I flipped over and swam away from shore, making for the closest float. My brisk crawl soon brought me within reach, and I tapped the top of the wooden frame to tick off another accomplishment. Grinning, I gave myself an imaginary pat on the back, then turned and paddled back to the beach.

My self-confidence growing with each test, I strode from the water. I dried off and pulled on my sundress, then sat and buried my heels in the sand. Laziness sunk into my bones.

"What an awesome day," I said, squinting at the lake.

The woman minding her daughters turned and smiled. "Gorgeous, isn't it?"

"Definitely." Times like this lived to be captured, and who better to record them than a photographer? Pulling my camera from my tote bag, I took pictures of the trees reflecting on the water. The little girls splashing on the shore. I zoomed in on a grasshopper climbing to the top of a blade of grass and, tilting sideways, took a selfie with the grasshopper. I tossed my camera back into my tote, grabbed my paperback, and was soon sucked into the story.

Until a crack rang out in the forest behind me.

Shifting around, I peered over my shoulder but saw nothing.

Another snap. As if something—no, *someone*—had stepped on a stick.

Rising, I gnawed on my lower lip while staring toward the woods. Where the sun barely reached, a shadow darted from one tree to another.

I gulped. "Who's there?"

The cry of a loon flew across the lake, and I jumped.

A quick look around told me that while I'd been absorbed in my book, everyone else had left.

I was alone.

Spooked, I stuffed my feet into my sandals. With my tote held against my chest, I rushed up the path. Not watching where I was going—too busy gaping at the dense woods surrounding me—I stumbled over a root, barely catching myself before falling. I groaned and hobbled on, pushing past my stinging foot like I'd pushed past the pain when a man snapped my wrist three months ago.

Dull thuds came up behind me, making me bolt. As my sandals slammed the ground, my breath came in frantic spurts, and my heart thundered. Reaching the end of the path, I raced across the open, grassy area in the center of the campground, making for the log cabin changing rooms in the middle. If I could get inside a room, I could lock the door. I'd be safe.

A gust of wind shot hair into my eyes. Campfire smoke swirled around me. A dog barked. But two giggling kids chasing a butterfly nearby made me slow my steps and come to a halt.

I gazed over my shoulder.

Nothing.

"Of course," I ground out. "It was just my imagination."

So much for challenging my fear.

My shoulders sagged, and disappointment burned like acid through my belly. Did I really think someone would harm me while I was out in the open like this? The campground was filled with people getting ready for the weekend. If I screamed, someone would jump to my defense.

Few jumped to your defense last time. The majority had looked away as if men kidnapping women off the street was part of an ordinary day.

I hated that a random sound in the woods could send me into a full-blown panic.

With a sigh, I started up the stairs, but tripped, landing on the deck. Rising, I rubbed my aching wrist. As I brushed the dirt off my knees, I stared toward the path. A man dressed in jeans and a hoodie stood in the shadows. Was he watching me?

Pulse jumping, I slunk against the plank wall, wishing I could melt through the panels. I reached back and pulled open the closest changing room door and slid inside, standing still while my vision adjusted to the dark.

My towel fell from my limp fingers, landing on the floor by my feet.

I'd walked in on a naked man.

He stood with his back to me, his wet swim shorts a tangled bundle near his feet. While my eyes widened, he lifted a towel and wiped his face. A bead of water trailed down his spine from his short, coal black hair. The tail end of a phoenix tattoo, created from more colors than a sunrise on Kilimanjaro, curved along his back and around the top of his shoulder.

He smoothed the towel across his chest, trapezoids flexing as he worked the material lower.

Leave, before he realizes you're here.

I eased my foot back, but it hit the metal trash can, making a clang ring out in the room. Spinning, I faced away from him. "Oh, shit, I'm sorry."

He grunted. "Thought I locked the door."

"I'm *really* sorry." My cheeks couldn't get any hotter if I'd spent a day at the beach without sunscreen. "I…I thought someone was chasing me on the path from the lake, and I didn't look before barging in."

"Chasing you?" Clothing rustled, and he came up beside me, the white towel slung around his narrow hips. A small towel, it barely covered his butt cheeks. Not that I was looking *that* closely.

Mortified, I kept my gaze directed downward.

"I'll take a look around outside. But first, here." He pried a small piece of wood off the rough-cut wall and handed it to me.

"Thanks?" I stared down at it. Shaped like a wedge, it was wide on one end and narrow on the other. "What do I do with it?"

"After I leave, press it in here." He slid his fingertip along the thin gap between the door and frame. "I *did* lock the door, but the lock must be broken. This'll keep anyone from entering without your permission."

Who was this man, and how did he think of things like this?

"You'll know it's me returning because I'll knock hard twice, wait three seconds, and then knock once softly."

"Okay." I tightened my grip on the piece of wood, savoring the control it would give me over the situation.

Like a knight in shining—well, white-towel—armor, he strode outside, leaving me alone in silence broken only by my thumping heart.

After using the wedge on the door, I turned and propped my back against the wall. Shoved my damp hair off my face. And tried to slow my pulse, which still raced double-time.

He returned and used the series of knocks, and I let him back inside. Hovering beside me, his chest rose and fell softly.

What should I say? The thought of meeting his gaze made me cringe. I'd already drooled over his backside. No need to get caught checking out his front. "Anyone out there?"

His hand lifted toward me before dropping to his side. "Nope. Didn't see anyone suspicious hanging around."

I'd heard his voice before, but where? Maybe in town or overseas. Traveling the world had introduced me to more people than I'd ever recall.

He cleared his throat. "Are you okay?"

I needed to pay attention to the conversation, not the gruff cadence of his voice. His abs. Or his hips, barely covered by the damp towel. Flutters sprang up in my belly and heat rushed into my cheeks, which had to be scarlet by now. Fortunately, while my brain had gone on vacation, my tongue was still on the job. "Yeah, I'm okay. It was probably nothing. I must've imagined the whole thing."

Just like all the other times, when I could swear I heard someone outside my apartment, only to beg my brother to come over for an investigation that revealed nothing. With each incident, I lost more of my pride. There was nothing worse than turning from a strong, independent woman into a whimpering, cowering shadow of herself.

The man strode toward the bench. "Let me get dressed. I'll wait for you outside while you change and then walk with you to your campsite."

How simple it would be to let everyone protect me. But I hadn't come here this weekend to let fear rule. "Thanks, but I'm all right." A glance over my shoulder sent me whirling back to face the door again because he'd dropped the towel and was lifting clothing from the bench. *Do not think about his cute butt.* I tugged on the knob. "I'll...umm, see you around?"

Wonderful. *See* you around. So much for possessing a working tongue.

I ran outside before he could reply and hurried down the steps. With my lower lip pinched between my teeth, I paused to scan the area, but no one looked my way. The hooded man was gone.

A stick lay half-buried in the grass by my feet. I hefted it, feeling incredibly stupid, but a heck of a lot safer. Weapon in hand, I headed for the shady section where my older brother, Eli, and I had set up our campsite.

Families bustled around me, erecting pop-up campers and screen rooms. Kids rode bikes and scooters on the path. Excitement rang out in the air. As a kid, I'd spent most of my weekends camping at Glenridge Mountain with Eli and Mom. Dad left us when I was five and Eli eight, so it had just been we three. Mom was away until next week, and it had been ten years, but Eli and I had decided to resurrect the tradition.

Two six-packs of soda sitting on the picnic table told me Eli had returned from his trip into town.

Feeling silly for carrying a stick, like I expected a pack of coyotes to attack any minute, I tossed it into the fire pit.

Eli emerged from his tent shirtless and limped over to the cooler. After coming too close to an IED in the Middle East, he'd been medically discharged. Regular PT had helped him maintain the bulk he'd gained during his years with the Navy, and leave it to him to flaunt it. A teenager almost ran into a tree while gawking over her shoulder.

"Hey," he said. "How was the water?"

"Chilly, but refreshing."

Eli slumped on a chair near the campfire ring, a soda can in his hand. He popped the top and took a long swallow. "I forgot to tell you earlier. One of my high school buddies is camping with us this weekend. Hope that's okay."

"Who?"

"Coop."

My heart flipped. Back in high school, Cooper Talon had been tall, skinny, and I could barely find his eyes behind his black hair and thick glasses. I'd been hyper-aware of him, unsure why my skin tingled whenever he came near. At fifteen to their seventeen, I'd been waiting forever to turn into the beauty Mom had predicted, one who could snag any guy I wanted. I'd wanted Cooper. There was something about the way he held his shoulders when he talked to my mom. How his tongue peeked from his mouth when he and Eli played Xbox. That cute nose wrinkle when he sat at the kitchen table doing homework.

I'd put on my best flirt whenever he was around, but it made no difference. He'd only grunted when I spoke to him. And he'd usually shown me his back, rather than his front, whenever I walked into the room. Talk about stomping on my burgeoning crush. I hadn't seen him since he joined the Navy—the Seabees—after he graduated from high school twelve years ago. Last I'd heard, he was stationed in California.

That voice in the changing room…Of course.

Eli nudged his soda can toward the open grassy area. "There's Coop now."

Naked-man strode our way, dressed in khaki shorts and a patterned brown tee. Eighteen-year-old Cooper Talon had given me heart palpitations. A fully mature Cooper might bring on cardiac arrest.

He stalled in front of me and grunted.

I blinked up at him, and my voice squeaked. "Cooper."

"In the flesh." His deep, raspy tone sparked through me. There was no mistaking the humor in his gray-blue eyes. Beautiful eyes he no longer hid behind thick glasses.

Stepping forward, I hugged him. His free hand slid around my waist, and his scent filled my senses with fresh air and warm skin, plus a subtle hint of spice.

"You look great, Ginny," he said by my ear. "Nice to *see* you."

I snorted. "Nice to *see* you, too." Eli's buddy and my old high school crush. I couldn't equate that shy teenager with this gorgeous man holding me now.

Releasing me, he stepped back. "No one was here earlier, so I left my things in my trunk. I'll go get them."

"Need help?" I asked.

"Nope, I've got it." He flopped his wet suit and towel over the line we'd strung between two trees and walked toward the parking lot above the campground.

I stared at his backside as he moved. Even clothed, he had a nice butt. Nice legs, too, with just the right amount of hair dusting his calves. "When did Cooper grow up?"

Eli frowned. "Huh?"

"Nothing." I shouldn't have spoken. No need to let on that my libido had locked onto this Cooper as easily as it had the younger version twelve years ago. Striding to the clothesline, I pulled off Cooper's suit and towel to hang them properly.

"You think Coop's changed that much?" Eli asked as he stood. Wincing, he rubbed his thigh.

I shrugged and clipped my towel beside Cooper's. I needed to get over my absorption with my brother's friend. For all I knew, he was married with three kids. Through the years, Eli had shared details about Cooper's deployments in the Middle East, but nothing personal. "You know if Cooper has a girlfriend?"

Eli's brow narrowed, filling me in on the fact that my interest had come across beyond casual. "You're not looking at Coop like that, are you? Don't even go there. You moved home—for good, you said. And Coop lives out west. He's career military. I doubt he's ready to move back to Crescent Cove when his battalion plans to deploy overseas soon."

"I only asked a general question."

Eli strolled closer. "I'm not warning you off—"

"Because you know I'd deck you if you did." Try to, anyway, if I could reach. My brother—and Cooper—had a good foot on my five-foot-four frame.

"That's not what I meant at all." He groaned and scratched his head, mussing his thick blonde hair that was much like mine, only shorter. "You can go out with whoever you want. You know that. But I'd hate to see you get hurt. Coop's…"

I couldn't read the emotions flicking across his face. "Cooper's what?"

"Not settling down material."

Ducking underneath the line, I eased past him. "Maybe I'm not settling down material, either."

"What about Zen?"

"He and I were nowhere near settled." I'd met Zen in Paris over a year ago, and we traveled together after that. At his urging, we'd gone to Croatia and then to Istanbul. I hadn't loved him. If anything, I'd stayed with him because seeking the perfect photo could be lonely, and he was a decent companion. "We broke up ages ago. Before…"

If only I could forget what happened in Istanbul as easily as I'd forgotten my former boyfriend.

The horror of that moment spiked through me. If Zen had been with me that day, those men might not have—

"Seems to me you've become the settling down kind, now," Eli said. "Bought a building with an apartment on the second floor. Opened a photography business that's doing great already."

I fumbled with my tent flap. "I didn't mean anything when I asked about his personal life." *Liar.* "I was just making small talk." *Double liar.* "I'm not interested in anything more than friendship with Cooper." I nodded to solidify my argument. A third lie piled on top of the others. From Eli's snort, I hadn't convinced him any more than I had myself.

Gravel crunched behind me, and I turned.

"I dropped my keys." Cooper bent forward to grab them off the ground. A speculative gleam filled his eyes when he directed them my way. "I'll go get that tent now."

Perfect. Nothing good ever came from gossiping about someone behind their back.

Squirming, I stepped into my tent and zipped the door closed behind me. Hunched over because I couldn't stand upright, I untied my bathing suit top and tossed it aside, and shimmied out of my bottoms. Looking around, I frowned. Where were my shorts and t-shirt? I could swear I'd left them on the foot of my air mattress.

The idea that someone had been inside my tent and moved them gave me pause.

"Do not do this to yourself," I whispered. "You've freaked out once today already. Your stuff's around here somewhere."

Calm words couldn't prevent my gaze from flicking around the tent interior, seeking someone lurking inside the tight space with me. Although it was humid, the warmth barely penetrated my skin.

My gaze was pulled to my pillow, where a mini-tile painting waited for me, and my body loosened. While I was swimming, Eli must've dropped off his latest treasure.

Moving around the mattress, I found my clothing lying on the floor beside it and dressed quickly. I flopped onto the bed and studied the tiny painting of the view from the top of Cadillac Mountain. It had been years since we'd hiked to the peak together, and I smiled at the memory.

As a teenager, Eli had started painting with watercolors before moving on to oils. One of his larger works hung in my living room. A few weeks ago, he'd started leaving me little painted tiles like this one. The last had been of Acadia Park, a place we'd visited a few times while growing up. I tucked the tile inside my backpack for safekeeping, planning to add it to my mini art collection.

While unzipping the tent flap to step outside, I renewed my determination to regain my life.

Istanbul was a random event.

It wouldn't haunt me any longer.

2

Cooper

I strode up toward the parking lot, where I'd left my rental car. Not paying attention, I almost ran into a hooded guy darting from another trail that connected with mine. I halted to let the man go ahead of me—it was clear he would've slammed into me if I hadn't. Breathing hard, the jerk elbowed past, heading in the same direction as me.

Damn hot for a sweatshirt, but what did I know? Maybe he'd just come from the lake and was cold. None of my business, anyway. I had other things to occupy my mind. Like setting up my tent and drowning my irritation about what I'd overheard in a beer or two.

Twelve long years should've cauterized Ginny from my brain. It wasn't like she'd haunted me or anything. After all, I'd slept with a woman I'd gone to boot camp with. I'd enjoyed my share of quick relationships between tours overseas. And I'd lived with and almost married Annie, a woman I'd dated while stationed in California, before we ended things a year ago. Plenty of women had passed through my life since I'd buried my desire for my best friend's younger sister back in high school.

We met in my junior year, and her honey brown eyes caught me up and dragged me down to the bottom of the deepest sea, where only she existed. To keep from staring at her all the time, I pretended she didn't exist. As if that would impress a girl. I'd wanted to act on my interest, but a seventeen-year-old making a play for his best friend's fifteen-year-old sister was a touchy matter. First, she might've turned me down, making every second I spent at their place torture. If things hadn't worked out, it could've ruined my and Eli's friendship. And Eli might've flat-out told me I wasn't good enough for her.

In my wildest dreams, I'd hoped to take her out someday. Show the world what she meant to me. Thirty hours a week at the supermarket brought in some cash, but after Dad took most of it for bills, I couldn't afford to ask her to go to the movies with me or even for ice cream. My hopes of getting closer to her crashed when my father kicked me out after graduation. The military offered me a new home, but it pulled me away from her forever.

Last I heard, she was still traveling overseas. I sure hadn't expected to meet up with her again while I was buck-ass naked in a campground changing room. When she told me someone was chasing her, my protective instincts kicked in. The awkward kid who'd itched to talk to her back in high school had emerged from the dark cave where I'd penned him, responding as if it had only been seconds since I'd last seen her.

And here she was again, as unobtainable today as she'd been back then. From her sisterly hug and the comment I overheard, she'd tucked me back into the older brother slot I'd filled when I was a skinny high school nerd. The military had toughened me up, and endless workouts had broadened my shoulders and chest, but the new me still wasn't enough to impress her.

Reaching the parking lot, I popped open my trunk. A car backed out a few spaces down and churned toward me, flinging dirt behind it. Brow narrowing, I shifted around to the side of my vehicle while it went past. Dust stung my eyes. When the vehicle reached the main drive, it picked up speed, sending rocks pinging around me. Local shrapnel. It was all I could do not to grab my nonexistent helmet and shout for my buddies to take cover.

"Slow down, asshole." Doubtful the guy heard me with the windows up. But, shit, this was a public place. Someone could get hurt.

The vehicle skipped the stop sign and squealed out onto the pavement, heading toward town.

Shaking my head, I returned to my trunk. I set my cooler on the ground and then looped the tent strap over my shoulder. Nothing like spending a weekend in a one-man pup tent. But I'd scrounged out worse places to crash in the Middle East, sleeping with my gun as my only companion. After locking the car, I grabbed the cooler and walked back to the campsite to put up what would become my new domain for the next three nights.

"I'll be right back." Ginny gestured toward the building housing the bathrooms the second I arrived. She tensed on the edge of our campsite, frowning. "You guys aren't going anywhere while I'm away, are you?"

"'Course, not," Eli said. Not sarcastic, just reassuring.

Clouds fled her face, replaced by a soft smile that punched me in the gut. The last of my air wheezed out.

"Thanks," she said while I relearned to breathe. "We should light the grill when I get back and start dinner."

"Sounds great." I doubted she heard me because she'd already spun away. Paying more attention to her than setting up, I fumbled with my tent bag, sliding out the sack with the poles.

Ginny as a teenager had been sweeter than cotton candy at a summer's fair. Doe-like limbs. Curves that only hinted at the lushness she'd grow into. And a sense of humor that lit a spark inside me that would never die down.

Stooped forward, Eli pulled the nylon tent from the bag. With a flick, he extended it outward beside one of the others.

"Coop." Eli grunted and said it again, louder, "Cooper."

"What?" I kept staring at Ginny.

"I'm gonna have to ask you to back off from my sister."

Had I been that obvious? I hadn't been the face-heating kind since Mom died when I was thirteen, but my cheeks sure burned now. My curt nod was worthy of a Master Chief disciplining me for due cause.

"Ginny's been through something traumatic recently," Eli said. "She's...vulnerable." Reaching across the canvas surface, he grabbed the poles from my unresisting fingers and began linking them together.

A growl rumbled in my chest. "Someone hurt her?"

"Yeah, but it's not my story to tell." Eli straightened and pulled the tent up, securing the pole in the ground stay.

I studied Eli's face but couldn't infer anything from the sun-creased lines.

"She needs to focus on finding herself right now," Eli said softly. He handed me the empty spike bag. "And you've got eight years left to serve before you retire."

More than halfway toward twenty years, I'd be a fool to cut from the military now.

"Yep." I could see where Eli was taking this conversation and didn't like it. Not one bit.

"You told me you were headed back overseas soon. Another tour in the Middle East?"

"Yep." Although I'd been sent on tour multiple times during the past twelve years, I'd volunteered for my last few deployments. A Seabee carried a gun and was called upon to use it, but I was part of a construction battalion. Though Eli had been discharged from the military after being wounded, combat wasn't the norm.

"You're only in Crescent Cove for a short time. It would be wrong to let my sister start thinking you could offer her more."

Valid point. Not that it would ever come to something like that. "I'm here long enough to get the house cleaned out. That's it."

Eli placed his hand on my shoulder and squeezed. "I'm sorry about your dad. Even though I know you two weren't close."

Something Eli and I shared, though Eli's dad had bailed on Eli's family when my friend was eight. Eli was still haunted by the loss, but I hadn't seen my father since he slammed the door in my face after telling me get the hell out of the house.

"Must be hard being in the place where you grew up," Eli said.

"Yep." Actually, it was easier than I'd thought it would be. But then, I'd only cleaned out the first floor, saving the upstairs and all the memories it contained for last.

"Here's the thing," Eli said. "Ginny's starting a new life here, and yours is on the other side of the world. We've been friends for years. You're a great guy. But I don't want to see either of you get hurt."

Even if I wanted to pursue this, Ginny had made it clear she wasn't interested. It was a non-issue. No reason I couldn't respect Eli's request.

"I'll let it go." I met Eli's brown eyes, only a shade darker than Ginny's. "Promise."

Shrugging away from my friend, I finished setting up the tent, which sagged worse than a sack of cow shit. I unzipped the flap and shoved my bedding inside, then climbed in after it.

It was time to deflate my lungs into the air mattress.

While trying to forget how perfectly Ginny fit in my arms.

3

Ginny

While I was walking from the bathroom to our campsite, a fluffy toy poodle came yipping across the grass and ran right up to me. Grinning at the cute, fuzzy face, I stooped down to pat the dog, chuckling as it wiggled beneath my hand.

"What a sweetie. And who are you?" I asked. The dog squirmed and jumped, trying to lick my face, unable to get enough of my touch. "I love your bows!" Pink ribbons were tied behind the dog's ears.

A blond man rushed up to us. "Thanks for grabbing her," he said, panting. "She slipped her leash."

I lifted the dog and passed her to him. "No problem."

"Not the first time my baby's gotten free," he said with an easy smile. He scratched under the dog's chin. "This girl was born to run, just like her mama. But I worry she'll get into trouble." He chuckled. "Also like her mama."

I smiled. "I understand."

"Hey," he said, a bright gleam filling his eyes. "Don't you remember me? We went out for a while back in high school."

He did look vaguely familiar.

His face scrunched, creating little creases around his eyes. "Come on. We were both in the photography club, too." Grabbing my forearm, he squeezed it. "Tom Prescott."

"Oh, yeah." We'd gone out in our senior year, but he started getting clingy, so I ended it. After graduation, he'd gone to tech school or the police academy. Something like that. With the flurry of buying my airline ticket for Europe, outfitting my backpack for a long stay, and convincing my mom I wouldn't be murdered my first night in a hostel, I hadn't paid much attention to what my classmates were doing.

The dog whined and strained toward me.

"Weird how she likes you." Tom studied my face. "She doesn't usually take to strangers. But you and my wife, Laura, could be twins."

"Maybe that's it."

"Must be." Tom turned and started back across the campground. "Thanks again."

"Nice seeing you," I called after him.

He waved but didn't look back. "You, too."

I continued on to my campsite. When I arrived, tension hung in the air thicker than smoke over a greenwood campfire. Since the cause was not readily apparent, I decided it must be a man thing. And while some might balk at doing what was often called a woman thing, I got out the grill and started preparing dinner. Eli took his turn at the bathrooms while I dumped hickory chunks underneath the grate.

"Want some help?" Cooper asked.

"No thanks, I've got it." This wasn't the first time I'd made dinner. While covering the globe one photo at a time, I'd stayed in hostels, welcoming stranger's homes, and even the occasional roadside shack. Being able to prepare a decent meal with what I could scrounge up locally had become both a pleasure and a necessity.

Cooper went over to his cooler and lifted the lid.

Stooped down, I tucked bits of newspaper among the briquettes, forcing myself to use my bad as well as my good arm. Broken by the kidnappers, I'd only gotten the cast off a month ago.

Use it like you normally would, my doctor said. *Don't baby it.*

But it still ached. All the time. Like my spirit.

Cooper straightened from where he'd been sorting through his cooler. "I brought dogs. You up for red skins?"

"I'm making pizza."

"On the grill."

"Yup." I smiled at his amazed expression. "Frozen bread dough I set out earlier to rise. Fresh tomatoes, herbs, and spinach from Mom's garden. Cheese. Artichoke hearts and Greek olives."

Could a grown man drool?

"I have enough for you," I added.

Cooper dropped his eyes to the packages of rolls and hot dogs in his hands.

I lightened my voice, letting my smile shine through. "Come on. You know you want some."

"I do." Huskiness whispered through his words.

Flustered by his tone, which I shouldn't read as sexy, I turned, hoping he wouldn't catch the color rising in my face.

Cooper came over to stand beside me. "Tell me what to do, then?"

"Inside the plastic bin in front of my tent, you'll find a cutting board and a bottle of oil. Grab them, plus the bottles of spices. When the coals are ready, we'll stretch out our dough." As he turned away, I said, "Would you

21

get the vegetables and pepperoni from the bigger cooler, too?"

Eli returned, and we popped open beers. While we grilled one side of our bread dough, we sat beside the cold fire pit in collapsible chairs and savored our brews.

I took pictures of the little girls I'd seen at the lake, who were playing with toy trucks in the dirt in the campsite next to ours. After, I pointed the camera my brother and Cooper's way. "Smile, guys."

Leaning his shoulder against Cooper's, Eli stuck his tongue out and screwed up his face. Call me sneaky, but I tilted the lens at the last minute to get a full face shot of Cooper. For posterity. Nothing else.

We flipped our dough, added toppings, and left them to bake. Nothing made a stomach rumble more than the smell of bread, melted cheese, and fresh herbs floating in the air. I zombie walked to the picnic table with mine, salivating. After sitting, I dug in, chowing my way through my dinner in seconds. We each made another pizza, but my pace slowed before I finished half. I dropped the rest on my plate.

"Busy this week, Eli?" I asked.

"A few shifts."

Eight months ago, when he got out of the Seabees, he moved home and took a job in security at a hardware store one town over from ours. He still hoped to find something that would use his military technical skills, but nothing had opened up yet.

I reached for the rest of my pizza, but found an empty plate. Cooper's eyes gleamed, and he licked lips. My eyebrows flew upward. "There's a fox in my hen house."

Total innocence filled his face. "What do you mean?"

"I can't believe you ate all of yours and the rest of mine. Where did you put it?"

He patted his flat belly. "I'm a growing boy."

I bit back my smile.

"I can make you another."

I'd only been teasing, something I couldn't resist. "Make one for yourself, if you want, but I'm finished." My stomach growls had receded. Roll me over to my camp chair, and I'd doze the evening away. I licked tomato sauce off my fingers.

"I'm full, too." His eyes followed my movement before he stood and grabbed my plate. "I'll do the dishes." He dumped them into the unlit fire pit.

"There *are* no dishes."

"I can wash the tongs, the cutting board." Basin and sponge in hand, he walked to the water faucet on the edge of our campsite.

"Who's up for cards?" I asked when he'd retaken his seat. "I'd love a game of cribbage."

"Not me." Eli grimaced at Cooper. "She wins every single time."

I grinned. "That's because I have precognition." Cooper lifted his eyebrows, and I giggled. "I always know what the cards are before they're flipped."

"Not possible." Cooper tossed a knowing look at my brother.

He didn't believe me, huh? I reached across the table and grabbed the deck. "Care to take me on, *big boy*?"

"I'd love to take you on."

His comment stirred up flutters in my belly, but I reminded myself he was only being friendly.

Eli stood. "Don't do it, dude. She'll slay you."

"Maybe I want to be slayed." Cooper turned on the bench to face me. "Two out of three sound good?"

"Sure."

"I'm going swimming." Eli rubbed his thigh. "The best

exercise for my leg, according to my physical therapist." He strode toward his tent. "You can massacre Cooper without me hanging around to witness the event, Ginny."

"I've been known to win a cribbage game or two back at the base," Cooper said. "I might prove your precognition theory wrong."

"We shall see, won't we?" I dumped out the pegs, then shuffled and cut the deck. Queen for me.

Cooper flipped a two. "See?" He sipped his beer. "You've got nothing on me."

Leave it to him to crow about it. I snorted and handed over the cards. "Your deal."

Eli emerged from his tent dressed in swim shorts, a towel looped around his neck. He bumped my shoulder as he passed. "Don't be too hard on Coop."

I chuckled and called out to my brother as he walked away, "If you hear him whimpering in his tent when you come back, ignore him. He'll need privacy to patch up his wounded pride."

After Eli left, Cooper did some slick moves with the cards, and I had to wonder if I'd be the one whimpering by the end of the evening.

"I'll show you, sweetheart," he said.

Sweetheart, huh?

"Guess I need to take an edge off this overconfidence of yours," he added.

"I dare you to try."

"Don't even go there."

I snorted. "What are you going to do about it, military man? Pull your weapon?"

"Utilize our Seabee motto," he said smugly. "Can do."

Lord, I wanted to explore what he *could* do. I flicked my hand at him. "Show me your worst, then."

He dealt, and I handed him two cards for his crib. I

split the deck, anticipating an eight or a seven to go with my run. In fact, I'd planned for it.

"Cool," Cooper said. "A five."

Not cool, because I'd given him two face cards. I led, and we placed cards back and forth, Cooper pegging last.

"Awesome." When he looked up at me through his long lashes, my heartbeat surged. "I'm in the lead."

"Just like in high school."

He cocked his head. "What do you mean?"

"You ran cross-country. Won first place in most of the school track meets."

"You remember that?"

I remembered a lot about Cooper.

He blinked down at his cards. "Hmm."

I cleared my throat before this got awkward. "My turn?"

"Yep."

The long look he gave me made me squirm, because it implied he saw through to that secret place inside me that still found him attractive.

"I think you're trying to mess with my mojo." My voice came out breathless, but I couldn't help it.

He slapped his palm to his chest. "Not me."

I shook my finger at him. "No fancy tricks."

We played a few more hands with Cooper maintaining an irritating lead. It matched his irritating smile that grew with each play. My card savvy had either fled for the evening or it had settled on Cooper, because the deck sure loved him. Not that I had *true* precognition, but I was able to predict the cards more often than not, to the frustration of my friends. It occurred to me that I might be eating my earlier bravado for dessert.

"Homestretch," he said with too much enthusiasm, moving his peg. "You'll never catch me."

I scowled, a gesture that lost some of its oomph when my grin slipped through. Squeezing the cards, I closed my eyes. *Give me a decent hand, please!*

"Looking for some of that mojo?"

My lips quivered. If he wasn't so cute, I'd growl. I peeked over my cards, hoping to read his upcoming moves on his face.

"How's that precognition working for you tonight?"

"I think it's on vacation. Or swimming with Eli."

"Who is no longer swimming." My brother emerged from the darkness and paused beside us.

"How was the water?" I asked.

"Warm." He tugged his towel from around his neck and stared toward the deep woods beyond our campsite. "When I was coming back from the lake, I could swear I saw someone behind our tents. But when I got close, I didn't find anyone there, just random tracks. Whoever it was must've heard me and took off."

Cooper frowned and started to stand. "Let's scope it out."

Eli dropped his hand on Cooper's shoulder. "Thanks. Already did."

"Just say the word, and I'm on it." Cooper squinted into the dark a moment before settling back on the bench.

"Probably nothing," Eli said. "The campground is packed this weekend."

"True." Cooper tapped the deck. "Pick a card, Ginny. This is your last chance to win this round."

"I'm getting creamed," I told Eli, pouting.

After the cut, Cooper dealt the last hand. "Warned you, didn't I?"

The scowl I sent over my cards would've made a lesser man squirm. "I can't figure out how you're doing it."

"Maybe I've got precognition." He tapped his temple. "The next card will be a six."

"Like that'll happen." I flipped the card over. Six. My exhalation shot hair off my face.

Eli set a water bottle on the table. He scrolled through his phone before tucking it into his pocket. "I'm going to bed." His gaze slid between us. "Don't squeal too loud when you lose, Ginny."

I stiffened. "I'm not losing."

"Looks like it to me." Eli grinned and entered his tent, totally missing the pretend stake I threw at his back. His air mattress squeaked as he settled his body for sleep.

"You lead." Cooper flicked the back of my cards.

I fidgeted during the next few plays but couldn't make headway.

"And home," Cooper said, pegging through to the end. His warm smile drew me in. "Another game?"

"I don't have enough pride left for more defeat." Rising, I headed to my tent for my toothbrush.

Cooper came around the table, meeting up with me. "Bed, then?" His eyes darted down my front.

Why did I picture us naked inside my tent? I'd never been a woman who hopped into the sack with someone without getting to know him first. But I knew Cooper. Or I had as a teenager. This man? Not as much as I'd like to.

"Sweetheart?" Cooper murmured.

"What's with the sweetheart talk?"

"Just being friendly." He leaned close to my ear. "You're sweet, so it seems appropriate."

With that parting shot, he ducked inside his tent.

4

Cooper

Flirting with Ginny thrust me deep into dangerous territory. Not only because I risked handing over that part of my heart she'd captured back in high school, but because of the promise I'd made to her brother.

Why had I agreed to leave her alone? At this point, I couldn't be with her a second without dying to touch her. I wanted to tilt her chin and cover her mouth with mine.

After ditching my clothes inside my tent, I settled on the air mattress and stared at the canvas ceiling. Moonlight filtered through the trees, creating camo patterns on the dark material.

Being back in Maine sure screwed with my head, which was why I'd never returned. Not that Dad sent an invitation. He'd cut me off completely.

When Mom was alive, we'd done family things together, like fishing and hiking. Once she was gone, Dad and I butted heads worse than cliffside rams. The one drink Dad normally had after work soon turned into straight-old drinking from the bottle. Hangovers made it hard to get up in the morning, and Dad lost his job at the mill. We'd lived on the settlement from Mom's accident until it ran out, but after that, only I could hold down a steady job. Working in a grocery store paid a few bills, as did his disability check, but what was left didn't do more than put boxed macaroni and cheese on the table.

Alcohol stole my loving father and turned a decent man mean.

Get your shit off the table, became my notice to finish my homework and go to bed.

I'm not footing the bill for your clothes, Dad said when I asked to use some of my own money for jeans or a shirt.

Don't shove that in my face, was my reward when I tried to show Dad the high grades I got in school.

Never should've bothered trying to impress my father.

After Dad skipped my graduation to blur Mom's memory with Johnnie Walker, I'd had enough. A cup of water woke Dad fast, and his blistering anger turned the final trick on my future. Dad kicked me out of the house, telling me never to return, that I was *crap-for-a-son* and that I could make my own way in the world. He'd been right. I'd done well in the military, moving up through the ranks, making Chief.

And I was a fool to keep rehashing this. My father was dead. Nothing could change now, except me.

Light footsteps crunched outside. I hadn't heard Eli or Ginny unzip their tents. When the steps crept closer, I frowned. A popping sound, followed by shuffling, suggested someone was going through our belongings. We hadn't brought much, but I refused to let someone steal what little we had. I slipped from my sleeping bag. Barefoot, I emerged from my tent in time to catch a dark streak running from our campsite.

"Hey," I yelled. Sticks gouged my feet as I raced after the man.

The guy entered the path leading toward the lake and disappeared into the shadows.

I pushed for speed, hitting the path at a dead run, but when I tripped, I slowed. I ran all the time, but not without proper gear. Give me sneakers, and the thief sure wouldn't outdo me on any day.

Someone rushed up behind me and hit me in the back of the head. Grimacing, I dropped to my knees, cussing. As quickly as he'd arrived, the guy faded into the woods. I struggled to rise, furious with myself for not sensing he was near. This might be a rural campground, but I could still get hurt. Not paying attention could see me killed.

I rubbed the back of my head and groaned. No blood I could tell; just a bump and a headache that would hit me soon. I squinted around, hoping to hear something that would tell me in which direction to give chase, but the perp appeared to be gone.

It would've been great to catch him. Then I could've returned the favor of a knock on the head before I made it clear I wouldn't tolerate stealing any more than assault.

Since there was nothing I could do, I limped back to the campsite, rubbing my skull while cursing every stick and rock my feet met along the way.

The plastic cover lying on the ground told me the guy had pawed through the kitchen bin outside Ginny's tent. The intrusion sent anger rumbling through my chest all over again, and I stooped down to pick up her things.

As I was returning to my tent, Ginny unzipped her entrance flap and tucked her upper body out. She'd braided her hair, and it hung past her shoulder in a thick, golden rope.

I straightened and faced her, doing my best not to notice how little clothing she wore. Just a skin-tight tank and what looked like minuscule shorts.

I wore even less, just cotton boxers.

"Everything okay out here?" she asked. "I heard something."

"Someone was going through your kitchen things," I said. "I chased them, but they got away." No need to mention the blow to the back of my head. I didn't want to worry her, and I wasn't truly hurt. The military had delivered harder hits in the past.

"Oh." She frowned and darted her gaze around. "You sure they're gone?"

"For now. Probably looking for something easy to steal."

"I didn't bring anything valuable. Whatever I can't bear to lose is locked up inside Eli's Jeep."

Smart.

Ginny fidgeted with her braid. "I guess things will be okay as long as you guys...oh." Her gaze slid down my body, and she blinked. "You're, umm..."

Wearing next to nothing. The moon didn't shed much light, but I could swear I saw color filling her face as her attention zoned in on the front of my boxers.

"I, uh..." I said. Maybe I should've thrown on more clothing before leaving my tent.

"You all right?" Her words came out breathless, but I was the one who'd been running.

"Sure." Absolutely not. I wanted to nudge her back inside her tent and beg to follow.

Her tongue touched her upper lip.

Groaning, I turned away. "Let me know if you hear anything out here, okay?" Without waiting for her reply, I bulled my way inside my tent.

"Night," Ginny called out softly as I yanked up the zipper.

I dropped onto my back on my mattress, ignoring the

sleeping bag. Chilling down had become a top priority. Swearing, I rolled onto my side and quietly hissed out a marching cadence until things returned to semi-normal.

Yeah, Ginny had noticed me. Who wouldn't notice a nearly naked man standing around in his boxers? While other guys might read her breathlessness as interest, I didn't dare take the chance. This wasn't just about the promise I'd made to Eli, but about my past.

Verbal abuse could gut a man. I didn't have a damn thing to offer a special woman like her, outside of leaving. Next week, I'd finish cleaning out my father's house and hand it over to a realtor. If there was anything left after I paid the back taxes, I'd buy myself a pizza. I'd soon deploy overseas and then return to my base in California to prepare for my next mission.

Ginny would continue her life here in Maine.

Without me.

5

Ginny

Rough hands grabbed my arms. A second man covered my mouth, smothering my cry. His fingers reeked, and my throat filled with bile.

They shoved me forward.

"Bizimle gel!" Turkish, and I didn't understand.

I couldn't scream. I had to scream. No! Leave me alone!

While terror liquefied my limbs, I was unable to kick or punch. Shock had frozen my bones.

The men dragged me across the sidewalk, toward their vehicle.

Loosened from my panic, I wrenched away from them, shrieking for help.

A fist tightened on my jacket, yanking me backward. The other man grabbed my wrist, twisting until bone gave way. Agony shot through me, and I screamed.

An arm tightened around my throat, making each breath wheeze.

Horror overwhelming me, I tripped, crashing to my knees. A shove sent me forward, and my left palm bit the pavement. My right arm hung limply, like the broken wing of a bird.

Whimpering, I curled into a ball while hands slapped, feet kicked. A boot connected with my ribs, and pain stabbed deep. Gasp-

ing, I squirmed, my fingernails breaking as I tried to drag myself across the pavement. "No. Please."

One of the men grabbed my foot and hauled me over to the curb-side vehicle. As they stuffed me inside, my head smacked on the open sliding door. Stars flickered in my periphery, and I worried I'd pass out.

They threw me on a bench seat and slammed the door.

As they jumped into the front of the vehicle, I scrambled to escape. My bloody fingers slid along the glass.

This couldn't be happening. Please…Oh, no, please.

I bolted upright in my tent, my lungs on fire. The rancid taste of the man's fingers filled my mouth as if the assault was happening now, instead of three months ago.

Early morning sunlight filtering through the nylon overhead, and a child's laughter nearby, brought me fully back to my senses. I flopped back on my mattress and rubbed my face. My sigh whistled from my throat.

In the woods, a raven cawed. A light wind stirred the trees, the leaves whispering calm. My nightmare slithered back into the dark corner of my brain where it lurked, ready to rise up and strike again. I was safe here. Eli and Cooper would hear my screams.

While my pulse slowed, I willed my breathing to relax. My body wouldn't stop trembling. I hadn't had a nightmare like this for weeks. If only I could put what happened behind me. Counseling had helped, but the best cure of all was moving home, where Eli and Mom enfolded me in their comforting embrace.

At least I'd escaped those men. When they pulled up to a stop sign, I yanked open the door. Before they could grab me, I stumbled out onto the sidewalk, and a couple of bystanders intervened. The vehicle took off.

By then, it was too late for me. Coming so soon after a break-in at my hotel room, my confidence had been shredded. In seconds, I'd changed from a self-assured woman into a weak, quivering mess. The police told me the break-in was someone looking for valuables or money or drugs. Thankfully, I'd had my camera, computer, and thumb drives in my backpack with me when they rifled through my things. It would've been horrible to lose the items most precious to me.

I wasn't the first American to have something bad happen, the police said. A few months earlier, a diplomat had been murdered. Muggings were common. Foreigners were hot commodities in Istanbul. For ransom or worse.

Worried it could happen again, I'd abandoned my career as a travel photographer. How could I roam the world alone when horrible things like this could hit me at any time? Retreat was my only option.

The incident still haunted me. For the past three months, I'd worked hard to put myself together again, but I was barely making progress. Which was so, so wrong. I wanted my freedom back. I wanted to go outside by myself without being scared.

I smoothed my hair, using the gesture to drive away the last of my shakes. Rising, I dragged on sweats and, with my bathroom bag in hand, I walked to the showers. A thorough soaking under the hot spray helped me put the past into perspective. I brushed my teeth and stuffed my things into my bag, slinging it over my shoulder.

When I stepped outside, I smacked into someone coming around the other side of the building. The towel draped across the back of Tom's neck told me he'd show-ered, too.

"Hey, I'm sorry," he said. "I didn't mean to run into you." His poodle whimpered from where she sat on the ground by his feet.

"It's okay. I wasn't looking where I was going."

"You must've just washed up, too. You look great." Tom's gaze traveled down my front. He stepped forward and slid a lock of my hair over my shoulder. Grinning, his warm gaze met mine. "Laura's hair was a lot like yours. She had the same height, facial features, and build, too."

Was? I'd thought his wife was alive.

I'd be foolish to ignore the prickles traveling down my spine.

"I need to get back to my campsite." I cursed myself for being creeped out by what was probably a simple inter-action. "I need to start breakfast."

"Wait." Tom reached for me, but I evaded his hand.

While the dog strained against the leash and barked shrilly, I rushed toward my campsite. Arriving and finding it empty, I put my bathroom things away in my tent. I was getting out the frying pan to make breakfast when someone came up behind me. Still spooked, I spun with the pan raised in defense.

Cooper lifted both hands and took a step backward. A wide grin revealed his straight white teeth. "Whoa. I never argue with a woman armed with a cast iron weapon."

I snorted and lifted a smile to match his. "Decent policy all around."

"I did tell you a Seabee is always prepared, didn't I?"

I had a feeling Cooper was prepared for just about anything.

Shoving off the uneasy feeling generated by Tom, I dropped the pan onto the picnic table and started the cook stove. Eli joined us as I was sliding eggs onto plates. By then, I'd had my first cup of coffee. Nothing cured an unsettled mood better than caffeine. We ate, and our easy joking drove away the last of my shadows.

Eli stood and gathered the empty plates. "I'll do kitchen duty this time."

"You about ready for our gold rush?" I asked while I tidied the campsite.

"I can't make it today," Eli said over his shoulder. "I'm really sorry, but Steve was in an accident. He's hurt."

Eli's employer had only three security guards. Normally, they alternated shifts, but they had to make up for each other if someone was sick or on vacation. Most of the time, Eli loved the overtime. He hadn't taken vacation time to come camping; this was his scheduled time off. Steve was one of the three.

"Is Steve okay?" I asked.

"Think so. The boss asked me to fill in."

I was disappointed, of course, because I'd looked forward to hanging out with my brother today. But I understood. When work called, you answered. Especially if someone was injured.

"We can go another time." Eli dropped the dish drainer on the picnic table and ducked into his tent to get ready.

"Okay." I nibbled my lower lip, wondering what I'd do to keep busy today. I'd ridden here with Eli and left my car at home. Even if I had a vehicle, the idea of going on the adventure by myself made my skin crawl. Maybe I could lounge in my tent and finish my book.

Cooper smiled my way. "I'm game for a gold rush. Whatever that is."

"Problem solved," I said, standing. "We can leave as soon as you're ready." I tapped my chin. "You'll need swim shorts and water shoes if you have them. I'll pack the rest." He started toward his tent, and I called out, "Oh, and bring a hat."

While he showered and changed, I made lunch and tucked it into my backpack. Cooper soon strolled back into the campsite wearing shorts and a tee, with a hat on his head, brim backward. It might do nothing to shade his face, but it sure sparked my libido.

After saying goodbye to Eli, we walked up the path to the parking lot.

"I'll be your chauffeur today." Grinning, Cooper pulled his keys from his pocket and dangled them in the air like bait. The teasing glint in his eyes hauled me in like a fish on a line. Every. Single. Damned. Time. "I'm an excellent driver."

I fanned my face, only able to nod.

We tossed our stuff on the back seat and climbed into the thousand-degree car, putting the windows down. The second Cooper started the vehicle, the radio blared. "…information about an American diplomat killed in—" He shut it off and eased the vehicle out of the parking lot.

At the top of the camp road, he slowed. "Where to?"

"Left." I'd printed a map. Tilting it into the sunlight, I squinted at the fine lines scrolling across the paper. "I think."

His eyebrows lifted. "I have GPS on my phone."

"Where we're going, even satellites can't direct us."

"The military gave me the highest security clearance. You can trust me with secret locations."

I rolled my eyes. "You just follow my directions, and you won't need to flash your high-security badge, Sheriff."

Chuckling, he pressed on the gas pedal, making the vehicle speed up. The stifling heat inside the car was shifted aside by a wave of cool air drifting from the forest on either side of the road. The scent of evergreen and earth overloaded my senses.

"Up here." I leaned forward, pointing. "Take a right onto that dirt road."

"The one with no sign."

"Exactly."

Cooper rubbed the back of his neck. "Where did you get this map, anyway?"

"If I told you, I'd have to take you down."

He sputtered. Talk about making my day. As far as I was concerned, the best kind of man was a man who was unsettled.

The car smacked over potholes as we inched along the road. We passed a lean, gray-bearded man dressed in overalls, carrying a fishing pole and tackle box. He paused and scowled while our vehicle drove by.

"How much farther?" Cooper ducked as if he worried low-hanging tree branches would plunge through the roof any minute.

"Take us all the way to the end."

Ten minutes later, we came to a roadblock with a thick forest beyond it. While the fence slanted, the sign showed little wear. *No Trespassing.*

Cooper put the car into park and stared through the windshield, tapping his fingers on the wheel. "This must be the wrong place."

"I have written permission to be here."

Unbuckling, he turned to face me, his gaze narrowing. That gleam I savored had reappeared in his eyes. "Sure, you do."

I struggled to maintain a serious expression. "I'm beginning to suspect you don't believe me."

"And what gave you that idea?"

"I've got a map." I waved it in the air and he tried to snatch it from me, making me tuck it behind my back. "Where do you think I found it, anyway?"

"On eBay?"

I sputtered, trying not to laugh, because this was the same reaction I'd drawn from him. Maybe a woman was also best when she was unsettled. "Trust me."

He spoke slowly like he was reserving judgment. "Okay."

We got out of the car and covered ourselves with bug spray before the mosquitoes carried us away.

"Hey." I pulled my camera from my pack. "Can I take your picture before we head out?"

"One last photo before I disappear off the face of the Earth?"

"Ha, ha."

"Let's do one of us together instead." He paused. "If that's okay. You can send me a copy."

I couldn't imagine another photo I'd rather take right now. "I'll use a timer." After setting things up on a boulder, I darted over to stand beside Cooper. His arm slipped around my waist. He was only being friendly, but it sure felt wonderful.

Picture taken, I tucked my camera back into my bag. I couldn't wait to look at the photo later.

Cooper glanced around. "Where do we go now?"

The map indicated beyond the fence. After striding through deep grass and around to the other side, I stopped and pointed to a narrow trail snaking downhill through the woods. "That way."

Cooper followed, and we eventually came to a river. More like a stream this time of year, since it hadn't rained in weeks. We stood on the bank, staring at the water trickling around rocks and clumps of vegetation. It looked deep in places, though not over our heads.

"Okay, gold rush," Cooper said, hands on his hips. "I was expecting…a jewelry store?"

I flung my arms wide. "Nothing sparkly out here but the great outdoors." After shrugging off my backpack, I unzipped it and pulled out a metal pan, handing it to Cooper. "Here you go."

He blinked down at it. "We making stir fry?"

"Only the inedible kind." I yanked off my tank but left on my shorts.

Cooper groaned.

Glancing up at him, I dropped my floppy hat back on my head. It blocked out the sunlight, but not his odd expression. "What?"

He stared at the ground, not at me. "Absolutely nothing."

I shrugged and popped the lid off my sunscreen, slathering some on my arms, legs, and chest. I nudged my head to the side. "Can you do my back?"

"Yep." His hand lifted away from his side slower than me in the morning before caffeine, as if...

Surely, he had no problem touching me. Because, if I unsettled him that way...How intriguing. My heart rate doubled, and I knew my words came out breathless. "I don't know if you want to take off your shirt or not." Might be better if he didn't because Cooper's bare chest shouted temptation. "I don't burn easy, but I'm not sure about you." Actually, from what I could see, his skin was a delicious, creamy tan—no doubt from time spent in deserts and the southern California sunshine.

"I'll take my shirt off."

Okay. I could handle this. Maybe. I handed him the sunscreen. "You do me, and I'll do you."

And, that had come out wrong.

His eyes drilled my lips before dropping to my breasts. The blue-gray spheres darkened, smoldering. Tingles shot through me, centering in all the right places. Maybe I was taking my teasing too far.

"Turn," he said abruptly.

I spun, my face overheating, because teasing him also teased me.

Cooper squirted cream onto his hands and rubbed his palms together. He placed them on my body and rubbed slowly, easing across my shoulders and down my back. This was better than sliding into a hot tub. I closed my eyes and acknowledged that him touching me wasn't a good idea. Well, it was a fabulous idea, but I was enjoying it too much. Savoring every caress, I parted my lips, unable to hold back my hum of pleasure.

Too soon, he laid the bottle on my shoulder. "I'm next."

I scrambled to locate my wits and turned just in time to catch him peeling off his tee, revealing that well-worked body I'd seen yesterday.

Other parts of his body looked ready for a little work-out, too.

Needing to speed this process up, I coated his back quickly, even though I ached to linger. It was time to jump into the icy river to chill off before I exploded.

"Let the gold rush commence." Pan in hand, I rushed around Cooper and picked my way down the embankment and into the water. After splashing through the shallows, I arrived at a small island.

"Panning for gold, huh?" Cooper stood on the shore. He'd slid on mirrored sunglasses, hiding his eyes, but their heat bored through me. It kept me flustered, hyper-aware of his presence.

"We may not find much, but there's gold in them there hills." I waved toward Glenridge Mountain. "It washes down here and is lying around for anyone to find."

"Have you panned before?"

"A few times. You?"

"Never, but there's always a first time, right?"

"There sure is."

A first time for everything.

6

Cooper

I reminded myself that Ginny was Eli's sister, not a sniper endangering my heart. But I couldn't stop thinking about the way her breasts filled her bikini top. The warmth of her skin under my palms. The clever way she teased me.

Grumbling about hasty decisions, I splashed into the deepest part of the river, pretending I was overheated—which I damn well was—and dropped onto my knees, submerging myself up to my shoulders. Nothing like a mountain-fed river to ice a man down.

Until I looked at Ginny again. Leaning forward, she shifted her ass while she gathered gravel into her pan. I couldn't muffle my groan.

She spun to face me. "You okay?" Concern filled her face. Sisterly concern, no doubt.

"I'm just cold." Like that was an intelligent statement. "Yep, the water's cold." Nowhere near cold enough.

"Come over into the sun, then."

Remaining underwater, I used rocks to pull myself across the riverbed to her side. Of course, when I arrived, this position put me crotch-level with Ginny. This was not a good idea.

She dropped to her knees and shivered. "Wow. Feels great. I was hot."

Not nearly as hot as I was.

Her smile curled up on one corner. If I kissed it, could I make the other side match?

"Let me show you what you need to do." With her pan, she scooped up a bunch of gravel. She added water and swirled the contents, creating a rich slurry. "See here?" Her movement slowed, and she flicked through the gravel, highlighting tiny, deep red stones. "Garnet. Where you find garnet, you find gold." Moving the pan again, she eased the lighter contents over the lip, leaving the heavier stuff—small stones and bits of dark granite—behind. "And bingo." She looked up at me with a big grin. A few tiny gold flakes winked in the sun, and she inched them across the smooth side of the pan and into a vial. "By the end of the day, we might have enough to buy a gum ball at the grocery store. If you're looking to get rich, this won't do it, but it's fun."

I rose to my knees. "Let me try." I scooped up gravel and water and started slopping it around.

"That's too hard." She placed a restraining hand on my forearm. "And you're going too fast."

"If you want me to slow down, you just say the word." So, my words came out cocky. Ginny wasn't the only one who could tease. From the color flooding her face, we could call this point one for me. And…at least ten points still for her. But a man had to start somewhere.

She dropped her eyes. When she raised them again, they'd darkened to the richest chocolate. She worried her lower lip with her teeth, drawing my eyes to the movement. Make that eleven points for Ginny. Hell, I didn't mind losing a round to this woman on any given day of the week.

Shit, I liked her. More than someone soon leaving the country should.

"Let me show you how to do it." She covered my hands and guided me in swirling the pan, tipping it forward to allow a trickle of water and gravel to sift into the river. Her giggle fell between us. Infectious. It pulled out my laughter to combine with hers.

Something squeezed tight inside my chest, before loosening.

"What are you laughing about?" My voice held a husky tone that betrayed my growing feelings.

"It's hard doing it backwards." Her laughter slowed, and she peered up at me through her lashes.

My heart thumped louder than a platoon leader's marching cadence as I fell into her beautiful eyes. I lifted a shaky hand to finger the tips of her soft, honey hair drifting around her shoulders. Dropping the strands, I ran my palm across the sun-kissed skin on her upper arm. Warm. Smooth. Total heaven.

Ginny was so close. So touchable. And infinitely forbidden.

I wrenched my gaze from hers and moved backward, letting my hand drop to my side. Being near this woman shredded my self-control, making it hard to keep the promise I'd made to her brother.

"I think I've got it now," I murmured.

Did I ever.

WE PANNED for gold until early-afternoon, stopping

when we'd partly filled the vial and our fingers were wrinkled from being in water. Sitting on the bank to dry in the sun, we ate the sandwiches and the chips Ginny had packed.

She ate the chips, that is.

"Dill pickle?" Scowling, I held one up in the sunlight. Was it green or was the light playing tricks with my eyes? I tossed it toward the river. The fish might enjoy it more than me.

"They're yummy." Crinkling her nose at me, Ginny reached into the bag and pulled another one out. She popped it into her mouth and crunched, closing her eyes and moaning while shifting her body as if she savored the finest delicacy in the world. Or a hot bout of sex.

I had to stop putting Ginny and sex in the same equation. We'd had fun together today. Like siblings—on her part, anyway. The last thing I wanted to do was make things awkward between us by showing my hand.

But I'd kill to lay her down in the grass and explore every inch of her body.

It was going to be a torturous afternoon if I didn't find a way out of the trench I'd dug. As soon as we finished, I stood. "How about a walk upstream?" I nudged my chin in that direction. "We can find another area to pan."

She squinted while resting back on her elbows with the sun bronzing her skin. "Is this a case of the gold being sparklier on the other side of the stream?"

I chuckled. "Maybe." And maybe things were golden right here. Damn near perfect, in fact. Which was why my body would soon be responding. I grabbed a pan.

"You go. I'll stay here." She twisted around and smoothed out her shirt on the grass. Was it just me, or were her hands trembling? She couldn't be scared. Not settling in like a cat prepared to soak up sunbeams. She stretched out fully on the ground and wiggled her toes. "I'm going to enjoy the warmth."

I'd enjoy dropping to the ground and warming her completely.

Time to hike this feeling out of my system. Exercise would be the best cure outside of a cold shower. "I won't go far."

Her eyelids jerked open, and her voice rose an octave. "You'll stay within shouting distance, right?"

There was more going on here than just below my belt. Eli said something in Ginny's life was holding her back. I wanted to ask her to tell me what it was, to take on part of whatever burden she carried, but asking would be wrong.

I'd be gone soon, leaving her to bear whatever haunted her alone.

7

Ginny

Sticks and leaves crackled underfoot as Cooper moved away.

My heart tripped.

Other than yesterday, when was the last time I'd been completely alone while outside my apartment? Not since before the kidnapping. The panic scrambling inside me suggested I chase after Cooper, use his presence to bolster my confidence. But the sun felt good. And I was so freaking tired of letting what happened to me rule my actions.

He said he'd remain within shouting distance, which meant I wasn't *really* alone.

Closing my eyes, I found a comfortable spot on the ground.

The river's flow lulled me. Leaves fluttered in the breeze. A bumblebee hummed nearby. The sun's warmth took hold of me and pulled me down, down, down...

Rolling onto my side, I snuggled a corner of my shirt beneath my chin. I slipped into a dream where I walked through a field beside Cooper, my fingers brushing the tips of tall, spiky grass. He smiled and said my name in such a sweet voice, I longed to lean into his chest, stroke his face, and pull his essence inside me.

Ginny.

I stirred and then drifted deeper. Cooper leaned closer...

Ginny.

The whisper pulled at my consciousness and I mumbled, rolling onto my back. The dream. I wanted to go back to the dream, but something deep inside me told me I needed to wake up. My eyes slid open to take in the sun. From the angle of the light slanting through the trees, I hadn't been asleep long.

Ginny.

That voice. It was insistent. And *here*.

I sat upright, then jumped to my feet. Spinning, I studied the dense forest. The river. The mountain range looming nearby.

Nothing. No one. I was alone.

Or was I?

"Cooper?" I called. In a normal tone, not loud and shrill like I yearned to do. He said he'd stay close, and I didn't want him believing he had to rush to my side every other second. I wasn't a puny, clinging thing who needed someone to save her, like I'd been when I moved home. The determination to save myself had been growing inside me for weeks.

Ginny.

The guttural whisper came from behind me.

I pivoted to face downstream. Anxiety spiked up my back and lifted goosebumps all over my body. I rushed over to where we'd left our things and shoved my feet into my sandals. Grabbing my shirt, I yanked it over my head.

Ginny.

"Who's there?" Turning, I tried to place where the

voice had come from. The river churned, and the birds…
Wait, the birds who'd chirped earlier had grown silent.
Like they did when something moved nearby.

Or when someone hunted.

"Cooper?"

Deep, coarse laughter echoed around me.

My heart lunged up into my throat. "Cooper!"

Unable to remember in which direction he'd walked, I
ran for the path. My arms pumped, and my sandals
smacked the dirt. Brambles raked my legs, slicing my
exposed flesh. I darted into the forest, and it hauled me
into its smothering embrace. Where the sun never reached,
darkness lurked. It waited.

The leaves quaked overhead, whispering, *you're not safe.*

I'd *never* be safe.

A guttural cry burst out of me. Racing forward, I
tripped over a fallen branch. My body flashed cold with
sweat. As adrenalin sank through me, my leg muscles
spasmed.

Footsteps hit the forest floor behind me. Heavy and
persistent. Coming closer. No time to look.

Go faster! I had to get to the car. The road. I needed to
reach Eli.

"No." Air wheezed from my lungs. Whimpering, I
glanced over my shoulder while pushing for more speed.

There was no one there.

Scrambling backward, I smacked into someone. My
shriek echoed through the woods, and I blubbered, trying
to wrench free.

"Ginny!" Cooper held me steady, his fingers snug on
my upper arms. His worried gaze locked onto mine. "You
okay? Your scream…You scared the shit out of me."

"Something is…Someone's after me." I spoke wildly,
and birds squawked and flew up from nearby trees. My

breath coming fast, I could barely speak. A quick look toward the river again showed no one was there. "Someone was calling my name. Chasing me."

Cooper shifted me to the side and strode down the path. "Wait here."

No way. I crept behind him, blood seeping down my thigh from where I'd scraped it.

Halfway to the river, Cooper dropped to his heels and stared at the ground. He traced his fingertip along an oval pattern. "Hmm." Standing, he took my hands and squeezed them. "Let's get you to the car. You can wait there while I look around some more."

"I want to stay with you."

"We can lock the doors. You'll be safe inside." Terror must've stood out starkly on my face, because he pulled me into his arms. "It's all right," he said into my hair. "It's going to be all right."

Sunshine had kissed his skin, and I soaked in his heat. His reassurance. And I told my heart to stop racing, my breathing to ease. Because I'd let fear drag me beyond control again. This could be nothing, just my imagination going haywire.

I shifted away from him and raked my hair off my face, securing it at my nape with an elastic. While my trembling lips might still give me away, I lifted my chin. "I can wait in the car. You'll go with me, though?"

"Of course." Taking my hand, he led me up the path.

We reached the edge of the forest and emerged into the sunlight. Crickets sang from the deep grass beside the road and in the distance, a lawnmower growled.

Normal sounds on a day when nothing felt normal.

Cooper opened the passenger door, and I dropped onto my seat. Though it was hotter than an oven inside, the warmth couldn't penetrate my shivers.

"I won't be long." Before he shut the door, he leaned in to cup my face and stare into my eyes. "You'll be okay. I promise."

Promises kept were rarer than gold in these hills.

I knew he only meant to comfort me, to lend me some of his strength, but I couldn't keep from grabbing onto his words and holding them close. They helped crowd out the fear.

"Watch out," I said as he shut the door.

He gave a curt nod before turning and striding back toward the woods.

I was left alone in silence broken only by a click when my finger engaged the car door's locking mechanism.

8

Cooper

Keeping my tread light, I made my way back to the path. I was soon engulfed in heavy woods where the creatures stilled due to my movement. I stopped to listen as they did. Silence greeted me, leaving me no clue as to what had recently gone on here.

Who the hell was messing with Ginny? Anger and frustration surged through me.

I cursed myself for wanting to hide my body's response to her earlier, because it had pulled me away from her side. I'd only been gone a short time, had barely rounded a couple bends in the river. I'd stopped and was thinking about dipping my pan into the small pool I'd discovered.

When she screamed, my heart flatlined. The thought that someone was hurting her froze my guts solid then sent blood roaring through me. I scrambled over logs and around trees, racing back to where I'd left her. Alone. Without my protection. At a dead run, I hit the area where we'd eaten lunch and found only her pack. No Ginny. As if someone had snatched her up and taken her away.

Hell, no.

Cutting through the woods in a direct route for the road, I'd plowed through blackberry thickets and leaped over fallen trees, eventually finding myself ahead of her when I reached the path. Seeing her approach, I'd called her name. As if she hadn't heard me, she'd slammed into me. It was all I could do to reassure her. Her body…She'd trembled in my arms. Only my anger at whoever had done this kept me from shaking along with her.

Time to track down the person responsible and demand some answers.

I came to the place where we collided and slowed. Stopping again, I listened. Only the shuffle of tiny animals further inside the forest and the soothing tones of the river reached my ears.

With a slower pace, I trailed Ginny's steps along the packed dirt, pausing to assess for other tracks outside ours. A few bent blades of grass here and a broken stick there, but nothing indicated anyone else had been this way except us. There'd been next to no rain for weeks, though, which made it difficult to find anything on the hard-packed ground.

I continued down the path, almost reaching the place where we'd put sunscreen on each other. Dropping to my heels again, I studied the ground.

There. A shoeprint. Lightly pressed into the soil. From today? Not any earlier than yesterday. But sometimes, it was hard to tell.

Tracking forward, I found another mark where the grass was lightly crushed. Then a spot where the deeper compression showed someone had stood for some time. Ahead, the river glistened through the trees. Someone could've watched me and Ginny while we panned for gold. When I stroked her arm and ached to kiss her. When we sat on the bank eating.

Crap. They might've stood here and watched while I left her to walk off my heat.

We'd passed an old guy carrying fishing gear on the road. These could be his tracks. He could've paused earlier in this very place for some random reason having nothing to do with us.

Which...didn't sound quite right.

Why couldn't I explain this away with the fisherman?

Ginny was waiting in the car, scared out of her mind. I needed to get back there and reassure her. Make her realize I'd keep her from further harm for as long as I could.

With nothing more I could do here, I grabbed my shirt off the bank and pulled it on. After gathering up our things, I jogged up the path.

Ginny's concerned expression smoothed when she spotted me emerging from the woods. I was sorry she'd been frightened with me gone, but it made more sense to leave her in the car while I looked around. If I'd come across someone, she was safer here.

As I approached, she unlocked the car and climbed out, wiping her hand across her forehead. "Wow. I was melting in there."

"See anyone?" I asked.

"Nobody but two red squirrels." Her shoulders relaxed and her eyes brightened, taking on that spark I'd savored on more than one occasion. She pointed to a few maple trees growing on the side of the road. "I think you pissed them off. They threw acorns at your car."

Her laugh loosened the limbs I'd held tight as I rushed up the path. The grin I released made my cheekbones throb. "Maybe I should make a citizen's arrest. Haul them into town for prosecution."

She laughed. "Good luck with that."

I tossed our things into the trunk, and we got inside the car, where I cranked the AC to high and put the windows down.

"What did you find?" she asked as I turned the vehicle around and started driving down the road.

"Not much. A few tracks that could've been from anyone."

"I heard someone. They called my name." My glance caught her lowering her eyes to her hands clenched on her lap. She kept massaging her right wrist as if it hurt. "I swear, whoever it was laughed at me."

"We saw a fisherman when we drove in." I pulled out onto the main road.

Her head tilted, and she squinted at me. "Do you think it was the fisherman? He could've come down to the river to fish." Hope bloomed in her voice. "Maybe I was mistaken about someone calling my name. I'd been dreaming and…"

I grumbled because I wasn't sure. But telling her I suspected anything else might make things worse. Before I spoke further, I needed time to analyze the situation. "Who could it be other than him?"

"I don't know. Not sure why he'd chase me, though."

Valid point. "Did you recognize the voice?"

She shrugged. "I was sleeping. It startled me awake." Her voice grew quiet. "I was scared."

Reaching across the console, I took her hand.

"Do you believe me?" The urgency in her tone told me my answer meant a lot to her. "That I heard someone calling me?"

"I do." Not sure why I didn't have doubts, other than I knew Ginny would never make up something like this.

"Thank you."

"I'm sorry. I shouldn't have left you, not even to take a walk."

"It's okay." The defeat in her voice made me want to put the car into park and gather her into my arms. Would she let me? Probably. Only because she'd had the fright of her life.

I was honest enough to admit I wanted it to mean more to her than comfort.

9

Ginny

I lowered the dish drainer onto the picnic table. "Guys, I think it's time for a fire."

After returning to the campground, Cooper had suggested we call the police, but what could I tell them? While I was napping in the sun, I thought I heard someone calling my name from the woods. But I didn't see anyone, and Cooper didn't find any tracks to speak of.

Oh, and I could tell the sheriff that I'd bolted like a fool, running and sobbing and screaming through the woods like a demented banshee. He'd probably question whether I'd been drinking, which I hadn't, but still.

I must've been mistaken. Waking from a dream, I'd imagined the entire incident. Panicked.

It seemed a shame to ruin our weekend over something so silly.

"A fire sounds great," Cooper said.

The sun had tucked itself below the horizon, dragging away the warmth I'd complained about earlier in the day. Shivers rippled along my bare skin. I'd need to grab a sweatshirt from my tent soon.

Eli had returned from work this afternoon, in time for dinner. His boss's son-in-law, the third security guard, was going to fill in here and there for Steve, with Eli covering the other shifts as needed. I'd suggested we return to town, but Eli wanted to get what he could out of the camping weekend, even if he had to work.

Cooper dumped the last of the grill coals into the fire pit, and the paper plates generated smoke signals. While he ducked inside his tent, I dragged our chairs closer to the pit.

"I'm going to run to the camp store before it closes." Eli tilted his head in that direction. "You want any snacks?"

"I brought plenty of junk food." I waved to my tote. "Popcorn, nuts." Oreos, but I wasn't mentioning my stash. If Eli caught a whiff of them, they'd be gone faster than beads of water in the sun.

"Not Fritos," he called over his shoulder, heading toward the lights twinkling in the distance. "Can't live without my corn chip fix."

Chuckling, I pulled a bag of salt and vinegar chips from my tote. Maybe Cooper would find them more appealing than dill pickle.

I turned and bumped into someone I assumed was Cooper.

Tom grabbed my forearms tight enough I dropped the chips.

"What are you doing? Let me go." I wrenched backward and cradled my wrist, which ached from his tight grip.

"I was looking for you." His breath slid across my face, dank and sour. "*Il mio amore.*"

While I didn't speak Italian, I knew *amore* meant love. My heart raced, a loud boom as dread took hold.

"You've got time to talk now, don't you?" Tom's eyes flashed around our empty campground. "No meals to slave over for that…other guy."

I edged sideways until I smacked my thigh on the picnic table hard enough, I flinched.

He followed. "Where you going? Every time I want to do things with you, you act like you don't even like me." His eyes glinted darkly in the campground lights. "And that's not what you said."

What was he talking about? My gaze fleeing his, I sought a way around him. I could run for my tent but didn't dare. What if he followed me inside?

He moved in so close, I could smell his sweat. "I saw you with him, L— Ginny." His voice rose. "I sent you chocolates. I've been giving you keepsakes from all the times we've been together. And those flowers."

Was he referring to the dozen long-stemmed yellow roses he'd sent back in high school? Totally blindsided, I'd been tempted to throw them away. Sure, they'd been pretty, but we'd only gone to the movies and played mini golf once. We weren't exactly a couple.

And then he brought me chocolates, one of those huge, heart-shaped boxes you couldn't finish before they dried out. I'd winced, because I'd actually been planning to tell him I didn't want to see him anymore.

He'd never given me keepsakes, and I sure hadn't asked him to.

Head rearing back, the whites of his eyes flashed. "I won't let you be with another guy this time, either. I keep what's mine."

"Enough, Tom." I clenched my fists at my sides. "I'm not yours."

"Everything okay here, Ginny?" Cooper came up behind me, so close, he warmed my back.

I barely resisted leaning against his chest to soak in the comfort he offered. Relief weakened my knees. "No. I...Tom."

"It's time for you to leave," Cooper told the other man. His hand dropped on my shoulder and squeezed.

Tom flashed a hot glance from me to Cooper, and his nostrils flared. "Who the hell are you, anyway?"

"I'm someone who watches out for Ginny." The steel on Cooper's voice suggested he'd gladly grind Tom into the dirt.

Tom slid his gaze down my body, making me wish I wore more than a tank and shorts. "You don't have any right to be with my girlfriend."

I sputtered. "I'm not your girlfriend. We broke up a long time ago."

"You will be again. And more." Tom waved toward the sky. "The moon's something else tonight, Laura. You always loved the moon. We could—"

"Go." Cooper started toward Tom, clenched hands rising.

"Okay, man. It's cool." Tom flashed his palms while slinking backward. "I'm leaving." His attention settled on me again, a lead weight around my ankle in deep water. "We'll talk later, Laura, when this asshole isn't around."

"I'm not Laura," I shouted. "Leave me alone."

Tom glared, and darkness flooded his face. "You're just a whore, aren't you? Just like with that other guy—"

Cooper started for Tom, but the man pivoted and ran across our campsite, only pausing to kick our trashcan over as he passed it.

Tom had a temper that surpassed my old boyfriend, Zen's. Come to think of it, Zen had acted possessive, too. As if by saying I was willing to be with him, I'd given him that right. He'd been creepy sometimes, too, especially when he chastised me in a fake voice—he had a knack for mimicry and could sound like anyone with barely any practice.

What was it with guys thinking they could tell me what to do all the time?

Tom shouted, "You'll regret not taking me back." He continued across the green and disappeared into the night.

"Well." I lifted a shaky hand to my hair, shoving a few strands behind my ear. "I'm glad that's over."

"For now."

Said like he thought we hadn't seen the last of Tom yet. My heavy sigh rang out between us because he was probably right.

"Who the hell is that guy, anyway?" Cords stood out on Cooper's neck, and his narrowed gaze remained fixed in the direction where Tom had entered the woods.

"Someone I went out with a few times in high school. We broke up." I tugged on my shirt and worried the hem. "He creeped me out. Started getting possessive. I told him I didn't want to see him again, and I thought that was it because he let it go."

"It's weird that he's acting like this now."

"What's even weirder is that he called me Laura." A knot of fear in my throat made it difficult to swallow. "I ran into him here at the campground yesterday and then again this morning when I went to the showers. He said he was married to someone named Laura but then he implied she was dead. Anyway." I lifted my chin. "I appreciate you backing me up."

"Anytime."

A frown pulled down my lips. "Do you think it was him in the woods today?"

Cooper scratched the back of his neck. "Hard to say."

Rumbles rose in his chest. "I'll talk to Eli. Tell him he needs to keep an eye out for that creep."

"I hate being a burden, especially to my brother."

"You know he'd jump off a cliff for you."

I'd do the same for Eli.

But I had no intention of spending the rest of my weekend slinking around. Life was too short not to make each moment fun. I reached into the rack of dried dishes, pulled out my trusty cast iron frying pan, and brandished it. "Maybe if I smack him with this, he'll get the message."

Cooper chuckled and the indigo faded from his eyes, turning them blue-gray again. "You think?"

"Let's hope I don't need to find out."

He grunted. "Won't as long as I'm around."

Which we both knew was only for a few more days.

Eli returned with two bags of chips, throwing one to Cooper, who caught it. Cooper filled him in on what happened.

My brother shot a concerned look my way and fisted his hand so tight, his chip bag crackled. "Ginny, I—"

"Cooper handled it."

"Still," he said. Tossing the chips onto the picnic table, he came over and gave me a quick hug. "I'll have a word with Tom tomorrow."

Stepping back, I wrapped my arms around my waist, holding in my shivers. "I appreciate it."

I ducked inside my tent for a sweatshirt. While rifling through my bag, I found another painted tile tucked between two t-shirts. My flashlight highlighted the scene: Port Clyde Lighthouse at dusk. When I tilted it, the tile slipped from my hand and landed on the floor with a soft thud. A black swirl, vaguely like a letter, was revealed on the back. Not Eli's name, like I'd expected, but maybe he preferred to remain anonymous and this was his mark.

"You want a beer?" Cooper was walking toward the cooler when I stepped back outside.

"Thanks." I popped it open and toasted my brother. "And thank you, Eli." Meaning the painting. I wasn't sure Cooper knew about my brother's artwork, so I'd keep that part quiet for now. "Remember that time we went to Port Clyde?"

Eli smiled. "That spring a couple years ago, when I was home on leave. It was an awesome day, wasn't it?"

Bright sunshine. Balmy weather. And the whisper of waves gliding along the shore. We'd sat and eaten our picnic lunch on large slabs of granite.

"We'll have to do it again sometime," I said.

"Definitely."

I took a long swallow of my drink and sat in one of the folding chairs.

The guys joined me and went caveman with the fire pit.

Scowling, Eli crouched and blew on scraps of newspaper. He'd mounded about half our woodpile on top of it. Leaning back on his heels, he grumbled, "Needs kerosene."

"C-4 works better," Cooper said from the chair beside me.

Really. Leave it to a military guy to come up with something like that. I widened my eyes. "You didn't bring explosives to a campground, did you?"

He wiggled his eyebrows. "Only fireworks. You're up for fireworks tonight, right?"

From the sparks shooting through my belly, there was no debating which kind of fireworks I preferred.

Eli finally got the fire going—without C-4, thankfully—while the campground quieted around us.

I dug through the tote outside my tent, locating the

ingredients for S'mores. While Eli toasted the marshmallow and made the usual chocolate and graham cracker
sandwich, Cooper and I ate our marshmallows plain.

"Toasting marshmallows is a true art form." I rotated
my stick until the marshmallow turned burnished bronze.
Lifting it, I slid the crusty, steaming outside off the gooey
innards and popped it into my mouth. Eyes closed, I
moaned while I chewed. Absolute bliss.

My stick wiggled, and I opened my eyes to stare down
at it. Somehow, I'd lost my marshmallow guts. Leaning
forward, I peered into the coals, wondering if it had
plopped off. No smoking white lump to be found.

"Problems?" Cooper licked a line of whiteness off his
upper lip.

Narrowing my gaze on him, I grabbed another marshmallow from the bag. "That fox is back in my midst. The
beast keeps making off with my goods."

Cooper pressed his broad shoulders against his chair.
"You accusing me of theft?"

I rolled my eyes and focused on my marshmallow.
Cooper kept my emotions in a perpetual tailspin. I had to
hold them in check, or I'd crash.

"Here you go." Cooper tilted his stick my way. Crusty,
golden yum steamed within my reach. I slid off the outside
and popped it into my mouth, chewing while he ate the
rest.

He reached for the bag. "Another?"

"If I eat any more, I'll slip into a coma." I poked the
fire with my stick. Flames licked along the tip, forcing me
to sacrifice it to the campfire gods.

Across from us, Eli stared into the flames. He'd spent
the last half hour nursing his beer and fiddling with the
pockets on his shorts. Eventually, he stood and tossed his
empty into the recycle bin. "I'm off to bed. The alarm

goes off too early. Wish I didn't have to work, though. You're…" His gaze cut to me. "You don't mind that I'll be gone after midnight, do you?"

He meant, did I mind being alone while I slept?

I waved. "Go. I'll be fine." Probably. I cut my gaze to Cooper who studied us both with a frown on his face. "Cooper's here with me, right?"

His concerned look faded, although his eyes remained flinty. "Sure am."

"Okay, then," Eli said. "I'll be back by four-thirty-ish tomorrow afternoon, okay?"

I nodded.

Cooper tapped his sneaker on the side of the fire pit, and I could feel the heat of his gaze, though I didn't look his way. I kept my face neutral, because, jeez, I hated letting him think I was scared all the time.

"You up for a swim?" he finally asked.

I shot him a quick glance. "It's dark out."

He chuckled. "You turn into a coach at midnight?"

"The story includes a pumpkin, and it's not even close to midnight."

He checked his phone. "Okay, ten."

"I should go to bed. Long day tomorrow." I needed to go into town for provisions, and I planned to test my resolve by swimming to the furthest dock in the lake alone.

"You can sleep in tomorrow."

It *was* time to move forward, right? "Okay, you're on."

10

Cooper

After changing, I walked with Ginny to the lake. At least Tom wasn't lurking around. If he moved on her again, I'd be all over him.

"Kinda chilly for a swim, isn't it?" she asked when we stopped by the water to stare.

A ton of stars filled the sky, and the nearly-full moon shot a wavering white line across the lake. We weren't alone. Swimmers were jumping off one of the floats farther out. But other than that, darkness had shut down the world.

"This is the best time to swim," I said. "When the air's cold, the water feels warm."

Ginny sighed. "If you say so." She lifted her sundress over her head and tossed it onto the towel she'd laid on the bank.

Moonlight outlined her body, and I had to remind myself she wore an ordinary swimsuit. I shouldn't be turned on just because small scraps of cloth highlighted inches of skin I ached to stroke with my fingertips.

Remember your promise.

Fuck the promise, my body said, stirring immediately.

Ginny had changed from the sweet but serious girl I remembered back in high school. The funny side I'd only caught on the sly had grown stronger, as if she'd settled into her skin and let everything inside her shine through. And while her shape might be more mature than I remembered, she'd maintained those curves that had fueled every damn one of my teenage fantasies.

She strode forward, splashing into the lake. Water swirled around her calves and kissed her knees and thighs. That sweet juncture between them.

So much for not turning rock solid. Good thing my body was hidden by the dark and the enveloping water as I followed.

Lifting her arms, she pushed off her feet and dove into the water. She emerged with hair sleeker than a mermaid.

I did the same, keeping pace with her slow crawl as she swam away from shore.

We stopped and treaded water with our legs.

Tipping backward, I floated, and she linked her hand with mine. Friendly, most likely.

"You're right," she said. "This feels great."

It had cooled me down, making it easier to behave.

We turned and swam to an empty float. I waved for her to climb the ladder ahead of me, but was unable to drag my eyes away from her tempting ass.

I was so screwed.

We dropped onto our backs on the wooden boards, staring up at the sky.

"Tell me about your travels around the world over the past ten years," I said, not only to distract myself, but because I wanted to know everything about her.

Talking wouldn't break my promise.

"Wherever you go, there are new people. New customs.

New food. You've traveled with the military, so you know what it's like."

"Not the way you have." It wasn't wise for military personnel to venture far from the base. And combat situations didn't lend themselves to exploring new locations. "I want to hear what you've been up to. You graduated two years after us and went to Europe, then Central America. Eli told me that." I'd kept asking about her until I heard she was living with a guy. Funny, I hadn't realized until now that I proposed to Annie after receiving the news. Coughing, I pushed aside that unwelcome insight. "Eli said you backpacked around for a while before heading somewhere else."

"Yes, Europe first. Then I met up with friends and we traveled from California to Panama. Costa Rica is gorgeous. So's Nicaragua."

"Taking pictures along the way."

She turned and propped the side of her head up on her palm. Moonlight lit up her face, outlining her high cheekbones and dimpled chin. "You know I'm a photographer."

"You're famous."

She snorted and tucked a strand of hair behind her ear. "Not so sure about that, but I've done well over the past few years."

"I bought all your books."

Her laughter rang out across the water. "I wondered who my solitary fan was."

"Your photos are awesome."

"Wow." Her pause made me wonder if I'd stolen her words. Her photos sure had stolen mine.

"I bought multiple copies of each book," I said. "Gave them to all my friends as gifts."

"Now you're telling me a tall one."

"It's true. I kept bragging about you. I know her. Check out this picture. I'd open to the one where the mother held her newborn child. Or the one of the man running from the bulls. His face, cratered with determination …Your pictures blew me away."

She blinked. "Thank you. You're making me feel, I don't know, happy, I guess. I didn't think anyone outside my family cared about the moments I've captured."

"Eli said you've sold to magazines. Life. Vanity Fair. National Geographic."

"Seems like Eli shared quite a bit of my life with you."

Did I read curiosity or irritation in her voice? In the dark, I couldn't tell. "Just some." Whatever information I could squeeze out of Eli without letting on I had more than a casual interest.

One corner of her mouth rose, centering my attention in that area. "Just some?"

"Enough." Never enough, actually.

Full-on teasing lifted her voice. "Then you're saying you don't need to hear more?"

Right now, I wanted to hear any secret she was willing to tell me.

"How about you?" she asked. "Eli told me you've been to the Middle East with the Seabees."

"A couple tours."

"Mostly desert deployments in tight areas, though, right?" She sighed. "I've never been to that part of the world. War zones aren't safe to travel through."

Her photos mostly featured faces. Some hardened by life, staring into the distance. A child in wonder. Old men hauling stick-filled packs up craggy hillsides.

"What's it like over there?" she asked.

"Beautiful. Shaggy mounds you can't see over. Dangerous during a sand storm."

"There's beauty in storms, too." She squeezed my hand. When had she linked our fingers together? "What else?"

"It's isolated. Lonely." My laugh came out like a croak. "I'm a mood killer, aren't I?"

"I don't mind. I want to hear." Her eyes gleamed, black pearls in the shell of her face. Lake water spiked her lashes, making them super long. I wanted to touch them, find out if they were as soft as they appeared. I wanted to touch all of her, if only she'd let me.

"There's no one in your life?" Her gaze flitted away from mine. "No one special?"

Reading more into this than casual conversation would be wrong. I'd encroached on the line I'd drawn in the sand today already. Crossing it would betray everything, including my honor. As grueling as this was, I needed to remember that.

"Not for over a year," I said. "I was engaged to Annie, but it ended."

"I'm sorry."

"Sometimes, things aren't meant to be." Even I could hear the sorrow in my voice, but I was mostly sad I'd let myself get that far into the relationship. Annie had called it off, but she'd made the right move. When it came time to take that final step at the altar, I would've frozen. There was no way I could've stood in front of our friends and told her I'd cherish her forever.

Because a tiny part of me was already taken.

Annie got married six months ago. She and her husband had a kid on the way. I couldn't be happier for her.

"How about you?" I wanted to sound her out about Eli's comment. Was Ginny still living with that guy? "You with anyone special?"

"Not any longer."

I borrowed her words. "I'm sorry."

Her teeth grazed her lower lip. "Me, too."

"Want to talk about it?"

"Zen's gone, and really, that's the end of it."

"In some ways, but not in others?"

"Maybe." She frowned as if she sought inward. "No. He *is* gone. I hadn't realized until now."

"You loved him?"

"That's just it." Her eyes fell into mine. "I didn't. Not the way I wanted to." She said nothing for a long while, just stared at me with heavy-lidded eyes. They dropped to my lips.

A hush descended, as if the kids playing at the other dock, the night birds swooping along the water, and even the wind itself stilled.

She shifted forward and placed her mouth on mine. Lightly enough I could pull away and say, *hell no*. Firmly enough to show me her need. It wrapped around me. Dragged me down until nothing existed except her. Us. Touching.

Unable to resist and cursing my soul for eternity, I opened my mouth and let her inside. She tasted of marsh-mallows, with hints of the teenager I'd been crazy about back in high school. Followed by the heady flavor of all woman. The one she'd become.

Deepening our kiss, I sifted my fingers through her hair and pulled her closer. I slid my hand along her waist, urging her up onto my body. I'd kill to feel her pressed against me. Her wet shape glided across mine, and she moaned.

An IED exploding nearby couldn't pull me away from Ginny now.

With my tongue, I parted her lips. While I might be

damned by my actions, I reveled in it. I couldn't resist touching every inch of her while I tasted. Easing her onto her back, I rose over her. With a reckless need driving me, I slid my hands up the slick skin of her waist to the underside of her breast. Teased the soft cup while stroking my thumb across her hidden nipple.

Whimpers rose from her throat, and her fingertips trailed down my back. I left her mouth, kissing my way along the sleek column of her neck, nibbling her shoulder. Licking. Sucking.

Her head tipped back in surrender. "Cooper." My name flew across the water.

Heat centered in my groin. The need to give her pleasure overwhelmed me. I shifted the nylon of her top and fondled underneath. Her nipple hardened to a pebble. I'd willingly drown for the chance to take that nub into my mouth and stroke my tongue across it.

A car horn blaring in the parking lot drove me back to my senses. It also reminded me that I'd promised this woman's brother I wouldn't make a play for her heart.

Even if it was already too late for my own.

With a growl that betrayed how much I wanted to be with her, I lifted my head. The vulnerability spilling across her face wrenched the insides right out of me. I loosened my arms and dropped onto my back beside her.

11

Ginny

I wanted Cooper badly. I'd scream if we didn't come together.

As a teenager, I'd crushed on a skinny, shy, eighteen-year-old Cooper. When had I let myself fall for the man he'd become? What I felt for him now surpassed anything I'd felt for any other guy I'd been with before.

Heady. Ecstatic. Aching.

"Shit, I'm sorry." His words sent an icy wave across my heart.

"What do you mean?" Forcing my limbs into motion, I turned onto my side to face him.

Grief etched lines in his face. "I'm sorry," he said again as if the first one hadn't taken. "That shouldn't have happened." He rose to his feet and stood in profile, glaring toward shore.

While I might be weak from his kisses, I wasn't taking whatever he had to say lying down. I got to my feet.

His words said one thing, but his body betrayed him, jutting his swim shorts forward.

"Is this about the woman you were engaged to?" I

hated saying her name. "Annie?" If he was stuck on someone else, I wouldn't stomp through and muddy up those waters.

He dragged his hands across his head. "I guess." A rod didn't come close to his stiffening spine. "Yeah, that's it. Annie."

What could I say to that? I wasn't Annie, and I refused to be a convenient substitute. This must be why Eli had warned me away.

"It won't happen again." Without waiting for my reply, he dove cleanly into the lake. His head cut the surface yards out from the float, and he lifted his arms and made for shore.

I followed, catching up fast. The fact that I could told me that while he was fleeing, he still took my safety seriously. At least he thought that much of me. Not that it mattered, because safety wasn't a fraction of what I wanted from him.

We reached the shore at the same time and walked out of the lake.

I snatched up my towel and wiped myself off briskly, wishing I could remove the memory of his hands on my body as easily as the moisture. With my dress clutched close, I left him standing by the shore and hurried to the changing rooms.

He followed.

After dropping down on the bench inside one of the rooms, I rubbed my mouth to eliminate any lingering trace of his kiss. The tightness in my chest couldn't be rubbed away.

Cooper waited for me outside when I emerged. No harm in admitting I was relieved. With Tom around, I'd been dreading walking back to the campground alone.

I strode back in silence beside him, resisting the urge to

say, *why did you have to kiss me back?* And, *why did you make me care for you?* He wouldn't have answers; I'd done this to myself.

After brushing my teeth at the faucet, I sought my tent. The air mattress bit into my back, my side.

No other reason I couldn't get to sleep.

SUNSHINE STABBED my eyes when I left my tent the next morning.

Cooper wasn't around, but it was just as well. My guards weren't high enough to deal with him yet. It was hard to say if they'd ever lift high enough for something like that. As the newly rejected, I'd decided not to speak with him—or look at him—ever again. Childish, but there it was.

I couldn't believe how hurt I still felt about this. Silly me for starting to fall for a man I could never have.

Since a note on the picnic table told me Eli had left for work after midnight and would be back mid-morning, I decided it was time to take on my next challenge. I changed into my swimsuit inside my tent and, with my towel looped around my neck, I left the campsite, my sandals slapping my heels. I paused when I reached the start of the path to the lake. The last time I'd come this way, I'd been at a run, terrified someone was following me.

Sunlight winked through the trees, and birds swooped through the air. Frogs cheeping inside the woods echoed around me. The everyday sounds sent calm through me. Hand tightening on my towel, I strode forward. A butterfly became my companion, fluttering beside me before landing on a flower.

On the path, I met up with a woman about my own age who walked with two small girls.

"Hi," I said as I caught up to her.

The woman lifted her hand. "Hey, I'm Brittany, your neighbor in the pop-up camper beside yours."

"Nice to meet you." I slowed to walk with her. The girls kept racing near the woods shrieking, then running back to the path. "Your kids look like they're having a great time here at the campground."

"It's been wonderful." Brittany's grin filled her face, and her blue eyes sparkled. "They wear themselves out and nap forever. Makes me think we should live here year-round." She winced. "Well, except the camper *is* unbelievably small. Perfect for a couple, but a family of four? Not for more than a week. While I enjoy the afternoon breaks, I'll be glad to pack up and head back to my three-bedroom house in a few days."

"You live around here?"

"In Farland. You?"

"On the edge of Crescent Cove."

"A short ride home for you, too, then." Her eyes lowered. "This might sound weird, but are you and your friends planning to hang out at your campsite tonight?"

"We are," I said. "I can't wait for the fireworks." The campground planned to set them off at nine.

"We were thinking of taking the kids to dinner then stop by my mom's place for a little while after. Would you mind keeping an eye on our campsite?" Brittany frowned. "Yesterday, I saw a man sniffing around. He took off when I called out to him but you never know about people."

My heart skipped a beat. "What did he look like?" I asked carefully.

Brittany shrugged. "I couldn't tell. He wore a sweatshirt with the hood up."

Why would anyone need heavy clothing in this heat? "Weird."

"Right," Brittany said. "Probably just some teenager goofing off. But I figured if you were going to be around, you might be willing to keep an eye on things."

"I'd be glad to." It wasn't like I had anyplace else to go tonight. "What time do you plan to leave? And when will you be back?"

"We hope to head out five-thirty-ish," Brittany said. "And we'll be back no later than ten. That okay?"

I sucked in my lower lip and nodded. "Sounds fine."

We reached the shore and dropped our things onto neighboring chairs. The youngest girl leaned against Brittany's side, her shy smile revealing gaps from missing baby teeth. So picture perfect, I captured her image with my camera.

Brittany stroked her daughter's tight, curly hair, before opening her bag and pulling out water wings. "If you want to go swimming with Melanie, honey, you have to wear these." She stooped down to get her daughter ready.

I pulled off my shorts and tank and dropped them onto my chair. After ditching my flip flops, I strode down to the lake. The crystal-clear water begged to be slipped into, and I splashed through the shallows until I'd submerged all the way to my waist. With a push off the bottom, I dove beneath the surface and only came up when my lungs begged for air. Setting a brisk pace, I swam away from the shore with no goal in mind other than the most distant float.

Passing the floats, I swam further, pushing myself to test my bravery. I swam far enough out, the girls' laughter faded. Until there was no one else around.

Energy spent and my body complaining from the activity, I floated on my back, savoring the cool water. I closed my eyes to shut out the blinding sunshine. My hair swirled around me, the strands tickling my shoulders. Tiny waves buffeted me, rocking me back and forth, back and forth like I lounged in a hammock on a lazy summer's day.

Nothing but the low hum of a distant motorboat disturbed my peace.

Why had I resisted being alone like this? Solitude brought calm and with it, growth in my confidence. Isolated in my watery cocoon with no one around but birds and fishies, I could rebuild myself.

I drifted, letting the water lull me. Not falling asleep, but sinking into a calm much like meditation. That was me, ready to hum, ohm…

A buzz grew louder as if a swarm of bees flew near. Noises were muffled when ears were underwater, but this seemed different.

It felt *wrong*.

I dropped my legs and lifted my head barely in time to catch a speed boat bearing down on me.

"Whoa!" Pulse leaping, I flung myself toward the shore, half drowning as I floundered and gulped in brackish water.

The boat zipped past, leaving a wake of churning waves that swept over me in a mini tidal wave. The vehicle turned and came straight for me again, its engine emitting a high-pitched whine. The bow smacked the water as the boat went faster. Low on the horizon, I couldn't see the driver. I couldn't see anything but my approaching death.

I waved my arms and shouted, "Stop!"

The boat kept rushing toward me.

Whimpering, I raced for shore, putting all of myself into moving my limbs.

What was wrong with them? Couldn't they see

someone swam in the water? They needed to slow down, back off. Take the boat in another direction.

Or I'd be hurt.

Breathless, I swam with every speck of my will, aiming for the nearest float. But the boat screamed closer behind me. It picked up speed, the engine's growl indicating the person gave it more fuel. I couldn't let them reach me. Pressing for more power, I dragged energy from somewhere deep inside my exhausted body.

Only a few feet further…

Closer.

I wasn't going to reach! No.

My legs screamed from my efforts. My arms trembled. With a burst, I shoved myself forward, scrambling my fingers along the float, wood splinters jabbing deep.

The boat soared past the dock and spun around to face me, spiking water high in the air behind it when it throttled in place. It growled like a ravenous beast.

Arms trembling, I hauled my shaking body up the ladder. I collapsed on the top of the dock, panting. But when the engine rumbled, I propped myself up to watch the boat.

The driver cranked the shifter back and drove the vehicle around to face the other direction. Blue smoke and churning water erupted from the rear, devouring a cluster of lily pads. The engine whined. With a high-pitched roar, the boat flew away, heading across the lake.

I flopped onto my back and blinked at the sky. My heart thundered in my ears. My lungs wheezed.

"Wow," someone said from nearby. "That was something else."

I half-opened my eyelids.

An older guy with long sideburns and a round belly stood on the float beside me, squinting to where the boat rocketed toward the opposite shore. "That driver out of his mind? He could've hit you." His concerned gaze fell to me. "You okay, Miss?"

"Yeah." I sat and shoved my sopping hair off my face. "I'm fine." Scared, but what else was new in my life lately? Shivers took over my body as reaction set in. Goosebumps competed with muscle spasms. My limbs trembled with exhaustion from my race through the water. It was all I could do to move, let alone think.

"Anything I can do for you?" the man asked. "Get someone for you?"

"I'm okay. Really."

I'd only been swimming. Floating. Had my body, spread across the surface of the water, been invisible to the boater? This could've been a simple accident.

Or had it been intentional? I'd be stupid not to consider a connection between someone chasing me in the woods yesterday and this boater today.

It might've been a fluke. Some guy not paying attention. While the majority of boaters acted responsibly while on the water, others were careless. Especially during the weekend, when they were drinking, having fun. Accidents like this happened all the time. Didn't they?

I was grateful I hadn't become another statistic.

While the man shuffled his bare feet, I sat up and crossed my clammy arms over my legs, hugging my quaking body. I rocked back and forth.

From now on, I'd have to be extra careful. Watch out for myself all the time because, when it came down to it, no one could do the job better than me.

"If you're going to be all right, then, I'm..." The man waved toward the shore.

Teeth chattering, I nodded, releasing him from his self-imposed caretaker duty.

With a grunt, he climbed down the ladder and eased into the water. His arms swirled around to help him maintain his position. "That asshole must've had too much to drink."

This early in the morning?

The man swam away.

Once I'd regained control of my body, I returned to shore. Brittany, occupied with her daughters, seemed to have missed the entire incident. She gave me a distracted smile as she toweled one of her daughters dry.

"I'll see you later," Brittany called out as I left.

I waved. Still a shaking wreck, I returned to my campsite quickly and changed out of my suit.

Nothing calmed an eventful morning more than strawberry pancakes. Placing the camp stove on the end of the picnic table, I leveled it with sticks. I set my cast iron frying pan down on the grate and whisked up the batter before plopping in a handful of sliced strawberries. I lit the stove and when the oil sizzled, I spooned batter onto the pan.

Rapid-paced footsteps approached, yanking my attention away from my browning breakfast. I braced myself, but it was Cooper running toward me.

While I'd promised myself I'd ignore him, I couldn't help staring. And what a view. He stalled beside me, lungs heaving, sweat cutting trails down his temples. More had created a broad line in the center of his brown tee. Writing on his left chest said, *NMCB 14*, and below it, *Seabees. Can do.*

Can't do, actually.

A charred smell kept me from asking him what—if anything—he *could* do.

"Watch out. It's burning," he said.

Like everything else in my life. Scorched sugar hit my

sinuses. I flipped my cake and held in my scowl. "I like it dark. Makes it crispy."

When the other side was done, I slid it onto my plate. I sat and coated the top with butter and launched my boat in a pool of syrup.

"Four miles. I'm beat." Cooper yanked his shirt over his head, revealing his delectable muscles. He tossed the garment toward his tent. Missed by a long shot.

I held in my snicker and focused on consuming my pancake. Otherwise, I might stroke his chest with my eyes, abandon my breakfast long enough to do something forbidden like trail my fingertips across his tattoo.

"Okay if I use some of this batter?" he asked.

Crimping my lips together, I waved my hand toward the bowl.

"I'm starved," he said. "I can shower later."

Sure, act like nothing happened last night, why don't you?

I nipped off the snarky thought before it slipped past my lips. While my night had granted me little sleep, it had given my perspective. It wasn't Cooper's fault I'd rekindled my crush. He was mourning the loss of a relationship, and that needed to be respected. I'd shoved myself into the void, essentially taken advantage of his vulnerability. No rebound romance for me.

He slid his perfectly golden cake onto his plate and joined me across the table.

While he doctored his breakfast, nearly naked-man struck again, dragging my lust out in heavy waves. I smacked that baby down fast. But I couldn't keep my eyes from gliding along his shoulders. His pecs. Focusing on his nipples.

Fortunately, Eli arrived before I could make a fool of myself by touching.

"Cool," he said. "Strawberry?"

I rose. "I'll have some ready for you in no time." Making more ingredients would occupy my brain. Should I tell Eli about what happened on the lake? Or go with the assumption it was an accident? The lines on my brother's face told me he was exhausted. I'd wait until after he'd slept. "How's your coworker doing?"

"Fractured his ankle."

"Oh, no!" I'd met Steve a few times. Nice guy. Married with a new baby. "How long will he be out of work?"

"Three weeks until his cast comes off. At least it wasn't a bad break."

"I'm glad to hear that." I slid a big pancake onto Eli's plate and handed it to him. "When do you have to work again?"

"Three." He dropped onto the bench where I'd been sitting and covered the cake with butter and syrup. His fork dug in, and he shoved a huge bite into his mouth. "This looks fantastic. Thanks."

"You're welcome." Pausing behind him, I smoothed his mussed hair. "I was going to go into town this morning for supplies, but I can wait until you get up." I needed ice and chicken breasts for dinner. Maybe I should make a list. What else would go well with the corn and the potatoes I'd brought from home? Some—

"I probably won't be able to bring you into town before I have to leave."

I felt bad the second he said it. He needed to sleep. While I could go alone, his Jeep had a manual transmission, and I'd never learned to drive a stick. "I guess I can get by without the supplies." What could I make instead for dinner? There wasn't much bread dough left, but we—

"I'll take you." Cooper set his fork on his empty plate.

I forced a smile. "Thanks, but I'm all set." I'd rather eat

leftover dough for dinner, washed down by warm beer, than sit in a car for twenty minutes with Cooper.

"I have to go to the base, anyway," Cooper said. "You can pick up what you need at the Commissary."

I hesitated. Did I really want to expose my fragile heart to Cooper Talon again this soon?

"It's not out of my way," Cooper added.

This might be a bad idea, but I really wasn't looking forward to a skimpy dinner and warm beer. I could handle an hour or so with Cooper, couldn't I?

I sighed. "Okay. Thanks." Riding into town with him had to be better than getting into trouble here at the campground while Eli slept.

12

Cooper

Ginny grabbed her things and headed to the showers while I cleaned up from breakfast. This left me and Eli alone at the campsite. I knew my friend was tired, but even my commanding officer with orders in hand couldn't keep me from pinning him down.

"I need you to release me from that promise," I said.

"I assume you're talking about Ginny." Eli set his toothbrush on the picnic table and scrolled briefly into his phone. When he looked up, grooves filled his brow. "Why?"

"Because...well, I kissed her."

"You've only been here a few days. Please don't tell me you and my sister have——"

"Nothing like that happened." Except, I'd stroked her body. And that kiss. Our kiss meant everything to me.

"I don't get why you're pursuing this."

"Here's the deal." I settled on the picnic table bench. "I like her and want to get to know her better." Go out with her. Talk about photos and gold. Joke about whatever came into my mind. I wanted to kiss her again. Touch her gorgeous breasts. Slide my fingers across her waist and delve into that sweet spot below if she'd let me.

"You're only here for a couple more days."

"*Eight* more days." It could equal a lifetime. Things didn't have to end there. We could—

"Like a few days versus eight matters?" Snorting, Eli crossed his arms on his chest. "You're deploying again soon. You'll be gone for months."

"Ten weeks, but I'll be back. Lots of deployed soldiers have girlfriends, wives."

Eli reeled back, his lips thinning. "You're not thinking that far ahead, are you?"

Was I? Hell, if I knew. "I just want a chance."

"To prove what?"

"I don't know." I groaned and raked my hair. "Maybe nothing will come of it."

"What if something does? What if Ginny falls for you, expects things from you?" Eli's stare bit deeply, messing with my resolve. "You prepared to give up your career? Move home and settle down? Because I know that's the only thing she can consider right now. Someone stable who'll be here for her. Not someone like that asshole she dated overseas. Guy wasn't around when she needed him."

Acid burned through my stomach at the thought of her and the other guy together, but I had no right to feel jealous. She didn't belong to me. She never would. Was I crazy to pursue this?

"Tell me what you can offer her, bro," Eli said.

"I don't know." I hadn't thought that far ahead. If things progressed, was I willing to leave the military and return to the town I'd run from? The thought of moving back to Maine created a dull, heaviness inside me like a boulder was crushing my chest. Moving back here would be the same as starting all over again with nothing changed, except I was older. Like the past twelve years had been wasted.

"Think this through. You might not have to move home, but what will you do if you two hit it off? Come back once or twice a year for a visit? Women want men who can be there when they need them. Ginny especially."

What was Eli saying here? "I get leave. We can Skype." I could barely keep my shoulders from caving. Even if Ginny let me into her life, could a long-distance relationship truly work? If I was a decent guy, I'd forget this. Step back and let her find someone else. A local man who could give her what I was unable to deliver.

A man who wasn't fragmented by the abuse from his past.

For whatever reason, I couldn't let this go. I rubbed my chest with my fist, but the spasm wouldn't go away. This wasn't about jealousy or getting to know her better. I wanted—

"Why not wait until you're back from your deployment?"

"I won't get leave again for almost a year. Used most of it up coming home to take care of my dad's place."

"So, you'll return to the base in California and my sister will pine for you here in Crescent Cove." Eli's words ground out. "Exactly what I didn't want to see happen."

I hated the way this conversation was going, but Eli was right. Again. Sure, I wasn't a teenager any longer, eking out a living from bagging groceries at the supermarket. As a Seabee Chief, I earned enough money to take Ginny out. Do things for her. Buy her that ice cream like I'd wanted to years ago. But with her here and me in California, I couldn't offer her what she needed more than anything else.

All of me.

Eli sighed. "You and Ginny, huh? You like my sister that much?"

"I did years ago, too." That same crushing disappointment I'd felt back in high school filled me now, magnified ten-fold. It made me question whether I'd get any further with Ginny this time around than the last. "She's special."

"Why didn't you ask her out back then? I wouldn't have minded. Much." Eli growled, but his smile emerged, showing he was only fooling with me.

"After Dad...Well, I had to leave," I said. "But I should've talked to her before I got on that bus for boot camp." Should've believed in myself. I should've gotten an apartment after my father kicked me out, a job at the mill, and asked her to let me into her life.

Too many should'ves and no way to go back and redo the past. I could only shelve my regrets and proceed from this moment.

"This isn't really up to me," Eli said.

"That promise." I refused to go back on my word. If Eli wouldn't release me, I'd need to forget her. As much as it might kill me to do it.

"I'm the last one to suggest you leave your feelings for a woman buried." Eli glared up at the sky, and I wondered who he was referring to. As far as I knew, Eli wasn't interested in anyone. "If you can find a way to make my sister happy, you have my blessing." He coughed. "Not that you need it from me."

"Ginny controls her own life," I said.

"Yeah." Eli rose from the chair and crossed the campsite to drop his empty water bottle into the bucket. "And probably everyone else's if they let her."

That prospect didn't intimidate me one bit.

Eli leaned against the picnic table and folded his arms

on his chest. The intensity in his gaze pinned me to my seat. "I want your word you won't hurt her."

"Of course." I stiffened my spine. "I have nothing but respect for Ginny. Always have."

Eli nodded. "That's all I need to hear."

———

EVEN THOUGH THE AC was turned off, ice ruled inside the car. I couldn't seem to find a way through it to find the Ginny I'd joked with yesterday.

"Once we're on the base," I said, "you'll need to stay with me because you have no military ID." My words came out pompous, but she wasn't working with me.

She grunted and continued to stare out the window like she'd done the past ten minutes while I drove into town. "I'm not planning on strolling around the military base by myself."

"I just thought I should mention it." How could I break through her hardened exterior and find the woman I'd held in my arms last night? Because things had changed. I could ...pursue her. See what happened after that.

"Would you mind stopping for coffee?" she asked. "We're going to pass my usual place up here." She pointed to Mr. Joe's on the right.

"Sure."

We coasted through the drive thru, each getting something to drink. After taking a quick sip, I set mine in the console holder and pulled back onto the main road, continuing south.

Ginny stared out the window while sipping her iced mocha latte.

And while I might be distracted by thoughts of her, I

could swear a car was following us two vehicles behind. It kept me glancing into the rearview mirror, my pulse jumping in my throat.

"What are you looking at?" A frown brewed on her forehead.

Directing my focus to the road ahead, I whistled through my teeth. Should I tell her? I didn't want to scare her without due cause. "What do you mean?"

She faced me. "Don't play around. You keep looking behind us."

"Watching traffic?" When her lips curled down, I said, "All right. I think someone's following us."

Eyes widening, she peered behind. "Which car?"

No mistaking her breathy tone. Crap. I had alarmed her.

"The black one." Much like the vehicle that had peeled away from the campground parking lot yesterday, come to think of it. Any relation to the man I'd passed on the path, the guy dressed in a sweatshirt with dirty blond hair? Details were adding up to…nothing. Not so far, anyway.

"I'll watch for you." She pointed a few minutes later. "Oh, okay. Whoever it was turned off. It was probably nothing." Slumping back into her seat, she redirected her attention out the window again.

"Someone *was* following us," I said. "For quite a distance."

"I'm a photographer. My biggest gigs right now are taking pictures of dogs in tutus. High school graduation photos. I'm not someone worth stalking. But you're military. They might be interested in you." Said like she wondered what I'd been up to overseas for the past few years. I'd laugh if I wasn't so eager to repair things between us. "If you're doing top-secret espionage, Eli didn't tell me about it."

"You asked Eli about me?"

"I didn't say that."

"Sure, you did."

Silence.

Interesting. I'd quizzed Eli about Ginny whenever I dared. Had she been doing the same with me?

Growling because I couldn't figure this out, I turned onto the base and slowed as we approached the gate.

An E3 stood outside the checkpoint dressed in camo, with a 9 mm strapped on her hip. I stopped beside her and handed over my military ID.

"What's your business here today, Chief?" she asked as she scrutinized it.

"Exchange. Commissary."

Ginny leaned forward and handed over her driver's license.

"She's going shopping with me," I said.

"Sounds fun." The woman handed our IDs back with a smile. "You're all set, Chief."

"Thanks." I put the car back into gear and drove along the tree-lined road until the dense vegetation gave way to open spaces filled with parking lots and squat cinderblock buildings. "I'll also need to be with you when you buy what you need at the Commissary." I glanced at my arm—a pale band encircled it. "My watch strap broke. I need to go to the Exchange for another, but if you're willing to wait, I've got a few things I need to get at the Commissary, too. Beer. Chips." My laugh came out weak, but I hoped she'd take the bait. "Bread dough."

"Pizza again?"

"What else could be on the menu tonight?"

"I plan to dry-rub chicken."

My rumbling stomach suggested I was hungry already.

"If I'm invited, then chicken it is." Her silence suggested assent, so I ran with it. "That sounds awesome."

She tightened her lips.

Okay, maybe things weren't that great, after all.

I pulled my vehicle into a space, and we walked inside the main building. Ginny aimed for the coffee shop while I went in the opposite direction, to the Exchange. After buying a watch band, I joined her at a table.

"What else do you need besides chicken?" I asked.

"Ice." Her brows knitted. "And a few other things."

"Like what?"

"Cookies."

"Any particular kind of cookies?"

"Eli found my stash of Oreos last night, but I'm not saying a thing, because a hard-working man like my brother deserves all the cookies he can put away. Anyway. I need more double-stuffed."

I couldn't resist teasing her, even though her mood still shouted *uncertain*. "What's wrong with the single-stuffed variety?"

Her face scrunched. "They're boring."

"Why?"

"Double stuffed are the perfect dessert when you eat them right."

A long paused followed while I waited for an explanation that never came. What had I missed? "I see."

Her eyebrows lifted, and her lips quivered. Her positive reaction made my body hum. Finally, I was making headway.

"You must know what you're supposed to do with double-stuffed Oreos," she said.

"Eat them?"

Her smile rose but faded from her eyes sooner than I'd hoped for. "Guess so." She stood. "You ready to go?"

Had my rejection last night driven away the Ginny I was dying to get to know better? I wanted—no needed—to see her happy again. How could I make it happen?

We dumped our cups and walked across the hall to the Commissary, where I held open the door and gestured for her to enter ahead of me. Inside, we wove a cart up and down the aisles, pausing to collect enough junk food to survive an apocalypse.

"Well, if it isn't Chief Talon," someone said from behind me. "How are things?"

That voice. I would recognize it even in dark terrain. I turned and shook the hand of the man who'd saved my ass overseas more times than I liked to admit. Flint had left the Navy eight months ago, though he'd stayed in the Reserves. "Awesome to see you."

Flint nodded to Ginny then gestured to our junk food-laden cart. "Looks like you're stocking up for a long weekend."

"Can't have enough Oreos," I said. "What's with the uniform?"

Scowling, Flint tugged on his starched white jacket. Formal gear was a bitch in this heat. "Wedding. The bride begged for an Arch of Swords."

"The ushers dress in choker whites and form an arch with their swords for the bride and groom to pass under-neath when they come out of the church," I explained to Ginny.

"Sounds fun." She shifted forward and smiled at Flint.

Why did my gut churn because she was being nice to Flint? Lots of people liked my friend.

Women, especially.

I ran my gaze down Flint, wondering what she saw outside the uniform. Dark hair cropped almost as short as mine. Bulky build, telling me Flint still worked out like he used to. Green eyes I'd once overheard an E5 say made her hot and bothered. Decent-looking dude, if I was into dudes.

My pulse slowed. Was Ginny interested in Flint? She'd just met him. And Flint was…last I'd heard, my friend was single.

"If you're here on the base, you're obviously still in the service," Flint said to me. "You grew up around here, didn't you?"

"Yep." Decent distraction, but all I could think about was Ginny and Flint together. A local guy, she could date someone like him.

"Last I heard…" Flint spoke to me but his grin took in Ginny. "You were stationed in California."

"Port Hueneme."

Flint squinted toward the entrance where a pretty red-headed woman in a yellow dress peered our way. Maybe she was his date. Or he'd gotten married, and I hadn't heard. The latter being the best scenario. "I wish we had more time to talk. But my sister's waiting."

Sister. Wasn't that wonderful.

"We came in for a card," Flint said. "And I snagged this." He held up a bottle. "Can't imagine a weekend without good bourbon."

"This is Ginny," I said, wanting to bite back the words the second I said them. Why was I introducing her to Flint? "She's Eli's sister."

"Eli Bradley?" Flint glanced around. "He here with you? Heard he'd been injured, discharged a few months ago. Already knew he was from Crescent Cove. I've been meaning to call him about a job."

"I can give you his number," Ginny said softly. When Flint handed over his phone, she typed it in. Her lips curled into the full smile I'd been seeking, though it wasn't directed my way. "Nice meeting you, Flint."

His chipped nod was directed Ginny's way, and I swore his eyes drifted down her body with distinct interest. "And it was nice meeting you." He glanced toward his sister again. "I should remind Mia that Eli lives local."

"Mia?" I asked.

"Don't believe you ever met my sister as she only came out to the base a few times and you were overseas when she did."

"You mentioned Eli," Ginny said with a frown. She studied Mia with interest. "Were he and Mia…"

"Not at all. But…" Flint peered over his shoulder at his sister. "When I got out, I decided to move here to Crescent Cove to make it easier to do my Reserve duties on the base. This part of the country is gorgeous, one of the few affordable coastal locations left in Maine. Mia and I are close. She moved up here a few months ago and took a job at Express Care on Main. She's a doctor. But I don't believe she knows Eli's around."

They *must* have history then.

"Anyway." Flint slapped my arm. "If you've got time over the next few days, come see me here on the base and we can talk. I'm doing my two weeks of active duty." He handed me a business card. "But I'm also…" He cut a glance at Ginny's as if he wasn't comfortable sharing with her. "At my new business, Viper Force, we're working on… recreational drones."

Military-related business then. A man might leave the Seabees but the Navy never left the man.

"Sounds intriguing," I said.

"I'd love to talk about old times."

Plus a few new things if I knew my friend. "Will do."

Flint walked away, and Ginny stared after him. "Gotta say, that's a hot suit."

"Choker whites are a killer in this humidity."

"Not quite what I meant, but there's that, too."

I squinted at Flint, who'd joined his sister. "You like the uniform?"

She wiggled her eyebrows. "I'd have to be dead not to like *that* uniform."

Almost made me wish I'd brought formal clothing along with me.

Ginny scanned the food in our cart. "All set, do you think?"

"Unless you want to grab a fourth package of Oreos."

Her scowl rose, but her lips twitched it out of place, lightening her face.

Got her. Finally, I was thawing the glacier she'd surrounded herself with.

At the register, we bought two bags of ice and took them from the cooler out front. We loaded everything into my trunk and headed back to the campground. As I drove, I pressed my lip-twitching advantage. "Eli says you've moved home for good." Glancing her way, I tried to sound out her expression, but read only neutral.

"I bought a building with an apartment upstairs and a studio on the ground floor. As I said, I do photography."

"For more books or just the graduation stuff?"

"For books but also portraits. Fashion. Wildlife if it holds still long enough. Weddings." She turned her gaze out the window, effectively shutting me out again. "I'm doing a big spread for a local author and his fiancée in August. He writes highlander historical romance. He's wearing a kilt and she's dressing in something Scottish, too. There will be bagpipes, you name it."

"Sounds fun."

"We don't have to keep making small talk. You're just giving me a ride into town."

I pulled up to a stop sign and eased out onto Route One. Bumper-to-bumper traffic awaited us, grinding my vehicle to a halt. I tilted my head toward the window. Construction ahead, but things appeared to be moving again beyond the paving equipment. "Maybe I want to get to know you better."

Those beautiful eyes turned my way, delving deep. "Why?" No mistaking the break in her voice.

If this meant nothing, I would come up with some half-ass statement. Turn this around and pretend my only goal was to make her laugh. But that would keep her at arm's length, the last place I wanted her to be. "Because...I care."

She blinked and softness flitted across her face before her scowl returned. She flipped her attention back out the window. "Could've fooled me."

I inched the vehicle forward, slowly approaching the paver. "You're talking about last night."

"I am."

"I kissed you back."

"Until you shoved me away."

The fact that I'd hurt her hit me in the chest like a sledgehammer. Not my intention at all. But, if I hurt her, it meant she cared, too. It wasn't much, but I could work with it.

We reached the intersection, and I turned onto the lake access road. The entrance to the campground was a half a mile down on the left, but I needed to have this out with Ginny before we arrived. "I didn't want to shove you away."

"You said you were still stuck on Annie," she muttered but kept staring out the window.

"I'm not." Frustration coiled in my gut. How could I get her to soften toward me?

I pulled into the parking lot. Before I could wrangle my seat belt loose, she'd undone hers and jumped from the vehicle. I climbed out from my side and stormed around the trunk, meeting up with her at the back passenger door. Unable to help myself, I pressed her against the metal, putting my palms on the car on either side of her shoulders.

"I lied," I said through gritted teeth.

Her chin jutted forward and challenge flared in her eyes. "About what, specifically?"

"About this." I captured her lips with the same hesitancy she'd used when she stole mine last night. Because I wouldn't push her or make her do anything she didn't want to do. If she shoved me away like I had her, I'd respect her wishes.

Her hands slid around my neck, and her mouth opened beneath mine. She strained toward me.

I tasted her with my tongue, exploring the smokiness of coffee and the sweetness that was all Ginny. She moaned and pulled me closer, fitting me against her body.

Damn, she felt wonderful.

A car turned into the entrance of the parking lot, proving this wasn't the best place to make out. With one last, lingering stroke of my tongue along hers, I lifted my head. "We need to talk."

She nodded. A little dazed; a fact that pleased me immensely.

The car pulled up beside us because herd mentality ruled in a mostly empty parking lot. A family climbed out and two kids raced for the path, their parents following at a more leisurely pace.

I backed away from Ginny. Remaining against the car,

her tongue touched where my lips had recently been. Where I wanted to put them this second.

In combat, having a strategy could make a difference between a life saved or lost. I'd need a plan for Ginny, because I was fighting for everything.

As soon as we unloaded our purchases, we'd sit down and hash this out.

Ginny started across the parking lot, bags in hand, and I followed.

"I didn't have a chance to tell you or Eli." Her throat moved with her swallow. She entered the path, speaking to me over her shoulder. "Something happened this morning. I went swimming and…" She paused as we approached our campsite. Her gasp slipped out as she stared forward, and her bags slipped from her fingers and crashed on the ground. "What…?"

I slammed through the thick weeds beside her then ground to a halt. Someone had trashed our campsite.

"I don't understand." Ginny's mouth opened before snapping closed. "Eli!" She rushed forward, toward her brother's tent. But the flaps were open, and he wasn't inside. Turning, she stared around frantically, ignoring the rubble surrounding her. "Where is he?"

I pulled my phone to send him a text but found one from him waiting. Must've missed it.

I got called into work early. Tell Ginny I'll be back to get her and her things in the morning. And that I know she'll be okay. She's got you to watch out for her.

She sure did. I read Eli's message out loud to Ginny, who nodded before gaping at the upended totes and her clothing strewn around on the ground.

Her eyes filled. "I don't understand why anyone would do something like this."

While I might not know the reason, I had a pretty good idea who'd done it.

Ginny's tears sent anger roaring through me, and I clenched my teeth tight enough they hurt.

"You want to wait in the car again?" I asked. "I'll take a look around and come back for you."

Her chin quivered, but her face tightened. "I'm going to start cleaning up."

I dropped our bags on the table and took her hands, barely holding back the rage boiling inside me. "You sure?"

The stiffness of her spine rivaled a Master at Arms during a vital inspection. "I'm okay." Releasing my hands, she went back for the bags she'd dropped on the path and placed them on the table beside the others. "I can handle this." No mistaking her dragging footsteps, however.

The human cyclone who had rushed through our site had focused their attention on Ginny. They'd dumped her totes onto the ground and scattered her possessions but left mine and Eli's things alone. Ginny's tent had been slashed—with a knife was my best guess. Her mattress lay limply beside the tent, a dusky blue, deflated balloon. Her clothing had been tossed around as if someone had searched her belongings.

Or like they'd done this in anger.

Tom. Who'd made a threat yesterday and carried it out today.

"Wait here." I shot across our campsite, aiming for the path across the green. I didn't know where I'd find the other man, but I damned sure wouldn't stop until I did.

"Where are you going?" Ginny yelled after me.

"I'll be right back."

My feet thudded as I charged across the grass. I darted around a couple of teenagers lying on a blanket, working on their tans. One lifted her sunglasses as I passed. A giggling toddler ran away from me when I came near, no doubt hoping I'd give chase. On any other day, sure, but not today.

It was time to teach an asshole a lesson.

I raced up a wide path leading to the other section of the campground and slowed only to inspect each site. Seeking Tom. I located the other man five sites down, conveniently emerging from his tent. Taking a nap after scaring Ginny half to death? Not on my watch.

I was convinced the other man had not only trashed her things but stalked her in the woods yesterday. Who knew what the hell else he'd done that we hadn't yet discovered? Payback would be sweet.

My anger flaming all over again, I ran up to him, grabbed his shirt collar, and shook him.

"What the hell?" Tom slapped my hands away and stumbled backward.

I stalked him, fists clenched.

Tom stopped when his back hit a tree. "What are you doing? You have no right to—"

"I'm going to tell you one last time," I ground out. "Leave Ginny alone."

Tom glanced to where two men stood on the edge of the campsite adjacent to this one, staring intently our way. Tom sneered. "You and what army?"

No reason I couldn't take this creep down all on my own. But I wouldn't turn this into a three-on-one situation. I had no issues with the other men. Scowling, I lowered my voice. "Going through her site is a crappy thing to do, and you know it."

Tom's stubbly chin lifted. "It's a free country. I can go wherever I want."

The hell with worrying about anyone else joining in. I

growled and advanced on Tom again, getting right up in his face. It pleased me to no end when he cowered and backed around the tree, putting it between us.

"Hey, Tom," one of the men called. "You need a hand there, buddy?"

"Nope." Tom grinned. He eased away from the tree and spat on the ground. "I can handle this."

"You just let us know," the man said.

A small poodle leaped into the air from where it was tied to a tree, barking shrilly at me. Tom stooped down and made soothing sounds as he patted the dog. He straightened and put himself between us as if he thought I might attack the pet.

"I should call the police," Tom said. "I was a cop before...my wife died. I've still got plenty of friends on the force who'd help me press assault charges." He waved to the others. "I've got witnesses, too."

"Try me."

Tom strolled around me and over to a cooler. He pulled out a drink and popped it open, the can hissing when he flipped back the tab. After guzzling, he wiped his mouth with the back of his hand. "How would an assault conviction look on your military record?"

Tom had snooped around. If I involved the police, I would find myself in deep shit. The military frowned on soldiers starting trouble, let alone doling out their own version of the law. But I'd do it all over again—and more —to protect Ginny.

I rubbed the back of my head that was still tender. "Seems you know more about assault than I do."

"I don't know what you're talking about."

Sure. "Don't come near Ginny again. Don't talk to her. Don't look at her. And don't touch her things."

"I haven't been near her things."

Like I believed him?

Color flared on Tom's face, and the sideways dart of his eyes shouted lie.

"And don't challenge me again." My heart slamming in my chest from the confrontation, I stomped to the edge of the campsite before I turned to face Tom one last time. "You won't like the outcome."

13

Ginny

All I wanted was to do was drop down onto the picnic table bench, lay my head on my arms, and cry. Ever since Istanbul, my life had been in tatters.

But collapsing now would let whoever did this win.

I aimed for normal and prepared the chicken. No reason to let it sit in the sun and rot. After cleaning it and dumping in the Cajun seasonings, I tossed the plastic bag into the cooler with the ice we'd bought. Then I turned and with a sigh, tackled the mess someone had made of my life.

After upending my tote, I knelt and placed my things back inside, brushing off dirt first. Nothing was badly damaged, not enough that I couldn't still use it. With my finger, I traced a place where a rock had scratched my favorite cast iron frying pan. To think a simple scrape could make my chest squeeze tight.

I popped the lid back onto the tote and picked up my clothing. Blinking back tears, I folded each item carefully, stacking it all on the table. I'd put the pile in Cooper's car. Or with Eli's things, in his tent.

At least my laptop hadn't been touched. I'd left it sitting on the picnic table bench, a sweatshirt casually tossed over it. While I should've put it inside Cooper's trunk when we went to the base, I'd been distracted.

Finally, I stood beside my flattened tent and deflated mattress. No making normal with these items. I cringed while dragging my sleeping bag to the side, where I shook off the dirt and draped it over the clothesline. While the creep had slashed a hole in it, it might still be salvageable after I washed it. No reason I couldn't sew the hole closed.

I wasn't sure why someone coming up behind me fast didn't scare the crap out of me. Maybe numbness had finally set in.

"We'll pack up and go into town," Cooper said, dropping a comforting hand on my shoulder.

Eyes closing briefly, I leaned back, into his warmth. "I'm staying." The words were dragged from deep inside me.

"Why?"

"Because I'm sick of cowering all the time." Hiding and flinching at every pin drop was killing me. I'd come camping to prove something to myself. To push my boundaries. Letting whoever did this chase me home could set me back weeks.

"You're sure?"

Biting my lower lip, I eased away from him, nodding.

"There's no repairing your tent."

"My mom bought it for me when I was ten." I'd been proud the first time I was able to set it up all by myself. "I'll sleep in Eli's." On the floor beside his air mattress.

Hands on his hips, Cooper glanced around. "What can I do to help?"

"Would you put my mattress and tent in the dumpster

behind the camp store?" I righted one of our camp chairs. "No reason to take them home."

He dragged them to the edge of our site before returning to stand in front of me. When his arms enfolded me, and he lowered his chin onto my head, my eyes stung. It was a major struggle not to let myself sob. My insides felt ripped wide open, laid bare to shrivel in the sun. I savored the comfort he offered and the warmth of his touch. The tickle of his breath across my hair.

How had I ever felt complete without him?

"Where did you go?" I had my suspicions.

"Just took care of a little business." His chest expanded, pressing against my cheek. "This won't happen again."

No reason to dig further. If Cooper said he'd eliminated the problem, I believed him. "Thank you."

"Any time."

We pulled apart.

"Since you don't want to leave the campground," he said. "Do you want to hike after we finish up here?"

The perfect distraction. "Sure."

"I won't be long."

As I was finishing tidying up, one of the girls from the campsite next to ours ran up to their camper and opened the door. She climbed inside while Brittany and the smaller girl set bags on their picnic table. Brittany waved at me. I was struck by the normalcy of the action so soon after someone had ravaged our campsite. My knees still shook, but I waved back. Reaction could set in later when I was alone.

Seeing Brittany gave me an idea, though.

Cooper returned and ducked inside his tent, emerging in shorts and a tee. The soft, light blue fabric stretched across his chest and highlighted his muscular build. Heat filled me, and I half-smiled at the thought that my head could spin so soon after the horrible thing that had recently happened.

"How about hiking up one of the mountain trails?" I said. "Some are over fifteen miles long. I doubt we'll go that far but we can take one of the shorter paths to the cliffs. There's a great view of the ocean up there."

"Sounds like a plan." He glanced at his watch. "Do I have time to grab something to eat before we leave?"

I nodded, and while he heated three hot dogs on the camp stove, I put my clothing inside Eli's tent and straightened his bedding. I puttered around the campsite while Cooper dressed three rolls with ketchup, mustard, and dill relish. He sat at the picnic table with a hearty sigh. Ravenous wolves couldn't have eaten the meal faster.

Amazing. "You *are* a growing boy." I slapped a hand over my mouth, my face hot after making the comment.

"You said it, sweetheart." Standing, he tossed his crumb-covered paper plate into the fire pit and grabbed an apple from the dish in the center of the table. His even teeth crunched through the red skin, and he spoke around the bite. "Let me grab a few things and we can go."

I was filling my water bottle at the faucet when Brittany came out of her camper. "Hey," I called out, striding over to her.

Brittany smiled. "How you doing?"

"Something happened you should know about." I winced. "When my friend and I were in town this morning, someone trashed our campsite."

Brittany gasped, her eyes widening. Leaning around me, she stared toward the gap where my tent had been.

"I had to throw a bunch of things away," I said, sad all over again about the loss. "Whoever it was scattered my things around, too."

"Did you call the cops?"

"My friend took care of it." Maybe I should've called the police. If Tom had been involved, it might teach him a well-needed lesson.

"That's terrible." Brittany's eyes softened. "We were down at the lake all morning. I'm really sorry. Here I've asked you to watch our camper tonight, but I'm not returning the favor."

"It's not your fault," I said. "I never thought someone would do anything like this."

Brittany clicked her tongue. "I just can't believe it."

"We're going hiking. I don't suppose you'd be willing to watch our things for the afternoon?" We'd return before Brittany and her family wanted to leave.

"Of course, I will," Brittany said. "I plan to read while the kids nap, anyway. And if I have to leave for even a second, I'll put Jamal on duty. Nobody will touch your things while we're around."

That would be a nice change.

"Thank you," I said. After shouldering my pack, I waited for Cooper to get ready. A sliver of darkness on the horizon to the west hinted at rain either tonight or early tomorrow. Hopefully, it would hold off until the fireworks were over. I was determined to proceed with the evening I'd planned earlier.

"All set?" Cooper asked. He paused and squinted toward the parking lot.

I followed his gaze, and my heart leaped with joy. Wasn't this lovely? Tom was loading bags into the trunk of a black car. "Do you think he's leaving?" That would make the rest of my camping trip complete. Even the glare Tom shot in our direction before climbing into his car didn't stop my stress level from dropping multiple notches.

"Looks like it." Cooper grunted but satisfaction filled

his face, much like a cat lying in the sun on a front porch. Evidently, he *had* taken care of the problem.

My mood lightened further as Cooper and I walked toward the back of the campground, our sneakers crunching on dead grass. Outside of strawberry pancakes, fresh air and sunshine had to be the next best cure for unsettled nerves.

"Have you hiked here before?" he asked.

"On some of the lower trails a few years ago." Back in my prior life, when I'd been bold. Complacent. Brave.

His eyes sparkled when he glanced my way. "Do you have a special map we're following this time?"

Kudos to him for making this fun. I could play along, too. "Forgot to buy one on eBay." I waved to the sign we approached at the base. "I bet we can figure out which trail to take when we get there."

We stopped and studied the map.

"I think we should climb Big Piney." I traced a dotted green line that led to the top. "It's three point two miles each way."

"What about Little Piney?"

I frowned, unable to find a trail marked Little Piney.

Oh. Of course. Snickering, I lifted one eyebrow his way. "Actually, I was about to suggest Middle Piney because I wasn't sure you could take on a three-mile walk. Since you ran this morning, you might not be up for anything more than a leisurely stroll." With all the indecision I felt lately, how did I find the nerve to tease him?

His voice deepened, and his eyes focused on my mouth. "I think I can handle any piney you're up for." Leaving me with sparks flickering in my belly, he started up the trail marked with a green slash of paint on a tree. He paused and looked over his shoulder. "Coming?"

Damn, but he *could* handle himself in a tease.

Fanning my face—solely from everything that had happened today and not because of the hot guy striding ahead of me—I caught up to walk with him.

The level trail gave way to gradual hills. As we progressed, our breathing deepened to accommodate the steeper inclines. Dense evergreen forest surrounded us, a cool, primeval landscape. Other than a few squirrels and chipmunks darting from the path and the occasional bird flying overhead, we might be the only two beings in the world.

I was itching to dig in and quiz Cooper about our kisses but the mostly single-file hiking didn't lend itself to meaningful conversation. I'd wait until the trail widened again and we could walk side-by-side. Then I could watch his face when he spoke.

But that didn't mean I couldn't ask him about other parts of his life until then.

"You joined the military right after graduation, right? What was it like? You got your diploma, and you were gone." I snapped my fingers. While Eli had shared some of his military experiences, I was eager to hear about Cooper's.

His calf muscles kept on flexing, carrying him up the trail ahead of me. I had to admit that running gave a man nice glutes. But other than frogs croaking in the distance, silence hung in the air. That might not have been a good conversation starter, after all. Instead, I could ask about—

"It was scary," he said.

Increasing my speed, I leaned around him and squinted up at his stoic face. "What do you mean?" If asked to describe Cooper Talon, I'd immediately say confident, capable, and methodical. Never scared. That was my role in life.

"We're talking about leaving Crescent Cove, population two thousand. I hadn't even been out of Maine before."

The path widened, and I strode faster to keep up.

"I wasn't planning on joining the military at first but they were willing to take me on…suddenly. They flew me to Chicago and bussed me to Great Lakes, Illinois."

"Boot camp?"

"Hell, by any other name." He chuckled but the sound came out harsh. "I was such a green kid. Wild hair. Glasses, remember?"

He'd looked pretty cute in those glasses. And his hair? I'd wanted to stroke it. Press myself against his lean frame while I ran my fingers through it. "You wear contact lenses now?"

"I had Lasik. Didn't want to worry about breaking my glasses."

"I've heard boot camp can be rough."

"Terrifying. The military becomes your home. You lose your identity when you put on that uniform."

"Camis?"

"And blues. But not right away. You have to wait until there are enough newbies around to form a Company. That held me back a couple of days and let me tell you, you want your Company formed as soon as possible."

"Why?"

"The regulars bully you constantly, and you stand out in your civilian clothing. But that's just the start. Once your Company forms, they house you in barracks and the real fun begins."

We walked around a bend in the trail and started up a steep, rock-strewn incline, winding our way around big boulders.

"Like I've seen on TV?" I asked.

"One big, open room with enough bunks for your entire Company."

"Which is…?"

"About one-hundred and fifty sweaty guys."

I could only imagine how much dirty laundry that group would generate. "Wait. You said all in one room?"

"With a second Company above us. Talk about snoring."

And farting if they were like Eli.

"Then comes the good part, right?" I said. "Stomping through tire rings and climbing walls." If climbing walls could be considered a good thing.

"No obstacle courses. Just plain old PT, running, and calisthenics. All on the Grinder." He must've noticed my frown. "Pavement. None of that fluffy grass for us. They want you tough and they make sure it happens fast." The animation on his face told me that while his training had been hard, it had made a major impact on his life. Maybe there had been some good mixed in with the bad. "They enjoy playing games with your mind."

"Why do that to a kid? You were only eighteen."

He held a branch back along the side of the trail until I'd passed. "Everyone needs to learn to work together. If you can't put up with whatever they throw at you both physically and mentally, you could freeze in a combat situation."

"Boot camp sounds like prison."

"Not much different, I guess. It wasn't all that bad." He paused. "But then, I'd already learned how to handle shit like that from a master." My puzzlement must've shown on my face because he halted on the trail. "Eli didn't tell you? My dad was super strict. What a freaking bastard. He handed out abuse on a regular basis."

"He hit you?" I stumbled, and he reached out to grab my arm, keeping me from falling. The idea of his father smacking him made me want to show the bully who'd raised him what it meant to be on the receiving end of a fist. It also made my throat ache so badly I couldn't swallow.

He released my arm and strode forward. "You don't need to hit a kid to make him feel like crap," he said over his shoulder. The pain of his past stood out starkly on his cratered face.

We walked in silence, me struggling to absorb what he'd said, Cooper probably trying to forget. I hadn't known that about his dad. Sure, there had been rumors around town his father drank too much but not this.

I wanted to go back in time and take the hand of that skinny teenager I'd crushed on. Hold him in my arms if he'd let me. Tell him he wasn't crap. The Cooper I remembered had been smart, sweet, and a loyal friend to my brother.

The trail widened again, and I drew up beside him. His face remained impassive, but his eyes had darkened to indigo blue as if the shadows of his past still tainted their beautiful color.

"I'm sorry," he said. "I wanted to talk with you about what happened last night, not drag up my ancient history."

History had a way of haunting the present. I hoped Cooper could someday find peace with what happened.

"I want you to be honest with me," I said. "About anything."

"I need to come clean with you about last night."

I sighed. "Look, if this is another let-her-down easy thing, I get it."

"You do, huh?"

The intensity of his gaze stilled my heart and dragged the truth from me in soft tones. "Actually, I don't."

"We've kissed twice."

Two wonderful kisses. Not that I was counting.

Actually, I was.

Stalling on the trail, he turned to face me. "You think that didn't mean anything to me?"

Whenever we were together, I scrambled to make sense of the heat that raged between us. "Maybe it was a spontaneous gesture on your part. This morning, that is. The other kiss, on the float, must've been a spontaneous gesture on my part." Shit, could I please stop babbling?

Taking my hand, he pulled me into his arms. "This is spontaneous." His mouth met mine, driving whatever words I'd been contemplating straight from my head. Whenever he touched me, I could only feel. Take. And give.

While my tongue darted out to meet his, I slid my hands around his waist, exploring his back. If only I could carve the feel of his skin into my mind. Then I could pull it out later and savor it all over again.

He lifted his head and gave me a crooked smile. "I guess you could say I'm a spontaneous kind of guy."

"I don't understand." Leaving the warmth of his embrace made my chest crack wide open, but I needed space. Otherwise, I couldn't think. "You pulled away from me last night and said it was because of Annie." Mentioning that cursed name dragged the woman's ghost out to float in the divide between us.

"It wasn't about Annie."

"Then why?" Pain leaked into my voice. "I'll lay it all out here. I like you." Too much, probably.

"You do?" The way he said it came across boyish and incredibly cute. As if I'd made his day and all the ones to follow.

"I can't be a rebound fling for you." Steel edged into

my words. "Or some girl in a port." Did Navy guys still do stuff like that?

He laughed.

Embarrassment crackled across the top of my head like lightning. I stormed away from him, marching up the trail.

"Wait." He caught up and pulled me to a stop. His arms slid around me again and his heart thumped wildly, much like mine still did from our kiss or any other time he came near.

"I'm crazy about you, Ginny," he said softly. "You were, like, my secret fantasy when I was in high school. In many ways, you still are." A quiet vulnerability filled his voice. "I hope it's okay to tell you that."

Rising onto my toes, I stroked his shoulders. I cupped his neck and urged him close. I needed to show him how my heart sang from his words.

"I really don't deserve you," he said after we pulled apart.

"It's not about one deserving another. It's about being together."

He stared deeply into my eyes before his lips thinned and he nodded. Like he'd waged an argument with himself, and my words had tipped the balance.

We continued up the trail. Dense forest slowly gave way to shorter, scruffier vegetation and then to rocks and cliffs. We held hands as if this fragile bond we'd created would float away if we didn't stay connected. Emerging from the woods, we arrived at the peak. We sat in the sunshine on a wide slab of granite with the ocean gleaming in the distance.

My phone vibrated with an incoming text from Eli. *Will you be okay tonight? I'm stuck here at work, and I'm not sure when I'll be back. Hopefully tomorrow morning.*

Poor Eli. And poor Steve, who'd been injured. They

really needed to hire more staff if one person being out could throw their schedule into such a tailspin.

Cooper's with me. I texted. No need to get into what happened at the campsite or the lake earlier. I didn't want him to worry.

Silence stretched long enough through the airwaves, I wondered if squirrels were jumping on the lines.

Okay, he finally texted.

I read acceptance in that one word. While I didn't need it, I was pleased to have my brother's approval.

"What made you decide to move here and buy a place?" Cooper asked while I put my phone away. "I love your photo travel journals. Your blog."

His arm slid around my shoulders and I leaned into his side, placing my hand on his sun-warmed thigh. Sharing this slab of rock, no, the world with him, filled me up inside. "You've read my blog?"

"Haven't missed a post since you started it eight years ago."

"Once, all I wanted in life was to find the next perfect photo. To capture a face overcome with grief or joy. But something happened."

Memories of that day crowded into my mind, dimming the sunlight. Bringing the stark reality of what happened back as if it flashed before my eyes this moment. I tightened my fingers on his thigh and tried to slow my breathing because I was gulping in air.

He lifted my hand and linked our fingers together, lending me strength. "Tell me."

"It happened in Istanbul. Three men..." My words choked past my lips in sharp gasps, bringing with them the penetrating fear that had consumed me that day. "They strode up to me on the sidewalk in broad daylight. I thought they were on some random mission, that they'd pass me by." Like they did every time I relived that moment, frustrated tears welled in my eyes. "They had a mission, all right. To abduct me."

Sheltering me in his arms, Cooper turned me to face him. His fingertips stroked my face before he pulled me closer. A growl rumbled in his chest. "You were kidnapped?"

"Yes. They…" I gulped. "They kicked me then dragged me when I fell. They kept shoving me and shouting in Turkish, but I didn't understand what they said. They pulled me into their van and drove away. When they stopped at a light, I was able to get the door open. I jumped out, screaming. People pulled me to safety. But the men broke my ribs and my wrist." And my spirit, which might never heal.

"They hurt you. I could…" His breath shuddered, and his arms tightened around me. "I'm glad you got away. That you're safe."

I pinched back tears. Would I ever truly feel safe? A big part of me had been stolen, and I worried I'd never recapture it.

"You've felt more secure here in Maine?"

"Yeah, but…"

Leaning back, he focused on my face. "What?"

"I've had a hard time with it. At first, I was afraid to leave my Mom's place." My rough laugh slipped out, and I couldn't hold his intense gaze. "I got counseling and it helped, but I'm not all me—yet. Not sure I ever will be. It makes me sad. Frustrated. Angry. Because I can control a lot of things, but I can't control my emotions."

"You've had a traumatic experience. You can't shove something like that into the back of your mind and lock it away."

"I wish I could."

"Don't we all?"

He must mean his father again.

"I'm sorry he was awful to you."

His gaze darted away. "Crap like that can shatter someone into a billion pieces. Leave them with nothing left to give."

Was he referring to me or himself? Maybe both of us. I cupped his face and kissed him, trying to show him with my touch that he mattered more than anything to me. That I'd never harm him or break him. His mouth took but also gave. I imagined he needed my reassurance as much as I needed his.

I faced the ocean again and leaned back on my palms. Heat soaked through the stone, radiating up my arms. The wind picked up, sucking dead leaves into the air. "Going camping is a big deal for me. It means stepping out into the world and holding back my fear. I take on the occasional wedding, which means going to wherever they need me. Because people are nearby during those times, I feel safe. But sleeping outside in a tent by myself? This is huge."

"You're brave."

"Hardly." I smiled up at him to reward him for the effort. "I don't like being afraid. It holds me back."

"Fear's a good thing sometimes."

The solemn expression in his face told me he'd been involved in things some people should never experience, situations worse than my abduction. "You don't seem afraid of anything. Look at you, going to the Middle East on a regular basis. It takes courage to put your life on the line. To sacrifice yourself to protect others."

"Sounds like Eli's been sharing a few secrets about me."

"I wanted to know. I still do." I lifted our joined hands

and studied his fingers. Long and lean, with closely-clipped nails. Tiny scars covered the backs, and he had thick calluses on his palms.

He tipped his head back to stare at the sky filling with heavy clouds. "Everything you could imagine in life waits for you once you move beyond the shadow of fear." A flash of sadness crossed his face.

"Are those your words?"

"I read them on a poster in my doctor's office but they stuck with me." His soft smile chased away the sadness lingering on his face. "The instinct to run is there to protect you but you've got to use it for your benefit, not let it overpower you."

Fear. That shadowy being that stalked me through my dreams and into the light of day. Its mocking face rose between us, telling me to flee from this, too. From Cooper. Because he was leaving soon, and I'd fall apart once he was gone.

But I was tired of running. Of letting worry about what might never happen control my future.

I rose to my knees and faced him, centering my palms on his shoulders. I stared into his eyes as if I could discover every thought, emotion, and nuance that made up this man. How could he know what I needed without my speaking the words and then offer it to me so freely?

The yearning on his face told me he craved me as much as I did him. It sparked heat in my belly.

His hands slid around my waist. "I don't know if I can give you more than a few days, Ginny." The passion in his words and the caress of his fingers on my back told me he placed himself in my hands.

Right from the start, I'd known we couldn't have forever. How could I assume anything else? He'd be sent on his next mission and then he'd return to California, while I'd remain here in Maine, where I needed to be.

Thousands of miles would separate us.

Could I give myself to him knowing I'd soon face his loss?

"I'll take days," I whispered. If that was all he could offer I'd find a way to make each moment last forever.

He caressed my face. Tender. As if he feared I'd shatter on contact. "I don't know where this is going or even if it can go anywhere, but I want you."

"I want you, too." Leaning forward, I kissed him, showing him with my lips and my hands that this time together meant everything. The heat of a million suns flew through me, making me melt. My limbs trembled.

He fell backward, taking us to the ground with me on top of him.

Nothing could drag my lips from his. The taste of him. His woodsy smell. He filled my senses to overload. With a moan, I straddled his waist and slid my hands underneath his tee to trace the lines of definition I'd seen on his abdomen.

His fingertips teased the sides of my waist. They reached my bra, where he slid them along the seam.

My past frightened me and my future remained unknown, but the present belonged to us. I hadn't been acting on impulse when I said I wanted him. I'd take this moment and make it something to treasure during the long days to come.

My commitment unleashed a fever inside me. I couldn't get enough of him. Breaking our kiss, I sat upright and pulled my shirt off. I reached behind, unhooked my bra, and tossed it away.

"You're beautiful." He rose up and kissed me. The

rough pads of his fingers stroked along my waist to fondle my breasts.

I moaned and tugged on his shirt, wanting it off so I could press my skin against his.

"Slow down," he said. He feathered his lips along the column of my neck. While his fingers rubbed my nipple, his mouth moved to suck my other breast. His tongue ran across the tip, and he gently bit down.

Fire shot through me, centering below my waist. I cupped his head, his short, bristly hair teasing my palms. Closing my eyes, I arched back, giving myself over to him.

"Damn, you're sweet." He smiled up at me, his breath hot on my breast, his eyes a dark, stormy blue.

My heart split wide open and let him inside.

"Take your shirt off," I said. "Actually, take all of your clothes off. I want to touch you."

"I'll give myself to you," he said. "Tell me how it should be." The sexy grin splitting his face shouted out his need. "Hard and fast?"

His feverish body rising above mine before pressing down.

"Yes," I breathed.

"We can do that. But right now." He eased me to the ground underneath him. "I want to touch every part of you. I think this time, it's going to have to be slow and deep."

I loved that he wanted more than one time. An ache pooled between my legs, one only he could satisfy.

"Condom?" I hadn't carried one for months.

"Got one." Red filled his face. "Got more than one, actually. When I bought my watchband. I…hadn't bought any in a while. Wasn't sure I'd ever need them but…"

"More than one condom is good." I winked. "Because slow and deep might not be enough for me."

His eyes smoldered. "Now, that's a challenge if I've

ever heard one." Devilment deepened his voice. "Lie back, and I'll see what I can do to convince you slow and deep is more than enough." He unbuttoned my shorts. "First, let's get these out of the way."

Why was he still dressed? I wanted to smooth my fingers across his chest, stroke his abs, and take his length into my hand. "Your clothes need to come off, too."

He chuckled and teased apart my thighs with his hand.

I was wet for him. But then, I'd been wet for him since our first kiss. No—back in the changing room the other day. Lately, all I had to do was think about him and I spun to the moon.

He kissed me, and our tongues met and stroked. Leaving me gasping, he kissed lower, pausing at my breasts. While he rubbed between my legs, I panted and writhed. He slid fingers into me, delving deep.

My breath stuttered to a halt and I ground myself against him, seeking more. His fingers felt so good, reaching and sliding inside me. My moan rose from my throat unrestrained, climbing for the heavens.

His mouth stalled on my breast and he rested his forehead against my chest where my heart thrummed wildly. "I've gotta…slow down."

"Not now." Arching up against his hand, I bit back my scream when this drove his fingers deeper.

"I can't do this. Not yet." His lungs expanded, and he ground out a sigh. "Just…give me a second."

I was close. He couldn't…no.

As if he'd recaptured his control, his fingers teased inside me again while another finger pressed at the top in hard circles. His mouth returned to my breast to suck. Each pull sent bursts of heat to my groin as each stroke of his fingers brought me closer.

I didn't want it like this. Well, I did but I had to have

him inside me, too. Slow and deep or hard and fast, whatever he wanted to deliver. In fact, I wanted them both.

"Cooper!" I meant to be firm, to tell him in no uncertain terms he had to be inside me but his fingers twisted and rubbed, driving me nearer to the edge.

His name came from me again in a gasp, because I was cresting. So unbelievably close.

His overheated breath sent prickles across my damp skin. "I've got to be with you. Now." Rising to his knees, he hauled off his shirt. While staring down at me with his gaze consumed with darkness, he shucked his shorts and boxers. Freed, his length strained against his abs.

He reached for his shorts—for a condom, most likely.

And the world exploded around us.

14

Cooper

"Keep down!" I dove forward, covering Ginny's body with mine.

Lightning arced across the mountain and thunder followed, the boom vibrating through my bones. When had the sky gone black?

Rain peppered my face and drummed the ground around us.

"A storm." I lifted my head and stared down at her, shock plunging through me. Water dripped off my chin. "We've got to get off the mountain. We're too exposed up here."

I helped her stand, and we dressed as quickly as we could in saturated clothing that resisted our efforts. Holding hands, we raced for the trail. In seconds, we were inside the woods. Not that the forest provided much cover. The rain nailed us, the heavy clouds delivering payback for the recent drought.

When Ginny slipped on the path, nearly falling, I slowed to a walk. I needed to get her to a secure location, but I couldn't stand it if she got hurt in the process.

Shielding my eyes with my hand, I looked around, desperate to locate shelter.

"Come on." Because the smooth surface was slippery, I pulled her off the marked path and into the deeper woods where sticks and fallen leaves provided traction. Thorn bushes and wild roses snatched at my clothing, but I shielded her behind me. I wouldn't risk injuring her fragile skin. Pressing forward, I was guided by lightning flashing across the sky in unrelenting shockwaves. The thunder of a thousand land mines rumbled around us—through my body, spurring me on.

Shit, for a minute up on the mountain top, I'd thought we were under enemy fire. I'd fallen on Ginny, frantic to protect her from harm. While counseling had kept me from reliving the worst moments I'd experienced overseas, I hadn't realized how on edge my career kept me. Instinct had taken control, and I'd let it rule.

A slice of darkness up ahead called me closer. I ducked underneath the broad branches of a cluster of evergreens where the rain only reached in infrequent drips. I brushed sticks out of the way on the ground and smoothed the pine needles, creating a soft spot where we could sit and wait out the storm.

I dropped down and tugged Ginny onto my lap, enfolding her in my arms. She shivered, either from reaction to the hell still raging through the forest like an invasion of giants or from the sudden drop in temperature. Didn't matter. I was determined to shield her from everything.

She wrapped herself around me and buried her face in my neck. Her essence pulled me in, a mix of rain, ozone, and woman. I drowned in the memory of her response back on the peak.

"We can stay here until it lets up." I rubbed her back,

trying to lend her my calm because she still trembled. Each shake dragged me closer to despair. A frantic need to make her feel safe forged through me, stronger than the storm roaring around us. "The weatherman said there might be thunderstorms late this afternoon."

"Might be, huh?" Leaning back, she grinned at me.

Shit, maybe fear didn't make her tremble. Maybe *I* did. The thought squeezed my heart until it bled dark red. Nothing and no one would keep my smile from my face. "I think the weather report got it right, don't you?"

"Not a common occurrence for them."

"They said the storm is supposed to go through fast."

Her low chuckle lifted the hairs on the back of my neck. "Hard and fast?"

Yeah, I wanted her. Badly. "I did promise you slow and deep, now didn't I?"

Palming my shoulders, she leaned near, and her lips stole across mine, stirring fire. "And you've yet to fulfill your promise."

"Far be it for me not to deliver on a command."

She slid her shirt over her head and unclasped her bra. Her clothing found its place on the pine needles. Hands on her hips, she smirked. "Well, soldier, what are you waiting for?"

Reverence filled me. To think this woman wanted me. Craved to be with me, even if only for this moment. I cupped her breasts and stroked her nipples, bringing them to hard peaks. They strained toward me, begging for my touch. She caressed my back and teased her fingertips around to my chest. Tension coiled tight inside me. Only she could bring the release my body begged for.

We kissed, long and with growing heat, the stroke of our tongues bringing our breathing to a feverish rush. My heart sent rocket fire through my chest. I'll kill to be with her.

As predicted, the rain slowed quickly. The late-day sunlight stabbed through the forest, seeking us. Highlighting Ginny in all her naked glory.

I had to have her. Take all of her. Immediately.

The world collapsing around us couldn't make me leave our haven now. Life—and all the crap that came along with it—crowded out sanity often enough. No reason to let it back in yet.

I'd have to catch a flight to California soon, and I didn't want to go. Leaving meant losing the one person I was starting to care for above all others.

Ginny stood and pulled off her shorts, urging me to do the same. Her smile—timid and bold, all at the same time—made my chest swell. She was the loveliest thing in the world.

I reached for her, pulling her against me, and we sank to the ground again, our bodies rubbing together. The sensation of moist skin on skin made me groan.

She leaned sideways, delved inside my pocket to pull out the foil packet, and held it up in the air like it was a prize worth fighting for. Guess it was.

"Slow and deep, right?" she said with the very devil in her eyes.

I could do that. Maybe.

She tore into the packet, and then rolled it down me, stroking along the way. She drove me insane with her fingers. Her laughter lit up her face, leading me to believe she knew what she did to me and reveled in it. I had no problem with that. But a beast was rising inside me, demanding the satisfaction only her welcoming body could give. Easing her back onto the ground, I rose above her, growling with endless hunger.

A goddess lay beneath me, her eyes half-lidded with anticipation. Her arms reached up and pulled me into her intoxicating embrace. Ginny was the past I never wanted to forget and the future I could never have. I shoved aside the bitterness that came with the realization. This *would* be enough. I'd find a way to make it so.

I took her lips with a need that outdid all others and reached between us to stroke her. Damn, wet again. Could I really hold back until she was fully with me? She needed to come before I gave into my own satisfaction.

She writhed and cried out my name, telling me with her sighs that she was as eager for this as I was.

Shifting my head back, I stared into her eyes while I sheathed my body inside hers, connecting us completely. Her legs rose to wrap around my waist, pulling me deeper still.

She closed her eyes and moaned. "You feel so good, Cooper."

Determined to make each of her cries last me into the next world and beyond, I pulled back and slid into her again. Her body was smooth and soft, yet like steel, pulsing around me. So freakin' wet. Like a horny teenager, I was going to come after only a few strokes.

Her fingers gripped my shoulders, her thighs held me near, and her head arched back on the ground.

Slow and deep, right? I deployed that rhythm, battling to keep from pounding into her until my body exploded.

"Faster." She lifted her hips to meet mine. Her head thrashed on the pine needles. "I want...I..." Her words dissolved into a moan.

"Yes." With a guttural sigh, I sped up, driving into her over and over, satisfying her need while giving into my own.

We rushed toward the peak together, and I echoed her

cries. Arms trembling, my body a shaking mess, I held myself back until she spasmed around me.

She pressed her face into my shoulder. "Yessss."

Shuddering, every muscle in my body forging into steel, I found bliss in Ginny's arms. And collapsed on top of her afterward, a massive wreck.

We breathed as one. Our hearts thudded together in a furious pace that finally slowed. I held her close and kissed her lips. Her eyelids. That tender spot where her jaw met her neck.

I might not have a whole man to offer Ginny, but I would shower her with every speck of myself I had left to give.

⸻

GINNY STIRRED IN MY ARMS, and I rolled onto my back on the ground beside her. The sting in my shoulder from the movement made me confident I had a mark—where she'd bitten down on my skin when she came.

She turned onto her side and propped her head up on her elbow. She traced my tattoo with her fingertip. It tickled, and I snorted. The soft smile she gave me shot joy through me. There wasn't anything more satisfying than the well-sated expression on this woman's face, except knowing I was the one who'd put it there.

If only…

I needed to ditch that thought immediately because there was no *if only* for me. Just *now*.

"I'm starved." Her words broke the stillness, pulling me back to the present where I needed to remain. "Someone I know had hot dogs a few hours ago. I, however, have burned up more than a pancake."

"You saying your tank's running on empty?" I stroked her shoulder, the side of her breast, and on to her waist. Satin couldn't compare to Ginny's skin. Nothing would make me happier than to touch her every single day of my life.

"In some ways." Her eyes darkened.

I wove my fingers into her damp hair and urged her nearer for a kiss. Groaning, I smoothed my lips along hers and stroked her lower lip with my tongue before biting down. Not long ago, I'd had more pleasure with Ginny than anyone else before. How could I want her all over again?

I couldn't get enough of her.

I had a feeling I'd never get enough of her.

15

Ginny

I lay with Cooper in the forest until the sun slanted along the sky, making me realize that, if we didn't leave soon, we wouldn't get back in time for Brittany and her family to leave for town.

To make the weekend extra fun, the campground planned fireworks tonight. I had a few fireworks I wanted to explore with Cooper in his tent afterward.

The rain may have quenched the ground, but it also generated humidity. Steam rose from the forest floor and swirled around our sneakers in silvery ghosts. We held hands and hurried, determined to arrive at the campground by five.

We *tried* to hurry, that is. I kept giving into my insatiable urge to stop on the trail and make sure I'd been right all along about Cooper's lips.

Goals met, we emerged from the woods just before five. While shimmering waves of yellow and pink spread along the horizon, we grabbed dry clothing and hurried to the changing rooms. This time, we shared space on purpose. We both had to change, and Cooper wanted to watch over me. Or plain old watch me. I couldn't resist turning this opportunity into another tease. Slowly peeling off my clothing, I shifted my hips in a rhythm older than time. I dropped the wet things onto the bench, exaggerating my bent-over movement, spreading my legs. It was all I could do not to laugh when he groaned.

His fingertips trailed along my hip, and he turned me to face him.

"You're going to be the death of me." His eyes focused on my breasts. His fingers ran across my skin like fire and centered on that place between my legs that ached for his touch.

I lifted my eyebrows. Need trembled through me. "Don't tell me you're worn out already?"

He growled and backed me against the plank wall. "I'll show you worn out." His mouth came down hard on mine. Or my mouth rose to press against his. Both equally satisfying.

When his fingers feathered down my body and delved inside me, we both gasped.

He pulled a condom from his pocket and put it on.

"Now," I said, my voice a full-on plea.

With my thighs spread wide and linked around his hips, he drove inside me. I moaned and arched against him, tension spiraling through me, building already. Would it always be this good between us?

Pulling out, he thrust forward again. When I moaned *yes*, he took on a rhythm that pounded himself into me over and over. My muted cries urged him on, sending us ever higher.

One thing was quickly becoming clear to me. While slow and deep might be a welcome part of my future, I was a complete fan of hard and fast.

We strolled back to the campsite, arriving just in time for our neighbors to leave.

"Nothing went on at your site while you were gone," Brittany said with a firm nod, her narrowed eyes scanning the area. "I made damn sure of it."

"I appreciate that."

"And thank you again for watching our camper." She and her family walked toward the parking lot.

I started the grill while Cooper stooped down and tinkered with the fire pit.

"Firewood's wet." Soot painted his face, turning him into a warrior primed for battle. "You *sure* we can't use explosives?"

Whining like a little kid. If he didn't stop upping his cute factor, we'd starve.

"None of that, now." I meant more than the fire. But the gleam in his eyes told me he'd read my thoughts as if I'd screamed them out loud. He lifted one eyebrow and nudged his head toward his tent.

Warmth pooled inside me. I wanted him again. How could I heat up for him this fast?

"You, Tarzan," I said breathlessly. "Make fire. Me, Jane. Make dinner." I spun away, giggling.

Abandoning his duty, his arms snaked around my waist while he shifted my tank strap to the side with his teeth. He nibbled on my shoulder.

Sliding my eyes closed, I tilted my head back and drank in the sensation of his lips performing magic. The bag of briquettes slipped from my hands and dropped onto the grill, making it clatter. My eyes popped open, and he left me with a deep chuckle, obviously aware of what he did to me. Of course, this game was best played by two, and I had no issue with increasing the stakes. But there were families nearby, even if our next-door neighbors were gone for the moment. Not that I couldn't cook up a few ideas for later. I was *also* eager to experiment with nibbling.

Heart thumping with anticipation, I got the grill going and wrapped potatoes in foil. I'd lay the corn cobs on the grate in their husks when the chicken was nearly done.

While our meal permeated the air with the scent of mesquite goodness, I got out the fixings.

Cooper proved himself worthy of the fire gods and had a roaring blaze going in no time.

"How'd you do that?" I couldn't keep the awe from my voice.

His chest expanded, and he chuckled.

My grin filled my face because making him happy made me happy. I was beginning to know Cooper Talon well.

Unsettled, I spun away, pretending I needed to check the chicken. I really needed to hide my fading smile because caring and knowing soon turned into loving, and we didn't have a lifetime to explore each other.

Just days.

We ate until we couldn't stuff in another bite. After, we washed the dishes at the faucet, laughing as we tried to steal the trickle of water from each other.

"I need to use the facilities," I said as I placed the dish drainer on the picnic table.

"I'll walk with you. While you're inside, I'll go get my sweatshirt from the car."

Nodding, I grabbed my tote, and we walked across the green. He left me at the wooden building that housed the showers and bathrooms and continued up the path toward the lot.

Since a crowd of teenagers filled the community bath-room—putting on make-up and styling their hair—I went around the side of the building to one of the family-style rooms.

The door refused to stay shut with the latch alone. Grunting, I yanked it inward and then made sure the lock clicked into place.

At the sink, I pulled off my tank and shorts. After wringing out a washcloth, I ran it over the important areas. Satisfaction filled me—something I hadn't felt in years, if ever—solely due to Cooper.

What would my present be like if we'd hooked up in high school? Would we still be together? I liked to think we would be. But if we had connected, I would've missed out on the wonder of my travels. The places I'd been, the people I'd met. But Cooper…being with him would be worth the loss.

He was different from my old boyfriend, Zen. Where Cooper was open—I could read his emotions on his face and in his actions—Zen had been secretive. Sneaking out during the night, never willing to tell me where he'd been. And his sudden flares of anger. I sure wouldn't miss that part of our relationship.

After drying my body and redressing, I brushed my teeth and combed my hair. The latter I left down around my shoulders. I packed my things inside my tote.

My phone rang, and I answered. "Hello?"

A long silence was followed by breathing. Great. Some-body was fooling around.

"I'm watching you," the person whispered.

Hot sparks flared across my skin, and my heart jumped. My muscles stiffened as if they were ready to flee.

"Tom?" I asked. It had to be him. Jerk.

He chuckled. And while a chuckle and a few whispered words might not reveal someone's identity, I recognized the voice. I'd heard this same laughter twelve years ago.

I'd been seeing Tom for a few weeks, and while I liked being with him, there were times when I'd felt unsettled by something he'd say or do. During this incident, Eli and I had been planning a surprise birthday party for my mom but Tom had wanted to go to the movies that night instead. We'd been sitting on the sofa together, me patting my cat, who lay beside me.

"I want you to ditch your mom's party and go out with me," he'd said firmly.

"I can't." Really, how could he have asked that of me? "It's her fortieth."

"That's not the point." His eyes had fallen to my hand that continued to stroke my cat. "You love that animal, don't you?"

My hand had stilled, and a trickle of fear had traveled down my spine. I'd said nothing, just gaped at him because he was teasing, right? It wasn't a *real* threat.

"Would hate to see something happen to your kitty just because you're not willing to do something with me." Then, as if it truly had been a joke, he'd laughed.

Like now.

I tightened my hand on the phone. "You need to stop!"

More laughter before the call ended.

Hands sweaty, I shoved my phone back into my pocket. I splashed my face with cool water again and dried it. I stood staring into the mirror until the horror faded from my eyes.

After gathering my things, I strode to the door. The lock clicked when I switched it to open, but when I pushed, the door wouldn't budge.

"Okay. Maybe you locked it, instead of unlocking it," I whispered. Great. Leave it to me to do something like that. At least no one had walked in while I was washing.

I clicked the lock in the other direction and shoved the door again, but it still wouldn't move. Was the lock broken? Or had the door swollen in the frame from humidity created by the storm? Which begged the question: how could moisture sink into wood that fast?

I dropped my tote on the floor and leaned against the door, wiggling the knob as I put all my weight behind my push. Grunting, I hip-checked it. Why wasn't it opening? I smacked my shoulder against the wooden panel and it shuddered in the frame but held true. The lock must be broken.

Or someone is trying to keep you from leaving the bathroom.

Someone like Tom.

The wild thought took hold. Sweat broke out on my forehead, and my pulse picked up while energy surged through my limbs.

"Get a hold of yourself," I hissed out. Tom hadn't locked me inside. It wouldn't make sense for him to do it.

Things like this didn't happen outside of horror movies, did they?

A line of moisture drizzled down my spine, reminding me of bugs crawling across my skin. Hands trembling, I rattled the doorknob, wiggling it back and forth. It turned, but the door felt frozen in place. Stuck.

Or wedged closed.

"Cooper?" My voice shook, and I fought the panic rising inside me. This couldn't be happening.

How long would it take for him to walk to the car and back? I'd been in here five minutes or more. That was enough time for him to go to his vehicle, retrieve his sweat-shirt, and return by now. Where was he?

"Cooper!"

Anxiety sunk through my bones. My breathing went ragged while my heart thumped against my ribcage, seeking escape.

I whimpered, the sound breaking the hush in the small room. That's when I realized I was behaving like a weak, cowering fool. If only fear hadn't stolen my self-control.

My mind flashed to the boater this morning. That person *could've* been trying to run me down. And he'd come after me again.

Someone was trying to harm me.

Wait a minute. Slow down. What an off-the-wall thought. Who'd want to hurt me? I was a photographer who took pictures of moms and kids and pets. Graduation photos. I aimed to please and was happy to retouch a picture if a client asked. No one would do this because of a bad photo.

I needed to think rationally about this. If I was capable of doing so.

Locking me in a bathroom wasn't exactly a threat to my life.

"What do you think will happen to you inside here?" I said firmly, ignoring the fact that my voice shook. "The worst thing that could happen here is that you'll stumble and fall head first into the toilet and drown. Or succumb to toilet fumes." Which *were* pretty bad. Even with the high window on the far wall, which was propped open to let in fresh air, a sharp odor permeated the tight space.

I banged my fist on the doorframe. Solid wood didn't give an inch.

Wood burned.

A quick sniff told me there was no fire nearby. Which only reassured me until I realized that if someone wanted to burn me alive, they'd need to kindle the fire first. After the rain, wood was wet. It would take time to get a solid blaze going.

Crossing to the window, I jumped, hoping to see through. The frame had been propped open on the outside, leaving a screen secured to the wall on the inside to keep bugs out. It would work if the screen wasn't torn. Trapped inside with me, a few moths dove and smacked against the single lightbulb mounted above the sink. Long-dead leaves wedged in the screen from last fall rattled in the wind.

With renewed energy, I returned to the door, determined to get myself out. Grabbing the knob, I turned it while hitting my hip against it. The wood protested but held true. Log construction at its best. Damn stuff held up for years.

I sagged and pressed my forehead against the rough panel. What was I going to do? If I couldn't find a way out and Cooper didn't return soon, I'd—

Skittering, scraping sounds behind me made me pause. Sweat trickled down my backbone.

Did I dare turn to find out what was behind me?

Lately, it felt like my life couldn't get much—

A thump was followed by a rapid crackling as if someone ran through a pile of long-dead leaves. Or a cluster of deep-throated crickets sang on hyper-drive.

I frowned.

With dread unfurling its wings inside me, I forced my shaking body to turn.

I screamed.

16

Cooper

I left Ginny at the bathrooms and cut back across the open area to reach the path to the parking lot. My brain buzzed; I couldn't keep from whistling. If I wasn't such a horrible singer, I'd crank out a tune.

Shit, but I had it bad.

My teenage fantasy was coming true. Not that I enjoyed being with Ginny solely because I'd had the hots for her back in high school. The depth of my feelings for her were stronger than that. I couldn't imagine not being with her all the time, which was crappy since I had to leave for the Middle East soon. When I shipped overseas, I'd have to find a way to live without her.

Except…Could we make a long-distance relationship work? For many reasons, I wanted to try.

As I approached the lot, I pulled my keys from my pocket and unlocked the doors. The headlight flash high-lighted something scattered across the ground on the passenger side. I stalled at the top of the path. What the…?

There was a gaping hole where the passenger window used to be. What happened?

Squinting, I looked around. The skin on the back of my neck prickled, the same sensation I got when somebody watched on me from a hidden location. This wasn't a combat situation but that didn't mean I should ignore my instincts.

I slid into the shadows beside a minivan and inched forward, studying the perimeter. Looking for signs of movement and listening for sounds that would indicate someone hid nearby.

Nothing stood out to me. Damn shitty lighting up here, though. The campground owners should consider installing more than one streetlight in the parking lot.

Was I alone or was someone spying on me? The tension creeping down my backbone suggested the latter.

Tom.

If that asshole had damaged my vehicle, I'd call the police and report him, and then fill the cops in on the incident that went on earlier at the campsite. To hell with the consequences for my actions. I'd confess I shook Tom and threatened him. The guy who got a thrill from scaring Ginny should be knocked down a peg or two or three on a regular basis.

I crept over to my car, remaining in the shadows as much as possible. No need to skyline myself. While it was doubtful anyone hovered in the woods with a gun, prepared to take potshots at me, I'd learned long ago to be careful.

My sneakers crunched on the fallen glass when I leaned forward to look inside the car. Shards covered the passenger seat but there was less on the driver's side, indicating a blow had come from this angle, shattered the glass inward. I didn't keep much inside the car worth stealing, nothing but the sweatshirt I'd tossed on the back seat. This had to be solely about revenge.

Since reassuring silence reigned in the woods around me, I straightened and went around to the driver's side of the vehicle to open the door.

A baseball dropped out.

Awesome. My heart rate dropped to normal in one beat. While I'd been gearing myself up to challenge Tom, the other man was probably sitting in a bar somewhere enjoying a beer, completely oblivious to what was going on out here at the campground.

Kids. Loved 'em, but they sure could get themselves into trouble.

I could picture it now. They'd been tossing a ball around in the parking lot. Someone threw it too hard, and the ball hit my window. Scared they'd get into trouble, they ran rather than reporting the damage.

Well, nothing I could do now but call the rental place. I couldn't drive the vehicle without a passenger window. Good thing I'd bought expanded coverage when I picked it up.

I grabbed my sweatshirt off the back seat, shook off the glass, and leaned my hip against the vehicle's back fender while dialing the rental company.

"Ace," someone said.

I explained the situation.

"Tell you what," the woman said. "We'll send out a wrecker to get the vehicle and drop a new one off for you at the same time if you want."

Decent of them, considering it was a weekend.

"We're short-staffed tomorrow, so it'll be easier to take care of this immediately. The wrecker can drop the vehicle in town at the garage where we have a repair contract. You should be fixed in a snap."

"I appreciate it." I needed a fully functional vehicle this week.

"No problem. We aim to please. It should take us…" She paused. "Give us half an hour or so, okay?"

Far better than I'd expected.

"Will you be with the vehicle when the wrecker arrives? He can offload the new one, give you the keys, and take the other when he leaves."

I'd have to run down to the bathrooms and let Ginny know what was going on. She could either come back up here with me to wait or return to the campsite to enjoy the fire. She'd told me earlier she was looking forward to the fireworks, and I'd hate for her to miss them. "I can wait."

"Thanks. You want a vehicle similar to what you have right now?"

Anything would do. "Sure."

"We'll be on it in a flash, then. Bye."

I pocketed my phone.

Rustling in the woods above the lot drew my eye, and I squinted into the gloom. Clear-cut of all but brush during the past few years, the area was mostly overgrown with tiny new evergreens and a few spindly birch trees. I could see well enough, unlike inside the dense woods near where we'd panned for gold.

Nothing big moved. The sound could've been a squirrel or a chipmunk. Or a skunk, although I didn't smell anything on the wind.

I checked my watch. Ten minutes had gone by. Ginny must be done by now. In fact, I'd—

A scream pealed through the night. The world—and my heart—stilled.

Fuck. I raced for the edge of the lot and barreled down the path. Legs pumping and my heartbeat flailing in my throat, I crossed the green, desperate to reach Ginny.

Maybe the scream had been someone else. But with everything that had happened lately…

I stormed into the bathroom, interrupting a bunch of girls doing things to their hair.

"Sorry."

A girl giggled while I backed out, my palms raised. No Ginny here.

Another scream. Outside?

I rushed out onto the decking and looked around frantically before loping around the side of the building, my feet rattling the pine boards. Where was she?

Whimpers to my left had me wrenching open the wooden door to a family room. Ginny fell out, into my arms. I clutched her to my chest, shaking with relief that she was alive and appeared unhurt. "Sweetheart, what's happening?"

"A s…s…snake."

"What?" I tried to peer around her but the door had smacked closed. I rocked her while she trembled. "Tell me what's going on."

"I was locked inside. And there's…there's a snake inside the bathroom. A rattlesnake!"

"Locked? A snake?" I blinked at the door. "Let me look." I started to ease her to the side, but she clutched my arm, holding me back.

"It's not safe in there." Her face gleamed with sweat, and lines of stress created shadows on her face.

"I'll be careful. I promise." At her tight nod, I moved around her, keeping her to my back. She crept forward with me to the door. I cracked it open and peered inside. Nothing so far. Opening it wider, I tucked my head in and scanned the room. "There isn't anything here." Stepping forward, I started inside, but she grabbed my arm again.

"Don't go in there. Let's call the police."

"I can't call them unless…"

Her shoulders curled forward. "You don't believe me."

"I do." She'd never make up something like this.

"I saw it. I did. And after that boater tried to run me down this morning—"

My mouth flashed dry. "Wait a minute. What are you talking about?" Shutting the door, I turned fully to face her. "What boater?"

"This morning, I went swimming. A boat came at me, almost hit me. If I hadn't reached the dock in time…"

"Why didn't you tell me?"

"We weren't…well, talking." The shuddering breath she took in only enhanced her shakes. "And the idea seemed so crazy. Why would anyone want to run me over? It couldn't be anything more than an accident. A guy on the dock said the boater was probably drunk, but now I'm not sure." Her gaze cut to the bathroom.

"I need to go inside and look around."

She worried her elbows with her fingertips but nodded.

Turning, I creaked the door open again. A distinctive rattle echoed in the room. Over near the sink, where light from the bulb barely reached, a grayish, circular shadow lay on the floor.

Shit. I backed out and slammed the door shut. Nothing else I could do but pin it in place with my foot. A quick glance took in a two-by-four lying on the ground some distance into the green. I waved toward it. "Grab that for me, would you?"

Ginny brought me the board, and I wedged it underneath the knob. I pulled my phone and dialed.

"9-1-1, please state your emergency."

It didn't take long to explain.

"A rattlesnake you say. Not many of them in Maine."

I grumbled. "I know what I heard."

"Are you injured? Bitten? Do you need medical assistance?"

"No one has been bitten, but this is a bad situation waiting to happen."

"Okay, sir. I don't see why we can't get someone over there to check it out. If it's a rattlesnake, someone could be hurt." She paused and the sound of papers shuffling trailed through the line. "This sounds like something for the game warden to handle, but I doubt I'll reach her on a weekend. Will the sheriff do?"

Anyone would, at this point. "Of course."

"He's been hopping all weekend, chasing down everything from lost grandmothers to lost dogs to lost boats. It could take him some time to arrive. That okay?"

"Yes."

"You'll wait with the…snake?"

Waiting here would mean tag-teaming between the parking lot and the bathroom until the wrecker arrived with my new vehicle, but Ginny could help. No way would I leave the bathroom untended. A kid could enter and be bitten. "I will."

"All right, sir. Sheriff Moyer should be there soon."

I gave the operator our location and then ended the call and pocketed my phone. "My car window is broken and the rental place is sending a new vehicle. They'll take the old one when they leave." Her eyes widened, and I explained about the baseball. "Which do you prefer? Snake patrol or parking lot duty?"

"A dark, gloomy parking lot surrounded by woods or sitting out here in the open, with lots of people around, guarding a locked-in snake?" The fact that she could chuckle loosened something in my chest and made me glad I'd helped her relieve some stress. "No choice." She dropped to the deck and tucked her legs up to her chest.

"You going to be okay?"

The quiver in her lower lip betrayed her dismissive wave. "Go. You need to be there when they arrive. I'll be all right."

Two seconds longer wouldn't make a speck of difference. I dropped to the deck and leaned against the building. Ginny didn't need any encouragement to crawl into my arms. I held her while she shuddered. "What a day you've had." The boater incident made me want to gnash my teeth and howl. Had it been an accident or something more sinister?

"I still can't believe it." Looping her arms around my shoulders, she nuzzled my neck, seeking my warmth and comfort. Knowing she could find it in me made my chest swell ten times its normal size.

Did all these incidents add up to anything, or were they just isolated events? Taken on their own, they appeared benign. Even the snake could've been a fluke. It was hot out; the creature could've sought a cool place to sleep. Ginny was lucky she hadn't been hurt.

I was damned grateful she was safe. Tightening my arms around her, I rested my chin on her head. "I'm going to do everything within my power to make sure no one harms you."

She leaned back in my embrace and lifted a shaky smile. "I'll do the same for you."

Ten times? Forget that. My chest had swelled twenty times its normal size. What the hell had I done in life to deserve her?

I soon headed to the parking lot. The wrecker arrived and made the exchange. Keys to a fresh vehicle in hand, I jogged back to the bathrooms. I found Ginny sitting in the same place, nibbling on her fingernail but minus those heavy creases on her face.

"Any sounds inside?" I asked.

She shrugged. "Maybe the snake's asleep."

"Maybe." I dropped to the decking beside her and checked the time on my phone. Eight-thirty. It felt like a lifetime had passed in a few minutes.

The crunch of tires in the lot announced a vehicle, and a man strolled down the path toward the bathrooms, a handgun strapped to his belt, keys or change jingling in his pocket. A woman dressed in a similar manner—khaki pants and a button-up shirt, a tan hat on her head— followed, scanning the area with narrowed eyes.

"Mr. Talon?" the man asked as he approached the bathrooms.

I stood and walked down to the grass, hand extended. "Cooper Talon. I placed the call."

"Name's Bill Moyer." The sheriff's solid gaze drilled into mine as if ferreting out hidden secrets. Since I had nothing to hide, I maintained the other man's gaze until the sheriff's dropped. He gestured to the woman, who nodded. "Deputy Franks." He removed his hat and scratched his head. "Dispatcher said something about a rattlesnake?"

I explained.

"You do know that there haven't been rattlesnakes in Maine for years. They're extinct. If I had my guess, we're dealing with a milk snake here."

I hadn't heard of a milk snake, but I'd seen my share of rattlers in other parts of the world. Their distinctive sound could never be forgotten.

Ginny came over to stand with us. "It rattled."

"Ma'am." Bill dipped his chin toward her. "Thing is, milk snakes shake their tails when they're threatened. People confuse them with rattlesnakes all the time. But milk snakes are harmless."

"I don't know." Ginny picked at her lower lip. "It sounded real to me. Terrifying."

Bill tugged on his belt and stiffened his backbone. "Well, there's no harm in taking a look, now is there?" He climbed the stairs and pulled the two-by-four away from the door, propping it on the outer wall. He opened the door and stomped inside, his boots creating hollow thuds on the floorboards. "Hmm. I don't…" The door slammed shut behind him.

I started to follow, but the deputy snagged my tee, holding me back. She lifted her eyebrows and pressed for a smile. "Pretty scary if there's a snake in there. But don't worry. Not much scares Bill."

Bill appeared at the door again, shaking his head. "Don't see anything inside. Looked around good, too." In no time, he'd wedged the board underneath the doorknob again.

Ginny clenched her hands to her chest. "There was a snake in there."

"I heard it as well," I said. "Saw something, too."

"I believe you, folks." Bill crossed to stand with us on the grass again. "Probably is a snake in there. But it could be hiding. Snakes are shy." He glanced toward the deputy. "I've got a tool pouch in my trunk. Want to go grab my hammer and a few nails? We'll nail 'er shut to keep anyone from going inside." He faced us. "You weren't hurt, were you Ma'am?"

"No," Ginny said. "Just frightened."

I put my arm around her shoulders and pulled her into my side. Her trembling had stopped, thankfully. I'd never been more relieved than I was now, knowing she hadn't been harmed.

The deputy returned with the hammer, and the sheriff secured the door.

"That'll keep anyone for going in there," Bill said. He nodded to us. "The game warden will come out and investigate this week. I'll let you know what she discovers."

"What if this was someone trying to hurt me?" Ginny asked.

"With a milk snake?"

She blinked. "You don't think it was a rattler?"

His shrug shifted the star badge on his chest. "I can't really say what you saw, Ma'am, but I doubt you'll find a rattlesnake in Maine."

"But Tom…"

I told the sheriff about Tom's threat and how he'd wrecked our campsite, only leaving out my confrontation with Tom. Ginny also mentioned a phone call she'd just received in the bathroom.

A phone call, too? My hand tightened on hers.

"Tom Prescott?" Bill's face tightened. "You sure about that? I worked with him before he left the force. He's a reasonable guy. If you said you weren't interested in him, Ma'am, I imagine he listened."

"He was pretty persistent. He made threats, saying I'd regret turning him down," Ginny said. "He…scared me."

The sheriff scratched his head again then replaced my broad-brimmed hat. "Well, I believe you about that, Ma'am." His gaze slid away. "You need to know that Tom's had a tough time lately which could make him act a bit out of character. Tell you what. I'll talk to him. Make it clear he's to leave you alone."

Talk to him. It was doubtful the sheriff would talk to Tom in the same manner I had. But at least law enforcement was involved. Maybe being questioned would make Tom back off, because this situation had gone on long enough.

"I appreciate it," Ginny said. "Another thing. This

morning while I was swimming, someone almost ran me over with their boat." She explained further.

"Ah." Bill held up his hand. "I know exactly what went on there."

"You do?" I asked. This man had an answer for everything. How could he know what happened here today? But then, this day had been one surprise after another.

"We got a bunch of calls earlier about someone going like a bat out of hell on the lake," Deputy Franks said, rocking back on her heels. "Caught the guy, too. Drunker than a skunk."

"He'll get a DUI for that." Bill shifted his hips, thumbs hooked on his belt. "You might've been the first he almost ran over, but you sure weren't the last. Ass—jerk, that is, almost ran over a couple kids near the shore. I'll add your name to the list of complaints if you want."

"I appreciate it." Ginny lifted a half smile my way, her face fully loosening. Just knowing she was less frightened relaxed my own joints. She linked her fingers through mine. "It looks like there's a good explanation for everything."

Maybe.

And maybe not.

17

Ginny

With the fire in front of us, I positioned our chairs to give us the best view of the upcoming fireworks display over the lake. We grabbed a couple of beers from the cooler to sip while we watched.

I'd contemplated packing up and leaving. Yet, everything that happened seemed to have been explained away. And what would I do if we went into town? Suggest Cooper stay at my place? I'd love to have him sleep over, but it might be pushing things too far. Our relationship was new. Fragile. My heart wasn't ready to test it. Tomorrow would be soon enough for that. Greedy of me, but I wanted more time with Cooper in a neutral setting.

We could keep each other safe for one night.

Leaning forward, I tossed more wood onto the fire. Hissing white ribbons slithered along the damp branches and steam rose, feeding moisture to the clouds for the next storm.

"You said you did an electrical program with the military?" I asked Cooper.

"Yep." He took a long drink of his beer then followed

the beads of sweat running down the sides of the bottle with his finger.

"Does that mean you're a master electrician?"

He shrugged. "The military doesn't give out the same licensing as the public sector. Sure, I have hours I could use—will use, I guess—when I get out in eight years. But I'll still need college classes and tests to get a master's license."

"You're sticking it out for the full twenty years?"

"I'm over the hump. I'd be foolish to throw away the retirement I'll get at twenty. At my paygrade, it's substantial."

Eight more years. Stationed in California, while I'd remain here in Maine.

My heart sunk, even though it shouldn't. He *had* said this was only for days. The thought stabbed deep, and I slumped lower in my chair. To avoid revealing the pain I had no right feeling, I sipped my beer. All I could do was hold on to my memories when he was gone. If only it didn't hurt so much to think of him leaving. "What sort of electrical work do you do?"

"I mostly work on the base doing public works, construction. Actually, I specialize in high voltage."

"Sounds dangerous." The words alone spiked my tension, because they suggested he was putting his life at risk. Not that the Middle East didn't offer danger all on its own. Eli knew that as well as anyone.

"Any job in the military is dangerous. You've got to watch your back all the time." He stabbed a stick into the coals, and they glowed an angry red. "I do my best to exercise caution."

"Stateside, high voltage must mean running poles and those thick lines. What sort of high voltage would you do in…say…the Middle East?" Why was I pressing this? Knowing the risk he'd be in once he returned to his duties should've made me hush up. I needed to tie my worry for him up in knots so it wouldn't bite me. What if he got hurt like Eli, only worse?

"Where the Marines go, the Seabees follow."

"I thought the Seabees were Navy."

He tilted his head and peered up at me from where he rested on his forearms. The fire made his dark hair gleam like a raven's. "We mostly work with the Marines. They go in, clean out a site, and we follow to build. Housing, medical facilities, infrastructure that's been damaged or destroyed. Whatever needs to be done to support the mission, we do."

Can do.

"With a gun," I said.

He directed his attention to the coals. "Always with a gun."

I tipped the dregs of my beer onto the grass and rose to dispose of the empty. That same fear that had haunted me after my kidnapping filled me now, except it had found a new purpose. Worry about Cooper. I opened the cooler and dug out two icy beer bottles and returned to my chair, handing one over to him. "High voltage means you're up on a ladder, or in one of those big buckets, working on a pole, right?"

With a sigh, he tossed the stick onto the flames. He set our new beers on the ground, took my hand, and squeezed it. "Unfortunately, yes."

"I don't like it." It would be wrong of me not to name it. He must know I cared. No, I'd *shown* him I cared. "They've sent you overseas a lot. You've done, what, three, four tours?"

"Five. I volunteered for my last few deployments."

"Volunteered? Why?"

"I guess…" Releasing my hand, he ran his fingers

155

across his hair which was too short to thread through. "They ask for volunteers. I'm single. Many of my friends have families. Why put them in the line of danger when it can be me instead?"

"Because then *you're* in the line of danger."

He chipped a nod, and his voice deepened. "I'm okay with that."

I wasn't. I wanted to shout out the words, declare it to the universe. Yet Cooper and I weren't committed. Hell, I wasn't even sure we were a couple. Which meant I had no say in how he lived his life. Staring into the flames, I tried not to think about him leaving for his next deployment, taking chances as if his life meant nothing. Because his life meant everything to me.

"Tell me about your favorite photograph," he said.

A subject change was the last thing I was interested in right now. I wanted to hash this out, make him grant me promises I had no right to demand. Dwelling on something I couldn't change wasn't doing me any favors, however. I cleared my throat. "I love all my photographs."

His lips curled up on one side, and his voice lightened. "Let me see if I can guess your favorite."

This might be interesting.

"I know." Cooper tapped his chin. "The one with the Japanese man seeing his wife for the first time."

"He knew her in advance."

"I meant how everything's brand new once you marry."

My smile conceded his point was valid and sweet. "You weren't far off. While the man met her through a traditionally arranged marriage called *omiai*, they dated before agreeing to marry."

Inside, I was free to judge other cultures. The outside me—the person I presented to the world—had to respect the beliefs of the country I visited. As much as I yearned to advocate for change, and I had in my own small way whenever I spoke to people while traveling, I was only passing through their land. If they invited me into their lives, I had to respect the way they chose to live them.

"That's not my favorite photo," I said.

"You're right. Not that one." He held up a finger. "I know. The old woman staring out the window across the fields rolling into the distance."

That one *was* special to me. "Not many people know the full story behind those lines on her face. Her reddened eyes." The woman had sat stiffly, her spine not quite touching the high-back chair.

"Her eyes sought something." He shook his head. "I couldn't tell what."

"Only her wrinkled hands, clasped tightly on her lap, betrayed her." My lungs collapsed with a long breath. "She'd recently lost her husband of seventy years. Dementia made her forgetful. In a quivering voice, she told me to watch with her. That he'd be home soon. That she'd have to get supper on the table when he arrived."

"I think I'm close, but that's not the picture, either."

Joy made my cheeks ache. While my family often told me how proud they were of my work, few people had taken the time to understand my photos like Cooper obviously had. The fact that he not only thought about the stories behind the pictures but also remembered the images to this day touched me. "You're close, though."

His hand tightened around mine. "Then it must be the one with the girl and her falcon."

Bingo. "How did you know?"

"That look...her arm raised. Her face filled with wonder. What's the story behind that picture?"

"Mongolia. I lived with the girl's family in their village

high in the mountains for over a month. So many wonderful images to capture. She raised the bird under her father's guidance. Once it was grown, she begged him to let her release it. I took the picture as she started to loosen the jesses."

"Yes," he breathed. "I loved that one the moment I saw it."

I had to wonder. Had he seen a bit of himself in the bird?

"Did she do it? Let it go?"

"She did. It soared high into the sky and circled over us. Its keening cry was the only sound outside our harsh breathing."

"No longer tethered."

"That's right." Except in its heart. "It only flew a few minutes before returning to land on her arm again."

Cooper's eyes rested on mine, his smoky blue from wherever his thoughts took him. "Maybe the bird preferred captivity over living without her."

"And while it remained with her, it always soared free."

As if to punctuate that statement, the first fireworks shot toward the heavens, making my body jolt. A splash of blue and red burst in a circle, followed by a sharp boom. Loud enough to jar my teeth.

Cooper jumped, as well. Groaning, he rubbed the back of his neck. "Sorry. I…sometimes things startle me."

"I understand." I rubbed his thigh. Boy, did I get it. It felt like the world startled me all the damn time.

He pointed. "Look at that one."

I let the bright colors chase away my heavy mood. We toasted each other with our beers. Like an eight-year-old, I clapped and gushed over the better displays. Cooper laughed along with me, but I had a feeling, by the weight of his gaze, that he watched me more than the fireworks.

Taking his hand, I clasped it tightly, not releasing my grip until nothing except the echo of the last bang lingered in the air.

"What a perfect way to end the night," he said.

"Almost."

He lifted one eyebrow, and his smile lured me closer.

It was a smile worthy of a kiss, which I delivered. However, while anticipation coursed through me, I wasn't quite ready for bed yet. My belly was snarling, and Oreos would make the evening complete. Fetching a package, I set it on my lap and peeled back the top to expose the long rows of black and white yumminess inside.

Cooper grabbed one and shoved the entire thing into his mouth.

I gasped and sputtered. "How could you?"

"What?" he mumbled around the cookie.

I shook my head. "You're not eating it right."

He smirked and brushed crumbs off his chest. "There's a right way to eat Oreos?"

"Let me show you." Pulling two cookies from the packaged, I set one on the arm of my chair. "Like this." With a sharp twist, I separated the sides, leaving the frosting behind on one. "There's an art to this. If it isn't done right, part of the frosting sticks to the blank side. It needs to be fast, painless, and clean."

Eyes gleaming with humor, Cooper mimicked my action. "And?"

"You do it with the other one, too."

He chuckled and peeled another cookie.

"Then, you have to eat the plain side." Dry, but it was a necessary part of the routine. The dregs stuck in my throat, and I washed them down with my beer.

Cooper bit into the cookie. He grimaced and tossed it into the fire where it smoldered.

"Hey." I sat forward, squinting into the flames. Poor cookie, abandoned so thoughtlessly. "You can't do that."

"Why not?"

"If you want your reward, you've got to pay the price."

His deep, throaty voice trilled through me. "Name the price, sweetheart. I'm all about rewards."

Actually, so was I. I couldn't stop laughing. Cooper brought out every speck of happiness inside me. Cookies. I needed to focus on cookies. "I meant you need to do it in exactly the right way or it's not as much fun."

"Lead on. I'm game."

"You have to pay your Oreo dues." I crunched through the second dry half and sighed with bliss when I could combine the white frosted sides. My long-overdue reward was at hand.

Cooper snatched my cookie sandwich away from me and stuffed it into his mouth. "Mmm." He chuckled as he took in my rising indignation. After swallowing, his grin filled his face, covering me like a soft, warm blanket. "I think you're on to something here."

"You cheated." I poked his chest. "Unless you eat the sides without frosting, you can't have the other ones."

"Why not?" He snatched two cookies from the package, unscrewed them, and tossed the plain sides into the fire. He consumed the second sandwich in seconds.

"Because…that's not how it's done."

He lifted one eyebrow. "I think there are many ways to see things done."

Damn. I loved innuendo.

18

Cooper

There was nothing I found more satisfying than teasing Ginny. Except tasting her lips, sweet from the cookies. Or feeling her hands, soft on my skin. Best of all, when she pressed her body against mine.

Getting her alone again was my top priority. But as much as I wanted her, I wouldn't make assumptions about the rest of tonight. She wanted to prove something this weekend, so she might want to sleep alone. Everyone needed their space. I'd respect that.

I glanced at my watch while she put away the half-finished package of cookies. "It's after eleven."

Her lips lifted, and her eyes darted to Eli's tent. "I'll get my toothbrush."

We stalled together beside the picnic table after doing our teeth.

"I think there's room on your mattress for two, don't you?" The laughter in her voice told me she knew what I'd been thinking but that she had the situation under control.

My heart, too, most likely.

She held out her hand.

I took it and ducked inside my tent right behind her.

———

SOME FREAKING BIRD was determined to mess with my sleep. Of course, it wasn't the bird's fault I hadn't closed my eyes until dawn. The real reason I was exhausted lay half on top of me, slumbering in my arms. Ginny.

What was I going to do about this? About her?

She shifted the question aside when she raised her head and gazed at me, her brown eyes smoldering. And she drove all thoughts of anything but her from my head when she climbed up my body and placed her lips on mine.

I didn't know what I'd do without her in a week. In a month. Or in a year.

Right now, I could only love her.

Later, we got up, showered, and cooked breakfast. I made my coffee last beyond cold because finishing meant it was time to pack our things and head into town. Reality was poised to kick me in the gut all over again.

Eli showed up as we were trying to force my tent pieces into the tiny bag they'd come in. Damned bags must shrink the second you emptied them. The haggard lines on my friend's face told me how tired he must be. I moved around the cold fire pit and put a hand on his shoulder. "You okay?"

Eyes older than they ought to be in a thirty-year-old stared back at me. Red-rimmed, cloudy. "Will be, once I get some sleep."

"Let's get the place cleaned up fast and then you can go home and go to bed."

Ginny took charge; exactly what we needed. "Eli, you take the empty bottles and trash to the bins behind the campground office." Her concerned gaze fell on me. "You can help me take down Eli's tent."

"I'm really worried about him," Ginny said while we continued to pack things up. "He can't keep going at this pace."

"You're right. Glad it's only a short ride home."

Once Eli returned, we finished packing and hauled everything to the parking lot and loaded the back of Eli's Jeep.

I filled him in on all that had happened while he was gone.

"You think any of this adds up to more than coincidence?" he asked with a frown.

"Hard to say." I was going to make sure nothing *coincidental* happened to Ginny while I was around.

The heavy look he fed me showed he'd caught my concern and magnified it tenfold. "You can bet I'll keep an eye on her."

Since reality made it clear I'd have no say in what happened to Ginny beyond the next few days, it was the best I could hope for. If only the military didn't own me.

"You want my tent?" I asked Eli, resting my hand on the back of the Jeep. I swung the tailgate up and secured the latch with a bang. "I won't need it again."

Ginny dragged her eyes away from mine. My belly spasmed when I realized the message I'd unintentionally delivered.

Leaving soon. Won't be back.

The tightness in her spine only rivaled that of her lips. It ripped me apart to think I'd hurt her already. But what could I do? I didn't have a future to offer.

"I'll put it inside the garage with everything else," Eli said, oblivious to the undercurrent of tension between Ginny and me.

"Later this week, I'm going to stop by and see Flint. He's out at the base, doing his two weeks active. He mentioned he wanted to talk to you about a job, so you might want to go with me."

Eli froze. "Flint Crawford's around?"

"Remember? He left the Seabees eight months ago. Stayed in the Reserves, but he started his own business, Viper Force."

Eli stared toward town as if he was already halfway there. "What about Mia?"

Ah. So, there *was* something between Eli and Flint's younger sister.

"Flint said she moved to Crescent Cove. Took a job locally."

"Really?" Eli said eagerly. "I...I'll have to look her up." His face tightened. "You mentioned Flint might have a job for me? What kind of business we talking about?"

"Recreational drones." Anything but. If I knew Flint, he was working with highly-classified devices. But Ginny hadn't missed Eli's interest in Mia, and she was hanging on our every word.

Eli frowned. "Ah. Of course. I'm definitely interested in talking to Flint, but I won't fit him in this week. Might find time before the month's through."

I had a feeling he might find time in the next week to look up Mia, however.

After slapping my shoulder and saying goodbye, Eli strode around to the driver's side, leaving me and Ginny alone for one final minute.

Insecurity made me antsy, and I swiped my palms down my face. It wouldn't be easy to let us go, but what could I truly offer her?

Ginny paused and gave me a weak smile. "You want to come to my place for dinner tonight?"

Ending this immediately would make it simpler, before I was all in. But I couldn't make myself say the words. Not yet. Maybe not ever. "How about tomorrow instead? I need to put some solid time in at my dad's place or I won't get it done before I have to leave."

Her expression tightened but she nodded. "Tomorrow, then."

Leaning forward, I kissed her. I drank in the way she clutched my shoulders. "Five okay?"

"Sounds great." She opened the passenger door and climbed inside. With her head sticking out the open window, she waved. The tires crunched as the Jeep moved across the gravel lot, heading for the main road.

Ginny blew me a kiss.

Reaching up, I caught it. I pressed my fist against my chest and released her kiss. Warmth spread through my body.

Damn.

I already was *all in*.

19

Ginny

I was grateful Eli chose silence on the way into town. Thinking had captured my mind.

Putting aside Cooper's comment about leaving soon hadn't been easy, but what could I do? He'd made it clear we were a short-term thing. He'd made no promises. Even though I'd told myself I'd accept what he could give and not pressure him for anything more, I'd gotten caught up in my feelings. Fed them, even.

Eli brought the Jeep to a stop in my driveway and shut off the engine. We both stared toward the shingle-sided gambrel building I'd bought down the road from my brother's place. The original owner had used the first floor as a garage, living in the small apartment upstairs. Since it was a one-bedroom and he and his wife had a baby on the way, he'd put the property on the market. I converted the first floor into my photography studio, complete with a dark room and office. Crescent Cove hadn't seen a working photographer since black-and-white fame, and my business had grown quickly.

Eli unbuckled. "I'll help you with your things."

"No need." It was beyond time I handled life all by myself. I opened my door and climbed out, turning to lean back inside. "It's only my clothing. My pillow."

He shoved his sunglasses up onto his head and squinted at me. "It's more than that."

That. "I locked up when we left Friday. I'm sure everything's fine." For the first time since I'd come home three months ago, I didn't have an overwhelming urge to drag him through my apartment to check every corner for threats. Fear wasn't controlling me at the moment, so I latched onto the notion and held it close.

"It's a lot to carry upstairs." He nudged his head toward the back of the Jeep.

I hated to keep him when he needed sleep. He still had to hang the wet tents on a line to dry. Clean the coolers. Put everything away in the top of his garage. Unless he chose to do most of the chores later, he wouldn't get to bed for at least an hour. "There's less for me to carry than there should've been."

He growled. "If that asshole comes near you again, he's dead meat."

"I believe Cooper took care of it." I hoped so, anyway. If Tom was wise, he'd seek out someone else, someone who didn't remind him of his dead wife. Even better, a woman who was interested.

"Decent of him, but I should've been there to take care of it."

Since I'd slunk home seeking whatever comfort I could find in my family, Eli had become my protector all over again like when they were kids.

A mix of frustration and warmth filled me. I hated that he felt the need to hover. "While I appreciate you guys coming to my defense, I'm going to start doing things for myself again."

He cocked an eyebrow my way then opened his door and climbed out.

I met him at the back of the Jeep where he lowered the tailgate and slid my plastic kitchen tote to the edge. I took one end so we could unload it onto the lawn together. The tote wasn't heavy, just awkward. "I'm going to take self-defense classes." An idea that had been hovering in the back of my mind for more than a month. I'd almost asked Cooper to teach me but he'd be gone soon. That squeezing feeling took up residence in my chest again. Had it ever left?

Focus on now, not on the empty husk you'll be when he leaves.

We dropped the tote on the lawn and returned to the Jeep for the second.

"How long is Cooper in town, did you say?" I asked as we settled the second tote on the grass.

"Didn't say." Eli straightened. "Ginny—"

Cringing, I held up my hand. "Don't. I just…It's okay."

His eyes probed deeply, but I raised my shields and projected an expression I hoped suggested *I can handle this*.

"You sure?"

My quick smile must've reassured him, because his shoulders loosened.

"I just forgot to ask him myself." Hadn't dared to, actually, because I had no right to that knowledge. But I ached to know. How long until I had to say goodbye?

"Five days," he said.

If I pressed them out flat, five days could feel like forever.

"How about you?" I asked. His eyebrow lifted again, but he damn well knew what I was talking about. He couldn't pull one on me. "Who's Mia?"

A soft rumble flitted through his chest. "Just someone I met before I got injured."

From the quick way he'd questioned Cooper, Mia was more than *just someone*. "She's Flint's sister."

"You know Flint?"

"Met him on the base when I went there with Cooper."

Eli leaned forward. "Coop said Mia was with him."

"Gorgeous. Long, strawberry blonde hair. Petite. That the one?"

"Hell, yeah." The words sighed past his lips.

From what Mom told me after I moved home, women had made it clear they were interested in my brother, but he hadn't been on a date since he was discharged. Was he holding himself back because of Mia? "Who is she to you?"

"It's not like I'm hung up on her."

"Didn't say you were." But he was. "Come on. Tell me."

"I met her when she came to stay with Flint in California, while he was packing to leave the service."

"Before you were hurt overseas?" He'd also been stationed at Port Hueneme for his last few years in the Seabees.

"I asked her out. She…shot me down. Said long-distance relationships never worked."

"And now she's living in Crescent Cove." According to what Flint suggested, Mia might be as interested in Eli as he was in her.

He glanced toward town, and the longing in his gaze made my chest tighten. "Maybe. Guess I'll find out eventually."

"I hope you run into her again."

"Doesn't matter."

Eli never could fool me. "If that was the case, you wouldn't have asked Cooper about her."

"Told you. She said she wasn't interested."

"Maybe and maybe not. Her feelings could've changed. You don't live on opposite sides of the country any longer." Assuming she was still single, she might give him a second chance. If she turned him down again, it looked like my brother was headed for heartache.

Like me.

It was tough tacking down hopes and dreams when the heart was involved. Something Eli and I shared.

I stepped around my camping things and hugged him. Maybe the first real hug outside of *hey, I'm heading out* we'd shared in ages. He patted my back, and I swore he started to say something, but his spine tightened and he clamped his lips together. He stepped away, and my arms fell to my sides.

He grunted. "I'd tell you not to hurt Coop but then I'd have to tell him the same thing." He coughed. "Already have, actually."

"Please tell me you didn't discuss us." Talk about making me squirm.

"Not too much."

Okay, so my life would be easier if I didn't explore this further. "If it helps, I don't know where this is going, either. If anywhere."

"I get it." He stared wistfully toward town again—where Mia might be living now, totally unaware that my brother hoped to meet up with her again. Returning to the back of the Jeep, he grabbed my bag of clothing and dropped it beside the totes. "I'll help you take your stuff up onto the deck."

I reached for one of the kitchen totes.

"I've got it," Eli said.

"Your…" I cut myself off. He hated when anyone suggested his injury made him less capable than the next man in doing whatever needed to be done. Keys and pillow in hand, I followed him down the stone path beside my house and up the back stairs to the small deck outside my home's entrance. He took the stairs carefully. Damn IED. Shrapnel nearly took his leg off. He'd recovered—somewhat—but his career in the Seabees had been over.

After dropping the first tote on my deck, he insisted on carrying the second up as well, while I muscled my bag of clothing, feeling particularly useless.

Eli dropped the second tote and turned to me. "Can you get everything inside from here?"

His red-rimmed eyes told me he needed rest more than he needed to breathe.

"Of course." I'd empty the totes and put them inside the storage shed in my back yard. My clothing, I'd dump in the washer.

"I'll see you around then." His sneakers thudded unevenly down the wooden staircase.

I reached toward my door, key extended, but stalled as I stared at the knob. "Eli!"

He paused and gazed up at me, studying my face. His soon reflected my concern. "What?"

"My door's open."

His expression tightened, and he stomped back up to join me.

"You know I always close everything up tight." Lord knows I was more than vigilant about security.

Eli peered around me, into the darkened space.

My skin crawled at the thought of someone violating my privacy, and my lower lip trembled. "Someone trashed my things at the campground, and now this." Said in a high-pitched voice, the one I'd perfected after moving home. Once again, I was clinging to my brother, something I'd determined to avoid. But what else could I do? The situation was freaking me out. My cheeks burned. "Would you mind making sure everything's okay inside?" Damn, I hated crumbling like this, but what if this was the real deal and I'd been robbed? Worse, what if someone waited for me inside? Two people were better than one measly woman who couldn't host enough defense to fight off a ladybug.

"I plan to." His chest expanded, and he breathed through tight lips. "Wait here." He pushed the door fully open and stepped into the entryway. "Looks okay so far."

I was grateful my home hadn't been destroyed like my campsite but my heart still competed in a road race of one. I followed Eli, but halted in the entry, darting my eyes around, seeking anything that would indicate someone had been here while I was gone. Nothing appeared out of place.

An island with bar stools separated the small kitchen from the dining and living areas, but the fact that it was only one large room made it easy to survey the area. To make the place cozy, I'd hung some photos on the walls. They weren't askew. Colorful pillows still lay scattered around on the furniture exactly where I'd left them. Beyond the living room was a huge, cedar deck—one of the major selling points of my home. I crept forward to look, and the furniture sat like I'd left it before going camping.

I owned two acres, which included a broad lawn with decent plantings, and a strip of woods behind. My nearest neighbor was a good shout away, giving me plenty of privacy if I wanted to sit out in the evening. Now, the lack of anyone nearby heightened my home's isolation.

Eli appeared from the hall leading to my bedroom,

poking his head into the half bath along the way. He strode up to me. "Everything looks okay." Scratching his neck, he winced. "I hate to mention this, but are you sure you didn't—"

"Could you look downstairs, too?" I nodded to the door leading down to my photography studio.

"Of course." He said it like he meant it, but I had to wonder. Was he getting tired of investigating all the time but never finding anything? Now that my initial fear had faded, begging him to examine every square inch of my house made me come across needy. Weak.

"I'm sorry."

When he glanced back at me from the top of the stairs, a hint of resignation lurked in his eyes. "It's okay. I don't mind."

Tingling spread up my chest and landed in my face, flushing my cheeks further. I slumped on the sofa, barely resisting the urge to curl into a ball and fiddle with my hair, something I hadn't done since I was a kid. I fiddled with the fringe on one of my pretty throw pillows instead. When would I be strong enough to handle situations like this by myself? Relying on Eli forever wasn't an option. He had his own life to live.

He returned from downstairs and braced his shoulder against the entry doorframe. "It's going to be okay."

"Do you think I'm making this up?"

"Not for a second. Your door was unlocked. But outside of kids painting graffiti on the side of the high school during basketball playoffs, Crescent Cove sees about one crime a year."

"What about the librarian, Mrs. Clark? She said someone broke into her house. Stole her purse."

"They found it in her car where she'd left it."

I'd forgotten that detail. I blew out a noisy breath. "I distinctly remember locking my apartment door."

"But you went back for your camera."

I'd locked up after retrieving it, hadn't I? Jeez, it was hard to remember now. Friday felt like a lifetime ago. "Maybe it didn't shut fully." Easy to say, but hard to believe. Mistakes like this happened to regular people all the time, maybe even to me. At least no one had entered my apartment to steal while I was gone.

Setting the pillow aside, I stood. "I appreciate you looking around."

"You know you can call me anytime." Said with the same solid voice he'd used since I returned home a total wreck. Was his patience holding true, or was I on borrowed time? "You're all set, then?" As in, did I feel secure enough so he could leave?

"Yes." I'd have to feel that way because he needed to sleep, not hang out and hold my hand. Each minute here was one less he'd have in bed before he had to return to his job.

"I'll call later this week to check in." He stroked a strand of hair off my face and pushed for a grin. "Mom will be home next weekend. We should get together for dinner."

I rested my shoulder against the white-painted door-frame. "I'd like that."

He stepped out onto my deck. The breeze stirred his hair until he stuffed his baseball cap on his head, squashing it. "Bye."

"Thank you again." I called out as he paced down the stairs, "And good luck with Mia."

His feet paused, but he didn't turn. His chuckle slipped out. "She's just a friend."

Like I believed that. I just hoped she had fond memories of my brother.

I watched as he got into his Jeep, started it, and then backed down the drive. With a beep of his horn, he accelerated, heading toward his home.

"Okay." I exhaled, spiking hair toward the sky. Time to get organized. But I had one thing to do first. Pulling my phone, I typed *Security Systems, Farland, Maine*, into the search engine. I doubted there was a company in Crescent Cove. My town was too small. One popped up on the list immediately. Could things get much easier than that?

I dialed the number. Why hadn't I put in a system the second I bought my house? Maybe because Eli told me I didn't need one, that my deadbolts and window locks would be more than enough.

The person who answered the phone assured me they'd send someone out first thing tomorrow morning to give me an estimate. No guarantee they'd get anything installed right away but—for a hefty fee—they'd accommodate my need for urgent building security.

Hanging up, I pocketed my phone. This wasn't just for my own personal safety. I had valuable items here. Special equipment and costly chemicals I used in my business. Cameras I'd hate to have stolen.

I reached for my camping things but paused.

Oh. Another tiny painting. Weird that Eli left it on top of my bag rather than just give it to me directly. But maybe he'd wanted to give me a boost after he left, knowing I'd find it and smile.

I'd have to ask him why he was so secretive about them. Sure, he'd been embarrassed about his artwork during high school, but this was just us. He must know I treasured each bit of himself he gave me.

This painting was of the Deer Isle Bridge. We'd crossed

it once during a trip to Little Deer Isle, stopping on one side so I could take pictures. I loved that he was recapturing our shared memories with art, and I'd put this one with the other two he'd given me on my mantel.

I slid it into my pocket and hauled my camping things inside, then slid the deadbolt. Staring at the locking mechanism longer than necessary, I assured myself I *had* locked the door. This time.

I was setting my camera on the coffee table when I noticed the position of my magazines.

My legs started shaking, and I lowered myself onto the couch.

The magazines lay in a scattered pile.

Not the tidy stack I'd left last Friday.

20

Cooper

The second floor of my father's place awaited me.

Parked in the drive, I stared toward the two-story build-ing. At one time, this place had offered me welcome. Love. A home. Now it only delivered backbreaking labor.

As promised, the dumpster standing in front of the one-car garage had been emptied late Friday. The black cavern inside waited to chew through the rest of my memories.

I locked the car and took the walkway toward the house where I keyed the front door, unsure why I'd both-ered to lock the place up. It would've been easier to put an *everything free* sign on the front lawn, rather than bust myself hauling it all out.

Who would've thought that a man who left his house only to buy alcohol could've collected this much crap over the past twelve years?

Grabbing a box from the now-empty living room, I strode into the kitchen to finish emptying the cabinets. Any nonperishable food would go to the food pantry. Pots and pans, too, because they told me they'd distribute everything to those in need.

"Damned shit." I dumped a drawer full of congealed spices into a box. Left over from when Mom was alive, most likely. Dumpster-fodder now.

An hour later, I'd finished up in the kitchen and was taking a breather on the front steps with a bottle of water in hand when Ginny texted, *Hey. How's it going?*

Just hearing from her brought my smile out in full force. *Decent. You?*

Okay. I've unpacked all my camping stuff, and I'm catching up on my accounting. Man, I hate adding up long columns of numbers. I think my brain's going to burst.

I wondered how her business was doing, whether she'd turned a profit yet, but wasn't sure I should ask. That felt personal. Like we were a couple.

Hell, I considered us a couple already. But what we had was only for a few days, not the beginning of what could turn into a lifetime. I didn't have the right to ask about every facet of her life.

Deciding to keep this casual, I texted, *We still on for dinner tomorrow night?*

Why had I put her off until tomorrow instead of taking advantage of every free moment I had to see her? I could've gone over later and begged her to let me stay the night. Instead, my lonely hotel room waited for me on the other side of town.

I can't wait to see you, she texted. *Hey, I was thinking about taking some self-defense classes. I'd ask you, but I know you're not here for long.*

I could almost feel her pause before the word *long* because it resonated in my soul, too. With a hefty swallow of water, I tried to shove down the lump in my throat.

I'm sure your 'can do' motto extends to skills like that, she texted.

My smile made my cheeks ache. There was a lot I wanted to do with Ginny the first moment I saw her. Self-defense training was a great idea, though. I'd leave a hell of a lot more comfortable knowing she was learning to defend herself. I only had a few more days, but I'd carve out some time to show her a few essential moves. How to break a choke hold, for one. And maybe we could talk about how to avoid tricky situations. Hopefully, she'd never have to use her new skills.

I'd be glad to show you some of my moves, I texted.

I'd like that. You'll be here at 5 tomorrow?

It felt like a thousand years away to me. *I'll be there.*

I pocketed my phone and checked my watch. Four-thirty. While I could start on the basement, I still wasn't feeling it. Hell, I hadn't been feeling it from the moment I started this project last week.

Not that my mood mattered. *Get to it.*

Hours later, I locked the front door and called it a night. I'd pick up something for dinner at the supermarket then go to my hotel. I could drop on the bed, put my feet up, and lose myself in a game on TV.

But when I sat in the driver's seat, it was all I could do not to plug Ginny's address into my GPS. My heart called to her like a sailor capsized at sea. Only she could provide me salvation.

I hated my conscience for setting boundaries on our relationship.

21

Ginny

The next morning, I placed a call to the police station to report the possible break-in into my apartment. Once the dispatcher determined there was no vandalism or anything missing, she said she'd send someone out to file a report. I wondered how that would go since I could barely convince myself that someone had been inside my apartment.

When I returned my personal camera to the fire-proof safe located behind a framed photo in my bedroom, I realized I'd left my current thumb drive in Eli's Jeep. Seven other dated drives lay inside the felt-lined safe, each filled with images captured during my ten-plus years traveling the world.

I stored my pictures on thumb drives as well as on my laptop hard drive, only avoiding cloud storage because I was crap at remembering passwords.

The drive I'd left in Eli's Jeep contained pictures from my journey through Greece, a mini vacation at the Black Sea with Zen before we ended things, and multiple shots taken during school visits in Istanbul. I'd topped it off with pictures from the camping weekend.

While coffee percolated in the kitchen, I parked on my sofa. I slid my laptop off the coffee table and turned it on.

"Okay." A blinking white cursor stared back at me, plus the unwelcome message, *No Operating System Found.*

My computer-savvy didn't extend beyond the basics, and this didn't look like anything I could handle.

Holding in the start button, I counted to ten then let the computer start like normal. The blinking cursor and message appeared again.

A dead laptop was not what I needed right now. Where had I left those recovery thumb drives? Not in the safe with the ones storing my pictures. Were they somewhere inside the piles of boxes inside my storage shed out back? I grumbled because the last thing I wanted to do was spend hours poring through the contents of boxes in my hot, dusty shed.

Maybe that department store sales flyer I'd opened last week had given my computer a virus. Or Windows had failed. Eli *had* told me I should buy a Mac. Now, I wished I'd listened.

The easiest thing to do was take the laptop into town to the computer place and see if they could make it functional again. If not, I'd buy a new one, because I needed to blog and upload photos.

The security firm would arrive soon. Since I hadn't scheduled photography business today, my morning was free. This afternoon was reserved for making dinner before Cooper arrived. And for plucking my eyebrows and shaving my legs. Important things like that.

Someone knocked on my door. Rising, I dropped my laptop onto the coffee table. I tucked the curtain to the side and peeked out. After verifying the security guy by the patch on his right chest, let alone the van parked in my driveway with *Bastile Security* stenciled on the side, I slid the deadbolt and opened the door.

"Ginny Bradley?" he said.

"Yes." I waved him in.

"I'm Stanley Bastile of Bastile Security. I understand you'd like a quote on a security system install?" He offered me a business card in one hand while juggling a clipboard and pen with the other.

"I need something done as soon as possible. Can you start today?"

He chuckled. "You *do* want something soon, don't you?" Creases appeared around his eyes as he took in the rooms with tight professionalism. "What exactly are you looking for?"

I crossed my arms on my chest and gnawed on my lower lip. "Your best system available."

"We charge extra for quick installation."

"I'm okay with that."

He tugged off his cap, smoothed his balding head, then replaced the hat. "We're a new business, but we're fully certified in the systems we install." He cleared his throat. "But there's no way we could get it finished by the end of today. How does late tomorrow sound?"

My bank balance might protest the rush job but feeling more secure was priceless. "That would be great."

"I need to get in touch of some guys, but they'll be over here lickety-split and we can get started right away. We'll have to be out of here by three today, though. Prior commitment."

"Getting started is enough for me."

He gestured toward the living room. "Why don't you show me around, and we can discuss exactly what you're looking for."

Leading the way, I gave him a complete tour of the

building from top to bottom. We talked about the system he recommended for my style of windows and doors, plus the cameras he thought would be best for monitoring the outdoors. After returning from the ground floor, we sat at my kitchen counter while he went through what he planned, checking boxes on a spreadsheet as he outlined the system he'd install. He added up the columns with his phone calculator, swallowed, and named a price.

Substantial but less than I'd feared. At least I could afford it.

He made a few calls and more men arrived. They walked around, talking as they laid out what needed to be done. After carrying boxes up from the van, they got started.

"I need to go into town," I told Stanley. "I shouldn't be long. Is that okay?"

Stanley looked over from where he was attaching something to the doorframe leading to my back deck. "Not a problem. I've got your cell if I have questions."

My lack of caffeine had announced itself with a throbbing in my temples. At least Mr. Joe's was on my way to the computer store.

I packed my laptop and purse in my backpack and left the guys working. Knowing I'd have a new barrier between me and the outside world made me happier already.

Out on my front lawn, I stalled beside my car and studied the road. Walk or drive? While it was an easy hike downtown, I'd never felt comfortable walking on the road. The sidewalk didn't extend out this far, and I'd have to use the breakdown lane. And my fear of being outside alone had kept me locked up in my apartment for months.

Driving was safer, and I was all about feeling safe. But jeez, when was I going to stop worrying about everything?

"Walk," I whispered. "If Tom comes around, you can

smack him. Besides, you said you were going to stretch your boundaries."

It was past time to show the world—and myself—I was fearless.

Pack on my back, I forced my sneakers down the drive and turned onto the road leading toward town. I told myself it felt great to be outside, to savor the wind rustling my hair, to swing my arms freely. But my heart wasn't entirely convinced.

A few cars cruised past me, giving me a wide berth. Birds chirped in the woods on the other side of the road and in the distance, a lawnmower hummed. A few bees buzzed by, seeking pollen, and I passed a cluster of butter-flies fluttering on yellow flowers. Enjoying nature was just one of the many fun reasons to walk. I used to love hiking. I'd taken it for granted.

The sun warmed my arms, and my sneakers scrunched pleasantly on the gravel peppering the breakdown lane. Heat stole through my bones, and my heart sang. Pure joy rose up inside me, the feeling I used to get when I arrived in a new country.

Walking had been the right decision.

Mr. Joe's was ten-minutes from my house. I was already savoring the caffeine rush to come. Since sweat trickled down my back, I'd get my usual summer drink, an iced mocha latte. Like I had each day last week and when I went to the base with Cooper. My mouth salivated already. To celebrate my new bravery, I'd reward myself with a second drink on my way home. My veins were going to sing with energy.

Reaching Mr. Joe's, I darted around cars in the parking lot and then strolled inside and up to the counter. Baristas tweaked fancy silver machines along the back wall, a few shaking their hips and whistling along with the music piped in overhead. The smoky essence of caffeinated yum dove into my senses.

Joe greeted me from behind the register. "Well, well, well. Nice to see you here rather than at the drive-through window, Ginny."

The best part about being a regular was that the employees knew my name.

I smiled. "It's too awesome a day to be cooped up inside a car. I decided to walk."

His eyes lifted toward the large windows spanning the front of the shop. "Sure is gorgeous outside. What can I get you?" He laughed and held up his finger. "No, don't tell me. An iced mocha latte. Medium or biggie this time around?"

"You know me too well. I think today's worthy of a biggie. With a squirt of whipped cream on top." I'd really live it up.

"I'll have it ready for you in no time." He turned to make my drink.

"Got it," a man said in a deep voice. His back faced me, making it impossible to see his face. Average build, a cap pulled down over his blond hair. He scooped up ice with a plastic cup and then hustled to the swirl station to add chocolate. Something about him felt familiar, which meant I must've seen him around town. Last week, Joe told me he was hiring more staff.

The man crafted my drink and handed it off to Joe, never turning my way. All I caught was his partial profile. Short beard, pointy nose like a lot of guys around town.

I traded my drink for my debit card, and Joe handed me the slip, saying, "Nice seeing you. Have a great day." Leaning around me, he spoke to the next in line, "What can I get you today?"

A stop at the creamer station gave me a chance to tuck

my purse back into my pack. I unsheathed a straw and pushed it through the whipped cream topping. Unable to resist, I took a long drink. Icy, sweet, and extra chocolatey. With a sharp kick of espresso. Pure heaven.

Outside, I tugged my pack onto my back. I took another long swallow, savoring the mix of flavors. A slightly bitter taste hit me at the end, almost like cinnamon and something I hadn't ordered. Obviously, the new guy had messed up. Should I go inside and ask Joe to make me another?

Why bother? If I complained, the new guy could get into trouble. And time was a-wasting. I had to drop off my laptop for repairs.

While crossing the parking lot, I sipped more of my drink. Cinnamon combined with chocolate gave it an unusual flavor, but I'd deal. Caffeine was caffeine, and I needed it badly this morning.

I turned onto the main road and sped up to a brisk pace, enjoying the fresh air as I moved along. Another sip of my drink should send energy zinging through my veins any second now. Why then, was I feeling sleepy?

"You were awake most of last night," I told myself. "That's why you're tired."

Have some more caffeine.

I soon left the busy area around Mr. Joe's behind and strolled beside the wooded section outside the city proper. In no time, my drink ran dry. By then, I could barely hold the cup. My fumbling fingers dropped it and I staggered, barely catching myself.

Man, was I tired. And super-relaxed. Like I floated on clouds, squishing one foot after the other on all that white fluff. Tried to, anyway. My feet weren't cooperating.

Head spinning, I giggled but cut the sound off by slapping my hand over my mouth. Good thing the houses in this part of town were set back from the road. Otherwise, people would think I was drunk. At freaking nine in the morning? Please. I never drank before ten.

Why weren't my legs working like they used to? One wanted to take me out into the road while the other favored the steep ditch to my right. I wished they'd make up their minds. Or learn a little cooperation, like good legs should.

"Move forward, Ginny. You've got a toplap to drop off." More giggles erupted from my throat. Toplap. Really? That was…That was…

Unease shifted inside me, awakening like a dragon after a centuries-long slumber. It reared back its head and whiffs of dread swirled from its nostrils.

Something was wrong with me. This was more than feeling tired.

The sound of a vehicle coming up behind me sent me pivoting around to face it. My feet tangled together and my thighs quivered so badly, I could barely remain standing. My head spun, and I had to grab onto the guardrail before I collapsed.

My stomach rolled, and my heartbeat slowed as if it was encased in mud.

Frowning, I squinted at the car roaring toward me. My hand lifted all on its own to ward off the vehicle. Sure, my hand could stop a black sedan.

The driver rode beyond the white line on my side of the road. Didn't he see me standing in the breakdown lane?

"No," I hissed out. Why couldn't I move? I needed to get out of the way. And why the hell was I so loopy? Had I been—

The car veered right for me. Gravel spun out behind the tires as the driver gave the vehicle more gas.

Screaming, I scrambled backward. My legs hit the guardrail, and my arms flew up. I leaned toward the ditch. Momentum hauled me over the guardrail. Slamming onto the ground on the other side, I scrambled to find purchase, but my hands wouldn't work. The ditch sucked me down, down. I slid, my feet jarring. My body flipped sideways and I tumbled down the slope, gaining speed, smacking against rocks and sticks. Guttural gasps burst out of me.

I slammed to a stop at the bottom of the ditch, flat on my back, struggling to breathe. Finally, I was able to pull in some air. The world spun, and I thought I'd pass out. My voice was frozen with shock, and my heart fluttered in my chest.

Silence reigned in the woods around me. Up on the road, tires squealed and an engine roared. The vehicle drove off, taking the corner on what sounded like two wheels. In moments, I was left alone.

I lifted my head and stared around with blurry eyes. A lizard perched on a rock beside me blinked and, perhaps thinking I'd seen him, scurried into the deep grass.

"Ohh." I rolled onto my side, assessing the damage. Nothing hurt too badly. My arms and legs were cooperating, although they flopped around after minimal effort. I was okay. Mostly. If only my brain would stop whirling.

I could have a concussion. No, wait. I'd been groggy before I fell, because I was overtired from lack of sleep last night.

Or from something else.

Dread sunk through my belly like a lead weight.

Another car passed on the road. Heat surging through me, I struggled to sit up while shouting for help. But the driver kept going. With their windows up, they must not have heard me.

If I wanted to survive, I needed to get out of this ditch immediately.

I scrambled to my feet and grabbed onto a bush when vertigo tried to toss me back onto the ground. But my legs held my weight, so I released the tree and staggered forward.

Blood trickled down to my wrist from a long scratch, and my left knee ached with each step. As far as I could tell, I hadn't broken anything in the fall.

Using bushes and clumps of grass for purchase, I made my way slowly up the hillside, finally reaching the guardrail after what felt like days.

Another car was coming this way. I waved my arms, and my voice croaked out *help*.

The vehicle slowed and the driver pulled to a stop beside me. A woman in the passenger seat lowered her window and gasped. "What happened to you, honey? Are you okay?"

"No." The world was flying around again. To keep from falling back into the ditch, I clutched the guardrail. But my knees crumpled, and I smacked against the metal. My stomach cramped, and I vomited up my coffee.

Darkness crowded in, hauling me away—only broken by an ambulance siren sometime later.

Through hazy eyes, I watched a paramedic climb over the guardrail.

"We were driving into town, and she just appeared on the other side of the guardrail," a woman said shrilly. "Like a bloody ghost! Scared the heck out of me. We don't know what's wrong with her, but she was breathing, so I didn't do CPR."

Another paramedic wheeled a stretcher up to the other side of the guardrail and lowered it to my level.

"You okay, Ma'am?" the paramedic on my side asked.

"I don't know." The spinning had slowed, only to be usurped by a blinding headache.

"Where do you hurt? Your neck, your back?" She ran her fingers carefully over my arms and legs. Does anything feel broken?"

"I'm okay. I climbed. Out of the ditch." My words stuttered from my mouth, because my tongue kept flopping around.

The woman frowned while strapping a white collar around my neck. "This is just a precaution." She unclipped my backpack and eased it out from underneath me, setting it to the side. As another paramedic approached, she nudged her head toward the ambulance. "We'll need the backboard." She said to me, "Can you tell me what happened?"

"I was. Walking. Into. Town. Car. Coming at me. I fell…into the ditch."

The paramedic reeled back, eyes widening. "Are you saying a car hit you?"

"No. Almost. Yeah."

The woman frowned. "Better let Sheriff Moyer know something's up with this one," she told the other paramedic. "He needs to meet us at the hospital."

"No hospital." I felt fine. Sort of. I struggled to sit, but the woman pressed me back to the ground.

"Lie still, please so we can help you. You could be injured badly and not know it."

The other paramedic stepped over the guardrail and lowered himself to one knee beside me. He strapped a cuff around my uninjured arm and with a stethoscope in his ears, he took my blood pressure. "Low," he said as he removed the cuff.

"I run low," I said.

"Not seventy over thirty, though, right?"

"No, never that low." My teeth rattled as shock settled in.

They log-rolled me onto my side, laid me back onto a hard, plastic surface, and strapped me in place. Taking one end each, the paramedics lifted me up over the guardrail and lowered me onto the stretcher.

"You want me to call anyone for you, honey?" the woman from the car said. She wrung her hands underneath my chin. "A husband. A friend?"

"No." I'd call Eli when I got to the hospital, and he'd come get me and take me home. Then I could collapse on my bed and sleep for three days. That was all I needed. Sleep.

They loaded me into the back of the ambulance. While one paramedic got into the driver's seat and started the vehicle, the other sat beside me. She fiddled with her braid while she wrote a few notes on a clipboard.

Lights flashing but without the siren, we sped into town. I'd wanted to go into town but not like this.

"You sure we can't let someone know what's up?" The woman scribbled some more.

Relenting, I let her call Eli.

"She's okay, really," the woman said into her phone to my brother.

Yells erupted from Eli.

"Tell him to meet me. At the hospital," I said. "I want to go home."

"All right, sir. She'll see you two there."

Two? Eli wasn't calling Cooper, was he? He was busy at his dad's place, and I didn't want to bother him for something like this. It was just a silly fall.

The ambulance pulled into the hospital, and they bustled me into the ER where nurses pulled me onto a stretcher.

My two favorite men arrived soon, rushing into the bay where I lay waiting while the staff 'worked me up'. Bumped to the head of the line, I'd already had x-rays, lab work, and they'd made me pee in a cup. Really, I was okay. Just unbelievably tired.

Thankfully, a nurse had bandaged my arm. I had no other injuries, although they said they were waiting for someone to read my x-rays before being sure.

Eli came around one side of the stretcher while Cooper took the other.

"Jeez, you okay?" Eli clutched my hand, his face lined with more concern than when I'd fallen off his skateboard when we were kids. Leave it to me to take on the steepest hill my first time out.

Cooper leaned over and kissed me. I savored his hands on my shoulders and his warm concern. He tasted sweet enough to cure whatever was wrong with me. If anything was wrong with me.

"I feel stupid for bothering you guys," I said.

Cooper brushed aside my words with a sweep of his hand. "Eli's call scared the shit out of me," he said. As if kissing my lips wasn't enough, he added another to my cheek. Being close to him made my heart sing. "Tell me what happened."

"I was walking into town to leave my dead laptop at the computer store. I think it has a virus." I scowled at Eli. "Don't remind me. I should've bought a Mac." With a sigh, I turned back to Cooper, who'd dragged a chair closer to sit. His thumb stroking the back of my hand was highly distracting. "I'll have to drop my laptop off some other time."

"Don't think about that right now." Anxiety lined his face.

"I can drop the laptop off for you later," Eli said.

I'd started to explain further when the sheriff parted the curtains and slipped inside. He pulled a small notebook and pen from his pocket. While nibbling on the pen, he narrowed his eyes on me, perhaps trying to assess my injuries through the white sheet. "Well, Ms. Bradley. You've had a run of bad luck lately."

More than bad luck. Something horrible was going on, and I needed his help. "Yeah."

"The paramedics said a car almost hit you while you were walking into town?"

I told him everything. My head had cleared somewhat, but my brain remained groggy and my words came out in stuttering gasps.

"So, let me repeat this." The sheriff tapped his paper after I'd finished. "You were walking in the breakdown lane, going to the computer store. You bought a coffee at Mr. Joe's, drank it, and had reached that sharp turn before Main Street when you—"

"I heard a car." Thankfully, my tongue was working better. "It came right at me where I stood in the breakdown lane. It was going too fast."

His brows drew together. "Did it hit you? Is that why you fell?"

"I jumped backward, but I fell over the guardrail and rolled down the hill. I landed at the bottom of the ditch."

Cooper squeezed my hand. If only I could go home. Take him home with me, actually. Spend the rest of the day snuggling with him on the sofa.

"Ginny, you're damn lucky you're okay." Eli rubbed my arm, his fingertips careful to avoid my bandage. "I can't believe this. That—" His voice choked off.

I winced and squeezed his hand, horrified I was worrying him.

"Did you get the license plate number?" the sheriff asked.

"No. But the car was black. A sedan."

"I see." He wrote again. "How about the driver's face? Could you see them through the windshield? Would you be able to describe them?"

"The windows were tinted."

"The front windows, too?" He scowled. "Not quite legal, but people are known to do that." His eyes narrowed on my face. "This sounds premeditated. Any reason to think someone's out to harm you?"

I blinked. "I told you Tom threatened me."

"We spoke with him. He denies coming near you after you told him to stay away. We didn't just take his word for it, however," the sheriff added. "I've had my deputy keep an eye on him, but he's remained in his house the past few days. I don't think Tom's involved in this."

Thinking Zen was involved would be a huge stretch. Sure, he'd been pissed off when we broke up, which surprised me since he'd never put much effort into making our relationship work. Besides, he was in Istanbul. Or somewhere else. We'd lost touch after it ended.

Before I could speak, a nurse parted the curtain and gave us a benign smile. She approached the sheriff and whispered something in his ear. His gaze darted my way, and his nostrils flared. "Excuse me, folks. I'll be back in a minute." He followed the nurse out into the corridor.

"You're sure you feel all right?" Eli asked. "When the ambulance called, I didn't know what to do. I thought about calling Mom, telling her to cut her trip short. For all I knew, you were dying. Jeez, Ginny." He slumped into a chair and rested his chin on the stretcher rail. I stroked his head while he stared at me with red-rimmed eyes.

"The woman in the ambulance didn't tell you I was okay?" I said.

"You know how they are. They don't give out much information," he said. "I broke every speed record getting here." His eyes slid to Cooper. "Him, too."

Tears welled in my eyes. If only I could find a way to convince them I was all right. "I'm sorry you were scared for me."

"Hey, don't fret." Eli leaned forward and kissed my cheek. His chest lifted and fell. "I'm just glad you're not hurt badly. Nothing else matters."

I wiped my eyes with my sheet. "I don't understand. I keep trying to get the details straight, but they're foggy, like my brain's broken. I bought my iced coffee at Mr. Joe's." I frowned. "Funny. It tasted weird, but I thought that guy put cinnamon in it by accident. Anyway, I finished it, but I was sleepy which is strange when I'd just polished off a biggie coffee. My legs wouldn't work right…" Nothing had worked right.

Cooper leaned forward, his brows narrowing. "What do you mean your legs wouldn't work right?"

"I had a hard time walking. And I kept giggling. I feel so stupid. I—"

The sheriff entered the bay and stalled at the foot of the bed, saying nothing. His intense gaze made me squirm, but I'd done nothing wrong. The twist of disgust on his lips didn't reassure me. "Your drug tox screen shows benzos, Ms. Bradley."

I gulped. "What?"

"Your pharmacy says you have a prescription for Xanax."

"My doctor gave it to me to help me sleep." Anxiety spiking through me, I turned to Eli. "Right after I came back to Maine. You remember what a wreck I was. I thought it would help." I'd tried it once, but it made me incredibly loopy. Which was the point, but I hadn't liked the feeling. And the thought of knocking myself out—knowing I'd have no idea what was going on around me—had scared me worse than the thought of being tired all the time. I drilled the sheriff with my gaze. "I haven't taken any for months. The bottle is sitting in my bathroom closet."

"Here's what I think happened," the sheriff said shortly. He slid his thumb and fingers back and forth along his jawline, pinching at the tip. "You were nervous this morning, so you took some of your Xanax. Nothing wrong with that. It's your prescription, right? You walked into town, but benzos can make you sleepy. They can mess with your reaction time, your mind. You thought you saw a car driving toward you and stepped backward, only to fall over the rail."

"Wait a minute." I sat up and the sheet dropped to my waist, exposing my stained t-shirt. Thankfully, my brain no longer spun. "I might have benzos in my blood-stream, but I sure as hell didn't put them there. My coffee must've been drugged. You need to go out there and look for tire tracks—the vehicle squealed away after almost running me over. Find the vehicle and arrest the driver. And figure out who drugged me. This is all connected."

"I'm sorry, Ma'am." Color filling his face, the sheriff stared down to where he spun the brim of his hat. "My deputy went to the scene already. Sure, there are tire marks in the area, lots of them. If this vehicle laid rubber, they weren't the first. But we can't find a car based on tire marks. And as for drugging you, are you sure you didn't take your Xanax?"

Irritation spiked through me. "I didn't. Somebody tried

to harm me." The coffee. It had to be the coffee. And that man behind the counter who—

"I can't do much without a plate number. You don't even know if the driver was a man or a woman, let alone the make of the vehicle. Lots of black sedans around town."

"My coffee was drugged."

The sheriff blew air past his tight lips. "I plan to stop by Mr. Joe's and ask them a few questions, but I doubt they added Xanax to your coffee. Think about it. Why would they do something like that?" He leaned forward and patted my arm like a patronizing grandfather. "You've got to be careful with benzos, Ma'am. They're strong. They'll knock you on your as— err, behind, if you're not careful." He stuffed the paper and pen back inside his pocket, and his gaze pinned me in place. "Tell me, Ms. Bradley. Did you take your Xanax the day you saw the snake in the campground bathroom?"

My muscles tensed. "Of course not. Besides, the game warden was going out there today, wasn't she? What did she find?"

"She looked around."

"And?" Eli asked. Fists clenched and leaning on his toes, he looked poised to take the sheriff down to the linoleum tiles. Like that would go over well. He'd be hauled away in handcuffs and charged with assault. I grabbed the back of his shirt before he acted on impulse.

Cooper, his brow pinched, flicked his gaze back and forth between me and the sheriff. I couldn't fathom what he thought about all this.

"The warden found nothing." The sheriff turned to leave the room but paused with his hand on the curtain. "There was no snake in the bathroom when she unnailed that door. Now, I have to wonder if you just imagined it."

My throat closed up tight. He didn't believe me. Maybe no one believed me. Cringing, I looked at Cooper. "You heard the snake, too."

Cooper stood. "I distinctly heard a rattle when I opened the door."

"It's been locked up since I was out there," Sheriff Moyer said. "The room's rustic, but there are no holes in the floor. If there'd been a snake in there, we would've found it. One thing I did notice was some dead leaves caught in the screen. Whenever the wind blew, they rattled. I think that's what you both heard." He shook his head, and I could tell he was dismissing this already. Dismissing me. My belly clenched into a knot. "Count your Xanax and call me if you find some missing." After smacking his hat back on his head, he strode from the room.

Why wouldn't he believe me?

Eli slumped in his chair. His gaze skimmed my face but, he didn't meet my eye.

My chest ached. "You believe me, don't you?" If I lost his trust—no, his respect—it would crush me.

"I know you think you saw a snake. And a car coming at you today. And it's damn clear you fell into a ditch." Reaching out, he stroked my hair, smoothing it off my forehead. "But you've been under a lot of stress lately. Are you sure you didn't take any—"

"I didn't take any Xanax," I ground out. Looking at Cooper was not an option, because I was scared of what I'd read on his face. Did he doubt me, too?

I'd been drugged. I knew that for sure. And I hadn't drugged myself.

Not that I remembered, anyway. I collapsed onto the stretcher, my body shaking. I hadn't taken any, had I?

Shit. Questioning my actions suggested I was out of

control. Could I have taken a pill or two and forgotten? The sheriff said they screwed with the mind.

No. I was certain I hadn't taken any other than that one time. I'd look in the bottle when I got home.

"My memory *is* kind of shaky," I said, unsure why I was considering this could just be an accident. "The driver could've been distracted, riding in the breakdown lane without realizing it. Maybe texting on their cell phone. They might not have seen me."

"Is that what you think?" Cooper asked.

I shrugged because I hated pushing this, begging everyone to chase down possibly nonexistent leads. I *had* been drugged, but had the car been involved? That was unclear. If only my mind would work right, then—

A nurse parted the curtain, a sheath of papers in her hand. "Everything checks out okay, so we're releasing you."

Eli rose and leaned against the wall, his arms crossed on his chest.

The nurse explained I needed to go home, go to bed, take it easy for a few days, and then added, "You've got to be careful with benzos. If your body isn't used to them, they'll knock you for a loop."

Something *had* knocked me for a loop. I just needed to find out what and who'd given it to me. The car might be explained away as nothing, but I was not relenting about someone drugging me.

"I'll take you home," Eli said as the nurse left the room. "I can drop your laptop at the shop for repairs on my way back into town."

Cooper looked to me for confirmation, and I nodded. Part of me wanted to beg him to bring me home instead, but how could I ride with him right now? Eli obviously doubted me. If Cooper shared the same opinion, my brain was too scrambled to defend myself.

"Okay, then," Cooper said, rising. "I'll get back to my dad's place. Plenty of work waiting for me there." He leaned forward for a kiss.

"You'll still come for dinner tonight?" What if he said no? What if he suggested we end things now? I wouldn't blame him if he didn't want to be involved with a person the sheriff had essentially branded a drug abuser.

He whispered by my ear. "I can't wait to see you again. But let's make it tomorrow night instead. You need to go home, go to bed, get some rest. I wouldn't miss seeing you tomorrow for the world."

That reassured me.

Somewhat.

22

Cooper

The sheriff might think Ginny was taking benzos whenever the urge hit her, but I was far from convinced. I knew her. If she said she hadn't taken the medication prescribed for her, then she hadn't taken it.

Seeing her lying pale and defenseless on the stretcher had shredded me. The lost look she'd given me when I arrived…I'd wanted to scoop her up in my arms and take her someplace safe where no one could harm her. To think some creep had tried to hit her while she was walking into town. What the hell was going on?

I was determined to discover what happened. The thought of deploying overseas before this was settled was killing me.

She'd mentioned feeling dizzy after drinking the coffee from Mr. Joe's, so that was the first place I drove to the next morning. I pulled into the parking lot and strode inside.

A man with a gray goatee greeted me from behind the counter. "Morning. What can I get you today?"

"I don't want to buy anything, but do you have time for a few questions?" I glanced around, pinning each of the baristas with an intent gaze. A man with his back facing the counter slipped into the room behind this one, maybe going for supplies.

"I'm Joe, the owner." He placed his palms on the counter. "What can I help you with?"

I narrowed my gaze on him. "I have a friend who bought coffee here yesterday. She was injured after she left and ended up in the hospital."

"My word. I hope she's okay."

"She is, but that's not why I'm here. She said that after she drank the coffee she bought here, she was dizzy. Had a hard time moving her legs." Joe's face held nothing but neutrality, but I'd learned people were good at hiding. If Joe was involved in whatever happened to Ginny yesterday, I would see him prosecuted to the full extent of the law. "I think she was drugged."

Joe lurched backward, lifting his hands. "Slow down there, sir. You've got to be kidding me. We wouldn't do anything like that to our customers."

"Not you necessarily, but someone else who works here."

Affront filled Joe's face. "I screen all my employees well."

"I'm sure you do." I didn't like accusing him of deliberately harming Ginny. But one of the first things they'd taught me in the military was to vary your behavior. Never leave home at the same time. Never drive the same route. Don't turn any action a habit.

Ginny told me she got coffee daily at Mr. Joe's. If someone wanted to hurt her, doctoring her drink would be easy, because she'd established a routine, one Joe could've studied. I wasn't leaving here until I assured myself Mr. Joe's had played no role in harming Ginny.

"Who was this customer?" Joe asked.

"Ginny Bradley."

Joe's eyes widened. "Not our Ginny. She's a regular here, the sweetest gal." He blinked down at the counter, his lips curling. "Wait just a sec. I didn't make her coffee yesterday. Tom did."

"Tom?" This had to be a coincidence. Tom was a common name. It couldn't be the same guy.

"I hired him a few days ago. Great work experience; his references—"

"Where is he?" I growled. "I want to talk with him."

Joe glanced over my shoulder. "Now, that's weird. He was just here. Tom? Tom!" Joe barged through the doorway into the room beyond but returned alone. "He's gone." He scratched the back of his neck. "I don't get it. Crew out back said he rushed past them and out the door. Didn't say where he was going or when he'd be back. I looked in the lot, but his vehicle's gone, too."

"Out of curiosity, what kind of car does he drive?"

Joe narrowed his brow. "Black Toyota Hyundai. With heavily tinted windows. You know how these young fellas are. Feel like they need to hide from the world."

Tom would not hide from me. These coincidences were adding up, and they all pointed to Tom Prescott.

"Thing is," Joe stroked his beard. "Tom would never do anything like what you're suggesting. He's a decent guy. From what he told me, he's had a hard time of it. Lost his wife, his job with the police department. He deserves a chance. But if he takes off like this, well, he might not have a job at Mr. Joe's any longer. The point is, what's his motive for drugging Ginny's coffee? He'd only wind up in jail. As a former cop, he knows the law."

Revenge came to mind immediately. Creeps became stalkers for fewer reasons than a simple rejection. Not that I'd share this information with Joe. I *would* share it with the sheriff, however. It was time the local law enforcement took Ginny seriously. Tom was playing a game with her, and I wouldn't let go of this until justice was served.

"Thank you for the information, Joe," I said. "I appreciate it."

"Anytime." I'd started to turn when Joe called out, "You tell Ginny I'm thinking about her; hoping she feels better. Tell her to come by again for coffee real soon—on the house. And when I see Tom, I'll have some tough questions for him."

I was willing to bet Tom wouldn't return to work. He'd achieved what he'd set out to do. Now I only had to figure out his final goal.

Because it wasn't just drugging Ginny.

———

SINCE I'D BROUGHT limited clothing with me, I needed to hit the laundromat. I dropped my clean things off in my room at the motel after and decided to drive out to the base to see Flint. My father's place could wait. Forever, if I had any say in it. I didn't have it in me to go back there yet.

Parking in front of Bravo Company, I went inside and walked up to the quarterdeck.

An E3 on watch at the podium looked up. "Help you?"

"I'm Chief Talon, here to see Senior Chief Crawford."

Her brow narrowed, and her professional gaze flicked down my front, assessing. "Can I see an ID, sir?"

I pulled my wallet and handed the card over.

She scrutinized it and gave it back. "One moment." Lifting the phone, she dialed and spoke to someone before hanging up. "He'll be out in a moment, sir." After giving me a level stare, she entered my name into the log and returned to the sheath of papers she'd been studying on the podium.

I strolled over to the door to stare outside while I waited. Cars streamed by on the road beyond the main lot. Three men dressed in camo walked past on the sidewalk, their strides stiff and purposeful.

"Chief?"

I turned to find Flint standing in the open doorway leading to a hallway. He waved. "Come on back."

I followed him down the hall. Inside his office, Flint shut the door and sat in the chair behind the desk, while I dropped onto the one in front.

"Glad you took me up on my offer to stop by," Flint said. He gathered some papers and set them on top of the stack on the side of his desk. "It was great running into you the other day. It's been a few years since we last hung out, hasn't it?"

"Eighteen months." I explained why I was in town.

"I'm really sorry about your father."

"Thanks."

Flint leaned back in his chair and stretched, clasping his hands behind his neck. "Hey, remember that time when we were on leave in Gulfport and we went out to eat at that shack? We drank gallons of beer and chowed through buckets of bugs."

Crawfish cooked in spicy sauce. My mouth watered at the memory. Damn, but they'd been good. Nothing compared to authentic Cajun food.

"After, we went to the casino and had a blast with those slot machines. Damned things were rigged, though, because I couldn't even break even with nickels."

Outside of cribbage, I couldn't win with any game.

We laughed and talked about times we'd shared both stateside and overseas then moved on to when we'd been stationed together in California. A few years ago, Flint had been one of my best friends. Shipping out as often as we did made it hard to keep up with everyone. Something I needed to remember with Ginny.

"You know, it's great seeing you again," Flint said. "But I didn't ask you to stop by just to shoot the shit. I wanted to tell you what I've been up to lately and see if it's something you want to be a part of." He lifted a pencil off the desk and flipped it end-over-end, studying the movement. "You know I'm out other than the Reserves."

I scratched my jaw. "I was surprised you quit. You've got twelve years in already." No one dropped out at this stage in their career. Who wanted to trade eight short years and a steady retirement income for the uncertainty of civilian life?

"I'll get my time in this way." He flicked his hand at his desk.

Leaning on my chair arm, I studied his face. Like whenever we played poker, it gave nothing away. "Tell me about the…recreational drones."

Flint chuckled. "Saw through that, did you?" He leaned forward, eager. "Nothing beats blowing things up for a living."

I did love C-4.

"My new business will offer something no one else can."

"In particular?"

"Think MacGyver meets James Bond, without the clichés. We'll still work for the government but on the civilian side. Testing new weapons, drones, whatever they throw my way."

"R & D, huh?" How cool that must be.

"Thought you might want in, too," Flint said. "There isn't anyone I'd trust more than you. Or Eli for that matter. I intend to give him a call, see if he's interested."

"I believe he will be." Eli had griped about his security job. It paid a decent wage but providing guard duty at a hardware store wasn't anything close to what Flint was offering. "He's working all kinds of hours lately. They're short-staffed after one of the guys got hurt."

"I'll text him. Tell him to stop by when things are settled."

Eli would be all over this. As for me…I couldn't say. The idea was tempting but it would mean leaving the service, something I wasn't prepared to consider.

"So, just military testing?" I asked.

"Protection of personnel and assets, as well." Flint shrugged. "We'll provide the same services as the government or police, but on a smaller scale."

"Like babysitting visiting dignitaries?"

"Not quite." He chuckled. "And mostly overseas. We took martial arts classes together in Port Hueneme. I imagine you've kept at it like I have. And we trained with the Marines in close quarters combat while we were stationed in North Carolina. Our skills will only be enhanced by this job." He chuckled. "Fuck, I'll be a happy man if no one asks me to crawl a mile through swampland ever again."

If Flint's memory of those days at Camp Lejeune were the same as mine, he was filled with a mix of shit-I-can't-believe-they-made-us-do-that and admiration for the skills those tough Marines displayed.

Flint steepled his fingers under his chin. "I'm transferring that training into civilian life. It's a chance to get out from underneath the government's beck and call. I choose what I do and where I go, now."

This wasn't a bad idea, really. A soldier, especially a Seabee, worked closely with the Marines. In addition to the construction aspects, he needed to train not only in multiple weapons but in defensive and offensive maneuvers. Transitioning those skills to the private sector could be turned into a decent career.

"You want in on this?" Flint asked. "I've got a few people lined up already but I know you'll fit in with my crew. Hell, if you've got some money to throw in, you might be interested in joining me as a full partner. I bought a building, top of the line equipment. Contracts are rolling in already due to Commander Rhodes."

Our former C.O.

"Sid's around?"

"Retired but he's still got his fingers in all the pies. Since I hired his daughter, Becca, he's eager to see me succeed."

I'd saved most of my wages over the past twelve years. Housing and meals were provided on the base. Chow hall food wasn't top cuisine, but I wasn't picky. There wasn't much to spend my money on, since I wasn't into flashy cars or vacations.

If I was closer to retirement, this offer would be beyond tempting. But my need to finish something, to give my twenty years, had driven me since I left Crescent Cove after graduation. How could I consider bailing on that goal now?

"I'm deploying soon," I said. "Middle East."

"You'll be back."

"Not for three months." I clenched my hands on the arms of my chair. The urge to say yes battled with the need I'd lived with for twelve years. I had to stay in. Not just to prove to my father that I had the guts, but to prove something to myself.

Flint's phone rang. "Excuse me a sec." He lifted the receiver. "Master Chief?" Listening, he nodded. "Okay, sure. Be right there." As he hung up, his green eyes met mine. "I've got to go help a few new guys out with Seahuts. They're doing an exercise this week and can't figure out how to put the damn things together."

I stood. With limited time, I needed to get back to my father's place, even if the urge to drive there still hadn't returned. I extended my hand across the desk and we shook. "It was great seeing you."

"You, too. And, about joining me in my new business? You don't need to decide right now. My offer's open indefinitely."

This idea didn't fit into my life plan. Except, it would bring me closer to Ginny. Maybe I *should* think seriously about Flint's offer. If I could wrap my mind around the thought of quitting.

Flint walked outside with me. "I'm this way." He gestured in the opposite direction of the parking lot. "You've got my number. Call me anytime."

"Will do."

After a friendly smack on my shoulder, Flint strode away.

Studying the ground—my thoughts ricocheting around with the possibility Flint had presented—I walked to my car. I sat in the hot vehicle for a long while, wondering what I should do but came to no decision. Shoving aside Flint's offer for now, I drove into town. The second floor of my father's place awaited me.

Before I went inside Dad's place, I called Ginny. "Hey, how are you feeling?"

"Okay. Tired and a little sore."

"I was thinking." This might be pushing things but it ate me alive every time I thought about how vulnerable she was. "Why don't you stay with me at my hotel?" Where I could watch out for her. Protect her.

"That's a generous offer."

More than an offer. I wished I owned a place where I could hide her inside. Then, no one could harm her. Like a fortress with state-of-the-art protection. High walls. Around-the-clock security guards.

Ginny continued, "I just put in the best security system money can buy."

Even if she stayed at my hotel, I'd be away all day. She'd be alone with only a flimsy door separating her from Tom. I sighed, realizing she might actually be safer locked behind her new security system. "Okay." No reason I couldn't check out what she'd had installed and make sure it met my standards.

"I appreciate it, though." Her soft words broke through my worry.

"I'd do had thrown a ton you safe."

"I know you would."

After we ended the call, I sighed. Nothing would make me happier than seeing this situation settled. I needed to be confident that no one would threaten Ginny again. Frustration surged through me, because there wasn't anything I could do. I'd have to trust she was safe inside her apartment.

And I really needed to finish cleaning out my father's place, or I'd have to hire someone to do it for me. I was determined to close the door on this part of my life before I left.

I sat on the front step and ate a sandwich, washing it down with bottled water. Because I couldn't resist, I pulled my phone and sent Ginny a text, *Hey. Miss you already.*

<3 *Miss you, too.*

Hell, if I was at her apartment, I'd show her how much I missed her. And then start all over again. *Everything still going okay?* The most delicate way I could think of asking if she was safe. If only I could keep her securely inside my arms 24/7.

I just finished taking some dog photos. That pup was so cute!

I loved dogs, too. *Are you a little or a big dog person?*

Can I say both?

A tiny dog and a really big dog at the same time would be a fun mix. I'd always wanted to get one, but deployments weren't fair to a pet. A few friends might be willing to take the animal for a week or two but otherwise, I'd have to board it. Cats were more independent, but they still needed love and care.

I could get Ginny a dog, though, something big and protective. Or a small, alert dog for her to cuddle. Or both. Maybe we could go to the shelter together and pick a few dogs out. A pack that would take down an intruder.

Oh! I've got to go, she texted. *My next client is here for pictures.*

I thought you were taking the day off?

I couldn't reschedule this one. But it won't take long. I promise to lie down after.

I wasn't sure how far I dared take this. I had no right to tell her what to do. But my insides were a mess. *I worry about you all the time.*

A moment went by, and I wished I could see her face so I'd know what she was thinking. Damn, hopefully I hadn't offended her.

Thank you.

I could almost hear the sigh in her words. It wrapped around me like a soft blanket. *I'll see you soon?* I texted.

It's never too soon.

That stilled my heart.

I smiled, happier than I'd felt for a long time. And even though I wanted to race over to Ginny's place and show her how she made me feel, she was busy. Hell, I should get busy, too.

After putting away my phone, I entered the house. Echoes of happier times chased me across the worn living room carpet, up the front stairs, and into my old bedroom on the right off the landing. Had my father been inside this room since I left? The dusty bureau and spider webs draped across the ceiling suggested he hadn't.

Taking one of the empty boxes, I began the task of dismantling my boyhood. The old clothing in the closet and bureau went first; none of it worth more than rags. Piles of marked-up school work, notebooks filled with scribbles, and a few antique textbooks were loaded into the second and third boxes.

I ripped my dusty old bedding off my twin bed, stuffed it into a garbage bag, and tossed it down the stairs. My teddy bear, fur gone in places and missing one button eye, was thrown in with the school rubble along with a few CDs I'd never listen to again. Board games. Puzzles. All piles of useless junk, not a bit of it worth shipping home to California.

The late-day sunlight filtering through the window sparkled on something, snagging my attention. I stomped across the room and stood over the mess.

Ahh. *This* sliced through my belly. But I rubbed where it pinched most, my chest.

The glass menagerie Mom had helped me collect through my childhood lay in fragments on the floor between the bureau and the radiator.

Her warm smile when she presented me with another figurine for my birthday crept across my soul. The first—a solemn basset hound—when I'd turned three. For my seventh birthday, she'd given me a lion, its head tilted back, its mane flowing along its neck. A gangly, spotted giraffe for my tenth. At twelve—and longing to *finally* be considered a man—I'd cringed when she'd given me the pony.

With a soft groan, I collapsed to my knees. I brushed at the scattered pieces. There wasn't enough glue in the world to put them back together again.

Where was my phoenix?

My fingers traced the tattoo inspired by the figurine.

A few days after Mom's funeral, I'd found the wrapped box resting on her bureau where her own hands had placed it. A card taped to the top opened to a free-hand drawn heart, my name, and hers.

My thirteenth birthday fell the day after that car swerved into her lane and took her. I'd barely drummed up the nerve to tell her I was too old to collect glass animals anymore.

After the accident, I no longer had to.

The bright yellow shard I lifted wasn't quite right for the phoenix's tail. Maybe it came from that canary she'd given me when I turned four. None of the orange or red pieces lying among the blues, browns, and grays looked like they belonged to that thirteenth birthday gift, either.

No phoenix.

A quick glance around the room told me the truth. It was gone. Like Mom.

How had my collection gotten broken? Had the cat slipped in here and knocked it onto the floor? Or, had Dad, in a drunken haze…No. I refused to go there. Closing this chapter of my life was my sole purpose here. No need to open the book and start reading all over again.

I thumped down the stairs and fetched the dustpan and

brush from the kitchen. Then I took care of the mess, dumping it into another box bound for the trash.

My old fishing pole tilted in the corner, faithful tackle box by its side, both untouched for more than half my life. Long ago—before Mom died—we'd gone fishing most weekends, the three of us piling into Dad's canoe after launching it into whatever lake or river was handy. We'd drifted across the water, our paddles dipping in rhythm, stopping to eat PB&J sandwiches in the shade. After, we'd throw out our lines to catch trout. Striper. Sometimes salmon. Mom would fool with our hair with pride gleaming in her eyes. When we got home, she'd cook our catch for dinner.

I stared at the rod, knowing that I wasn't going to mail it to California.

But I wanted to.

Overriding that directive, I carried it downstairs, out the front door, and chucked it into the dumpster. I turned my back on it before I weakened and drove downtown to buy packing material for shipping.

Back upstairs, I boxed up my old books to donate to the library. I'd already arranged for the Salvation Army to come for the usable furniture. I dismantled my bed and hauled it and the bureau down to the garage, placing them with the other things stored there. That left a rickety lamp and side table in my room. Not much value in those.

Hefting the table, I'd pivoted to haul it downstairs when my eyes caught the writing on the back. I set it on the carpet and stared, remembering the day when I'd carved my initials and Ginny's inside a heart on the back. I'd only known her a few months. I'd been overconfident, obviously.

Stooped down on my heels, I traced those letters. And, with a sigh, I carried the side table down to the dumpster.

Before tossing it inside, I pulled open the drawer to make sure I hadn't missed anything important. A pack of gum. A long-dead calculator. Multiple chewed-on pencils, a habit I'd shaken in boot camp.

And, stuffed way in the back, *the picture*. I'd forgotten I'd snitched Ginny's photo from her mom's house all those years ago.

Her thick blonde hair hung half in her face, scattered there by the wind. But her big brown eyes gleamed as she smiled for the camera.

All sweetness and innocence and totally not for me.

The guilt brought on from stealing it had eaten away at me for months. I told myself it was okay; it was just one old photograph. Not something her mom would miss. That the albums lying around her house held more images of Ginny than her mom would ever need.

While I only had one.

I stroked her face with my thumb, remembering how desperately I'd longed for this girl. Still longed for her.

I pulled out my wallet and tucked the picture inside.

Hours later, I'd finished my room and the upstairs bath. The basement still awaited me and would likely take more than a day to clean since Dad had thrown a ton of junk down there. After that, I only had one room left to work on before I could call an end to this farce. I'd clean out my father's bedroom—that final, straggling piece of my past—at the end. My flight home was booked for early Sunday morning.

After locking the front door and pocketing the key, I drove to my hotel where I showered and dressed. After, I headed to Ginny's place for supper.

Damn, I missed her. It felt like a lifetime had passed since I'd last seen her. Touched her.

Even though it was still eighty outside, I turned off the

AC and lowered the windows. Fresh air cut through the car, slicing through the cobwebs from my past.

All I wanted to do tonight was bask in Ginny's glow.

With her new security system in place, and me there beside her, nothing could get to her now.

23

Ginny

I couldn't imagine why my pulse hammered in my throat or why my breathing was ragged. I'd done nothing but putter around my house for hours.

Cooper.

It wasn't as if I hadn't cooked a meal for a man before. Even this man. Why had I vacuumed and changed my sheets? Did I truly believe his presence tonight meant…something?

There was no harm in making the place look decent. After he'd seen the wreck I was in yesterday, I wanted to make a decent impression. That was all this was about.

Silverware and plates sat on the table. Cheese and crackers waited on the hutch near the sofa. I'd sliced up a loaf of crusty bread and loaded it into a basket. Butter sweated on a pretty plate beside it. The marinara sauce I'd made this afternoon steamed on the back burner, and hints of oregano, basil, and tomatoes swirled in the air.

I drained the pasta a few minutes before six and not a second too soon, because the doorbell rang. With my usual caution, I peered around the curtain.

The tightness in my chest told me how much I'd missed him. I smoothed my hair, placed a welcoming smile on my face, and unlocked and opened the door.

With a crooked grin, he thrust out flowers that looked suspiciously like ones I'd seen growing on the side of the road. He held up two bottles of wine in his other hand. "Wasn't sure if you liked red or white or either."

"Either, but red will go perfectly with dinner."

He shuffled his sneakers on the welcome mat. The light scent of shampoo drifting between us told me he'd showered recently. I wanted to tug up his dark green tee so I could taste his skin with my fingertips.

My intentions must've been obvious, because his lips lifted and his pupils dilated. He cleared his throat. "Some people believe life's unbalanced unless things come in threes."

I juggled the bottles and bouquet in my arms while he shut and locked the door. "Flowers. Two bottles of wine. That's three."

He took the flowers and wine from me and dropped them on the counter, and then nudged me backward until my butt pressed against the wall. His palms captured my face. "This is three."

And four, five, ten, and a thousand. I deepened our kiss and put my hands to good use on his shoulders, his neck, his back, and his butt. Pulling him into me while teasing his tongue with mine.

He lifted his head, and his eyes glowed. Mine probably did, too. "Nice seeing you tonight, sweetheart."

"You, too." Damn, but my head was whirling again.

He sniffed the air. "Something smells good."

"Spaghetti."

"Sounds awesome." Releasing me, he glanced around, taking in my home. "Nice place."

"Thank you." While I'd joked about Cooper being my only fan, I'd done well with the photographs I'd taken during my travels. Who would've thought journals filled with folksy posts and colorful pictures could sell for so much money? Even after I'd donated to orphanages and women's organizations, I still had enough tucked away for my future. Sure, I had a mortgage, but the payments were low. Living above my business was the best. No drive to work, and I could scoot downstairs whenever the urge to process film hit me.

"Have a seat." I waved toward the living room. "Do you want wine or iced tea?"

"Tea sounds great." He settled on the couch.

"Lemon or lime?"

"Lime?"

"It tastes good that way."

"Lime it is then." He thumbed through a magazine while I bustled into the galley kitchen. Joining him in the living room a moment later, I dropped our glasses onto coasters and brought the cheese and crackers over from the hutch.

For whatever reason, my excitement had fled, driven aside by sweaty palms and an urge to gnaw on my lower lip —something I hadn't done in years.

I wanted him here. All night, if he'd stay. But I didn't want to cling or say something awkward that might drive him away. The rules for our relationship had been set in stone. It just hurt, because the wall on my side was sharp and cut deeply. While I wanted to make each second with him special, I couldn't stop focusing on when I'd have to say goodbye.

Leaned into his side, I peered at the magazine over his shoulder until he closed it and pushed it away.

He turned to face me. "What did you do today?"

"Oh, this and that. I tried to lounge around like the nurse told me to, but I like keeping busy." Actually, I'd spent a lot of time dwelling on him. On us. On how there would never be a us. I'd started to mourn his loss already.

"I get that." He stroked my arm and ran his gaze down my front as if assessing for wounds. Even though they still smarted, he wouldn't find them. They lurked inside me, hidden away from the world. "How are you feeling? Better?"

"Much." My face overheating, I darted my eyes away. "After the drugs wore off, that is."

"No injuries other than your arm?"

I shrugged. "My right knee was stiff this morning, but I stretched and that helped." Could we let this go? He was leaving in a few days. Spending our precious time together talking about what happened yesterday was the last thing I wanted to do. Hell, I was embarrassed about the whole thing. "How about you? How have things gone at your dad's place? I know you've been busy."

"Yep." He lifted his tea and took a long swallow. "I like the lime."

My smile rose as thanks for the comment, but it fell short when I thought about all the work that must still wait for him at his father's home. "Do you want help? I have free time this week." I picked up my glass and sipped. "I could come over tomorrow afternoon. I'm also free Friday. I have a sunset wedding booked for Sunday, but that's it for the week."

"Tell you what," he said. "What time are you free tomorrow?"

"After two."

"Instead of working on my dad's place, let's do something together."

"What do you have in mind?"

He glanced toward my back yard. "How about we take advantage of that big lawn and play croquet?"

A game a grannie might be familiar with, but not me. "Umm…"

His gaze narrowed, but his eyes twinkled. "Your card luck doesn't extend to lawn games?"

"I toss a decent bean bag, and I've played badminton once or twice."

His grin widened. "Then you're sayin' I might stand a chance at whooping your ass at croquet."

I curled my lips. "You already whooped my ass at cribbage." A fact he'd mentioned more than once already.

"Made you whimper, didn't I?"

In so many ways.

"I think I can stand a little croquet whooping." Or any other kind of whooping that might come along with it.

The heated message my hormones were putting out must've transmitted to Cooper, because he took my iced tea from my hand and lowered it onto the table.

"Ginny," he said, his voice gone husky.

"Cooper."

"Anything on the stove we need to worry about?"

"I shut everything off before you arrived."

"I love how efficient you are." Leaning forward, he kissed me, his lips tasting of lime.

I moaned and wrapped my arms around him, giving in to the response he pulled from me every time he touched me. I wore a simple white top and a striped cotton skirt over bare legs. He stroked my thighs, his fingertips inching up underneath my skirt. Higher. Higher. While I ground my mouth against his and nearly shredded his shirt to reach skin. This man wore too much clothing. All the time.

His fingers stilled and he leaned back and panted,

staring down at me with widening eyes. "Aw, hell. You're gonna kill me."

He'd discovered I wore no panties.

"Scooch your hips forward and lay back on the cushions, sweetheart."

I pointed. "My bedroom's down the hall."

"No time."

My laugh burst out. "More hard and fast on the agenda?"

Growling, he tugged my hips forward and flipped up my skirt. "You are so going to get it."

I could only hope.

His head lowered. He parted my thighs and tasted me, his tongue soft and scratchy and twirling all together. Desire flooded my limbs as his tongue dipped inside.

I trembled and tried to keep from lifting my legs, pulling his head closer, and jutting my hips up at him. When he thrust his finger into me, while his tongue kept moving, we both groaned.

He looked up at me from where he'd crawled between my legs. "You don't mind if I spend a little time here, do you?"

My heart skipped, and my breath choked off. I couldn't say a damned thing, because he'd rendered me speechless.

Some sound must've slipped from between my lips because he nodded. "I'll take that as a yes."

He sucked, drawing that crest of me inside his warm mouth. While I writhed and thrashed my head on the cushions, he loved me with his fingers and his tongue. I'd reached for the peak when he stalled. His head lifted, and he patted my thigh. "I think it's time we slowed this down, don't you?"

No way. I was ready to speed things up, actually. Speechless still, I quivered.

He shifted back, leaving me splayed out before him. Once standing, he extended his hand. I took it, and he pulled me onto my feet. For as long as that lasted, because he swept me up into his arms.

"Bedroom," he said.

I waved, the only action I was capable of performing.

With firm strides, he carried me down the hall where he lowered me onto my bedspread. He climbed over me and braced himself with his arms. Need pinched his face. "I want you."

"You already have me."

ONCE I WAS confident my legs could support me, I padded naked out into the kitchen and turned on the burner underneath the spaghetti sauce.

The pasta lay in a glob in the strainer, but I might be able to salvage it by cutting it into chunks. Some would suggest this was a ruined meal, yet I wasn't complaining.

When hands settled on my hips from behind, I jumped and let out a squeak.

"Shit. I'm sorry," Cooper said.

He'd crept up on me, only betraying his presence when he touched me.

He wrapped me up as if he could cocoon me in his reassurance, but the sliver of a frightened girl inside me only curled tighter.

I hated this. Hated that fear ruled my life.

He kissed me, stroked my hair, and stared into my eyes —his heavy with sadness.

Embarrassed by my reaction, I pulled out of his embrace and turned away. "I'm sorry. I shouldn't have behaved like that. I…" The lump in my throat wouldn't go down, no matter how hard I swallowed. Why couldn't I let this go? The last thing I wanted was to give Cooper the impression I feared him when he had my complete trust.

"I'm the one who messed this up," he said. "I should've—"

I placed my fingertip on his lips and shook my head. "It's okay. Really."

We dressed and returned to the kitchen. Cooper leaned against the counter and watched me while I finished getting dinner ready.

I'd thrown a bucket of water onto our sexy moment and needed to fix things fast.

"Why don't we eat on the deck?" I said. If nothing else, it would be warmer out there. Eyes stinging, I kept my focus on arranging the food on our plates.

With a soft sigh, he tilted my chin and studied my face. "I'll be more careful from now on."

I nodded, unable to speak. I didn't want him accommodating me. I wanted to be free of my screwed-up past.

He released me and lifted the corkscrew I'd set out earlier. "Wine?"

Accepting his welcome distraction, I made busy at the stove. "Love some."

He took glasses and place settings out onto the deck while I hacked up the pasta and settled lumps on each plate. I spooned marinara sauce over the top. Our dinner looked oddly volcanic, but it would taste fine.

He whistled through his teeth as he approached, giving me fair warning. Coming up behind me, he paused and kissed my neck, wrapping his arms around me from behind. "Spaghetti's one of my favorite meals. It smells fantastic."

We took our food out onto the deck and sat across from each other.

Making an effort to ditch my embarrassment, I laughed as I stared down at my spaghetti mountain. "Jeez, I'm sorry. I'm not usually this bad a cook."

"The sauce is excellent," he said around a big bite.

"We won't discuss the pasta."

"Hey, I'm enjoying my I-got-to-drag-Ginny-off-to-bed pasta. It's a meal I'd be happy to savor any night."

The sparks zipping around in my belly told me I'd be glad to share lumpy pasta with him most any night, too.

We finished and loaded the dishwasher. Returning to the deck, we collapsed on chaise lounges and finished the bottle of wine.

I caught movement beyond the rail and sat forward, scowling. "There they go again." As I jumped and flapped my arms in the air, Cooper's eyes widened. "My turkey neighbors have come for dessert," I said. Like that explained things.

Frowning, he squinted through the railing. "Wow."

"Impressive, aren't they?" Below, multiple turkey parents herded numerous half-grown chicks—a generous term on any day for these butterballs—across the lawn. The turkeys trailed across the grass, pausing to snatch up bugs. "Only one problem. They keep eating my strawberries." I leaned over the railing, shouting and waving my arms. "Go!"

Like I'd fired buckshot into the air, the beasts let out squawks. Wings flapping, they scattered back into the woods.

Cooper chuckled. "You sure scared them."

"For all of twenty minutes. I picked berries today but those beasts'll clean me out of the rest if I let them."

He came over to stand with me, moving his feet on the wooden decking in a way I couldn't miss. I doubted the turkeys would miss him coming. I cringed, realizing I'd brought this between us. No, my fear had brought this between us.

"Did you mention strawberries?" The glint in his eyes banished my irritation somewhat.

My pulse fluttered in my throat, and my breathing stalled. "For later."

"Squirt whipped cream, too?"

"Yes." The word lasted twice as long as it needed to. Was he thinking what I was thinking?

"Why don't you get them, and we can share dessert."

Anticipation pooled in my belly.

I wasn't gone more than a minute but when I returned to the deck, he sat on the deck, reclining on a mound of pillows.

Cooper Talon wore buck-naked well.

He patted a place beside him. "I think berries with whipped cream is about to become my favorite dish outside of lumpy pasta."

THE NEXT MORNING, I encouraged him to join me in the shower. After, we enjoyed breakfast on the deck, laughing about the sticky spots on the boards. I would hose the wood later, but for now, I cupped the memories those spots contained and pressed them like summer flowers inside my heart.

Cooper's face grew serious. "I went by Mr. Joe's yesterday. Questioned him about your drink."

"What did you find out?"

His finger circled around the rim of his coffee cup. "Joe was upset."

"He's a nice guy. And he didn't make my drink."

"You remember that, huh?"

"A different guy made it. His back faced me, and I couldn't see who he was."

"The man's name was Tom. Lots of Toms around, but this feels beyond a coincidence."

I shook my head. "Tom Prescott made my drink?" The man had looked familiar, but the scruffy beard and back made it hard to identify him. Rising, I stomped across the deck. "That asshole drugged me." I halted and held up my hand. "Hold on a sec."

I ran inside and retrieved the bottle of Xanax from the bathroom closet. Pills clicked as I strode back to Cooper. I sat and shook the bottle then placed it on the table between us. "This is the Xanax my doctor prescribed me. Nine pills left because I only took one." I flapped my hand at the bottle. "Go ahead and open it. Count them."

"Don't need to." His quiet reassurance slowed my racing pulse, but the certainty in his eyes squeezed my heart. That he believed me meant everything.

"Thank you," I said. "Why do you think Tom did it?"

Cooper shrugged. "Who can say? Revenge, probably. Or maybe he hoped to follow and take advantage of you."

"Instead, he almost ran me down." I snaked my arms across my chest and shivered. "Why won't the sheriff believe me and do something about this?"

"I called him, let him know what I discovered."

"What did he say?"

"That he'd question Tom, get back to me." Leaning back, he snorted. "Then he chastised me for doing my own investigation."

"If he'd do his job, you wouldn't have to do it for him."

Cooper rose and pulled me up from my chair. With his arms wrapped around me, all was right in the world. What was I going to do once he was gone? Not just about Tom— although I was determined to keep him from taking advantage of me again. But losing Cooper would be worse than anything that had happened to me over the past week.

He eased back in my embrace and kissed me. "I wish I could stay with you all day, but I've got lots to do, starting with Dad's basement. I want to get it done so I can come back to you this afternoon."

If only he could come back to me every day. But that daydream was as real as unicorns. I clutched the front of his tee, the only tangible thing I could hold onto. "I can still help at your dad's place if you want."

"You have your own work here. I'll be back with the croquet set later." I followed him to the front door where he paused with his hand on the doorknob. "Let me make dinner tonight?"

That should be interesting. "As long as it's not red hot dogs."

He turned and leaned against the door, splaying his arms wide. "Hey. I'm a decent cook."

I couldn't resist taking the space between his arms. Like I'd planned, he wrapped me up and pulled me near. Kissed me.

"Far be it for me to suggest a man not show off his cooking skills," I said.

"I think you'll be pleased."

"I'm already pleased."

"Then my job here is done."

Eli parked in my drive as Cooper backed out in his rental. The two men spoke before Cooper continued toward town. Eli stared after his friend then climbed the stairs and came inside. I engaged my new security system behind him, smiling at how confident I felt now that it was installed.

"Good to see you," I said.

"Wanted to stop by and make sure you were okay after yesterday."

After filling two cups with coffee and adding a splash of milk, I lowered them onto the kitchen island, and we sat.

He sipped his coffee but then plunked the mug on the tile hard enough the creamy brew slopped over the lip. If he kept after his hair with his fingers that way, he'd have knots. "I really don't like thinking about you and Coop doing…"

"Jeez, Eli. I'm not thirteen." A la Scarlett O'Hara, I slapped my palm to my chest. "You do know I'm not saving myself for marriage." My eyes flashed fire at him. "I know you didn't come over here to defend my non-existent virginity."

His groan filled the room.

Payback was sweet. Sometimes, I just had to wait for it. He was lucky I didn't remind him of that time he'd snuck his high school girlfriend into his bedroom after Mom went to bed.

"I came over here because you're female," he said.

"I think we already established that."

"I need advice."

"Mia."

His coffee mug received all of his attention. "Yeah, Mia." He breathed her name.

I couldn't even handle my own love life. How he thought I could help with his was beyond me.

"I thought you were going to look her up," I prompted.

"I plan to. Sometime."

My sigh bled out. "If she's here in town, I don't know why you're here with me, moaning and groaning about her."

Shoulders couldn't cave more than my poor brother's. "What if I ask her out again and she turns me down?"

"Then you'll know to move on."

"Yeah."

"You've got it bad," I said.

"From the moment I met her."

"You might get somewhere if you took this beyond thinking." I just wanted to see Eli happy. If Mia could do that for him, I'd welcome her with open arms. "Call her."

"Don't have her number."

"Then get it from Flint."

"She's his sister!"

"I'm yours and I'm seeing Cooper."

"It's not the same."

I lifted my eyebrows because he very well knew it was.

"I spoke with Flint. We're meeting up next week to talk about a job. He'd be my boss."

"You think that'll make Mia off-limits?"

"It could get sticky."

"Hardly matters if you don't get to the point of asking her out."

He lifted his coffee and took a long gulp. "That's why I'm here. Because I thought you'd know what I should do."

No way would I give him the keys to the woman castle.

"You think I should send her flowers?" he asked as he ruffled his hair some more.

"That would be a nice start. But..." I frowned, remembering the roses Tom sent, how they'd creeped me out. "Keep it simple. Don't come on too strong."

He stiffened as if I'd offended him. "I'm more than prepared to back off if she tells me to get lost. I just saw her being in town..."

"As a chance," I finished for him.

"Exactly." His lips quirked up on one side. "But I think she'll like flowers. A guy knows these things."

Heaven help womankind.

"Then go for it. Do it today."

"Today?" He reeled back in his chair. "So soon?"

"Jeez, Eli, it's been half a year. If you're lucky, she still remembers your name."

"Hell, do you think she's forgotten me?" He sounded horrified at the thought.

I sighed. If Mia was anything like me with Cooper, my brother was still foremost in her mind. "Sometimes, women do like a man to pursue them. You'll have to read the signs when you talk with her. Watch for…Oh, I don't know. Fluttering eyelashes, color in her cheeks, the way she holds her body. If she's leaning toward you or fully facing you, especially if her voice is breathy, you'll know she's interested." Curse me, but I *was* giving him the keys to the woman castle.

Sorry, womenkind.

"I *could* send her flowers," he said, perking up. "Once I, uh, find out where she is. I could ask Flint. Sound him out. If he hints I need to back off, I'll respect that."

"At this point, things can't get worse, can they?"

"Actually, they could." He slumped in his seat. Poor Eli. His heart scraped across the floor. "Before I do anything, though, I've got to drive to Allagash."

I blinked. "That's six-hours from here, isn't it? What do you have to do up there?"

"My old high school friend, Jefferson, called. I've been meaning to look him up now that I'm back in Crescent Cove. He asked if I could give him a ride. Said he was sorry, but he'd already asked everyone he could think of already. His mom's in the hospital in Portland. He lost his job a few months ago, and his vehicle isn't registered. I'll go up, spend the night, and we'll head out first thing in the morning. At least I'm off work until tomorrow afternoon."

Downstairs, my bell rang.

"That's a client." A reunion family had arrived. I stood and took our empty coffee cups to the sink. "I've got to go."

"So do I. It'll take me a while to get to Allagash."

"It's nice of you to do that for your friend on your one day off." Especially a friend he hadn't seen in a long time. I walked with Eli to the door and gave him a hug.

"We go way back. He'd do the same for me."

There was no favor Eli wouldn't give if someone asked. I swung open the door, and he stepped out onto the deck. "Let me know how the flower venture goes with Mia."

"I will." He paused in the doorway and turned back to smile. "Thanks. You're the best."

24

Cooper

A short distance down the road from Ginny's, I parked in the breakdown lane and pulled out my phone. Tom Prescott's address came up on my screen after a brief search. I put my car into gear and followed the GPS directions.

On the opposite side of the road from Tom's residence, I shut off the engine. I studied the light green ranch house, watching for movement. No car parked in the driveway, but it could be inside the garage.

My pulse spiked, and my clenched fists ground against my thighs. It was past time to get this situation settled.

Since none of Tom's neighbors appeared to be around —hopefully all at work—I got out and strode across the road like I belonged here. A quick scan told me no one peeked around curtains or stood on their porches staring my way. While I could get arrested for trespassing, I couldn't help it. This had to be done.

Heart galloping along with the danger riding inside me, I slid between the hedge on the side of Tom's property and his garage. On the other side of the vegetation, a dog barked wildly. Hopefully, the neighbor wasn't into pit bulls.

I paused by the garage's side window and squinted through the dusty glass panes. Empty inside except for a lawnmower and a bunch of junk. No Tom, no car.

At the back of the house, I darted along the crushed stones placed to catch runoff from the roof. I paused at a window to glance in. No lights on, and not a soul in the entryway connecting the house to the garage.

Tom was either somewhere else in the house or he was away. Out seeking another opportunity to get at Ginny? Not if I had anything to say about it. Frustration grew inside me, displacing the tingling unease I'd felt while snooping. If I ran into Tom right now, I'd drop him to the ground and call the police.

After donning thin gloves, I tested the door leading out onto a small back deck. Locked but that was okay. I scanned the fenced-in backyard again to make sure no one was looking my way before I dropped down to my heels and grunted with satisfaction. Tom might be a former cop, but he didn't watch out for his assets. Even a toddler could pick a pin tumbler lock like this in under a minute.

I pulled my small set of tools from my pocket and began with the tension wrench. Then added a pick. In no time, a click sounded. Standing, I stuffed my tools back into my pocket. I turned the knob and slowly creaked the door open, peering inside to find the kitchen empty.

The stained linoleum squeaked under my feet as I carefully shut the door and locked it.

I took in the spotless kitchen. With no evidence around —dirty dishes, for example—it was hard to tell when Tom had been here last.

Taking a deep breath, I strode to a door on the right wall and opened it. A dank, musty smell hit my sinuses.

The basement. I crept down the wooden stairs. At the bottom, my sneakers hit a dirt floor. Likely built over a hundred years ago, the foundation had been constructed with granite slabs and mortar. A thready trickle of water bled down one wall and sank into the soil at the bottom. I skirted the staircase but other than the furnace, a water heater, and a jumble of sealed boxes stacked on wooden pallets, the room was empty.

I returned back upstairs and listened a moment before striding into the small dining area. Papers lay in tidy piles on the table but I didn't stop to scan them, moving instead through the open archway, where I found a living area spanning the building from front to back. Black shades had been pulled down tight as if Tom was a freakin' vampire. Older couch, recliner, and a standard TV. Nearly empty bookcase. Beyond the living room, I entered a hall. I snuck along the carpet, keeping my footsteps light. My pulse drummed in my throat because this could be it. Four closed doors lay ahead, and Tom could be hiding behind any one of them.

The first opened into a bathroom. Nobody inside. Two doors on the left led to a study and a bedroom. Each had nearly-empty closets. Only one door left in the hall. Was Tom inside this room, or would my search be a complete waste of time?

Sweat trickled down my spine, and my hands grew slick. Anticipation and caution waged a war inside me. If I closed my eyes, I could picture myself back overseas evading hostiles with my weapon drawn, my buddies at my back.

Back plastered against the wall, I carefully turned the doorknob. My mouth flashed dry as I thrust open the door and tumbled into the room, coming up on one knee, poised to dive to the side if Tom shot.

No Tom. Rising, I approached the closet and yanked the door open.

Nothing except carefully pressed shirts and pants draped over hangers.

Was there an attic?

Back in the hall, I found the hatch and pulled the rope, dropping a narrow set of stairs leading to a low-ceilinged room containing cloth-draped furniture and sealed cardboard boxes stacked in a neat row.

Except on one end.

"Fuck," I whispered, the word echoing around me. Pay dirt. Not Tom but as far as creep factor went, this shot everything else through the roof.

I approached the freakin' shrine. Pictures of a woman who looked very much like Ginny. Multiple candles, some burned to the nub. A plastic bag with a lock of golden hair tied with a pink ribbon. And a photo album filled with newspaper articles chronicling every event from a woman's life since she was a child.

I studied the photos. Laura and Ginny could be twins. In the pile, I found wedding pictures featuring Laura and Tom, plus a series of candid shots of her posing in various locations, most recognizable as tourist spots in Maine.

Clipped newspaper articles crackled as I sorted through them. Laura had gone missing a year ago. The police had questioned Tom, but his alibi appeared solid. The most recent article, dated three months ago, indicated they'd questioned Tom again and told him the case was still under investigation.

A brand-new photo album lay in the center of the display, and I flipped back the cover. I grimaced at an enlargement of Ginny's face. She sat in a beach chair at the campground, reading a book. Other photos showed her puttering around at our campsite, swimming, walking toward the central bathroom buildings. One had been taken when we'd stopped for coffee at Mr. Joe's.

Tom had been watching us, spying on us. This was fucking wrong.

I needed to end it. It was all I could do to beat back the urge to gather everything up and stuff it inside a garbage bag. Throw it in a dumpster. But this was evidence.

I returned to the ground floor and made sure everything looked as it had before. Outside, on the deck, I locked the house again. I returned to my Jeep and told myself to cool off and get control of my anger. Fury was making me shake. I clenched my steering wheel and stared at the house. If I could, I'd burn it to the ground, but that would not deliver the justice Tom deserved.

One thing was clear. Only when Tom was locked up forever would Ginny be safe.

I called the sheriff. "I'm checking in on your investigation into Tom," I said.

"Spoke with him. He denies everything."

"Of course, he does. Do you think he'd—"

"He's in Massachusetts, visiting his dad. Hasn't been around for days."

It was only a few hours' drive from Crescent Cove to Massachusetts, and family made the best alibi because many were willing to lie. "I think you should search his place."

A long pause ticked through the line. "Why?"

"Because you might find evidence."

"Of what?"

"That he's…" Shit. I couldn't come right out and tell the sheriff what I'd found in Tom's attic. "I feel like you'll find something in his house." Which sounded lame, but it was the best I could come up with at the moment.

"Can't do that without a warrant, and no judge would

grant one based on a hunch. We're doing all we can. Already told you that." His voice rose. "Don't tell me you've…" I could almost see him shake his head.

I wasn't admitting or denying anything.

"I'm telling you again," the sheriff said firmly. "Leave this to me and my crew. We're conducting a thorough investigation. If there's any validity in Ms. Bradley's claims, believe me, we'll act."

"Thanks," I growled. I'd have to be satisfied for now, because I couldn't say anything else without incriminating myself.

After hanging up, I dialed Eli and told him what I'd found.

"This guy…I fucking want to kill him," Eli said. "We need to keep this from Ginny. She's getting better, but this could set her backward."

"Yep." I could only imagine the horror she'd feel knowing Tom had been stalking her for over a month. I also had a good idea how Tom's former wife had gone missing. "I'm not letting him anywhere near her."

"I'm up north, in Allagash. Ginny's got her security system which should keep her safe but I'll call her, tell her to remain behind locked doors."

"I'll be at her place within a few hours, after I work at Dad's."

"Good. You'll keep anyone from bothering her. Can't tell you what it means to me knowing you're with her, ready to defend her from that creep."

I'd do everything I could for Ginny until I had to leave. Anxiety clawed through me. Would I be here long enough to see this finished? I couldn't leave her while she was in danger. I'd have to somehow convince the sheriff to issue a warrant for Tom's house. Once they discovered the shrine in the attic, they'd lock Tom behind bars.

I sat in my car, fuming for a moment before driving out to my dad's. Might as well vent my frustrations on the rubble inside. The sooner I finished, the sooner I could be with Ginny.

As I cleaned out the basement—and put the old croquet set in the trunk of my rental—I crapped on myself about what happened in Ginny's kitchen last night. Despite my efforts to protect her from everything, *I'd* been the one to scare her. Sneaking up on her for fun, when I should've realized she'd jump, was the worst thing someone could do to a person with PTSD. She hadn't named it, but I'd be foolish not to see it for what it was. Enough of my buddies got counseling for it after serving overseas. Me, too. While she was everything strong on the outside, inside, she was fragile. The kidnappers had broken her. If anything, the recent incidents had only heightened her stress.

Once Tom was out of the picture, she could heal and finally be free.

I rolled up my shirt sleeves and got to work.

Later, as I was dragging a file cabinet across the basement floor, my phone rang. Pulling it from my pocket, I squinted at the screen.

"Bill," I said. A Chief from NMCB 3. We'd shared at least one deployment together.

"Coop. How you doin'?"

"Should be back Sunday, as expected. Another few days will see this through." More work on the basement tomorrow. Then Dad's room. Saturday was all for Ginny, if she could fit me in. I had a feeling she would.

I wanted to talk. See if we could work out something long distance. I didn't have much to offer her, but I couldn't say goodbye. The thought of never laughing with her again…never touching her again…never hearing her soft sighs again…I couldn't stand it. I had to find a way to be with her always.

"It's about Sampson." Bill's words pulled me away from my dreams of a future with Ginny.

"Sampson?" A friend who'd deployed to the Middle East a few weeks ago. "How's that newborn son of his? He's super proud of that kid." I would be.

"He's dead."

I groaned as I slumped against the wall.

"Sniper." Bill's chipped word carved through the echoing silence, stabbing deep.

"How's his wife?" She'd be devastated. *I* was devastated. I pressed my fingertips against my brow to center myself and focused on Bill's words.

"Her mom flew in to take her and the kid home."

The crushing pain of lost opportunities hit me. Sampson was gone way too soon, leaving the rest of us behind to mourn. The man's son, Trooper. Poor kid would grow up without ever knowing what a great guy his dad had been. And his wife. Plain as day that woman loved him.

"He shouldn't have gone." I choked out the words. *It should've been me.*

"He volunteered. You know how it is."

Volunteering was for single guys who had nothing to lose. *Broken men, like me.*

Bill cleared his throat. "We all do it. They make you need it. You know it's a part of us, more than just a job."

No one could stand back and watch their buddies risk a firefight without going in with them. To protect them. Pull them out if the situation turned bad. Cover their backs.

Who'd been covering Sampson's back?

"I thought you should know," Bill said. "Better to hear it this way than casual-like on the base."

My throat clamped tight. "Thanks."

After ending the call, I stuffed my phone into my pocket and turned and pressed my forehead against the wall. I slammed my fist into the concrete wall. Again. Until my knuckles stung, protesting the abuse I delivered. Facing the dank room, I stared around with blurry eyes. I couldn't believe it. Sampson. Hell, I'd miss my friend.

Gathering myself together, I forced my misery back into that dark place in my mind where everything that had gone sour in my life hid. This was why we signed up. Why we went wherever the government sent us. To protect our country.

But right now, I couldn't remember why it mattered.

━━━

I PULLED into Ginny's drive shortly after two. Reaching into the back seat, I hooked my fingers through the grocery bags, then I climbed out and grabbed the croquet set from the trunk.

Ginny stood at the top of her steps, wearing a flowery, strappy dress that teased her calves. Bare feet. A big smile on her face.

Just looking at her made me want to rip my heart out and hand it to her.

The wind blew her hair and for an instant, the girl from that photo I'd stolen years ago stood above me. Waiting for me, her arms spread wide.

I took the stairs fast and bowled her over on the landing, nuzzled her neck, making her squeal. With my hands full, I couldn't touch but I sure could taste. Drink my fill.

She pulled back and fanned her face. "Welcome, sailor. You in port long?"

If only I was in port forever.

With a bright smile, she opened the door and I went in ahead of her. She took the croquet bag from me. "I'll set this on the back deck." After, she returned to the kitchen. "What's in the bags?" Her fingers snaked toward one sitting on the counter.

I dragged them out of her reach. "No snooping."

She pouted. "Come on, I'm curious. Whatcha making for me tonight?"

I'd wanted to buy her ice cream like when I was seventeen. Gallons in every flavor imaginable. Someday, I'd buy her *all* the ice cream and tell her why.

"Nothing fancy," I said. "You'll have to wait until it's served to find out."

That subtle tilt of one eyebrow, followed by the siren glint in her eyes, made my pulse surge.

"I'm not sure I'm the waiting kind," she said in a breathy voice.

Squeezing her hands, I kissed her. Honey. Hints of mint. That moan I died for worked its way up from her chest. My reward. As if having this woman in my life wasn't reward enough.

I was completely gone for her. So gone, there was no pulling me back. I'd willingly slay for her.

"You drinking iced tea?" I asked when I lifted my head. "I taste lime."

"Want some?" She nodded toward the fridge, keeping her arms snug around my waist. Her hands were underneath my shirt already, but I was more than okay with that. I planned to get underneath her dress as soon as was decently possible.

Croquet was overrated. Would she be open to spending the afternoon in bed?

"No, no, no." Her fingertip tapped my lips, and she gave me a heady smile. "You've promised me a croquet whooping this afternoon, and I won't be dissuaded." Leaving me floundering in the trench I'd dug all on my own, she strolled across the room to the deck where a second set of stairs led down to the lawn. The steamy look she threw over her shoulder made my knees weaken. "You never know. I might wind up giving you a whooping, too."

Where she led, I followed. Catching up to her, I tapped her sweet ass and leaned close to her ear. "I think you just issued me a challenge."

"What do you plan to do about it, soldier man?"

"Pull my weapon?"

Nothing beat watching the color rise in her face.

"You." She hefted the croquet set which I took from her. "I think if you had your way, we'd spend all our time in bed."

"Actually…"

She fed me a stern look but her lips quivered. "Croquet."

"Lead on."

We reached the lawn.

"How do we play, anyway?" She squinted at the bag in my hands.

I dumped out the supplies. My mom had worked at the supermarket when I was a kid but was always there when I got home from school. After homework, we'd do puzzles or play board games. The outside drew me in like a fish to a lure, and we'd spent a lot of time in our backyard. Badminton. Horseshoes. Bowling using weighted soda bottles for pins.

And always croquet.

I pulled out the instructions. It made me sad that I couldn't remember the set-up off the top of my head. With a mallet, I drove in the home peg. "You need to hit your ball through these hoops." I held one up to show her. "In the right sequence in one direction and then back the other way. Whoever returns their ball to the home peg first wins."

Her gaze hovered on me as I laid out the hoops across her lawn.

"What's my prize if I win?" she asked.

I returned to hand her a mallet. "Sweetheart, you need to be thinking about my prize because I'm gonna win."

She smirked and shoved her hair off her face. "Feeling overly confident today, aren't you?"

I puffed my chest and leaned in for a kiss. "Confidence is my game."

Mallet flipped onto her shoulder, she nudged a yellow ball toward the starting point with her foot. "Maybe I'm the croquet queen of Crescent Cove, Maine."

I put on my sunglasses so she couldn't read my intentions. "Any neighbors around outside of your turkey friends?"

She shrugged. "A few deer. Next house is at least a mile away."

"Decent." I held back my smile and waved my mallet. "You can go first."

She curtsied. "Generous of you. What do I do?"

"Hit it."

"How?" The scowl twisting her pretty face begged for a kiss, which I delivered.

"Well, there's the golf-swing, the side-stroke, and the between-the-legs hit."

She smirked. "I believe the last might interfere with your game."

I needed to remember never to underestimate Ginny. "I'll show you how to hit. It's actually called a stroke."

More color flooded her cheeks, telling me she was fully vested in the game I played within the game. Fair-skinned,

Ginny's complexion showed everything. The pink on her cheeks was only heightened by the color above her dress, a dress that hinted at the softness underneath. This tease was going to do me in. I'd have to make sure I took her along with me.

I moved behind her and encircled her with my arms, placing my hands on her forearms to direct her motion. "This is the golf swing." We swung out to the right before bringing the mallet back to connect with the wooden ball.

"And the side swing." Demonstrating, I led her to sweep forward from behind.

"I like this game," she said. "I think I'm going to have a lot of fun playing croquet." I swore she wiggled, shifting her butt squarely across my groin. Thankfully, I wore loose shorts. It was a stretch to think my groan could be interpreted as agreement but she ran with it. "Like this?" She swept the mallet, smacking a blue ball, sending it flying. She followed the hit with more butt wiggles that made my knees tremble while other parts became rock solid. If she kept this up, I'd be unable to resist my urge to bend her over, hike up her dress, and drive myself home.

Was she wearing anything underneath her dress? Sweat prickled on my forehead at the idea that she might not be. Could a guy delicately ask a woman a question like that?

I scrubbed my face with my palm. This was a simple game. I *couldn't* turn it into another sex-filled romp. Could I?

What sounded like a snicker slipped from Ginny's lips, bringing my brain back into focus. Wait a minute. Ginny dominated me far too often. I needed to maintain the upper hand at least once.

I stepped backward, putting space between us. Otherwise, thinking was out of the question. "There's one more stroke, but I believe you've already mastered between the legs, sweetheart."

Her eyes drifted downward. "I believe I have." Her half-smile begged me to kiss her until it achieved a full-on blaze. "So, I hit the ball through these two hoops?" A sharp crack sent her yellow ball shooting through the wires.

I blinked.

"Wow," she said. "Imagine that. I believe that *stroke* gains me two more hits, am I right?"

At my befuddled nod, she strode forward, her dress shifting across her curves. I squinted, seeking panty lines.

Stop it.

I gathered up enough brain power to speak. "Yep. Two strokes."

She glided forward but paused to peek over her shoulder. "Oh, and *sweetheart?* In case you were wondering, that's a no to panties." Her hot ass sashayed over to the ball, and she hit it with a stroke worthy of a golf pro. Another quick lob drove it through the next wicket. "My, my, my. I guess I've earned another stroke, haven't I?"

I'd definitely been had. If I was wise, I'd concede defeat and numbly follow her. Kiss her heels then move my lips up further as soon as was decently possible.

She missed the center wicket and groaned. "Damn. Your turn."

It was time to up my game, or I'd get caught with my pants down. Mallet centered, I hit the ball. It skittered forward and smacked against the first wicket. Crap.

"Hard luck," Ginny said. "Guess that means it's my turn again."

One would think I hadn't played croquet more than a thousand times in my life. But my skills were sliding, driven away by the vixen who smirked my way.

"Some people might believe I have no internet in this

neck of the woods, that I'm not able to watch training videos." She sauntered back to where I stood next to my lonely ball and closed my mouth with a fingertip under my jaw. She followed the gesture with a quick kiss to seal my lips. "My turn again?"

"Yep."

Crack. Her ball shot through the hoop on the right. She jumped and squealed, waving her mallet in the air. "Another free hit." Her ball flew through the end wicket and smacked against the far post. If she kept this up, I'd still be waiting at the starting point when she finished.

With one lifted brow, she strode over to stand in front of me. "I think your mallet has a malfunction."

The functioning of my mallet was *not* in question.

At my growl, Ginny backed up, giggling.

I caught her in three strides and scooped her up in my arms.

Smugness bloomed on her face, and she linked her arms around my shoulders. "I think it's past time you gave me that whooping you promised."

25

Ginny

Complaining about caveman tactics was the furthest thing from my mind while he carried me up into my apartment and down the hall to my bedroom. Without getting winded. I appreciated his stamina.

After lowering me onto the bed, he stripped off his tee. My mouth watered as I took in the flex of muscles across his chest and shoulders. His boxers dropped to the floor and like this was our first time all over again, my body thrilled with anticipation.

My naked man had struck again, and he wanted *me*.

"Your turn for a tease." His lips coiled up on one side. "Payback is going to be fuckin' sweet." His feet padded around to the foot of the bed where he stalled and raked his gaze down my body in a heavy caress. His erection jutted forward, and he stroked himself, making his length extend further. From the way his eyes smoldered, I knew he did it just to watch me heat up.

I swallowed and darted my tongue out, and he groaned as his eyes traced the movement.

He lifted my foot off the bed and kissed the back of my

heel, bringing out my laugh. Not only because it tickled but because his light bristle felt scratchy-good on my skin. With one knee braced on the bed, he worked his mouth upward slowly, kissing to my mid-thigh. My other leg was given the same attention.

I'd never thought leg-kissing could be so hot.

I was about to demand my hard and fast dues when he spread my legs apart further and climbed in between them. His warm palms stroked up my thighs, taking my dress along with them. The fabric pooled at my waist, leaving me exposed to his view. He watched my face as he rubbed where I ached for him most. Heat waves jolted through me, and I moaned.

"I'm ready," I shouted.

His grin blazed. "Nowhere near ready enough." He lowered his head and replaced his fingers with his mouth. His tongue swirled. He sucked.

I cried out his name in urgent gasps while his fingers performed magic, sliding in and out. Unrestrained, I bucked. My whimpers grew high-pitched, filled with endless need.

He climbed off the bed and went around to my nightstand for a condom. With one eyebrow lifted, he crooked his finger. "Come over to the edge of the bed, sweetheart."

I'd dive off a cliff to give in to his call.

I scooted over and sat. His body called to me, straining my way. So gorgeous. A drop of fluid glistened on the tip of his erection. I took him in hand and slid my fingers along his length from the base to the tip and back again. Eyes closed, he tipped his head back and leaned against the wall. He groaned. Beyond tempted, I repeated the action with my mouth, my tongue swirling, tasting, flicking.

I needed to show him everything trapped inside me. He always gave of himself, making sure he met my needs before considering his own. The thought that he'd sacrifice like that solely for me squeezed my chest tight. Taking was enhanced by giving, and I wanted to show him I could give, too.

With tilted head, I watched the urgent lines on his face deepen, shouting out his satisfaction. His lungs heaved. He groaned and strained. His muscles stood out in rigid, sharp definition.

He cupped my head and stroked my hair back then gently braced me while he pumped, his body tightening, laboring. A pearl of sweat trickled down his brow. His body shook. Creases filled his face and he gasped, a harsh, guttural sound of pleasure.

He shuddered while he strove for control, and he pulled out of my mouth. "Hell, Ginny. I've gotta be inside you."

When his eyes met mine, I saw myself there. Us. The world.

With trembling hands, I pulled my dress over my head and flung it on the floor.

He encased himself with the condom. "Lean back," he said hoarsely.

I moved my butt to the edge and he lifted my thighs, his fingers sinking, gripping tight.

Watching my face, he slid himself inside, all the way to the hilt. "Ahh. You feel…"

Unable to think, focusing only on the sensation of him filling me, I moaned. I braced my heels on the wall and strained toward him. He pulled out, slid back inside, and then took on a slow, languid rhythm that drove me insane.

While rubbing between my legs, he chased me ever higher. I closed my eyes and thrust up to meet him. My heart thrashed, and my panting breaths echoed around us, fusing with his.

He groaned and drove me on, maintaining his exquis-itely slow pace, his pumps pinning me to the bed. As if he sensed I was close, his fingers moved up my belly to stroke my breasts. Each pinch of my nipples sent heady spasms through my limbs. I climbed the peak. My body thrilled, high-strung and tense.

"Cooper. I'm gonna…"

"I'm with you."

With his arms braced on either side of me, he moved in and out, smacking us together. His muscles bulged. His eyes slid closed. And his body convulsed.

We plunged over the top and tumbled down the other side together.

I LAY across Cooper's body, my legs entwined with his. His arms held me close, and his breath sighed against my hair. Nothing could get better than this.

I loved him.

And I wanted to tell him. But we only had a few more days left together. Did I dare risk driving him away by sharing my feelings?

His fingertips swirled on my back in soft patterns.

It might be best to wait to speak and savor each moment like it was my last. But if the right time came, I'd tell him, because I wanted him to know even if nothing ever came of it.

"I'll be finished at my dad's house soon," he said. "You said you were free Saturday?"

I tilted my head and looked up at him. "Can we spend it together?"

His eyes stroked my face. "I want that."

So did I. "What should we do?"

"Let's think on it. We can decide over the next few days. All I know is that I need to spend every minute with you."

"Me, too."

His belly groaned. "Hey, you hungry?"

"Famished. I'd say you are, too." I smoothed my finger-tips across his abs, and he huffed out a laugh. Ticklish, eh? What a nice surprise.

His fingers wove through my hair. "I feel like I'm always starving you. Let me cook."

"I'll help." I started to rise.

He stilled my movement with a caress to my side. "Nope. Totally my treat tonight."

Every second with him was a treat.

He shifted out from underneath me. Staring down, his eyelids hooded as his gaze slid along my body. "Stay naked for me, would you?" The husky need in his voice called to me. If he used that tone all the time, I'd crawl through molten lava to reach him.

Whistling through his teeth, he left the room. Bangs rang out in my kitchen, leading me to believe he was concocting a four-course meal.

I curled my back, savoring the stroke of the sheet on my bare skin, and stretched like a well-sated cat. My limbs ached but in all the right ways.

He appeared in the doorway wearing only a ruffled apron and a grin, holding up two glasses of iced tea with lime which he placed on each nightstand. Humming, he sashayed out of the room, his bare butt wagging behind him. He was so cute, I was sure he'd be the death of me.

He returned with a tray. "Dinner is served, my lady." He climbed onto the bed and settled beside me before lowering the tray in front of us.

Oh, yum.

He'd hollowed out a round loaf of bread and stuffed it with slabs of cheese, sliced avocado, red peppers, lettuce, and turkey before replacing the top. The sandwich was sliced into pie wedges. Bowls on the tray held grapes, fresh pineapple, and double stuffed Oreo cookies. Cooper knew me too well.

With a grin, he laid a napkin on my lap and swept his hand toward the tray. "Dig in."

I popped a grape into my mouth and munched, savoring the sweet, juicy flavors bursting on my tongue.

He hefted one of the sandwich chunks and bit into it with gusto. His eyelids slid shut as he chewed. "Mmm. Mmm."

Fine cuisine had nothing on a meal prepared by Cooper. The sharp cheese and rich avocado complimented the peppers, and the crunchy-chewy bread was delicious enough it could be enjoyed all on its own. We divided the mega-sandwich and devoured it down to crumbs which Cooper eyed as if he wanted to lick them off the plate.

No need to be civilized on my behalf.

I thoroughly enjoyed caveman.

―――

ELI CALLED the next morning after Cooper had left for his dad's house.

"I need a favor," he said.

I sipped my coffee. With only fifteen minutes before my first corporate client came knocking, with her hair sprayed well enough to survive a hurricane and a business suit in hand, I'd need the caffeine. "Is this more of that *you're a female* thing?"

Silence in the airways suggested this might not be the

time for joking. I leaned forward. "What's happening? Are you okay?"

"My Jeep's in the garage in town, and I'm stuck here."

"Oh, no!"

"Weirdest thing. When I arrived, there wasn't anyone here. I couldn't reach Jefferson to find out what was going on. Since I went hunting up here with Jefferson a few times back in high school, I knew where he hid the key and let myself in. Spent the night, but my Jeep wouldn't start this morning. I need to get back as soon as possible. My boss said he'd cover until I can get there. A garage hauled my Jeep into town, but it needs a carburetor and they won't get one in for a day or two. I'll have to come back up later in the week when it's done." He paused. "I hate to ask but can you come get me?"

In Allagash. I'd have to leave my apartment and drive alone for hours.

"I know what you're thinking," he said. "But the sheriff said Tom's in Massachusetts."

Which did little for my anxiety. I could only hope Tom remained in Massachusetts for the rest of his life. "I have work lined up for today, but I can call everyone and reschedule."

"Normally, I'd call Mom or Steve, but you know Mom's still out of town and Steve's hurt. And Coop's time is limited here. I hate pulling him away."

"I can do it," I said, my voice growing stronger. "I should be there in, well, you know, six hours or so. I'll make those phone calls and head out right away."

"Thanks."

I grabbed a pen and paper. "Give me the address so I can plug it into my GPS." The last thing I needed was to get lost trying to find Jefferson's place after a long drive. I repeated it aloud to make sure I hadn't messed up the street number before I hung up.

A shifting sound on my deck drew my attention and I spun, staring toward where I'd cracked my French door to let in the breeze. My pulse thumped in my throat, and my hand compressed the paper with the address. Was someone out there?

I crept forward, skirting around floorboards that creaked. With my back hugging the wall, I peered outside but saw nothing moving.

My breath whooshed out. The sound must've been the wind fluttering the deck umbrella I'd left up. My gaze skimmed over my storage shed sitting at the back of my lawn, and I blinked. My heart stilled. I'd shut the door after putting my camping things away days ago. But now, the door stood open.

"It's nothing," I whispered. "The wind blew it open."

But I was convinced I'd dropped the bar to secure the door.

Maybe Cooper put the croquet set away inside before he left earlier but didn't secure it well enough. He'd said he wasn't taking the set with him.

Go out there, close it, and make those phone calls.

"It's just a shed door." It was broad daylight. With Tom out of town, no one could harm me.

Just in case, I grabbed a kitchen knife before I slipped out onto my back deck. I paused, listening. As if winter plunged down on me, my skin pebbled with gooseflesh. But only trees shifting in the wind reached my ears. Damn wind.

Creeping down the back stairs, my pulse chugging like a freight train in my throat, I reached the lawn. Yesterday, when Cooper and I played croquet, my backyard had been a happy place. Now, the isolation chilled me to the bone.

I could call Cooper. Without question, he'd come over and shut my shed door. But jeez, was I really that much of a coward?

I'd handle this on my own. Chin lifted, I strode across the lawn, my flip flops smacking my heels. Announcing my presence. Crap. I slipped out of my sandals, abandoning them, and continued toward the shed barefoot.

Panic spiraled inside me, but I shoved it away.

A cavern of darkness waited for me inside the shed. I stood a short distance away from the opening, my sweaty hand barely holding onto my knife. My lungs hauled in air and rasped it back out so fast my head spun.

Did I dare peek inside?

In the scary movies I'd watched as a kid, nothing good ever came from being a nosy woman. I had no interest in repeating their mistakes, but it would be silly not to make sure everything inside was secure. What if I'd been robbed? I not only kept my camping gear here but odd treasures I'd picked up through my travels and hadn't had the chance to sort through yet.

I inched forward until I stood in the doorway.

Utterly black. Still, too. My eyes slowly adjusted. Had the boxes along the back wall been moved? If so, why would anyone bother?

Taking a deep breath, I stepped into the gloom. Cool metal seeped up from the floor as I moved forward. It sank into my bare feet and made me shiver. But other than the boxes looking slightly out of place, nothing appeared missing. I'd been in a hurry to put my camping things away the other day. I must've hit the boxes when I dropped my gear.

That was it. No one was here and no one had been inside my shed outside of me. I turned to leave.

The door slammed closed, trapping me alone in the dark. My heart jolted against my ribs, and the nightmare of the snake dropping inside the campground bathroom rushed through me. My skin prickled, and I whimpered. I shoved the door, and it flew open, banging against the outside wall. On the lawn, the turkey flock scattered like I'd created a shockwave, squawking and flying into the woods with their necks outstretched.

The knife slipped from my hand, and I groaned and rubbed my face. A sob caught in my throat, but I lowered my arms and sputtered. My shaky laughter burst out. Damn freakin' turkeys.

Back inside my apartment, my pulse finally slowed. I shut and locked the French door and curled up on the sofa to regroup. I needed to reschedule today's clients for next week, but I couldn't stop trembling. And hysterical laughter kept leaking through, because I'd taken on a shed, plus a flock of turkeys today, and come up the victor.

Leaning forward, I scooped up my phone from the coffee table and made the calls.

Before I left my apartment, I called Cooper and explained about the shed, proudly telling him about my turkey rout. I laughed so hard along with him, tears filled my eyes. It felt good to find humor in everyday things again like I'd done before my life fell apart. Maybe I was finally coming back together.

Purse in hand, I locked my front door and started down the steps. If I timed it right, I could reach Eli by late afternoon. While my butt would protest getting back in the car, I'd make the long trip home immediately to get back to my apartment by midnight. Cooper had a key and said he'd come over the minute I got back.

When I jumped into my car, something hard poked my side. Leaning over, I fished out the object—another painted tile. This one showed a large river surrounded by an evergreen forest. I didn't recognize the scene.

Had Eli left it for me before he went to Allagash?

Wait. That wasn't possible. I always locked my car.

My shoulders tightened, and a skitter of awareness chased down my spine. Peering around, I didn't see anything but trees swaying in the wind and a few butterflies flitting across the wildflowers overrunning my lawn.

These tiny paintings…I'd assumed they came from Eli, but we hadn't specifically talked about them. What if my brother hadn't left them for me?

I flipped the tile over, expecting to find the same scrolling swirl I'd seen on the other but instead found a distinct letter A.

Cold sweat broke out on my body. I didn't want to know what this meant, did I?

I raced back up to my apartment and approached the mantel where the other four tiles were displayed in the center. With trembling hands, I scooped the tiles up and sat on the sofa, chucking them onto the coffee table as if they were bugs squirming across skin. They skidded, and one flipped over.

Not a scroll. The letter L.

Don't look at them. Throw them away.

I couldn't do it, because ignoring this meant I chose hiding. I had to know if this was my imagination or something more sinister.

With infinite care, I turned each tile over, laying them in a line in the order I'd received them.

LAURA

I GASPED, and my heart fluttered in my chest. Tom's dead wife's name. He said Laura had looked exactly like me.

Revulsion churned through my belly, rising up into my throat. Tom had been giving me pieces of his and Laura's past in painted form as if he thought I'd treasure them. I never should've assumed they were from Eli.

I flung my arm out, scattering the tiles. As if messing up the name would make it go away.

Tom was never going to go away.

Pulling my phone, I dialed Cooper's number, but he didn't pick up. And this wasn't a message I could send in a text.

I pressed my fist against my lips hard enough I winced and squinted around my apartment—the place where I'd felt safe since returning from Istanbul. My security system was infallible, wasn't it?

I'd left my bottle of Xanax on the coffee table after bringing it inside. Opening it, I poured the pills into my palm. Six. Not the nine that should be left after I took one of the original ten. Someone *had* been inside my apartment and they'd stolen my Xanax, only to force feed it to me after.

Not *someone*. Tom.

My stomach dropped through the floor, and I shot my gaze around the room but only silence greeted me.

Standing, I swept up the tiles and stomped to my kitchen, where I tossed them into a drawer. While I wanted to throw them away, they were evidence. I dumped the rest of the Xanax down the drain and ran the garbage disposal. Then I ran to my bathroom and threw up.

MY CAR BUMPED around the last corner of the shady

lane leading to Jefferson's camp late that evening. While I'd been tempted to remain in my apartment after discovering the meaning of the tiles, Eli needed me.

And I was done cowering. It was time to fight back. No, to take back my life.

It figured I'd get a flat tire along the way here, though. Fortunately, a woman stopped and helped me change it. Eli and I would have to get back on the road, and not just because he was needed at work. Each second with Cooper could be my last.

I shut off the engine and staring at the rustic log cabin sitting on a grassy knoll ahead of me. Other than the small clearing surrounding the building, dense woods spread out in all directions. From my GPS, I knew the lake sat beyond the house, but I couldn't see it from here. No Eli around, but I hadn't expected him to be waiting outside when I arrived.

I got out of the car, locked it, and squinted toward the house. Keychain in hand, I started forward, my shoes nearly silent on the pine-needle covered drive.

Dull thuds sounded behind me, making me skitter forward a few steps. Fear crawled up my back but before I could turn, someone shoved me hard. I cried out and stumbled, nearly falling. The person kicked me, and my right knee gave way. Arms splaying wide, I barely caught myself again before I fell on the ground.

Shrieking, I flailed out, trying to hit the person behind me.

An arm snaked around my neck and clenched tight. I clawed at the arm, and a man grunted and yanked me against him. His arm tightened, putting me in an inescapable chokehold.

Tom growled near my ear. "It's over, Laura."

26

Cooper

After finishing the basement, I dragged myself upstairs to complete my final chore, my father's bedroom. I'd put it off until last because I dreaded entering the space my father had claimed for his own after Mom died.

Dear old Dad. If I'd taken bets, I would've put my money on the alcohol killing the old bastard, not a brain aneurysm.

I stood outside the door and rubbed my face with hands that shouldn't be shaking. Only the thud of my heart and my rough breathing broke the quiet on the landing. I felt like a teenager all over again, creeping upstairs to ask my passed-out father for a favor. One I already knew would be denied.

I didn't know what to expect inside, because I hadn't opened the door since I arrived back in Maine.

Taking a deep breath, I shoved the door open and glanced around, relieved to see Dad hadn't overloaded the room with junk like the rest of the house. No alcohol bottles were strewn around, either. Big surprise there. Other than a thick layer of dust, it was almost tidy. The room wasn't arranged the way Mom had kept it, with patchwork quilts, cross-stitched pictures on the walls, and a china doll sitting on a chair in the corner. Dad must've given away Mom's things, because I hadn't found them anywhere.

He'd replaced her presence with framed pictures of hunting dogs, a generic bedspread, and simple furniture.

Cleaning the room Dad had died in should've been the toughest chore of all, but even in this, my father denied me. Throwing away the last bits of Dad's life should've meant I'd finally evict the man from my life. Yet, Dad had stolen that from me, too.

A spurt of anger ran through me. Why was I pissed off about this? Did I really need more hours of back-breaking labor to make it feel real? I grumbled, acknowledging that Dad had at least made the task easier. Not much personal junk hanging around for me to go through before I called this done. Dad's possessions were meaningful only for this moment.

A bed, a side table with a lamp, a bureau with drawers vomiting old clothing, and the closet. It was anyone's guess what was inside there.

Anticlimactic. I doubted I'd find anything of value inside Dad's private domain. Why had I expected otherwise?

Garbage bag in hand, I crossed the room to the bureau to get started.

Four bags later, I'd stripped the bed and tossed the bedding and Dad's clothing into the dumpster. I'd removed the dog pictures from the walls and hauled the furniture down to the garage. Chucked the mattress out with the rest of the rubble.

A vacant room stared back at me when I returned upstairs. Only the closet remained. After cleaning it out, I could lock the house, hand the key over to the realtor, and put my crappy existence here behind me.

"Great, more clothes," I said when I pulled open the door. More garbage bags to haul down the stairs and stuff into the overflowing dumpster.

The empty coat hangers clinked together when I moved them, as if Dad's ghost played an off-key tune for me alone. I stuffed them against the wall to silence their eerie melody.

On the top shelf, I found a small cardboard box about four inches high and twelve inches long. I slid it forward, bringing with it enough dust to make me sneeze. The box rattled. Must be more knick-knacks Dad had packed away and forgotten about. Taped shut. Scrawled across the top in black marker, Dad had written, *For Cooper*.

As if he knew I'd find it one day.

I wasn't sure I had the energy to open it. If I was wise, I'd chuck it into the dumpster and forget about it. But before I decided to break the seal or dispose of it unopened, my phone rang.

Not Ginny this time. She'd called this morning, and I didn't expect to hear from her again until late tonight.

The call was from California, someone in Bravo Company. Better not be more bad news.

With my arm braced on the wall, I answered. "Yep."

"Hey, Chief. This is B6. How you doing?"

What was this about? "Doing fine, Lieutenant. You?"

"Could be better, but we all deal, right?"

I grunted. Get to it, B6.

"I know you're on leave. Sorry to hear about your dad."

More social niceties. "Thanks."

"I didn't just call to chat, though. Senior Chief asked me to communicate something. Get your input."

"Okay."

"Things have changed. Kuwait's out for now but…we need you. There's somewhere else on the agenda."

Somewhere else. Loose lips sink ships. Sometimes, I didn't know my full assignment until the helo dropped me on location.

"It's our favorite desert destination, but we'll transport you from there."

Meaning Bagdad—and beyond. "I'm listening."

"This is actually TAD." Temporary Assigned Duty. A brief assignment to fill in for someone who'd been hurt or needed emergency leave. "We need to drop someone in for a short stint."

"How long's this one?" I pulled a strand of cobwebs off my head. Must've brushed against them when I—

"Twelve days." B6 cleared his throat. "We're thinking of sending Chief Mayfield…"

A married friend who had three kids under the age of ten. Absolutely not.

B6 continued, "But we—"

"I'll go." I would do anything to prevent another death like Sampson's.

The Lieutenant's chuckle burst through the airwaves. "Damn. Lord knows why I took that bet. Senior Chief said you'd be all over this. Now I'm out two movie tickets. I just need your okay."

What he meant was I had to volunteer. A loose term in the military. "Any deets you can share about the mission?"

"The other Chief was going in behind the Marines to look at infrastructure and put together a plan to get things up and running again. That's all I can say."

Probably an ISIS stronghold if the Marines were involved. A dam or a power plant? Either would mean back-breaking work bringing in power for lights, establishing water, supply routes. I'd spend days assessing what the situation needed, making recommendations, and digging into the grunt work until the other assigned Chief could return to duty. All while exposing my back to hostile attention. My spine flinched already.

"You in?" B6 asked.

I stalled and then crapped on myself for my hesitation. What was up with me? I'd never balked at doing anything the military asked before. "Of course, I'm in." I cleared my tight throat. "Just said I was, didn't I?"

"I'll put the papers through right away, then."

"Sounds good." Actually, for the first time in my career, it didn't. The danger might be heightened, but this wasn't the first unplanned maneuver I'd been asked to take on. Why did I view this one differently? "When do you need me?" Hopefully, it would—

"You need to be on the base within twenty-four hours. You'll ship out immediately after that."

Hell, no. I'd thought late next week or the week after that.

I couldn't leave. Ginny needed me. I still had to convince the sheriff to get serious about Tom. Ginny was scared, worried the other man would hurt her, that—

"Chief?"

No choice. I'd volunteered. If that was what this was called. My approval wasn't actually needed; it was just a formality. "All set."

"Right, then. We'll see you soon."

I hung up and ditched my phone on the floor. Rubbing my face, I groaned. I didn't want to leave Ginny, not when we didn't know what was going on with Tom. And things were unsettled between us. We needed to talk about what we had, if anything. I wanted to find a way to stay together.

To be on the base within twenty-four hours, I'd have to catch a red-eye tonight or a flight first thing in the morning, though I'd cut it close with the latter. That was nowhere near enough time to speak with Ginny, let alone ensure she'd be safe once I left.

What did I think I could do if I stayed in Maine, anyway? Ask Ginny for something she may have no intention of giving? I cursed myself, because I'd been the one to lay down the ground rules. But she'd agreed, which could mean she didn't want anything more from me than a few days.

Staying here to figure this out meant bailing on my duty. The government threw soldiers in military prison for shit like that. How could I consider giving up all I'd worked so hard to achieve?

My buddies overseas needed me. Twelve-years-ago this June, I'd joined the Navy. Because my re-enlistment was coming up, I'd put in my chit already.

The government owned me for another four years.

27

Ginny

I kicked and tried to bite Tom's arm.

His hot breath rushed past my ear as he struggled to maintain control. He punched me in the lower back, and I gasped. My knees trembled, and tears sprang up in my eyes. The blow hurt bad enough to steal my breath.

"Stop fighting, Laura," he said. "You're coming with me."

"Eli!" I shrieked, struggling to get away. I squirmed, sweat and tears streaming down my face. I had to get free, but Tom's hold didn't slip an inch. "Help!"

Where was Eli? Why hadn't he come to me? Shit. Had Tom hurt my brother? If he was lying somewhere unconscious or worse, I needed to go to him. Get him help.

I made myself go limp, praying I'd slip from Tom's grasp and fall. Better to give him a dead weight to drag than cooperate. If his hold loosened, I'd run.

He released my neck only long enough to clamp a hand over my mouth, cutting off my screams. His other arm wrapped around my waist, and he started dragging me down the drive. "I don't know how you got away. How you crawled out of that hole I put you in. But I'm going to make sure you don't escape this time."

Crawled out of a hole? Whimpering, I struggled to get away.

He tightened his grip and hauled me along, my sneakers dragging in the dirt. "Let's you and me go for a little ride, like before."

He'd killed his wife. Horror burst from my skin, because I knew I was next.

Anger charged through my veins, giving me the will to wrench his hand off my mouth. I lifted my keychain, tilted away from Tom and glared at him. "I'm not Laura!"

He snarled. "Shut up, Laura."

I shot a stream of police-strength pepper spray at Tom. Filling his face. His mouth. His eyes. I held the plunger down until he released me, my hands stopped shaking, and I regained control of my lungs. His arms dropped away and I staggered backward, my body a wreck from spent adrenaline.

Hands cupping his face, Tom shrieked. He backed away and stumbled. Snot dripping, eyes tearing, he tripped over a log and collapsed. Flopping onto his side, he writhed on the ground.

Some people would've run, but I was determined to make sure this threat was taken care of for good. I was sick of Tom thinking he had the right to chase me, drug me, scare me. No longer would I remain passive while he took advantage of me.

What to do about him now? I whipped my head around, looking for something I could use to immobilize him, but saw nothing. My car. Eli had insisted I stock a bag filled with all kinds of things in case I ever broke down. I clicked unlock as I ran toward my car. In the back, I dragged the bag close and dumped everything out onto the rubber mat. A coil of rope. Perfect.

The first piece I cut from the bundle secured Tom's wrists. I bound them tightly behind his back, making sure he couldn't wiggle free. While he moaned and sniffled and acted like he was going to die, I grabbed one ankle, then the other. I yanked them together and tied them in a double knot. He wouldn't slink away this time.

There. Leaving him lying on the ground, I stood. Shivering, I wanted to drop to the ground, curl into a ball, and cry. But I had to find Eli and make sure he was safe.

It was over. Finally. Not just with Tom, but with me, too. I'd conquered my fear and saved myself.

I staggered and nearly fell. A mix of joy and anxiety charged through me.

Skin bright pink from my efforts and my legs a wreck, I raced for the house to look for my brother. At the door, I pulled my phone and called 911. After explaining that someone had tried to kidnap me, the dispatcher promised to send the state police right away. I hung up and put my hand on the doorknob, paralyzed by the fear of what I might find inside. Eli would've taken on a T-Rex to save me. Why hadn't he?

"Please be okay." Harnessing some strength from deep inside, I swung open the front door.

A large, open living room with a kitchen galley along the back wall greeted me. A loft with a wooden railing stretched across the upper portion of the cathedral ceiling that was highlighted with light racks created from antlers. Rustic furnishings had been placed around the living room, and a moose head stared back at me from above the stone fireplace.

The floorboards creaked when I took a step forward. "Eli?"

Shuffling and muffled groans drew my attention to the sofa sitting along one wall. A long coffee table had been placed in front of it. The table rocked and fell over, revealing Eli lying on the floor behind.

He grunted and peered over his shoulder, his eyes blazing, the color in his face rivaling a volcano's. A rope encircled his ankles and wrists tight enough his hands had blanched white. Blood dripped from where he'd struggled ineffectively to get free. He wrenched his body back and forth in an effort to loosen his bonds, and his muffled cries slipped from behind the gag wrapped around his head.

I rushed over to him but I couldn't loosen the rope.

Panic raged in Eli's expression. He thrashed while I raced to the kitchen for a knife.

Ropes cut, Eli rose to his knees and grabbed me in a bear hug. "You're okay. I was freaking out with worry. Thought Tom would get you, too." His head pivoted, and he peered around me. "Where is he?"

"Tom did this?" How? My brother not only outweighed the slighter man but he also had the strength of a thousand lions.

Eli's eyes cut to the side. "I was asleep on the couch. Somehow, he got inside. Hit me." He rubbed the back of his head and winced. "Stunned me, then tied and gagged me before I could fight back."

"Let me look at your head."

He leaned forward and I parted his hair, finding a big bump that had bled a bit before clotting off. "You could have a concussion. We'll need to get that looked at as soon as we get home." Overwhelmed with relief that he was okay, I rested my head on his shoulder. "Tom attacked me outside."

"Hell, no." Eli released me and stormed to his feet. He

staggered before finding his balance, and I leaped up and grabbed his arm.

"Where is he?" Eli shouted. "I'll kill him."

"I pepper sprayed him and tied him up."

Eyes widening, Eli hugged me again. "Wow."

"Would you mind checking on the ties for me?" Tremors filled my voice. "I'd hate for him to get loose."

"Gladly." His feet unsteady still, Eli rushed outside.

I followed slowly, my legs as unsteady as my brother's. Reaction was setting in, and I couldn't stop shaking. Turning back, I collapsed on the sofa. I drew my legs up and wrapped my arms around them and rocked. I couldn't stop crying.

Eli appeared in the doorway. "You did great, Ginny. I'm proud of you. Of what you've done." He wove across the room and dropped to the cushions beside me. His arm dragged me close, and we sat together in silence until the wail of a siren approached.

I rose and wiped my face with the edge of my tee.

"You okay?" Eli got up and took my hand.

Lower lip wedged between my teeth, I nodded.

We went outside as the police pulled into the drive. Eli stood beside me on the porch, his arm around me, lending me much-needed support. The cop car pulled to a stop beside Tom and officers exited each side of the vehicle and approached him.

We joined them. Tom's eyes had stopped watering and he no longer moaned. The glare he gave me could've impaled me to a tree.

"I'm Officer Riggs," one of the state cops said. "You two called the police?"

I explained what happened and then elaborated on all that had gone on during the last week, from the boater who'd tried to run me down, to my drugged coffee, to the painted tiles Tom had left for me.

Eli added what happened with Tom before I arrived. "I think he lured me up here solely to draw you out, Ginny."

"What?" I gasped out.

"I couldn't reach Jefferson. I think the original call came from Tom, not my friend. It's been a long time. Makes sense I wouldn't remember the sound of his voice. And, after I arrived, Tom must've disabled my Jeep, leaving me no choice but to call for help. He took a chance I'd call you or maybe he didn't. If he's been watching, he knows Mom is away, that my co-worker, Steve's injured. It was you or Cooper. And if Cooper had come, it would've left you vulnerable. His plan was set either way."

"Clever," one of the officers said. "People surprise me all the time." He went to his vehicle for a first aid kit to wrap Eli's still-bleeding wrists.

"Sounds like this man has been busy," the other officer said, helping Tom sit up.

Tom growled at me, straining to break free of the ties binding his wrists. "Yeah, I chased you in the woods," he said. "Even followed you and that asshole to the base, but I didn't do any of that other shit. You know that, Laura."

Like he'd admit if he had? Besides…

"I'm not Laura," I shouted.

"Who's Laura?" Officer Riggs asked, his penetrating gaze scanning the area. "Anyone else here?"

"Laura was his wife. His dead wife." I frowned. "I think he was involved in her death."

The other cop nodded. "We'll certainly look into it."

"I wasn't going to hurt you again, Laura." Tom whimpered. Tears leaked down his face. "I was just doing what you asked me to. You kept calling, saying you wanted to be with me. Why did you have to sleep with that other man?"

"You might want to shut up right there, buddy." Office Riggs tightened his hold on Tom's arm. "You're incriminating yourself."

The other policeman cuffed Tom and then cut the ties I'd wrapped around his wrists and ankles. The officer nodded my way. "I assume you want to press charges."

"I do." I lifted my chin. "For everything."

"I'll put Tom in the back of the car and then we can get the paperwork done."

―――

THE COPS HAULED Tom into town, and Eli and I went back inside the house. By then, it was after eight.

"It looks like we're stuck here overnight," I said. "While I'm tempted to leave immediately, I'm worn out from what had happened and I don't think I can handle a six-hour drive."

Knowing he'd be worried, I tried to call Cooper, but he didn't pick up.

Eli dropped onto his side on the couch and groaned into the cushions. "My head is killing me. I'd drive if it wasn't."

"I'm really sorry. Let me see if there's ice in the freezer." Finding some, I sealed it in a bag and wrapped a thin towel around the package and gave it to him. He pressed it against his head, wincing.

"Is it okay with Jefferson that we stay here tonight?"

"Yeah. Finally reached him while you were in the bathroom. He's in Florida. The lost job, him unable to register his car, even his sick mom? All made up by Tom. I let the police know the latest details."

I shook my head, unable to believe the lengths Tom had gone to in order to trap me.

Fortunately, the cabin was decently stocked. I located food in the fridge and linens in a hall closet, which I used to make up a bed in the loft. Eli would sleep in Jefferson's room. After eating, I climbed between the sheets, exhausted.

Tree frogs cheeped outside the open window. In the woods, a barred owl hooted, long and lonely. The wind stirred through the forest, whispering something I couldn't quite understand.

I tried to call Cooper again but while the call went through, he didn't pick up. At the beep, I left a message, explaining briefly what happened with Tom and how relieved I was that the horror I'd lived with over the past week was finally over.

We could talk about it tomorrow.

Tomorrow would also be the perfect time to tell him my feelings. I wanted to talk about us, about trying for something more.

Whatever he was willing to offer.

28

Cooper

The thought of this mission made my gut expand to the point of explosion. Unsteady, I stalked my father's room, the boom of my pulse louder than the thud of my feet hitting the hardwood floor.

I didn't want to do it, because getting on that plane meant a whole lot more than shipping out. It meant leaving Ginny. This wasn't just about keeping her safe. I wanted to be with her in every way possible.

We hadn't talked about a future. I knew she liked me, but was this only a short-term thing for her? I loved her but my love could be one-sided.

What was I going to do? My time had run out. A job waited for me, and I had to heed the call.

Boarding that plane, then a chopper that would transport me from Bagdad to beyond meant leaving her behind to worry. I couldn't even to tell her where I was going or what I'd be doing. Or even when I'd be back.

With our relationship unsettled, I couldn't ask her to follow me to the base to wait for my return. She'd be alone with no family to lean on. If something like the events of this past week happened to her, she'd be scared, and I'd be unable to do a damn thing to protect her. It would kill me to think she needed me and I couldn't be there for her.

And I'd do it all over again with my next mission. This current one was short but most were a minimum of twelve weeks. Hell, six months was the norm.

Each subsequent deployment would drain more from her and steal her growing confidence. My eight years left in the military would mean eight years of Ginny's life given over to fear of being alone. And fear of losing me.

I raked my scalp with hands that shook worse than when I'd stood outside my father's door hours ago. The pain inside me surpassed the anguish I'd felt when I walked down the front walk after graduation, knowing I was on my own, that I could never return.

I didn't want to leave. I wanted to stay here and—

The box my father left me lay on the floor by my feet, barely discernable in the dark. I couldn't deal with whatever was inside now. I couldn't deal with *any* of this now. If I was wise, I'd toss it into the dumpster where it could wallow with all the other crap from my past. Once the physical memories were gone, the intangible ones could finally be laid to rest.

Picking up the box, I carried it downstairs. When I propped tucked it under my arm while locking the door, small things shifted inside.

Ginny would've picked Eli up by now and they'd be heading home. The only question was, would I be here to greet her when she returned?

An ache pressed on my lungs, making each breath a struggle.

I drove to my hotel, planning to pack the box in my

suitcase. The decision to dump it or not could be dealt with later. In the parking lot, I sat and tapped my hands on the wheel.

If I was an honorable soldier, I'd book the red-eye flight to California. I'd go inside the hotel, stuff everything into my bag, and return the rental. I'd call Ginny from the airport. Explain…something.

There was no reason I had to go back to my father's house, but my body took me there anyway. Like a raven blown astray in a storm, I sought a familiar place to land. Shutting off my vehicle in the drive, I stared at the house. Light from the road glinted on the chipped paint. The roof shingles were in need of repair. A shutter hung askew. The building was worn but not broken.

Unlike me.

I opened my water bottle and took a long swallow.

Look around inside one more time. It's your last chance.

Drink in hand, I forced my feet up the walk and into the house. My footsteps echoed in the dark, empty rooms, but the ghosts who'd lingered since death visited must've fled along with Dad's possessions.

From upstairs, my phone beeped. Shit, I'd thrown it on the floor after taking that call. I retrieved it and saw Ginny had not only tried to reach me earlier today, but that she'd left a message.

After listening, I slumped against a wall. Wow. She'd fought Tom off and protected herself all on her own. I grinned at the image of her taking the other man down with a face full of pepper spray.

Ginny was stronger than she gave herself credit for.

Damn, but she'd come far already. In no time, she'd be free. This chapter of her life was just about over. Once convicted of the charges Ginny had filed—let alone the possible murder of his wife, Tom would be locked up for a long time.

Did Ginny really need me around any longer?

I lowered myself to the floor and leaned against the wall. Staring forward blindly, the phone fell from my hand. I lifted the water bottle in a silent toast to my past.

I'd only intended to say goodbye to my childhood home one last time but memories of all that had been and all that should've been crowded back into my mind.

Mom. Dad. Me. If I'd asked Mom to stay home that night, she'd still be alive. If I'd begged harder, Dad wouldn't have lifted a bottle. If I'd done more, been more, achieved more…

Throwing everything away had made no difference. I couldn't dispose of my past. I carried it with me wherever I went, a sack of regrets on my back.

Ginny. My heart played a tune only she understood.

I smudged my burning eyes with my palms. Why had I thought a fragmented man could give her what she needed? That the limited time I had to offer would be enough? She was moving beyond her past, finding a new future for herself here in Maine. Stress for me would only drive her backward.

And I'd force her there.

I loved her. But, if I *truly* loved her, I'd let her go. I'd leave her to find someone who could be there for her always.

Just do it.

I called the airport and arranged my flight. It would leave in just under three hours. Shoving my phone into my pocket, I stared around wildly.

Do it.

At my hotel, I packed my things. I dumped everything

into the trunk of my rental. After dropping off the car, I took a shuttle to the airport where I checked my bags and slumped in a chair to wait for my flight.

Why aren't you doing it?

My sigh bled from my lungs, because I didn't want to say what needed to be said. I'd hurt her, something I'd been determined never to do.

It would kill me.

I stared at my phone for a long time before dialing her number.

She picked up at the first ring.

"Cooper! I'm so glad you called. Reception's crappy here but I was going to keep trying until I got through to you tonight. Did you get my message?"

"I did. Are you okay? I wanted to jump into my car and drive to Allagash…." I still did. Staring blankly around the terminal, I tried to shut down my emotions. Being numb might be the only way I'd be able to say anything. I'd never be able to do this to her if I let myself feel.

"I can't believe I handled Tom all by myself," Ginny gushed. "That pepper spray worked better than I ever expected. Thank you for suggesting it."

The realization that she hadn't needed me for protection sank through my bones. She was saving herself all on her own.

"I'm stuck here tonight," she said. "It's late. Eli's already asleep. Tom hit him, gave him a big bump on his head. He's—"

"Hey, I've got some news." That was putting it mildly.

Just spit it out.

"What's up?"

"I got called back early."

Her breath caught. "The military?"

"Yep. I'm actually at the airport, waiting for my flight." The numbness I'd aimed for wasn't working. The knot in my chest grew tighter as if a steel fist surrounded my heart. With my throat spasming, it was all I could do to breathe. I didn't want to—

"I see."

She inhaled but before she could say whatever was on the tip of her tongue, I jumped in. "It's probably for the best. We knew this wasn't forever." I wanted it to last forever. Why was I saying this? Ripping us apart? But leaving a letter would've been an asshole move, and I owed her the truth. "You knew I was leaving on Sunday, anyway. That I was deploying again soon."

Silence stretched through the lines so long, I wondered if she'd hung up. It would serve me right if she did. How could I pretend for even a second that she meant nothing to me?

When she meant everything.

Her clearing throat brought me fully back to the present. "Should I say have a nice life? Tell you good luck?"

The usual messages from a stranger but not from the one I loved. If she'd started to have feelings for me, I was killing them now.

The fist around my heart clamped tighter. *Do it.* "I'm sorry. I wish we could've had a few more days together. But you're in Maine, and I'm wherever the military sends me." Trite, but ending it like this was for the best. I had nothing to offer her except myself, and that would never be enough. Overhead, they called my flight. "Hey, I've got to go." If I didn't hang up, I'd take back my words, leave the airport, and find her wherever she was. I'd beg her to let me share even a tiny fraction of her life.

But I couldn't do that do her. She deserved more.

"You're a special woman, Ginny," I said. "I hope you find someone as special as you. Someone who can give you what you need."

Before she could reply, I ended the call.

29

Ginny

Eli and I hit the road bright and early the next morning. Eli had rested somewhat last night. Between rehashing my conversation with Cooper and checking Eli every hour to make sure he didn't have a serious head injury, I'd gotten no sleep.

We stopped in town for coffee and a box of donuts, planning to consume breakfast along the way home. After finishing his drink and half the donuts, Eli slept. His head was feeling better, and he was determined to go to work the moment we got home.

Being alone with my thoughts only made things worse until numbness descended. I welcomed it like a long-lost friend. Otherwise, all I could do was feel. I drove on, and the miles skipped underneath the car, marked only by the occasional road sign or vehicle coming from the opposite direction.

A while later, Eli stirred. We'd be home in just under two hours. At this point, I'd hold off telling him about Cooper. Next week or even a month from now would be time enough to unload that news.

"How's the head?" I asked when he fully woke up.

"I've had worse days." He sighed and directed his gaze out the window, where endless trees and a spattering of fields blurred past. When he looked my way, creases hung heavy on his face and his hair needed of a good combing.

Pressing down on the gas pedal, I passed a car, the only one I'd seen for miles.

His chest lifted and fell, and he shoved his clenched fist against his forehead. "I should've been there for you yesterday. It's killing me that I wasn't."

"He essentially knocked you out. Tied you up."

"Which never would've happened if I'd been paying attention." After wiping his face, he stared at me, his eyes glistening. "I'm freakin' Navy. Some kind of security guard I'm making now, huh? He never should've gotten the drop on me. I'm sorry. I failed you when you needed me most."

I couldn't deny that it would've been great to have him beside me when Tom attacked. While I'd handled it myself, the situation could've turned worse. But I hated to see him beating himself up about it. "For months, you've been my rock. The only sure thing I can count on in my life."

Eli placed his hand over mine where it gripped the wheel and squeezed. He unbuckled and slid sideways enough that he could put his arm around my back. He rested his head on my shoulder like I'd done with him when I was three to his five. When my big brother was king of the neighborhood, the best friend I'd ever have, and the person I wanted most to be.

"I'm proud of you," he said. "I couldn't have been as strong as you've been through all this."

"That's not true. I admire you more than anyone." I tilted my head to touch his, bridging the gap between us. "You're my hero."

He swallowed deeply. "And I'm sorry if you thought I

doubted you about…well, the drugs. The boat. You know. I didn't really believe you'd do anything like that, but I should've told you."

"I appreciate you saying that." More than anything.

Shifting back to his seat, he re-buckled. "You're the real hero here."

Three months ago, I wouldn't have dared drive this distance alone. But yesterday, even after discovering the meaning behind the painted tiles and taking on the challenge of an open shed door, I'd set out alone for a long drive north. My brother needed me, and I was determined to be there for him.

With Tom arrested, I'd finally be able to put all of this —and Istanbul—behind me.

It was late afternoon by the time I dropped Eli off at his place.

"Call me," I said through my open window.

"I will." Leaning inside, he kissed my cheek. "You take care. I'll come see you when I get out of work in the morning, on my way home." He tweaked my nose with his thumb like he'd done when we were little. I'd hated it then but I was okay with it now. Where would I be in life without my big brother?

I watched while he went inside his house. He'd shower then take a cab to work. I was glad he'd been able to sleep during the ride back to Crescent Cove.

I drove home and made something to eat. Not that I could stomach a bite. I watched the news. And wished…

My heart would appreciate it if I gave up wishing altogether.

After I did the dishes, I lifted the bag of leftover doughnuts off the counter, where I'd placed it. I should've chucked them out or made Eli take them. I sure didn't need the empty calories. A piece of paper fluttered to the floor, a poorly made paper airplane.

Instructions for how to play croquet. I'd meant to give Cooper the directions the next time I saw him.

Saw him. The realization that I'd never see him again gutted me. Shudders made my limbs give way. I slid down the wooden cabinets until I joined the paper on the floor. My hands flopped on my lap, palms exposed and quivering as if my dreams were being sucked away to the sky. My heart split open and seeped.

With a sob, I buried my wet face in my hands.

30

Cooper

My flight landed in California, and I took a cab to the base. I hauled my bag into my tiny apartment where cold silence awaited me. My harsh sigh filled my tiny bedroom as I unpacked and threw my dirty clothing into the hamper. If I found the time, I'd wash it before shipping out. Otherwise, the hell with it. I'd deal with it when I returned. Assuming I returned.

The box my father left me sat in the bottom of my suitcase. A long flight home should've been enough time to decide if I wanted to waste my time opening it or if I'd be better off tossing it into the trash. Since I'd spent my flight going over my conversation with Ginny multiple times, I hadn't thought about the box at all.

Common sense told me I didn't *really* need to know what was inside. The cringing teen I'd been suggested I didn't dare find out.

Box in hand, I walked to my kitchen where I pulled some crackers from the cabinet and dumped a couple onto a plate. Breakfast was served. Grumbling, I took the box and plate into the living room. Might as well put my feet up and eat fancy.

My bones groaned when I sank onto the plush couch. The crackers found their place on the coffee table and the box on my lap. I stared down at it. Pretty much flinched from it, if I was honest. Was it possible for my father to scream at me from the grave?

I shook my head. Why was I worried about this? It was probably more useless junk from my past. I'd look over whatever was inside and then stuff it onto the top shelf of my closet.

Get it over with.

With my pocket knife, I slit the tape and flipped back the top.

Curiosity might kill cats, but I was confident no booby trap awaited me inside. Why then, did I hesitate before reaching in? Did I think something would rise up and strike me?

Enough.

I pulled out yellowed newspaper clippings first and unfolded them one by one, leaning sideways to see better in the light. The clippings included pictures taken by the press of me at my graduation from boot camp. As I was honored for moving up in rank. Notices of citations and awards I'd achieved. A few photos from the ceremony when I'd made Chief. Newspaper articles after my successful missions overseas.

My father had actually taken the time to track them down and save them. Why? Dad had hated me. Scorned me.

Thrown me away.

This made no sense.

Underneath the clippings lay my high school diploma displayed in a solid, wooden frame. Report cards with circled As. Even a note from my supermarket boss telling me what a great job I did. A paper chronical of my life.

I found an envelope next and lifted it out. Staring at the seal on the back, I wondered if I had it in me to explore this further. Seeing these things now only brought my pain crashing to the forefront all over again. My father had gathered the best parts of my past in one place as if they had meaning.

When they never had before.

After tearing through the envelope's seal, I spilled out the contents. Old photos taken during happier days when Mom was alive. I flipped through them, and her smile shined up at me.

I set them carefully on the sofa and pulled out a small box. The lid popped back easily, revealing my glass phoenix sparkling inside. I held it up and admired the yellows, reds, and oranges all swirling together. It was as beautiful today as when I discovered it on Mom's bureau seventeen years ago.

Not gone, after all. Only tucked away for safekeeping.

But why?

I lowered the bird to the coffee table where it seemed to stare up at me. Watching me. Judging me?

Wild emotions rose up inside me, overcoming me and pulling me down, down, down in a spiral of agony. The pain crushing my chest was too much to bear. After ending things with Ginny—no, tossing her aside—I couldn't take this shit. My breath wheezed, and my chest wall pounded.

While I held my face in my hands, tremors took over my body. My world rocked as if a magnitude eight earthquake shook the planet, leaving me stunned. Bruised inside and out. The wrenching inside me was too much to bear. Why had Dad done this to me?

Come on. These things were nothing more than useless

bits of crap. Not true memories. They couldn't hurt me or steal away my future. I could throw them away.

But I didn't want to.

Only one thing left in the box, an envelope with my name on it. Maybe Dad *could* rise from the grave and hack away a few more pieces of my soul.

With shaking hands, I tore it open. I'd be done with this soon. Then I could set this part of myself aside and move on. Compartmentalize it away like I'd done after high school graduation.

Like I'd done with my feelings for Ginny.

I unfolded the paper Dad had tucked inside.

Cooper,

If you find this letter, I'm gone with no time left to explain. For that, I'm sorry.

I wish I could go back and have a do-over. Then I wouldn't snap at your mom over stupid things that no longer mattered. I wouldn't have picked up that first bottle. I would've tried harder to be the father you needed.

And I would've found the guts to call you home and tell you how proud I am of you.

I know I didn't show it, but I've always loved you, kid. Wish I'd had the chance to tell you to your face.

Dad

Stapled to the note was a picture taken before Mom's accident, when the three of us went fishing. In it, Dad and I held up our catch. Dad stared down at me and in his eyes, I saw hints of the man who'd loved me and Mom. And hints of the man I'd become.

Some good memories crowded back in, shoving aside the bad. Like when Dad coached my little league team. And ruffled my hair when we took turns hauling our newly-cut Christmas tree home from the woods. Evenings out on the back porch when Dad taught me to play the trumpet—the same one Dad played all through high school.

In this picture, our grins matched.

But that look on my face. It stilled me. This boy couldn't see how soon his innocence would be shattered. He'd only lived for the moment, not realizing how important it was to cherish what he had.

I leaned back on the couch, closed my eyes, and groaned while rubbing my face. The letter fluttered to the floor while my hands flopped to my sides.

Pain lanced through my chest and something inside me shifted. As if all the scattered pieces in me slid back into place.

AFTER I SPENT a night at a podunk base in Somewhere, Iraq, the call came through on the radio, *Code Name Snoopy is secure*. Time to move out.

The Marines had gone into the location, cleaned out any hostiles, and established a secure perimeter. Time for the Seabees to perform their own variety of magic. In other words, let the grunt work begin.

Not long after that, I sat strapped inside a helo with at least thirty other soldiers, a mix of Marines and Seabees—engineers and construction personnel going in to perform salvage. Overhead, the blades ground loudly, steel on steel. Even with ear protection, the high-pitched scream nearly deafened me. Standard digital camis in blocks of gray, green, and tan covered my body from my neck to my ankles. I'd buried my feet inside thick, black boots. A matching helmet pressed against my scalp, strapped tightly underneath my chin. My standard-issue 9 mm hung on my hip. Like everyone else on board, I wore dark, non-reflective safety glasses.

Tugging off my glove and glasses, I reached inside my pocket and pulled out my wallet. Before I went in, I needed one last look.

While the vehicle rocked, I stared at Ginny's face, memorizing the shape of her cheekbones, the rich color of her hair, and her deep brown eyes that seemed to sparkle only for me. The realization that I'd never see that happy expression directed my way again clawed my insides wide open.

I'd been right to end things, hadn't I?

The Lance Corporal sitting across from me leaned the butt of her rifle against her inner thigh and reached over, indicating she'd like to see. With reluctance, I passed over the picture.

She stared it and nudged her chin my way. I lip-read, "She your daughter?"

Did I really look that ancient? Hell, sometimes I felt that ancient. Especially lately.

"Just an old friend," I shouted, my words barely reaching above the noise.

"Most people don't carry pictures of old friends." Her smile rose. "The grown-up version a part of your future?"

Not any longer. With a shrug, I took back the photo. I stared at it some more until the helo landed and the door slid wide. Welcome to duty.

"Go," someone shouted over the diminishing whir of the blades, and we all jumped out onto the hard-packed desert floor. Most of the crew rushed toward distant buildings. Dust and sand created a hurricane around me. Through it strode the Captain in charge of the perimeter.

He pointed for me to follow, leading me away from the noise.

We paused beside a Seahut, the overhang barely blocking the merciless sun. Must be over a hundred-and-twenty in the shade. Sweat streamed down my face, and my uniform had plastered itself to my back, drenched through already. I'd be rubbed raw in no time. The norm for deployment in the sandbox.

"We got a problem, Chief," the Captain said. "Hostiles on the west end. Stay away from that location until rein-forcements arrive. You gotta go anywhere, you take a detail. Got it?"

"Will do, Captain. I'm only here for a few hours today. Just long enough to do an eval of what's needed."

"Fine. I've assigned a few men to you. We'll have things secure by the time you return."

And I would be back. Our mission was to get an airstrip fully functional. Glancing around at the bombed-out buildings and teetering powerlines, I could see I had my work cut out for me.

I realized that I still held Ginny's picture when I almost dropped it. Why hadn't I put it away? Stupid. Business should be everything now. With one last stroke of her face, I tucked it inside my wallet and made it secure in my pocket.

I kept repeating the words in my head.

I made the right decision.

"Down! Down!" The ping of a bullet ricocheting off a tin roof made me grab my helmet and duck. Adrenaline shot through my veins and I flinched, but no sharp pain followed.

"Go!" The Captain pointed toward the building in front of us.

I raced for cover.

31

Ginny

It took me three days after Cooper left to step out of myself enough to become partly functional. I made the effort because I needed to move past this. Past him.

I did my job by rote, smiling when it was expected but never feeling more than the motion. My heart hurt so much, I kept curling up on my sofa and crying. Not the best way to impress my customers.

Every second I spent in my apartment only made it worse. Cooper's scent clung to my sheets, but I couldn't bear to wash them. I found creative ways to shop for groceries to avoid pushing the cart down the aisle containing red hot dogs. When I stumbled over the packages of Oreos left from camping, I pressed them to my chest and keened. I spent my days with gummy eyes, an endless ache in my throat, and the realization that I was becoming a hollowed-out core.

Mom returned home and invited me to dinner. She hugged me after I told her about Cooper. "It's going to get better, honey," she said with a sympathetic smile.

That was doubtful.

"With time, your feelings will fade."

At twenty-eight, I wasn't sure I had enough time left for that to happen.

"Eventually, he'll just be a fond memory." She dished more mashed potatoes onto my plate as if food would solve everything. Even chocolate wasn't going to take away this heartache.

When you've been mortally wounded, even a can of squirt whipped cream will rip you to pieces.

I talked about my loss with my counselor. She assured me it was natural to feel as if my world had collapsed. But I didn't like how I was behaving. Staying in my apartment all the time was unhealthy. With all the progress I'd made, I hated slipping backward.

The realization that it was time to make permanent changes hit me when I found myself writing yet another text message to Eli, begging him to come over to peer into every corner in my house for shadows.

I kept hearing sounds outside. Eli kept pointing out the turkeys.

While I couldn't make myself forget Cooper, I was done waiting for life to get better all on its own. I needed to stretch my horizons. I desperately wanted to find myself again.

The first thing I did was sign up for self-defense training. I didn't like the clinging person I'd become since Istanbul and empowering myself was the only way to fix it.

Five days after Cooper left, I drove to the YMCA for my first lesson.

"Nice to meet you," Jan, my private instructor said, holding out her hand for a shake. "On the phone, you told me you'd been kidnapped."

I explained what happened both in Istanbul and with

Tom. His actions had dragged my nightmares back to the surface.

"You know you may not be able to stop something like that from happening again."

I winced.

Jan patted my arm. "Odds are, no one will try to kidnap you again in this lifetime, let alone break your ribs and wrist. Two kidnappings are more than anyone else usually experiences. But sometimes, no matter how cautious you are, things get out of hand. That's why you're here now." Jan's smile widened. "I'm going to teach you some techniques to reduce your odds."

I might not always have pepper spray handy. "That would be perfect."

Jan walked me through basic safety rules like being aware of my surroundings, trusting my instincts, and looking the part—meaning walking with purpose as if I knew where I was going, even if I felt uncertain. I learned the wrist sweep—bringing my elbow in and twisting my arm to break a hold. And how to thwart a bear hug in a way that would injure the assailant and give me time to run. We practiced defensive moves until they became seamless.

Six days after Cooper left, I parked in town. I walked up and down the streets, making eye contact with people I passed. I even went to Mr. Joe's and sat on a wooden bench at the park to enjoy my iced coffee. I sought out outdoor photography opportunities as my go-to assignments.

Seven days after Cooper left, I drove to the campground. I climbed the same green-marked trail to the top of Glenridge Mountain. Other hikers walked with me, keeping me company. My sneakers crunched through fallen leaves. In the woods around me, tiny creatures stirred but they only brought comfort, not fear. When I reached the top, I stood in the same spot I'd staked out with Cooper, staring toward the ocean glistening in the distance.

While the wind tugged my hair, I stooped down and gathered a handful of pine needles. Lifting my clenched fist to shoulder height, I opened it, my palm facing the sky. The breeze took everything away, including the sharp edge of my memories. As the last strand fluttered on the breeze, I closed my eyes and pictured his face. Pain shot through me, almost more than I could bear, but the agony was followed by a steady calm.

His words came back to me. *Crap like that can shatter someone. Leave them with nothing left to give.*

What had he meant about not having anything to give?

I couldn't puzzle it out. All I knew was that while I'd miss him forever, I needed to find peace.

Ten days after Cooper left, I biked to my brother's house. I kept my new bottle of pepper spray handy but I was making strides. Months ago, I would've been a wreck walking to my mailbox.

"I brought cookies," I announced when I swung open his front door. At the rate I was making desserts lately, I was going to gain a thousand pounds.

"White chocolate, macadamia nut?" Eyes gleaming, he limped over to meet me in the entry and grabbed the bag.

"What else would I make? You love them." I hugged him, making him grunt when I squeezed extra tight.

He set the bag on the kitchen table and poured us coffee. "You sure know how to pamper your favorite brother."

I took a seat at the table. "You're my only brother."

His grin widened as he placed my coffee in front of me. "Still your favorite, though. Am I right?"

"Always." I shook my head but smiled along with him.

We talked about town gossip and made some plans for next weekend, a barbeque at Mom's house.

"What are you up to this week?" I asked.

"Well, one good thing came out of us being stuck in Allagash. My boss has hired more staff. Two guys and a woman will start training soon."

"Great. You'll get to catch up on your sleep." I sipped my coffee and nibbled on a cookie. "How's Steve doing?"

"Cast should be off soon. He's eager to get back to work. Almost as eager as I am to have him back." He paused, looking down at his hands holding his coffee. "I... called Flint."

I leaned forward. "And?"

"Got her number."

"Awesome."

"And Flint wants to talk. He's out of the military now, except the Reserves, and he said he has an opening for me at Viper Force."

"Making recreational drones, right?" I tilted my head. "Would that actually interest you?" My brother was mechanically inclined, but I had a hard time picturing him tinkering on tiny robots.

"I'll be traveling with the company, too. Doing security."

"What does that have to do with drones?"

"More than you need to know."

"Oh." I huffed. "Military-related stuff, I assume? You'd have to kill me if you told me any secrets."

His chuckle might imply he was brushing aside my joke, but I knew my brother and I recognized the sharpness in his eyes. "Just babysitting visiting dignitaries. Escorting high-ranking officials on visits to the U.S."

"I see." Actually, I did, but it wasn't seeing my brother strolling around with foreign diplomats. From his evasive expression, there was a lot more to this job than he was saying. "Will you take the job?"

"Think so." He shoved half a cookie into his mouth and chewed, washing it down with his coffee. "It's an exciting opportunity. A chance to prove I still have what it takes." He rubbed his thigh.

Reaching out, I stilled his hand. "You've always had what it takes. You don't let anything slow you down." Damn IED.

"Thanks. I sure try not to. And now that my boss has hired more crew…"

"You can leave. I'm happy for you. I know you've been bored with your current job."

"How about you? Photography business doing well?"

"Better than well. I put fliers up around town and I'm booked solid for the next few months."

"You've filled a void here in town."

I leaned back in my chair and studied his face. "What about Mia?"

He ran his fingertip around the rim of his coffee cup. "Ah, Mia."

"Have you ordered those flowers yet?"

"Can't." His eyes darted up to meet mine before returning to his drink. "She's out of the country."

I blinked. "She didn't move away, did she?"

"Nope. She'll be permanently in Crescent Cove come September. But right now, she's in Mexico doing a medical mission. She's a doctor."

"When will she be back?"

"A month."

"Okay. So, you have time to think about flowers." I laughed when he groaned.

"Nothing may come of it, you know."

"You're right." Lifting his hand, I squeezed it. "I just want to see you happy. With Mia or whoever."

He grinned. "Appreciate it."

———

THIRTEEN DAYS AFTER COOPER LEFT, I sat in my living room watching TV, my plate of dinner resting on my lap. The weatherman finished telling everyone the bad news: rain tomorrow. And the good news: sunshine for the rest of the week.

"Now," the TV announcer said. "We take you to Bagdad, where our overseas reporter, Wang Le is covering the latest from the Middle East."

Another war story meant pictures of soldiers in uniforms. Seeing men in camouflage would scrape the scab off my fragile beginning. I'd muted the remote and was lifting a bite of chicken toward my mouth when the soldiers appeared on the screen. My fork hit my plate and fell onto the carpet, taking a cluster of peas along with it.

While some might suggest uniforms made soldiers blend together, I'd recognize his face even if I was ninety-two and had cataracts.

My heart cried out his name.

Fumbling with the remote, I sat forward. I turned the volume up so loud, the news report shouted through the room. My plate tipped, dumping rice and chicken onto the floor but I couldn't care less. I had to know what was going on.

Wang Le was speaking. "...such a dangerous mission, Captain?"

He held the mic out to a tall black man. "We're just doing our part to make the world a safer place."

Wang Le straightened his camo helmet that had slid

down his brow. "We're talking an airstrip, here. One formerly in ISIS hands. A dangerous situation for you and your men. I heard you've been fired on regularly. It's been a hairy situation, hasn't it?"

The Captain nodded curtly. "I'm sorry. I can't confirm or deny that information."

Someone firing on them regularly? Hairy situation? And Cooper had been in the middle of it. Had he been hurt? I scanned his body for anything that might tell me he was injured, but the picture was too grainy to pick out important details.

"Everyone's talking about it," Wang Le said. "How you took your men in, established control, and how you're getting the place up and running. Once restored, this airstrip will open more zones for troop deployment. Medical missions. Supplies. You're heroes."

"We appreciate our country's support but we're just doing our jobs."

"What's next? More action or are you folks planning on a little R&R?"

The Captain glanced over his shoulder at Cooper. "It's really hard to say where we'll be next."

"I see, I see. Makes sense you can't release information about where you're going next." Wang Le faced the camera and smiled, the mic poised in front of his mouth. "And there you have it. Another step forward for our military. I'm Wang Le, reporting live from Bagdad." He glanced to his left.

The screen cut to a commercial, and I turned the TV off. I cleaned up my spilled meal and dumped it in the trash. My appetite had fled.

That night, I lay in bed listening to the rain tapping on my roof. Memories kept me awake. The touch of Cooper's hand on mine. The warm light in his eyes before he kissed me. The way he always put my needs before his own.

It all meant something. Something bigger than me or him. Something that must mean…*us*.

Crap like that can shatter someone. Leave them with nothing left to give.

There was a message in his words; I just needed to find it.

I refused to believe we were truly over.

His last words rang out in my mind, *I hope you find someone special. Someone who can give you everything you need.*

Maybe he hadn't meant that he was tired of the drama surrounding me like I'd assumed. Or that he considered me a burden.

I cringed when I remembered how frightened I'd been at the campground and how he felt he needed to make noises whenever he approached me. The way I'd jumped at any sound. Had I driven him away?

Someone to give you everything you need.

What if this had been about him all along and not me? Did he consider *himself* the burden?

Everything you could imagine in life waits for you once you move beyond fear.

Rolling onto my back, I squinted up at the ceiling. The soft swirls in the paint told me nothing, but a strong suspicion was crowding into my mind.

Everything you need.

Finally, it hit me. It was simple, really.

I just needed to tell him.

━━

AFTER CALIFORNIA'S time zone caught up to a decent

hour the next morning, I called the base. No one would tell me when Cooper would be home. In fact, no one would confirm or deny that Cooper Talon existed.

I researched airline tickets but with security tight, it was doubtful they'd let me onto the base even if I slammed my fist on the door. After forty-five phone calls…well, really only four, I was able to find someone who would talk to me.

"Yes, Ma'am," the man said. "If you send it to my attention, I'll make sure he gets your letter."

Until Cooper returned home and read it, there was only one more thing I could do.

I called a realtor.

32

Cooper

Dog tired, I dragged my bag through my front door and dropped it onto the rug. I kicked the door shut with my heel while I clicked on the inside light. The smell of stale carpet and emptiness greeted me.

"Welcome home," I said.

My eyes were blurry from exhaustion, and my thigh ached from where a bullet had grazed it the week before. Nothing would make me happier than collapsing on my bed and sleeping for three weeks.

Throat parched worse than the desert I'd left behind, I walked into the kitchen for a glass of water. Liquid sputtered from the faucet and swirled around as it filled my cup.

I'd asked a friend to collect my mail and leave it on my counter while I was gone. A teetering pile awaited me. As far as I was concerned, it could keep on waiting.

I drained the water, set the glass in the sink, and stumbled down the hall to my bedroom.

I slept for twelve hours. Waking late the next morning, I scrubbed my long-overdue teeth, showered, and threw on a pair of sweats. I padded barefoot out to the kitchen to make coffee. While the pot sputtered, I got out a mug. With the smell of caffeinated goodness filling the air, I leaned against the counter and sorted through my mail, chucking fliers and credit card solicitations into the trash as I found them.

In the middle of the pile, I found a letter from Maine. I stared at it for a long time but the white exterior refused to tell me what was hidden inside. Did I really want to know?

When the coffee was ready, I poured a cup and took it and the letter into the living room. With slow hands, I made myself drink half the cup before I set it on the side table.

My gut coiled tighter than during any of my prior missions. Letters from home had been a sore spot for me lately, but I had to know what was inside this envelope.

I tore into it and pulled out the slip of paper inside.

Cooper,
You said you hoped I'd find someone who could give me what I need.
Don't you already know?
All I'll ever need is you.
Ginny

Almost two weeks ago, when I'd poured through the box my father left me, I'd remained stoic. Untouched. But this...

Aww, Ginny.

I couldn't...I shouldn't.

I cried.

I PLACED a brief phone call to my commanding officer. After, I left Flint a voicemail—and a job acceptance.

Too many torturous days later, after pulling my chit and completing the necessary paperwork, I packed my bags and left the base for the last time.

The remainder of my possessions would follow.

33

Ginny

Seventeen days after Cooper left, I sat on my back deck, cheering the turkeys that swarmed my blueberry bushes. Since I'd picked what I wanted, I'd let them have the rest. No reason not to be neighborly.

After, I ran over to Eli's place to pick up my computer and thumb drive. The thumb drive had been in his Jeep glove compartment while we were camping and I kept forgetting to get it. Eli had arranged for the computer store to repair my laptop, and I was eager to download my pictures.

I made a quick stop at the supermarket for essentials and returned home. With my arms full as I entered my apartment, I let the spring-loaded door shut on its own. I'd engage the lock once I had my hands free.

Of course, I dropped the carton of eggs while putting everything away. I cleaned up the gooey, sticky mess, grumbling.

A roll of paper towels later, I sat at the kitchen counter and turned on my laptop. A bit compulsive, I knew I'd feel better once I'd transferred the pictures on the drive onto my laptop then emailed them as attachments to myself. Unfortunately, the computer guy hadn't been able to restore those files.

The computer hummed as I popped the drive into the port. I clicked into it and sorted through the pictures, skipping past the ones from the camping weekend, unable to look. Seeing Cooper's face would undo whatever progress I'd made since he left.

While hope had bloomed in my heart when I sent the letter, I'd heard nothing from him. I worried I'd been too late. Or that I'd read our situation completely wrong.

My phone rang, and my heart jumped. Would it be Cooper? Or Eli?

Unknown number. Normally, I'd ignore it. I got too many spam calls already. But what if it was something important?

I picked it up. "Hello?"

Silence, followed by a click, then dead air.

"Hmm." I dropped my phone back on the counter and returned to my computer. Opening my mail, I found a new note from Zen. Well, sort of a note. Two lines and an attachment.

In addition to telling me I should've bought a Mac, Eli had also told me never to open attachments, that they could do funky things to my computer. But this was from Zen and not some random solicitation.

Hey, Zen said. *I ran into an old friend the other day. She says, "hi".*

Curious, I opened the picture—a woman we'd met in Crete over a year ago.

"Weird." I scrunched my face as I closed out the photo. "Why did he think I'd be excited about seeing her again?" The woman hadn't really been a friend, just an acquaintance I'd exchanged maybe twenty words with when we dined at her restaurant. With a shrug, I deleted the email.

I highlighted and dragged photos from my Istanbul school visits into a new folder on my desktop.

My editor had seen a series of photos I'd published in a magazine shortly before the kidnapping. Excited, she'd asked for another book. I'd email her a few of these pictures to see if she found them as interesting.

Next, I opened the folder with the pictures from Zen and my trip to the Baltic Sea almost four months ago.

Secret pictures, mostly. Although, a few had made their way into that magazine article.

Zen had asked me to leave my camera at home while we spent the day at the beach. He'd wanted our time to be solely about us, not about my never-ending quest for the best shot. Silly man. I could never leave my camera behind when the perfect light, the perfect view, or the perfect moment awaited me. I'd snuck it inside my bag and nodded when Zen asked if I'd obeyed.

We'd driven to the coast. After sharing lunch, we'd lounged in the sand and watched the waves lap against the shore.

Numerous pictures I'd taken on the sly showed Zen tossing rocks into the waves, kicking sand, and later, talking to a man he'd encountered while strolling along the beach. Early spring, the wind whipping off the water made it extra chilly that day. I'd been surprised to find anyone but us braving the cold long enough to stare at the water.

The men argued, which was odd considering they'd just met.

I took pictures the entire time they talked. Even zoomed in for close-ups as Zen and the man walked toward the pier. Their voices carried, although I hadn't been able to make out many of their words.

Money. Or honey, for all I knew. And someone not liking…something. Maybe the honey?

I'd laughed and dismissed the idea from my mind, although I kept taking pictures even when the men went underneath the pier. They'd stayed there for some time until Zen emerged alone, brushing sand off his jeans. When he strode toward me, I tucked my camera away. While Zen had made a decent traveling companion, he'd had a temper. I hadn't wanted to irritate him by proving I'd disobeyed his request.

I never told him I'd gone behind his back and taken photos that day.

Shrugging, I scrolled through the pictures, smiling at some of the prettier ones. When I came to the ones where Zen spoke to the other man, I opened them one by one. For some reason, one of under-the pier photos called to me.

Funny. I'd seen the man Zen spoke to somewhere else, but where?

Curious, I zoomed in on his face. Maybe he was someone famous like a politician or a movie star. No, maybe a diplomat, because he wore a stiff suit.

Ah, yes. That was right. An American diplomat. I tapped my chin as a memory slipped through my mind. An American diplomat who'd…The thought hovered beyond my reach.

I closed the picture and opened the ones taken after the men disappeared underneath the pier. I enlarged them one-by-one, hoping something would trigger rest of my memory.

In the last, before Zen emerged brushing sand from his jeans, I found a picture where the other man appeared to be lying on the sand. Had he fallen? Or had…Oh, shit. Had something happened to him?

I'd seen the man's face in a recent news report. In it, the U.S. government stated they were looking for...I opened the internet and typed in American Diplomat+Istanbul/Baltic Sea+the date to bring up the post.

...where the government was looking for any information about the murder of an American diplomat in Turkey. His body was found underneath a pier at the Baltic Sea.

My mouth drier than desert sand, I ran through the events of the past few weeks.

Tom had confessed to chasing me through the woods and following Cooper and me to the base. But he'd remained adamant he'd done nothing else other than trail me to Allagash and attempt to drag me to his car, which was bad enough.

The boat near-miss had been excused away by the sheriff as a drunk driver. I'd assumed Tom trashed my campsite in revenge. The sheriff said the rattlesnake never existed. Someone had entered my apartment while I was camping and stolen my Xanax. My coffee had been drugged. Someone had tried to run me down right after I drank it.

When Cooper investigated, Joe told him the employee who'd made my iced mocha had been named Tom.

If a person wanted to cover their identity, they'd use a fake name. Tom was blond. But so was—

What if the more sinister incidents had been caused by...someone who could mimic voices. Tom's voice. And Jefferson's. Even mine. Tom suggested I'd encouraged him, called him, told him I wanted to be with him.

Chills zipped up my spine. Maybe Tom was telling the truth. Yes, he'd chased me and followed us to the base, and then tried to grab me in Allagash, but maybe someone else had...

Behind me, the interior door swung wide and banged

against the wall. No breeze could do that. Hands trembling and lungs on fire, I turned.

Zen strode into my apartment, that smirk I'd always hated filling his face. "Ginny, Ginny, Ginny."

Unless he realized I'd taken pictures that day at the sea, he couldn't know I was on to him. Pictures…Shit. I'd published some of them in a magazine article that went live two days before the kidnapping.

Zen must've been involved in that, too.

I rose and faced him. *Act casual.* "What are you doing here?"

"Cute." He cracked his knuckles, another habit that got on my nerves. "But you never were stupid."

I backed up until my butt hit the counter. Could I make it to my bedroom? Then I could lock the door and keep him out for as long as the flimsy lock held true. My top-of-the-line security system only covered the exterior of my apartment. I never thought I'd need to barricade myself behind my interior doors.

Zen scanned the living and kitchen areas then narrowed his eyes on me. "I knew the moment you searched online that I would need to change my plan and pay you a visit."

"Searched online?" I shook my head and chuckled but even to my own ears, I sounded lame. "What are you talking about?"

"I planted a virus in an email attachment. Remember that picture of our dear friend?"

The attachment I'd opened and dismissed as nothing.

"While you looked at the picture, my program invaded your computer and waited unseen." His thick lips twisted. "The program was set to trigger if you searched certain keywords. American Ambassador. The date we went to the Baltic. Or even Derek Cushman. I didn't think you'd catch on this fast, however. The alarm sounded, and I knew it was over. I liked you, Ginny. We had some fun times together. I really hoped it wouldn't come to this."

Like his feelings played a role in this?

"You're not making sense." Inching sideways, I eased around the end of the counter. I needed a weapon. My knife set was opposite the sink—and too far away. A meat mallet was tucked into the cutlery jar sitting in the center of the island. Could I reach it in time?

Keep him talking. Find a way out of this.

"It's been nice seeing you again, but you'll have to leave now, Zen." I flipped my hand toward the door. "I have work to do."

He snorted.

So much for that idea.

His boots made hollow thuds on the carpet as he advanced into the center of the living room. "When you and your boyfriend left the campsite that day, I deleted your photos from your laptop and crashed your hard drive so they couldn't be restored."

That was why my computer wouldn't run. Zen had torn through my campsite, looking for...

"Then I needed you incapacitated so I could take out the final threat to my livelihood. If I could eliminate every copy of the pictures from that day, you'd never realize what happened. But the others were on that thumb drive." He growled. "Which I couldn't find anywhere."

All this time, we'd blamed Tom when, in reality, Zen had done most of it. "You drugged me, didn't you? Almost hit me with a car."

"Figured that out, huh?" Greasy didn't come close to describing his grin. "When I saw Tom snooping around, stalking you, I let him take the blame. I even used his identity to get a job where you always bought coffee. I knew my chance to feed you your Xanax would arrive soon."

"Are you out of your mind?" We'd been friends once. Had I ever really known this man? "You drove that boat. You could've hit me."

"If you were hospitalized overnight, I would've been free to search this place thoroughly. The mailman almost caught me the last time I was here. But I knew the thumb drive had to be in your apartment somewhere." As if this was a casual social visit, he paced over to my French doors and squinted through the glass.

Run! I raced for my front door, but Zen moved in front of me, arms splayed wide and teeth bared. Like a predator about to take down prey.

I backed up again and eased around the kitchen counter. "You had me kidnapped in Istanbul, didn't you?" Tremors leaked through my voice. I had to get away. But how? "They broke my arm, my ribs." *My spirit.*

"I sent my guys to get the thumb drive. They would've let you go once they had it." He took another step closer, a cat stalking a wounded sparrow. Now, he'd rip out my throat. "You deserved the pain for all the trouble you've caused me."

"You're a sick bastard."

Glancing around, his gaze fell on my laptop sitting on the counter. "Where did you hide it? It wasn't with your camping stuff or inside the safe."

He *had* been inside my apartment more than once. I rubbed my arms but couldn't chase away my shivers.

"No more chatting." Zen pulled something from his pocket, but I couldn't tell what it was. "You know about Derek Cushman which means you're another loose end I need to take care of. Destroying the thumb drive won't be enough any longer."

"He was an American diplomat." The game was up. Anger burst through me, making me stiffen. It fed my determination to get out of this situation. Zen would not win. "You met up with him that day at the beach. Killed him. What kind of person are you?"

"The kind of person who takes care of problems for wealthy customers."

A hit man? "You killed him underneath the pier, didn't you?"

He shrugged. "It was a lucrative job."

"You're an animal. No, worse than an animal." My voice rose, and I backed toward the hallway leading to my bedroom.

"I like that we're alone here, Ginny."

"We're not." Centering my feet, I clenched my fists at my sides. One step closer, and I'd punch his nose. Then run. "There are people waiting for photos downstairs."

He chuckled. "I've been watching for days from your shed, waiting to get inside, but you rarely left. There's no one here but us."

And I'd left my door unlocked, inviting him in.

Had he been hiding in the shed when I went outside to close it?

With one leap, he had me, his hand clenched around my forearm. I screamed and yanked sideways, but his grip tightened. He hauled me around to face him and lifted his other arm. "Don't struggle, and I'll make this easy on you."

Like I'd welcome death? I smacked his face, missing his nose but scraping my nails across his cheekbone. Jerking my knee up, I aimed for his groin. He grunted when I hit his thigh but renewed his hold.

"Take the thumb drive. It's in my computer. I won't say

a thing." Wrenching away, I backed down the hall. "We were friends. Together for a year."

"Why do you think I traveled with you?" Appearing confident I'd never escape, he stalked into the center of the living room and turned. His cackle lifted goosebumps on my arms. "You were a decent fuck but you were an even better cover."

There. On the small table in the hall. A stone woman with her arms wrapped around a child. I grabbed it. "Someone will figure this out."

"Not when you commit suicide. Your boyfriend's gone, and you're grief-stricken from the breakup. Your Xanax bottle will be empty instead of missing a few pills. No note for your poor family, but they'll be convinced you ended it."

"You can't make me swallow those pills." No need to let on I'd already disposed of them.

"I don't have to." He held up a syringe. "I brought my own supply. Amazing what you can buy on the street. There's enough here to take care of one final inconvenience—you."

Tightening my grip on the figurine, I reached for the door leading downstairs. My sweaty hand slipped along the knob, and I groaned. Open, damn it!

Zen leaped across the room and slammed me against the door.

My back spasmed, and I screamed.

34

Cooper

Twelve hours after leaving the base, I pulled my rental car into Ginny's driveway. The vehicle ticked while I stared toward the still building. Was she inside? And if so, would she welcome me when I knocked on the door? Or would she slam it in my face, as I deserved?

A *For Sale* sign had been posted on the lawn. Was she moving?

I got out of the car and walked toward what I hoped—no, prayed—would become my future. Our future.

If she'd have me.

A scream inside the apartment sent me storming up the back staircase. The door stood open, and I rushed inside. Some creep had pinned Ginny to the door leading to her photo studio while his other hand lifted something that glistened in the light. While Ginny smacked him and shrieked, the man lowered the weapon toward her.

Not on my watch.

I dove across the room and ripped the man away from Ginny.

The guy struck out, but I dodged the blow. My kick

connected with his hip, shooting him sideways. This gave me the chance to take him down onto the floor in the hallway. Our bodies tumbled against a small table, sending it crashing. Whatever he held in his hand flew up in an arc and skittered across the floor toward Ginny's bedroom.

Grunting, I grabbed his arms to pin him in place. But the guy bucked, and I was flung backward, my shoulder hitting the wall hard enough the drywall shuddered. I leaped on him again, pulling him back to the floor as he scrambled toward Ginny.

He flung his fist out, hitting my throat and making my breath wheeze while I wrangled for a better hold. Damn creep was slippery.

He shoved me off again, sending me reeling backward. I righted myself and kicked out, catching him in the knee with a solid blow. He groaned and clutched his leg, staggering while shooting a glare my way.

I jumped to my feet. Panting, we faced off in the narrow hallway, our arms spread wide. If I could get close, I'd end this.

Backing away from me, the man glanced at Ginny. Not done with her yet, obviously.

When he reached for her and she slapped his hands, I leaped forward, driving him into the wall. He grunted and slid down partway before he righted himself. I shifted Ginny around behind me.

"Zen, stop," Ginny yelled. "It's over."

Her ex-boyfriend? What the hell?

Zen's eyes darted toward his weapon—a syringe lying on the hardwood floor. Too far away to reach, Zen growled and rushed toward us instead.

I turned and yanked his arm forward and flipped him over my hip. The asshole hit one of the island chairs, sending it sideways. He smacked onto his back and groaned.

With my knee and entire body weight, I pinned him at the throat, cutting off his ability to breathe. Flailing, he punched my thigh, but he could die right here in Ginny's kitchen for all I cared. An overwhelming need to end this now, to make sure Ginny would always be safe, filled me. It blinded me to everything except Zen's ruddy face.

His arms flopped to his sides, and his eyes rolled back. He gurgled.

Thrusting myself up and off him, I wrenched him over onto his stomach. He gasped and hauled in big gulps of air, his sides heaving as I pinned his hands behind his back and wedged them in place with my knee.

"Grab something to tie him up," I said to Ginny. "And call the police."

Ginny tossed me an extension cord and rushed to the kitchen island for her phone. While she made the call, I secured Zen's wrists to his ankles, trussing him up tight.

"I can't believe you're here," Ginny said after she hung up. When she reached toward me then dropped her hands back to her sides, I worried I'd come too late. Not to help Ginny but for us.

Sirens drew closer, and the sound of multiple sets of tires squealing into the driveway was soon followed by stomps on the back staircase. The sheriff raced in through the open door, his gun in hand, the deputy right behind him.

"What the hell…?" The sheriff stalled in the living room and took in me still pinning Zen to the floor. His gaze slid to Ginny standing behind the kitchen island wringing her hands. "Care to explain what's going on here, Ms. Bradley?"

Ginny filled them in on who Zen was and what he'd

done. She produced the internet post and her photos as evidence.

"She's lying," Zen ground out.

From the sheriff's snort and raised eyebrows, it was clear the local law didn't believe him.

I was as astonished about this as the sheriff. I berated myself for believing it had been Tom all along. Would Ginny ever forgive me for leaving her unsafe?

"Well." Sheriff Moyer scratched his head. "I guess I better take this man to the county jail and book him. I'll notify the state police and they can fill in the feds."

The deputy bagged the syringe for evidence and held it up into the air, snorting. "Crap like this can kill you."

"You'll need to come downtown to make a statement, Ms. Bradley," the sheriff said. "And we need to take your thumb drive as evidence."

"I'll be down later." Ginny's eyes skimmed over me, intent and serious. Shit, would I be able to convince her I'd made the worse mistake in my life? I never should've left her without telling her how I felt, how much I still want to be with her.

I had no problem begging to make amends.

She tapped her lower lip and avoided eye contact. "I need a few minutes with Mr. Talon first, Sheriff."

A fist wrapped around my heart and squeezed. She probably wanted to tell me off and ask me to leave.

"Don't take too long." The sheriff nudged the brim of my hat. "Ma'am." He cleared his throat. "We'll…get right on this right away. I promise."

She nodded and shut the door behind them.

I brushed my hands on my pants and tried to straighten my clothing. I was a mess, not the picture I'd wanted to present to Ginny. Assuming she'd even look at me.

Her gaze lifted, and her tears wrenched my guts sideways. Was she crying because of the terror she'd just lived through or because I was trying to bumble my way back into her life?

When she lifted a shaky smile, my heart exploded.

Because maybe, just maybe, it was because of the latter.

35

Ginny

After the sheriff left, he and the deputy dragging Zen between them, I leaned against the door, letting a smile fill my face.

A gorgeous man stood in front of me, dressed in full military choker whites, looking a little worse for wear. Lines of hesitancy creased his face. He lifted his hat off the floor, brushed it off, and then tucked it underneath his arm.

Cooper Talon was a knight in shining armor. My very own Seabee knight, dressed in white armor. And his eyes gleamed only for me.

"Well, hello there, sailor," I said. "I don't think we've had time to speak since you arrived."

"I was somewhat busy."

I chuckled. That was an understatement. "Tell me. Are you in port long?"

The unease on his face disappeared, and his grin chased all my shadows away.

Light streaming through the French doors gleamed on his white uniform. Shit, but he looked hot. So hot, I needed to fan my face.

"I…" He cleared his throat and took a step forward. "Look, I…"

I clamped my lips together. It was obvious he had something to say and even if the world exploded around us, I'd hold still long enough to hear it.

He eliminated the space between us and dropped to one knee. He took my hand.

While my eyes widened and my heart pattered furiously, he kissed the back of my fingers, his lips warm and tender.

"Cooper." My voice squeaked. If my legs trembled any more, I'd fall. I wanted to squeal. No, jump for joy. Even more, I wanted to tug him up and cover his face with kisses.

He'd arrived in time not only to save me but to save *us*.

"I love you, Ginny," he said. "If you'll let me back into your life, I'll do my best to give you everything. For as long as you want me."

Tears stung my eyes, and my breath choked in my throat. How could he think I wouldn't want him forever?

Unable to go another second without touching him, I pulled him to his feet and nestled against his chest where his heart beat only for me.

I looked up at him. "I love you, Cooper Talon. I want you today, tomorrow, for always."

"Shit. I love you so much." With a groan, he pulled me close, wrapping himself around me, filling my senses with his scent. His touch. While his lips stroked mine, he cupped my face. The warmth of his hands moving down my back told me how much he loved me. How much he'd missed me.

When he lifted his head, his sexy grin heated me from the inside out.

I tugged on his sleeve. "You didn't travel all the way from California in this outfit, did you?"

"Would it impress you if I did?"

"Consider me suitably impressed already." My heart fluttering, I tilted my head. I pressed my lips together to hold back my intense joy, but I knew it spilled through. How could it not?

His lips covered mine again, urgent and loving.

"I left a message for Flint," he finally said. "I'm taking him up on his offer of a partnership in his new business."

I'd have to tell him Eli was contemplating working with Flint, too, but later.

"Other than the Reserves," Cooper said. "I'm done with the military. I won't get a full retirement until I'm sixty, but I've made my peace with that."

"A new job." And a new life for us.

He nodded and cleared his throat. "I'm home for good."

"Perfect. Because my home is with you."

36

Ginny

Three weeks later

OH. My. God.

Eight handsome men dressed in white Navy uniforms stood at attention as I emerged from the woods. Hunk, hunk, and even more hunk. A group of Navy men dressed in choker whites was enough to give me heart palpitations, but what were they doing here?

I peered around. Through the trees to my right, the ocean glistened in endless swirls of rich blue capped with white. The granite underneath my feet radiated heat from a day of intense sunshine. But other than a light breeze stirring the evergreens and a few butterflies flitting from one flower to another, it was me and eight Navy guys alone on the peak of Glenridge Mountain.

I recognized Flint, and Eli also stood among them. The sly grin my brother shot my way made me wonder what was in store for me next.

Cooper had asked me to meet him on the top of

mountain. Our special place since this was where we'd fallen in love.

While my eyes widened, the men strode toward me in two uniform lines, one man calling out, *march, march,* and *halt.* At *center, face!* They pivoted toward each other, then paced backward a few steps at the next command. In unison, they pulled their silver swords and notched them at their sides.

My breath caught, but before I could speak, my eyes were drawn to the opposite side of the peak, where an even hotter military man emerged from the path. Eli and the other guys looked awesome in their starched uniforms, but Cooper blew them out of the water, much like his favorite C-4.

When he stopped near his friends, his hesitant smile twitched his lips out of place. Why did he look nervous?

When someone shouted *Present!* the men thrust their swords up and forward until the tips met.

Thank heaven I hadn't worn yoga pants. This was why Cooper had casually suggested I meet him up here in my favorite dress. And that I wear my three-inch heels. While I'd strode up the path with my skirt swirling around my calves, I'd worn sneakers. If nothing else, I was practical. I'd ditched my sneakers and slipped my feet into my heels before I left the trail.

Cooper's hand lifted, and he beckoned me forward. I'd never ignore his plea.

His smile grew stronger as I walked toward him beneath the arch of swords.

Stopping in front of the man I knew I'd cherish for the rest of my life, I swallowed back the solid lump of joy in my throat.

"Well, hello there, sailor," I said in a raspy voice. "You're looking mighty hot in that suit."

His laughter burst out. "Choker whites can be a bitch in this heat."

But he'd worn it for me. His friends had, as well. I wasn't sure my heart could take much more without splitting in two.

His face grew serious. "Ginny." As he swallowed deeply, and some of the color left his face.

Really. Didn't he know there was nothing he could say or do that would drive me away? Trust and love for him filled me to overflowing.

He dropped to the granite on one knee.

While my fingers fidgeted at my side and my breath came in great gulps, the guys put away their swords and formed a circle around us.

With his gaze locked on mine, Cooper reached into his pocket and pulled out a small box.

"I love you," he said. In his deep, sapphire eyes, his emotion shone true. I knew he'd feel this way tomorrow, next week, and even seventy year from now. "Will you marry me?"

Tumbling to my knees, I wrapped my arms around him and bit back my sob. "Yes. Yes. Yes!"

While the guys cheered, we kissed. Couldn't get enough of Cooper's kisses. We pulled apart, and the happiness stretching my cheeks made them ache. I wiped my eyes, but my tears kept flowing.

"I love you," he said again as he slid a sparkling ring on my left finger. "Always have, always will."

"I love you, too."

"After we're done here, I want to take you somewhere," Cooper said.

"In your dress whites?"

"I'll wear them 24/7 if it makes you happy."

I leaned close, speaking solely for him, "Actually, I

wouldn't mind helping you remove them, but where do you want to take me first?"

"To the moon and back, actually." He laughed. "But for right now, I'd like to go back in time to when we first met. I'll take you to the prom. The movies. I'll buy you flowers and candy and whatever your heart desires. Instead of taking off for boot camp, I'll beg you to let me share your life."

"I don't need all those things." Choked up, it was all I could do to speak. "All I'll ever want is you."

"I feel the same." His voice dropped, low, deep, and husky. "There's one last thing I need to ask you, though." We stood, and he gave me a quick kiss.

Forget holding back my tears. Every wish I'd ever had was finally coming true. All I could do was nod. Because, really, there wasn't anything I wouldn't do for this man.

In his eyes, I saw hints of the sweet, vulnerable boy I'd crushed on twelve years ago. That expression cracked my chest wide open. I wanted to stroke his face, hold him close, and tell him he was worth a thousand moons and all the stars combined.

But he had something to ask me, and I wanted to hear it.

His hands clasped mine tightly, and he swallowed again before saying softly, "Do you want to get an ice cream with me?"

If you enjoyed Fearless, I'd love to hear your thoughts. You can leave a review on Amazon and Goodreads. And THANKS!

To find out what I'm working on next, sign up for my *newsletter.*

Look for my time travel romance, *Twist of Fate,* on Amazon, and Mia & Eli's story, *Ruthless.* I've included their first chapter here. Just scroll through and jump back into the Viper Force world.

~Marlie

———

Marlie write books with heart, humor, and a guaranteed happily-ever-after. When she's not writing romance, you can find her in Maine, where she works as a nurse. She lives with her own personal hero, her retired Navy Chief husband. They have three children, too many cats, and a cute Yorkie pup.

You can find me via my website,
Twitter, and on Facebook.

Other Books by Marlie May
YOU CAN VISIT MY AMAZON PAGE

Crescent Cove Contemporary Romances
SOME LIKE IT SCOT (link)
SIMPLY IRRESISTIBLE (link)

Other, Independent Titles
TWIST OF FATE, May, 2019
(A time travel romance set in ancient Pompeii)
On Amazon & in Kindle Unlimited

Crescent Cove Romantic Suspense
FEARLESS
RUTHLESS
RECKLESS, coming soon!

━━

Did you know?
I also write young adult under
the pen name, Marty Mayberry

DEAD GIRLS DON'T LIE,
A mystery/suspense
On Amazon & in Kindle Unlimited

CRYSTAL WING ACADEMY
A suspense set in a Harry Potter-style world

Outling, Book One

Dragonsworn, Book Two

Unraveler, Book Three

Scroll ahead to read the first chapter of RUTHLESS…

**Only Eli, a wounded ex-Navy man,
is ruthless enough to protect Mia
from someone lurking in her past
who's determined to destroy her.**

Doctor Mia Crawford moved to Crescent Cove, Maine to
escape an abusive—and now jailed—ex-boyfriend and
forget what happened one night on a dark beach in
Mexico. She settles into the peaceful coastal community,
psyched to be close to her brother, Flint, who runs Viper
Force. An added incentive is Flint's new employee, Eli
Bradley, a man who asked her out eight months ago when
she couldn't ever imagine dating again. When someone
stalks her, she turns to Eli.

Eli never forgot Flint's younger sister, Mia. Sure, she shot
him down, but they now live in the same town and she says
she's open to more. Things soon heat up between them,
and she offers a future he never thought he'd have. When
someone breaks into her house while she's sleeping and
writes #1 on her bedroom mirror, he'll stop at nothing to
eliminate this threat. A kidnapping attempt is followed by
#2 painted on her front door, and he fears it's only a
matter of time until Strike 3.

No way in hell will he let anything happen to Mia. But her
past overshadows the present—and a shocking revelation
puts her in the sights of a murderer. It'll take Eli's consider-
able military skills and the MacGyver tricks he's picked up
at Viper Force to keep the woman he's falling for safe.

Chapter One - Mia

Waves crashing on the Mexican beach masked all sounds —except for the footsteps coming up fast behind me.

My skin crawled with fear. Earlier, someone had shadowed me as I shopped for souvenirs in town. I'd tried to lose the creep and only after I'd raced down an alley and jumped into the back of a cab, shouting for the driver to *go-go!*, had I escaped.

No one was ever going to hurt me again.

Inhaling sharply, I pivoted and swung out my beach bag, smacking the person's shoulder.

A man dropped to his knees on the sand, releasing a surprised curse. As quickly as he'd fallen, he burst to his feet, his feral gaze trained on me. His hand flew to his thigh. A weapon?

"Crap!" I backed away quickly. The setting sun eclipsed his face, making it impossible to make out his features. Had the man from earlier found me?

My heart thundered in my chest, and I instinctively took the stance my military-trained brother, Flint, had drilled into me. Fists raised. Feet squared. Ready to kick.

My snarl collapsed when I got a better look at my opponent.

Double crap.

"Eli?" I gasped out. Horror and embarrassment surged through me like a red tide. Eight months ago, after Flint's engagement to Julia abruptly ended, I'd flown out to Port Hueneme, California to help him pack up his things. He'd needed a change and was discharging from the Navy. His friend, Eli, had been stationed there. He'd asked me out but I turned him down, telling him long-distance relation-ships never worked, especially with a man who was career military, getting ready to deploy overseas.

It was the only excuse I could come up with. I couldn't tell him the real reason.

"I'm sorry I hit you," I said. "I thought, well…"

Eli brushed sand off his jeans, wincing when his hand encountered his right thigh. He huffed, but from the sparkle in his chocolate brown eyes, I could tell he also found the situation funny. He swiped his hand through his thick, dark blond hair and laughed. "Flint said you'd be down here, staring at the waves. Gotta say it, Mia, you sure know how to greet a guy."

Figures. The first time I meet up with the man I'd thought about almost continuously for months, I nailed him with a sack of books. I'd never live this down.

"I'm *really* sorry," I said. "What are you doing in Mexico?"

My brother, Flint, and his employees, Jax and Cooper, were in Puerto Morelos on assignment for my brother's business, and I'd opted to join them for my last night before flying home to Maine tomorrow.

Eli was an anomaly.

"It's your birthday, and I wanted to surprise you," he said.

"Consider me surprised." I grinned, and my unease drifted away like dandelion fluff on the wind.

"Thought about sending flowers."

My eyes widened. "Here? In Mexico?"

"Well, back home." Color rose in his face. Damn, it made him even cuter. "You might not know it yet, but I'm done with the military. Moved home to Crescent Cove six months ago. Just took a job with Flint."

He lived in Crescent Cove? My heart rate doubled. "What made you decide to get out?"

His hand twitched on his thigh. "It was kind of a mutual decision." He nudged his head, indicating we should walk, and we started down the beach with waves rushing up the shore beside us. A storm at sea last night meant the surf was still high.

His gait...Did I detect a subtle limp? *Mutual decision,* he'd said. A medical discharge? Since I could tell the topic made him uncomfortable, I let it go. "You said you work for Flint now. What are *you* going to do at Viper Force?" My curiosity about what went on inside that huge warehouse my brother bought had been gnawing through my bones, but Flint had dodged my questions so far. Maybe I could tease a few details out of Eli. "Viper Force is an awfully lethal name for a company that builds and sells kiddie drones." Flint's lame explanation.

"Kiddie drones. Yeah," Eli said slowly. "That's what I'll be working on." Stopping, he bent over to pick up a pale pink shell and presented it to me.

I smiled and pocketed it, and we continued strolling. The setting sun warmed my back and other than a few birds trying to outrace the waves on spindly feet, we were alone. "Flint said you guys will also do simple security jobs on the side, such as the one here in Mexico."

Like I believed my brother was involved in anything

simple? The drone thing made sense. Flint had been an Explosive Ordinance Disposal Technician in the Navy. When he was twelve, he'd built a rocket and launched it into our neighbor's backyard. Mrs. Johnson's shriek made my mom jump. Mom's shriek sent Flint running. "Last I knew, Seabees didn't spend their time learning combat skills with the Marines only to provide guard duty for the local convenience store. I'm thinking that part of Viper Force sounds more like James Bond."

His gaze flicked toward the houses lining the board-walk on our left before returning to the ocean. "That's all there is to it, I'm afraid. Convenience stores." I could almost hear the groan in his words. "But, hey, Flint said you'd just finished a month-long medical mission here?"

Decent subject change. My curiosity about Viper Force might not be satisfied today.

"I'm a doctor. When Flint moved to Crescent Cove to be near the base for his Reserve duties, I visited and fell in love with the area. And because of what…" Wincing, I pinched my lips together. When I left Massachusetts, I chose to focus on the future, not the past. "Anyway, I followed Flint and took a job at Crescent Cover General Hospital, though I won't start until after Labor Day. I'd already set up this volunteer opportunity in Mérida, and I'm presenting my findings at a conference in western Maine next week."

"What sort of findings?"

"Cardiac risk in older women. I worked with the Juniper Foundation's mission here, providing free educa-tion and testing to women who might not otherwise receive the cardiac care they need." My volunteer work meant even more to me after what happened with a woman I was unable to save back in Crescent Cove.

"That's really admirable."

"Flint set it up, actually. He's friendly with the head of the Foundation, as you may know. He mentioned the connection, and I signed on to volunteer."

"I do remember meeting Peter, the head of the Foundation. And, well, Flint's fiancée, who was somehow also associated with the Foundation."

Julia had been a nanny for one of the Foundation board members. She'd bailed on my brother and left no forwarding address.

"When Flint asked me to fly down here to provide extra cov—uh, support on this job, I mean, I was hoping we'd run into each other." The crooked smile Eli sent me made butterflies flit around in my belly. "Didn't expect to find myself dusting the beach with my knees, though."

"I'm sneaky like that," I teased. As we slowed and studied each other, I tried to ignore the warmth radiating off his skin, let alone his scent, a heady mix of fresh air and spice. This man was hot enough to make my head spin.

He tugged on the bag still dangling from my hand. "What do you keep in that thing, anyway? Cannonballs?"

I held it up, smirking. "A girl can never have too many books when she's hanging out at the beach."

"Can't be just books," he said, chuckling. "No way would a couple of paperbacks deliver that solid a punch. I'd say you've got…A twelve-pack of beer in there, too."

"Really." I tucked my hand on my hip and lifted one brow. The humor in his gaze tickled through me. "You think I'm lugging a bunch of beers around at the beach?"

He shrugged. "I would."

I rolled my eyes. "Figures." Just like a guy. "No beer."

"What are you reading, now? Last I remember, you spent some time out at Port Hueneme curled up on Flint's sofa with a romance."

"Or at the pool. We can't forget that little pool incident." When he'd come up behind me as I sat on a folding chair with my feet the water, absorbed in a particularly steamy part of my book. He'd been going wide to catch a football thrown by Flint, only to stumble against my chair and send us both flying into the water. I'd been wearing a sundress, not a bathing suit. He'd rescued me—Flint's words, not mine—but I'd been drenched through.

Eli's soft gaze drifted down my front, and his voice deepened. "Not sure I'll ever forget the pool."

Was he remembering how our clothing clung to our bodies as we stood in the shallow end, close enough I could hear him breathe? A white sundress became transparent when wet and I'd gone braless. He'd only been wearing low-hung shorts and his bare chest, broad and rippling with muscles, had gleamed in the sunlight. I'd been unable to drag my gaze away.

"I still love romances," I said in a squeaky voice, overcome by the memory of how I'd felt back then. "But mystery is on today's menu."

"You sure it's not romances?" he asked. "With sexy covers?"

"Not you, too," I grumbled. Too often, Flint teased me about my choice of reading material.

"No way. I'd be the last to pick on you for that. Besides, I read romance novels, myself."

I halted and stared up at him, my jaw dropping. "You read romance novels?"

"Love the Highlander ones the best. You read any by that author who lives in Crescent Cove? Dag Ross. *Highlander's Fury* is the first in the series."

Who was this man, and why did I not know this about him?

"All those swords and battles." Eli wiggled his

eyebrows. "And hot sex."

"Wait a minute." I scowled. "You're joking with me, right?" My voice grew hushed. "You don't really read romance novels." As I gaped up at him, I pushed my wind-blown hair off my face. Damn curls kept getting in my eyes. "Do you?"

He snagged a particularly unruly strand and tucked it behind my ear. "You should check out my bedside table." Whistling, he started down the beach again.

Bedside table? That took my brain in a steamier direction. I stared after him before rushing to keep up, shaking my head about his comment. "Hold on." Grabbing his arm, I pulled him to a stop. It was impossible to ignore the nice play of muscles underneath my palm. Was the rest of him still as ripped as I remembered from eight months ago?

A crazy thought occurred to me, and I frowned at the ocean. Aw, shit. Did I dare? After all, I did sort of owe him.

"Hey, Eli," I said slyly.

He turned and walked backward. Yes, he did have a limp. So subtle, it would take someone who knew about injuries to notice. "Yeah?"

"About that pool incident."

His brow narrowed as if he hoped to read my intentions in my face, but I was a better poker player than that. The word came out again, slowly, "Yeah?"

Giggling, I rushed him, my hands outstretched. But I tripped and tumbled forward, into his arms that wrapped around me.

Momentum sucked.

Eli lost his balance. As we fell, he pivoted and I landed on top of him, my dress hiked up, my legs straddling his waist.

Now, wasn't this a delicate position?

A wave flew up the shore and crashed over us before receding. Sputtering, I pushed my sodden hair off my face and wiped the salty sting from my eyes. "I'm sorry," I said. "You okay?"

"More than okay." He rose up onto his elbows, grinning at me. "Damn, girl, you *do* know how to greet a guy." His heated gaze traveled down my front.

Of course. There was nothing like a wet white sundress.

━━━

AFTER CHANGING, I met up with Eli, Flint, Cooper, and Jax outside the restaurant where we'd arranged to celebrate.

"Mia," Cooper said with a nod. "Happy Birthday."

"Thanks. Congratulations to you and Ginny on getting engaged," I said.

His smile grew wider. "Thanks."

"What's this I hear about you and Eli going in for a swim, Red?" Flint asked me with a big grin. He ruffled my hair.

Big brothers could be a major pain in the butt. "My hair is strawberry blonde, not red," I insisted for what had to be the thousandth time since I'd learned how to speak. "And you know I hate that nickname."

"Dude," Jax came up behind Eli, sporting a smirk wider than the sea. He nudged Eli's shoulder. "When you say you're gonna surprise a woman, you sure don't hold back." Chuckling, he came around to lay his arm on my shoulders and smoosh me into his side. "Happy B-Day, kiddo." He kissed my cheek. "Heard about the tote bag incident, but I must've missed the swim. Where did you learn that move, huh? Not from my boy, Flint, here, because he's too much of a softie to encourage a sweet-as-honey girl like you to dance in the ocean with a man like Eli."

Sweet-as-honey. The nickname Jax gave me after I brought a batch of cookies into Flint's office. Despite the endearment and kiss, Jax and I were only friends. Actually, I had a feeling he was *sweet* on my cousin, Haylee, who also worked for Flint. Not that he'd acted on it as far as I could tell. Whenever she was around, he went all broody and barely said a peep.

"Glad the book incident wasn't directed my way," Flint said, rubbing his shoulder. "I'd be the last one to creep up on you on your birthday."

"Yeah, sure." If Christmas hadn't stopped him from tossing water balloons off the loft while I sat on the sofa underneath, why would my twenty-ninth birthday be any different? From the slick look Flint sent Eli's way, I had a feeling I'd been pranked after all, even if Eli was unaware of the role he'd played in my brother's latest trick.

"Let's go inside, shall we?" I said, waving at the door. "How about a cease-fire from teasing on my birthday?"

Flint held the door open for me to enter first. "Don't see no white flag."

"As if. I'd never surrender."

We were soon relaxing on the restaurant's deck overlooking the ocean. Eli and I sat on one side of the wooden table, opposite Jax and Flint. Cooper took a seat on the end. We chowed through numerous plates of burritos and nachos, washing the crispy-cheesy goodness down with tall glasses of cerveza.

"What happened to your leg?" I asked Eli quietly.

His hand flew to his right thigh and he rubbed. "Just a little encounter with an IED."

"Femur?"

He nodded. "Put me out of commission for a while."

A painful injury, then. "I'm sorry."

"It's okay. Not much I can do about it now."

I could tell the topic made him uncomfortable, the last thing I wanted to do. A quick subject change was in order, stat. "So, tell me about those romance novels you love. Are the Highlander ones really your favorites?"

"Shit, bro. Romances?" Flint reeled backward with pretend horror plastered across his face. "Don't tell me you're into that stuff, too?"

Color landed squarely in Eli's chiseled cheeks. Blushing only made him look hotter because it hinted at his vulnerable side. He straightened and yanked on the neck of his t-shirt. "I've read a few."

"That's a complete betrayal of mankind." Jax's words came out serious but the sparkle in his deep blue eyes indicated he was only poking fun.

Flint sipped his beer and then cocked one eyebrow Jax's way. "Maybe if you read a few romances, you'd learn how to talk to women. Then you wouldn't find yourself blanking at inopportune times."

"Burn," Eli said with a grin. His glance between the men made it clear he was enjoying the show.

"Women like to go out with me. Talk to me," Jax said with a huff. "I..." His gaze met mine, and my mind shot again to my cousin, Haylee. "Yeah, sometimes."

Haylee's eyes followed Jax whenever he was around. Didn't he see that? Maybe I should share my favorite cookie recipes with her.

Eli turned to me. "As I was saying earlier, I really like Dag Ross's books. There's something awesome about a spunky woman who can put a beefy Highlander in his place in two seconds flat."

Repeat performance: my jaw dropped. I leaned toward him, eager to share my favorite books, but Flint abruptly pulled his phone and answered an incoming call.

He listened for a moment, then said, "Okay. Hold tight. We'll be there right away." As he put his phone away, he directed an intent gaze to me. "I'm sorry but something's come up on the job. We have to take care of this now."

"Showtime." Cooper tossed his napkin on his empty plate and stood.

So much for Flint's "cushy" security assignment here in Puerto Morelos. Fluffy security jobs never called four ex-Navy guys out on a Friday night.

I tried not to pout, because I hadn't seen my brother in over a month and I was enjoying getting to know Eli again. "I thought you were off until tomorrow."

"In my business," Flint said. "I'm never off duty."

Kiddie drones, right?

"Trouble?" Eli asked quietly, his forearms braced on the table.

Flint's gaze slid away from mine. "Someone's...gone missing." Standing, he dropped a bunch of cash onto the table. "We've gotta go."

Rising, Jax's hand darted around to his back as if he needed to make sure he was still packing.

Stop. He wasn't armed, was he?

My gut clenched. What was going on here?

Eli joined them on the other side of the table, saying so softly, I barely heard his words, "I'm in if you need me."

"Thanks."

Cooper nudged his chin toward Eli. "Talk about new employee orientation, huh? Nothing like jumping into action your first week on the job."

"Action?" I glanced back and forth between the men

but their expressions might as well be carved from granite because they gave nothing away. These military guys sure held their secrets close.

"Well, no, not really action." Cooper coughed. "It's—"

"You'll go to the hotel immediately, right?" Flint said to me.

Getting up, I grabbed my clutch off the table. "Crack of dawn flight, so I guess so?" Since the celebration was over, I might as well spend the rest of my evening with a good book. After all, I had a *twelve-pack* of them waiting in my room.

Flint came around the table and hugged me. "I promise I'll be back in time to take you to the airport in the morning."

"Wait." Stepping back, I frowned. "You think you'll be gone all night?"

"'Course not," he said. "This is nothing." He rubbed my arms and stared down at me. "I'm sorry this job's ruining your birthday, though."

"It's okay." I pressed for a smile because it wasn't like he could help it. "It was still great to see you. We can catch up once you're home."

"Definitely."

Cooper nodded. "See you back in Maine."

Jax came around the table and bowled me over with a hug, saying by my ear, "Stop by the office soon, will ya? I've missed you."

I chuckled. "Chocolate chip?" Definitely needed to enlist Haylee for cookie duty.

He grinned. "Double batch, if it's not a problem."

"Deal."

We walked out front, and Jax, Cooper, and Flint strode toward my brother's rental parked in the lot and climbed inside.

Eli remained with me.

"Well," he said, his attention focused on the pavement. "It was nice meeting up with you again despite the unexpected dip in the sea." He reached into his pocket and held out a small white box. "Happy Birthday."

"Oh, wow." A thrill ran through me. He'd bought me a gift? "You didn't have to get me anything."

"Eli?" Flint called, standing inside the open driver's door. Brows lifted, he nudged his chin toward the black SUV. "Any time, bro."

Eli ignored him. "It's just a little something I thought you'd like."

My smile got bigger, because…nothing. This couldn't mean anything, could it?

"Eli," Flint said again, firmer this time.

Eli watched me, his lips teasing upward.

"As I said, I'm back in Maine for good, now." His intent gaze remained on my face. "I imagine we'll run into each other sometime?"

Excitement rushed through me at the thought of seeing him on a regular basis. Maybe…Was it possible things could be different this time? After all, I'd moved hundreds of miles away from Russell and the two men were nothing alike. "Sure, I'd like that."

He nodded and strode toward the SUV.

My pulse racing too fast from such a simple conversation, I watched him—couldn't help watching him, actually—until he'd climbed into the vehicle and Flint squealed out of the parking lot.

Dropping onto a bench nearby, I opened the box.

My breath caught when I saw what he'd given me. The delicate silver chain winked beneath the streetlights when I dangled it. Tossing aside the box, I smiled at the pendant—a small sterling silver daisy.

Did he remember that time I'd picked a daisy and spontaneously given it to him when I'd stayed on the base to help Flint? He'd turned redder than the horizon the night before a storm.

With a soft smile, I fastened it around my neck, then rose and crossed the road to my hotel. But once I'd reached my room and sat on the bed with my book open on my lap, I sighed. It seemed a shame to spend my last night in Puerto Morelos cooped up in a stuffy hotel room. The ocean would be gorgeous now that the moon had risen, and the sultry-salty air would give me one final taste of Mexico.

As I left the hotel, I looked around to make sure no one followed. The creepy guy in town must've been an isolated incident. Someone looking for an easy tourist mark.

Arriving at the entrance to the public beach a short time later, I kicked off my sandals. I fingered my necklace as I strolled beside the water, my mind skipping with thoughts of meeting up again with Eli once we were both back in Maine.

My smile fled and my pulse kicked into overdrive when I tripped over a man lying motionless on the sand.

The metallic tang of blood hit my sinuses.

———

IF YOU ENJOY my adult romantic suspense novels, you'll love my twisty young adult suspense, written under my other pen name, Marty Mayberry, that opens with a bang and keeps you on the edge of your seat until the shocking ending.

Here's the first chapter of *Dead Girls Don't Lie*. You can find it on Amazon.

Dead Girls Don't Lie ˜ or do they?

Seventeen-year-old Janie Davis was found wandering a Maine beach with second-degree burns and no memory of what happened. An accident on a yacht caused it to sink, taking her parents and best friend down with it. Recovering, Janie returns home under the watchful gaze of her new guardian—an aunt who had been ostracized by Janie's family.

Snooping uncovers the accident report. She's horrified to learn the deaths could be murder and is determined to solve the crime. Selective breaking and entering leads her to two suspects: her father's shady business partner who profited from Dad's death and her aunt, a woman with a sketchy past she's eager to hide. Unsure where to turn next, Janie enlists the help of Emanuel Sancini, a fellow high school senior who thinks doing community service in the library means he can call himself a librarian.

Their investigation leads them to crash a party where they uncover more evidence in the homeowner's office. Discovered in the act, they're forced to conceal their crime by pretending—sort of—that they snuck into the room to make out. Then Janie's brake lines are cut and only a quick plunge to the tile floor keeps an overhead lamp from impaling her in the school library. This, and the warning, *You're Next*, proves Janie's getting closer. With Janie targeted, she and Emanuel must race to expose the murderer. Or Janie could wind up dead.

Chapter One

Aunt Kristy insisted I was strong enough to go to school today, but my heart, a tiny bird trapped in my chest, disagreed. I climbed from her SUV and pushed the door shut, steeling my expression as pain shot up my arms.

My aunt came around the hood and thrust out her hand. "Give me your backpack, Janine. I'll take it inside for you."

"It's Janie," I said.

"What?"

"I told you before. Everyone calls me Janie." I tightened my hand on the strap looped over my shoulder. "And I can carry my own bag, thanks."

"Well. Okay. If you're sure. Janie." She worried her necklace, releasing a sigh, then pivoted on her heel and hurried up the walkway. I imagined she was dying to get to the teacher's lounge to put away her things. Gulp down a cup of coffee before she had to convince a bunch of teenagers that chemistry was fun. Or maybe she just wanted to get away from me.

Two months ago, Aunt Kristy moved into my home

and applied for a job at my high school. She'd done her best to be a parent since. Few people would take on raising a niece they barely knew. Considering she and Dad hadn't been close since before I was born, that said something.

"Hey, there you are," someone said from behind me.

Turning, I hugged Sean, my remaining best friend from before.

"Whoa, aren't you a rebel? I like it," he said, taking in my dark green skirt and white tee. At Finley Cove High School, we were expected to wear white collared shirts and khakis, and 'keep our appearances tidy'. Sean could be a poster child for the school dress code.

"That's me, living dangerously." I'd tucked my shirt into a skirt that landed above rather than below the knee. While my outfit would challenge the school board rules, it still felt awesome wearing something other than ratty shorts and a tee. "I, well, you know, lost weight. Nothing else fits. Think I can get away with it until I hit the mall?"

"I won't tell." His gaze fell away from mine. "You ready to hit the gauntlet?" At my tight nod, he shoved his backpack strap higher on his shoulder and held out his arm. A few months ago, he would've held out both arms. One for me and one for his girlfriend. Brianna.

The doctors said I should be grateful because I'd only received second-degree burns. Third-degree would've been worse because the nerves would be shot and I'd never regain sensation. Those doctors didn't know a damn thing. Pain could be swatted away like a pesky fly. Losing the people I loved had gutted me.

We caught up with a bunch of girls who stalled and grew silent when they saw me. I'd known most of them since elementary school, hanging out together more times than I could count to talk about hot guys, TV shows, and make-up. Frivolous stuff, but I'd been frivolous back then.

Marley's lips twitched as she took in the red patches on my pale skin and the puckers from my grafts. Another girl pretended to gag, not realizing that while my arms and hands might've been burned, my eyes worked just fine, thank you very much. Back home, I'd convinced myself my scars were battle wounds proving I'd survived when everyone else hadn't. Seen through the eyes of these girls, I was repulsive, a thing that should be hidden. I yanked my sleeves down around my wrists, wishing I could pull the material over my fingertips, as well.

"So, Janie. You still have—" Marley made air quotes. "—amnesia?"

"I don't remember much about what happened that night if that's what you're asking." The doctors said my memory might never return.

"But, but…" Marley's mouth dropped open. "What if *you* caused the accident?"

The other girls released muted giggles, savoring the drama.

"I didn't." My heartbeat pulsed in my throat.

Like my personal Pitbull straining against his leash, Sean bared his teeth and snarled.

"Kinda hard to say if you're to blame or not, now isn't it?" Marley smirked. "Considering you don't *actually* remember."

Anger slammed through me like a semi hitting a paper-thin wall. "I wouldn't hurt my parents or Brianna."

Sean elbowed himself between us. "Get lost, Marley, would you?"

With a huff, she spun and continued toward school with the other girls clustering around her feverishly whispering.

"Thank you," I said, grateful all over again I still had Sean in my life.

"Any time." We continued toward school. "Umm, about swimming. I thought about it a lot over the past few weeks." His footsteps paused before picking up speed. "Decided I'm going."

Sean, Brianna and I had been on the swim team together and had made a game out of competing for the best times. While Sean could literally swim laps around us due to his male body structure, Brianna also beat me at every meet. A foster kid, she'd worked twice as hard as me to get ahead. If only I'd appreciated that fact sooner.

"Swimming?" A shiver went through me. "How could you—I just can't."

"Going to the pool will be one of the hardest things I'll ever do but it's what she would've wanted. Yeah, I mourn her." His eyes squeezed shut. When he opened them, they glistened. "I'm going to miss her forever. But she would've wanted us to keep going."

My aunt had been after me to jump back into 'activities you used to do before the accident,' but I didn't see how I could. Going to classes without Brianna would be tough but it would ruin me to do anything else we used to share.

"I'll feel closer to her when I swim. Like she's still with me," he said.

Whenever I thought about getting into the water, my brain flashed to memories of me struggling in the sea…my head going under…our boat lighting up the night as it was consumed by flames.

"Hey." Sean peered down at me. "You look pale. You still up for this? 'Cause, we can bail, if you want."

Like that would do me any good? My grades were skating too close to the edge already. I pushed for a smile. "I'm okay. Let's go."

Crossing the lobby, we walked down the hall to the

wing lined with lockers where I ditched my backpack and pulled out a notebook.

Sean slouched against the wall. "*Are* you starting to remember what happened that night?" The hope in his voice tugged my insides sideways. If only I could give him one more memory of Brianna, a tiny speck he could hold on to.

"Some." I fiddled with a pen before stuffing it inside my pocket. "It's sporadic. Which is frustrating." Fear came through in my words. "Do you think I'm blocking it out because…"

"Janie. You weren't responsible. Forget what Marley said."

A worm of doubt kept wiggling through me, spreading its poison.

"Fireworks caused the fire. That's what the police said." He pulled out his phone and glanced at it. "Damn. I've gotta get to AP Chem." Not that Sean needed to worry about angering my aunt by being late to her class. With our school's highest GPA, he was the top candidate for the Upstanding Citizen Award, which came with a full college scholarship. If I knew Sean, he'd finish with the best grade in the class.

Unlike me. I'd be thrilled if I got a C in basic chem.

I went in the other direction, toward calc. Inside, I took my usual seat—front right and next to the window so I could look outside if I got bored.

The teacher clapped her hands. "Okay, everyone. Let's get settled."

Since I couldn't start school with everyone else in September, Sean had brought me my assignments, but I was barely squeaking by in some of my classes. It was time to get to work. I opened my notebook and clicked my pen.

When I looked down, my heart stopped. I stared at the

top corner of the white laminate desk surface where someone had drawn a tiny hummingbird in dark blue ink.

My hand flew to my right hip, and I traced the identical pattern. Brianna and I had used fake IDs to get matching tattoos earlier this summer. The fact that this one looked exactly like mine was just a coincidence. It couldn't mean anything.

An intense longing for my friend rushed through me, and tears swam in my eyes all over again. Jeez, I was hopeless.

The teacher's sympathetic gaze sliding my way only made things worse. She nudged her head toward the hall and lifted her eyebrows.

Running from the classroom, I went to my locker and dumped my stuff. I pressed my forehead against the cold metal until my ragged breathing eased.

This…wasn't going to work. Not today, anyway.

Slamming my locker closed, I ran.

———

I shouldn't be afraid to go downstairs. This was my house now that my parents had died.

The creak of my bedroom door sent a quiver down my spine. Old houses have rusty hinges, plumbing that sputters, and wooden floorboards that protest whenever you walk across them. History, my dad used to say. No, it felt creepy. Out on the landing, I peered down. My aunt had left a light on in the dining room, and a yellow beam bled across the carpet covering the entryway and glinted on the table where my parents had always dropped their car keys. Where Aunt Kristy dropped her car keys, now.

Somewhere deeper in the house, a man spoke, but I couldn't make out his words.

Barefoot, I tiptoed down the staircase to the first floor. While I could poke my head into the study—where I'd determined the voices came from—and tell my aunt what I was doing, why bother? I could dart into the kitchen, drink fast, and scoot back to my room without her knowing I'd been near.

"…haven't told her?" the man said.

Abandoning my thirst, I slipped through the living room and hovered against the wall beside the almost-closed study door.

"… need to know…" my aunt said. "I…best if she *never* knows. Janie's…fragile."

Great. She was talking about me with some man.

Nothing good ever came from eavesdropping, especially when you were the subject of the conversation. Part of me wanted to run back upstairs and jump under my blankets. Hide.

Curiosity only killed cats, not teenage girls.

I leaned forward, tilting my head to place my ear closer to the opening.

The hardwood floor groaned as the man shifted. "I think you—"

"This is a closed subject," Aunt Kristy said crisply. "Are we clear?"

A long moment passed. "You *are* her guardian." She'd applied for that honor a day after the police called her.

"Legally," the man added, "It's up to you to tell her or withhold the information."

"Exactly," Aunt Kristy grated out. "Is there anything else we need to discuss before you leave?" A chair screeched across the floor as if she'd shoved it back to stand.

"No," the man said. "Just doing my duty, delivering the report as requested, now that—"

"Thank you. I appreciate your efforts on our behalf."

"Anytime, Ma'am."

"Let me walk you out." Footsteps approached, and my heart leaped against my ribcage. Pivoting, I raced into the living room and stared around frantically before diving behind the sofa. I landed on the carpet, jarring my hip against the wall. Breathing fast, I lay still, listening. As my aunt and the man crossed the living room, my hands grew clammy with sweat.

"Thank you for coming," Aunt Kristy said. "I know you're busy at the station."

Station? I crept forward to peer around the end of the sofa.

Aunt Kristy unlocked and pulled open the front door.

A cop stood with her in the entryway. After dropping his hat onto his head, he grunted. "Let me know if there's anything else we can do."

"Thanks." My aunt's hands twitched as he stepped out onto the porch. His footsteps retreated, and a car door slammed. The engine fired.

Aunt Kristy shut the front door and slumped against it. She swiped her dark hair off her face with trembling hands. "Just what I needed," she growled. The click of her heels echoed as she strode into the study.

Because I didn't want to get caught snooping, I waited until she went upstairs, shutting the lights off behind her. Rising, I crept to my father's study and clicked on my phone light. Dad's oak desk sat sentry on the opposite side of the room with two windows overlooking the inky back-yard behind. My heart pinching, I crossed to the back of his desk where I pulled out his chair and sat.

This chair had hosted my pretend rocket launches to

Mars. My buggy rides down shady lanes. And Dad used to spin me around in it until I laughed and got dizzy.

When I closed my eyes, I could almost feel him.

Nothing lay on the scarred wooden surface except a green blotter and a few pens. I pulled open a drawer and pawed through pencils, a stapler, a billion paper clips, and a small framed picture of me taken when I was ten. Bank statements, a few thumb drives, and a folder with copies of letters Dad had sent to various businesses and the government. Nothing worth bringing a cop to the house at night.

The bottom drawer wouldn't budge, but I wasn't stopping now. When I wiggled a letter opener in the lock, it clicked open.

"Bingo." Inside the drawer, I found a green folder containing a letter from Dad's lawyer dated July 18, a week before the accident. Two pages of tiny print ended with Dad's printed name—he hadn't signed it yet.

My breath caught. He'd never sign it, now.

Mr. Somerfield's name jumped out at me. If I read this correctly, Dad had been planning to dissolve their business partnership, which was odd, because we'd gone boating to celebrate the upcoming release of an app Dad had designed for the company. But they had argued a lot.

Had Mr. Somerfield known about this?

Stuffed in the back of the drawer, I found a yellow envelope with *Davis Accident Report* scrolled across the front.

Ah. This was what my aunt was talking about.

I stared down at it for a long time. Did I dare look? Going through the details would make my grief fresh all over again, but looking might also drag my memories closer to the surface. I wanted to remember what happened that night, didn't I?

Raking my teeth across my lower lip, I separated the top of the envelope and reeled back when I found pictures.

They're not people you love.

The whimpering part of me insisted they were nothing different than photos I'd see on TV, but I couldn't stop the tears from filling my eyes.

When I upended the envelope, the images slid out onto the desk. Black and white and with the bodies carefully posed, the photos looked like graphic art. A gruesome nightmare played out before my eyes because they *were* the people I loved. No use pretending otherwise.

I traced my fingertip along the burned arm of the person in one photo. Long limbs. Gutted belly. Face a blackened skeleton. Horror rushed through me, making me weak.

Leaning closer, I squinted at the writing along the bottom. *Male, approximate age early-twenties. Burned beyond recognition.* One of the crewmen of the rented yacht?

Another photo: *Male, approximate age mid-forties. Burned beyond recognition.*

Dad.

My keen echoed in the room. This charred carcass with bits of flesh clinging to its bones wasn't my dad. This…this thing wasn't the man who'd rocked me to sleep when I was little and read me stories when I was sick.

If I was wise, I'd go upstairs, take a sleeping pill, and sink into a medication-induced coma. In the morning, I'd convince myself this had all been a dream.

Next picture. *Female, approximate age forty. Burned.*
Mom.

A whiff of Chanel No 5 drifted through the room. If I closed my eyes, could I pretend she was still with me or would I see flames?

Clumping the pictures together, I shoved them back into the folder then pulled out and skimmed through the accident report.

Approximate time of death of the passengers: 23:00. Four hours after we left Finley Cove, where Dad had rented the boat.

If only I hadn't talked my best friend, Brianna, into coming with us. But it had been her birthday. I'd wanted to celebrate it someplace special. I couldn't have known she'd die.

Cupping my face, I peeked through my fingers at the report.

Location of the wreck: ten miles offshore, due east of Big Berry Island. They'd found me wandering the beach after I escaped the boat and swam to shore.

A witness, Andrew Smythe, reported seeing a bright light at sea he dismissed as boaters setting off fireworks. He eventually became concerned about ongoing flashes and called 9-1-1.

The Coast Guard rushed to the scene but found nothing. It took divers and a thorough search to drag up the final evidence.

Highly combustible fuel source suspected. The heat of the flames killed the victims almost immediately. And, *the yacht burned through to the outer hull before sinking underwater, taking everyone down with it.*

I wiped my eyes, but they kept tearing. Bringing my phone closer, I stared at the last bit of information in the file.

My harsh cry rose from deep in my belly and burst into the room.

Possible homicide. Investigation is ongoing.

No, no. This couldn't be true.

Homicide?

Mom, Dad, and Brianna had been murdered.

FIND D*EAD GIRLS Don't Lie* here.

Made in the USA
Monee, IL
26 April 2020